Carol swayed a little as he held her, as if to music that played in her heart, and he smiled. The mommy dance. That little rocking motion, his mother had said, came from holding babies. He didn't know how true that was, but Faith swayed sometimes. Grace never did.

"This is probably why, don't you think, for now anyway?" He laid his hand on Carol's stomach, feeling the warmth of her skin through the cotton blouse she wore with capris. "I don't know why things happen, especially bad things, only that they do. You and Grace have both had more than your share, but you're carrying her baby for her, so that she'll hear that music you hear. She'll rock back and forth like you do, and it will be because of what you gave her."

"Maybe so."

He thought of his conversation with Dillon, of Becky and Davis Rountree and what they were facing, of moving from a two-bed-two-bath apartment to a house with more than six thousand square feet not counting the carriage house turned into a garage.

"And it's time, Carol."

She angled her head so she could see his face. "Time for what?"

"Time to drive the Mustang."

Praise for Liz Flaherty

The Healing Summer

by

Liz Flaherty

The Healing Summer

Cover Art by *Kim Mendoza*

The Wild Rose Press, Inc.
PO Box 708
Adams Basin, NY 14410-0708
Visit us at www.thewildrosepress.com

Publishing History
First Champagne Rose Edition, 2019
Print ISBN 978-1-5092-2845-4
Digital ISBN 978-1-5092-2846-1

Published in the United States of America

Dedication

To Denee, Pam, Cindy, Abby, Beth, and Megan,
the stylists—both past and present—at Hairtique,
the place that gave birth to Carol's Clip Joint.
Thanks for the cuts, colors, advice,
and the laughs you have shared—
and for talking me off the ledge every time I think
shaving my head might be something to consider.

Chapter One

Steven Elliot didn't lose many patients, especially young ones. This was why, in addition to *gifted young surgeon*, the term *miracle worker* got bandied about in journalistic circles. So did sexy blond ponytail, sexy dark eyes, and sexy lean build. Those were downright embarrassing, so he tried not to give them too much thought. Usually. Then there were the articles that had more to do with his sexual prowess than his surgical skill. He avoided them when they came out, but the fact that one of his sisters kept a scrapbook didn't help that evasion tactic at all. Sometime, when he went home to Peacock, Tennessee for a weekend, that scrapbook was going to come to an abrupt and fiery end.

Some of his patients were either celebrities or their relatives or just people who lived in the kind of communities no one in Peacock ever visited. Or, truth be told, wanted to.

Operating on famous people added to his notoriety and, his wife had mentioned more than once, his ego. Just as it was his ego that made him say, "Sure, I can do that," whenever he got invited to a radio or television talk show. But when he wanted to talk about heart surgery and affordable healthcare, the hosts always changed the subject to his social life. As if he had one.

But people watched and listened and bothered him. Because he wasn't a particularly private person, they assumed he had no right or wish for personal time or space. So it shouldn't have been a surprise when he left the hospital the morning seventeen-year-old Jameson Edward Scott III died before he'd even been wheeled into the surgery suite, Steven was greeted by reporters and cameras.

With a brusque "no comment," he sprinted across the parking lot and got into his truck, pulling his phone out of the pocket of his lab coat as he ran. He only had to slide a finger over the screen of the phone to call someone, but that wasn't enough today—he needed an old flip phone he could jab angry fingers at.

Teenagers weren't supposed to die. They were supposed to be pains in the ass who stayed out too late and did stupid shit and drove their parents over the edge. They were not, no matter who they were, supposed to freaking die.

It took him more than one slide of his finger, but he caught the chief of cardiology on the golf course. He blurted out the news of the Holt-Scott heir's death and finished with, "You know that time off you said I needed? I'm taking it."

"How long?"

"I don't know. Maybe for-freaking-ever."

"Steven, it wasn't your fault. It wouldn't have been your fault if he'd died on the table. He was on borrowed time most of his life. It just ran out."

"You're a surgeon, Mitch. Do platitudes really make you feel better when you lose one? For one damn freaking minute?"

"No." Mitch sounded both patient and tired. "Not one. Take your time off. You've earned it. Go back to that little town on the mountain and let your sisters remind you you're human."

"You're a good man, Dr. Mitchell."

"Actually, I'm a pissed-off one. I was all set to sink an eagle on the fourth hole, and you totally ruined it. I've been playing this godforsaken game for five years or so, and I've never gotten an eagle. Never a single time, and you just blew this one."

"Sorry." And he was. Mitch *was* a good man, a good friend, and an excellent surgeon when he wasn't being roped into hospital politics. "If you come over to Peacock sometime, my brothers-in-law and I will take you fishing up at Grant's cabin. Once you get to know him and Dillon, you'll be grateful I'm the only member of the family you have to contend with."

"I met them when…a few years ago."

When Promise died. Steven heard the unspoken words and remembered that a whole contingent of hospital personnel had come to his wife's funeral almost three years ago.

He stared sightlessly through the windshield. Three years. How could it be that long? The wound still felt as raw as it had the June day Promise Delaney Elliot was buried.

"But I'd like to come." Mitch spoke briskly in his ear. "Call me when it's a good time. For now, just go home for a while. We all need it sometimes."

Home.

Within an hour, Steven was on I-40, his golf clubs in the bed of his pickup. They were still there from a game he'd scheduled but never played a week ago, when springtime first started poking around in eastern Tennessee. That was the day Jamie Scott came into the hospital, his heart in shreds.

3

"Keep him alive until a transplant is available," his father had ordered tersely. Then he'd given his ghostly pale, cadaverously thin son a quick nod and left the hospital. His demeanor hadn't changed over the heartrending days since. He'd sat in Jamie's room sometimes, glancing at his watch every few minutes and talking on his cellphone. Whenever his ex-wife entered the room, he left without comment.

What a son of a bitch.

Steven eschewed the shorter, flatter route to Peacock and drove over the mountains instead. An oldies station played quietly on the radio, leaving him alone with his thoughts. Alone and feeling a little peaceful, which didn't happen often, especially on days like this, days when someone he should have been able to save had died.

The last time he spent more than a weekend in Peacock was when Promise was ill. Even then, at her insistence, he spent part of every week in Knoxville. He'd do surgery one day, patient care a day and a half, then head back to his wife, driving his Harley hard and too fast in a fruitless attempt to outrun the breast cancer that was taking Promise away from him.

On the weekends he went home after the battle was lost, he hung out with his brothers-in-law and a few old friends, avoided heartfelt conversations with his sisters, and visited the cemetery. He spent some professional time at Elliot House, where he'd grown up, which was now an assisted living residence its tenants referred to as the Old Farts' Home. It gave Jake, the facility's visiting physician, a break and allowed Steven to stay close to the residents he'd known all his life.

Sometimes he went to church. He'd sneak up to sit

in the choir loft so no one gave him pitying looks or asked him to join them in the basement for coffee after services. Of course, his sisters were in the choir, but he wasn't scared of them. At least, not very. Usually.

After church he'd kiss them goodbye and go back to Knoxville. He knew they worried about him, especially Grace, and he was sorry for that. He'd tried pretending, once in a while, that he'd stayed alive after Promise's death, but they'd known better.

Alive or not, a probably unhealthy fondness for caffeine decided a stop at McDonald's for a large coffee. He played peek-a-boo with a four-year-old whose silky red-gold hair reminded him sharply of Promise's. Even the little girl's eyes were the same clear blue—they were bright and laughing when she jumped around her father's legs to "scare" Steven. The coffee lasted the two-hour drive to Peacock, but by the time he pulled into Grace and Dillon's driveway, his stomach was growling angrily.

His sister, her short, curly hair the same mess it always was, waved from her vegetable garden. "You're here in time to help make rows and do a little planting," she called when he got out of the truck. "April's coming on fast and I'm sneaking in a few plants. Dillon will be so relieved. I think he called his publisher and asked for a pressing deadline so he wouldn't have to help."

"You know I have a black thumb." Steven kicked off his shoes at the edge of the driveway and walked into the freshly tilled earth. "Hi, Gracie." He pulled her slender body into a bone-crushing hug. "How you doing?"

"Fine." She drew back, her nutmeg-brown gaze

5

straight and serious on his. "It's the middle of the day in the middle of the week. What are you doing here?"

"Just needed time off." *Don't ask me now.*

She didn't, although he knew his sister well enough to understand the reprieve was temporary. "Okay. I've got chicken and wild rice soup for lunch and Dillon's sure to have beer. Sound good?"

"Sure does." He went back to his truck for his duffel bag. "I brought some laundry with me. Mind if I wash it here?"

She rolled her eyes. "Surprise, surprise. I'll do it."

He grinned at her. "Will you hang my clothes outside in the night air the way you do Mrs. Willard's?"

"You're a pain in the ass, Dr. Elliot."

"I try."

"Hey!" The voice came from above them, and they both looked up at the second story of the once-a-carriage-house-now-a-garage. Dillon Campbell, best-selling author, Grace's husband, and Steven's best friend since before they were housebroken, leaned out the window. "We didn't know you were coming."

Steven waved. "Neither did I."

"Wanna play some golf?"

Grace's hands rested on her nearly nonexistent hips as she looked up at her husband. "What about that deadline? You know, the one that's keeping you out of the garden?"

"Well, honey, there are gardens and then there are golf courses, and the twain really shouldn't ever meet." Dillon's midnight blue eyes crinkled when he grinned at her. "But I'll be down to work in the garden. The tall guy can help, too."

"Hey!" Steven held up his hands. "What if I

damage these?"

Grace shrugged. "What if you do? They're insured, and they'll heal."

He looped an arm around her neck. "You're a hard woman."

Her gaze sought his. "You all right?"

It was no good lying to her. Grace dug everywhere, not just in her garden, and she had absolutely no qualms about yanking scabs off places that still hurt if she thought it would help in the healing. "I lost one. A young one." He tightened his arm just a little, taking the comfort she offered just by being there.

"Was it something you did?"

No one but Grace would ask him that question. To his face, anyway. God bless her.

"No."

"Something you didn't do?"

"No."

The weight lifted. Just a little. He tightened his arm again and kissed the top of her head. "I've got six to eight weeks of vacation coming. Can I stay here?" He had more than that, actually, but he didn't want to scare her too much to start with.

"As long as you want. You can not only help prepare and plant part of the garden, you can hoe and clear things, too. Dillon will be so glad for your help."

"Didn't you mention lunch?"

She rolled her eyes. "Come on in. Bring that laundry. I'll get a load in before we eat."

Dillon was already in the kitchen, setting bowls of soup on the table along with a platter of sliced ham and a loaf of the fresh bread Grace baked every week. He reached to shake Steven's hand, his eyes sharp. "What's going on?"

"I've been thinking about buying a house." Steven wasn't sure where that answer came from. The apartment complex, complete with tennis courts and a pool he never used, but close to the hospital, suited him right down to the ground. Promise had hated it.

"It's like a hotel. If I wanted to live in a Holiday Inn," she used to say, "I wouldn't have become a schoolteacher or fallen in love with a doctor."

She hadn't fallen in love with a doctor, he'd reminded her. That came later. She'd fallen in love with a badass with a ponytail who *became* a doctor with an attitude.

An attitude but no house. She'd always wanted one, and they'd planned what they would buy or build when Promise got better. But she hadn't gotten better, and since he hadn't even learned to fully function in a *room* without her, he'd never considered a house. But maybe it was time—he'd turn forty in December. Although he thought the wife and family ship had sailed without him, that didn't mean he had to spend the rest of his life in the Holiday Inn, no matter how convenient it was there.

"In Knoxville?"

Grace's question brought him back to the present, to the autumn-colors kitchen that managed to be both large and cozy. "No." *Really?* "In Peacock. I have privileges at the hospital in Kingsport. I can open an office there. Or I can work here in town, for that matter, if Jake's looking for a partner. We could do a hell of a duet at 'here I come to save the day,' like Mighty Mouse used to do in cartoons."

"You can stay with us as long as you like. You

know that. Grace didn't mean it when she said you couldn't put a pool table in the guesthouse." Dillon grinned at him, but his eyes were full of questions.

"Yes, she did, and you know I'm scared of her." Steven took several quick spoonfuls of soup. "This is good, Gracie." He laid down his spoon. "I can't feel like this whenever somebody dies. Every damn time…it's like losing her all over again. I know that doesn't make sense. It doesn't to me, either. For a long time, I thought it was okay this way—I'd just keep working till I keeled over. But that would piss you guys off. Faith's twins would inherit my motorcycle and my truck, so they wouldn't mind so much."

Dillon scowled. "I thought I'd get your motorcycle."

"Nah, you're married. You don't need to be cool anymore. Grace wouldn't let you drive it anyway and while it's true I'm some scared of her, you're completely cowed."

"Cowed?" Dillon's brows rose. "Since when do you use words like 'cowed?' If you don't watch what you're doing, you'll end up sounding completely literate."

Steven sneered at him. "Just because you left your southern accent in that fancy-ass apartment where you lived in Boston, not to mention a few years in France, doesn't make you literate, Campbell. Just makes you talk funny."

"*I* talk funny?" Dillon pointed to himself in outrage. "At least if I start mentioning body parts, people know what I'm saying, and I'm not even a doctor."

Steven snorted. "You can say that again. You

barely passed first year biology in high school. You didn't mind practicing it, but you didn't know what you were doing. And all those body parts you mention in your books? You got the names from me."

Grace passed around plates with slices of chocolate cream pie on them. "You boys want to take it outside? You can work off your hostilities in the garden."

It felt good to sit in Grace's sunny kitchen and squabble with his best friend. For a while, as he forked decadently rich dessert into his mouth, life felt as precious and sweet as the pie. He watched as Dillon and Grace touched each other with the expressions in their eyes. They weren't big on public displays of affection—never had been—but the love in the way they saw each other was almost palpable.

Sometimes Steven's ache for Promise was…less. He'd go hours at a time without remembering the scent of her, the throaty whoop that was her laughter, the perfect ovals of her fingernails. Occasionally he even slept straight through the night and woke without reaching toward the other side of the bed. But all it took was the sight of a redhead, or clear blue eyes, or a red Mustang like the one she'd left to Grace, and he was lost again. Lost and alone and…oh, God*dammi*t, aching like there would never, ever be an end to it.

He put his lunch dishes into the dishwasher. If he didn't give in to the ache, it would go away. For a while. "Let's do the garden thing," he suggested briskly. "I want to go to the cemetery."

A couple of hours later, he straightened from hilling soil up around pepper plants to glare at Grace. "You know, a good sister would have said I was tired and needed my rest. She wouldn't have me out here in the blazing heat—"

"It's sixty-seven and breezy. Way warmer than it should be this time of year," Dillon interrupted from a few rows over, where Steven observed he'd just killed an heirloom tomato plant. He was going to be in trouble for that one. "But in that biology class I flunked, I'm sure we discussed the temperature when heat became blazing."

"Biology, huh?" said Grace mildly, hoeing her way down the row, covering seeds as neatly as if she were stitching a seam. "Now we know why you flunked it, don't we? And you owe me a tomato plant. A Cherokee Purple. They cost the earth."

Dillon grabbed the shoulder strap of her overalls and pulled her to him. "Put it on my tab, Mrs. Campbell."

Steven sighed loudly. "Do you two need time alone? I can always go—"

"Oh, bite me." Dillon buried the broken plant in the soft earth. "But we probably are done, aren't we?" He grinned at his wife. "That deadline, you know. I need to—"

She gave him a push. "Get going, doofus. You too, Steven."

Released from gardening duties, Steven pilfered an armload of daffodils and tulips from Grace's flowerbeds and stole Dillon's bicycle from inside the garage and set off toward the cemetery. It was a good day for a ride anyway. He waved at Jeff Confer and Parker Wendell as he rode through town, promising himself to have a beer with them later.

Once inside the cemetery, he left some flowers on his mother's grave and more on Promise's mother's before lowering himself to the ground beside his wife's granite marker. "Hey," he said, leaning forward to straighten the flowers he'd stuffed into the vase on the base of the stone, "what's new, darlin'? I had a rotten morning, let me tell you."

And tell her he did. Not only about this morning but about the six weeks since he'd last been here. He knew people who swore their dead loved ones talked to them, but he never expected that. It would have scared the bejesus right out of him if Promise answered his ramblings, although he knew what she'd say.

Get a life, Desperado.

He wanted to. Some days, anyway. Other times, most times, he didn't give a good damn. If he hadn't realized the depth of losses his sister and his best friend had already endured, he'd have considered an "accidental" overdose a long time ago. They wouldn't forgive him if he offed himself, and God probably wouldn't either. Steven didn't always attend the church in which he'd been raised, but he believed in the hereafter, and he certainly didn't want to piss off the One who ran things there.

The cemetery was shadowy with approaching evening by the time he straddled Dillon's bicycle again. The air had cooled considerably. He was exhausted, wrung out by the emotional merry-go-round the day had been. With any luck at all, the weariness and the quietude of home would make for a good night's sleep. Peacock wasn't referred to in travel brochures as a "sleepy little town" for nothing.

That was, in retrospect, the only possible reason he could come up with for not looking either way before he rode the bicycle into the one-lane road that dissected the cemetery.

****

Carolina Jessamine Whitney sat in her car, her eyes closed, and her bottom lip sucked between her teeth, as the painful throb pulsated through her calves and into her knees. It was always a relief to get off her feet, but the first few minutes were killers. She hadn't intended, when she went to cosmetology school the semester she should have been a high school senior, to still be doing hair twenty years later. Standing on an expensive anti-fatigue mat fifty hours a week and smiling in the mirror at customers even when she didn't feel the least bit cheerful.

She hadn't intended a lot of things.

Somewhere in the dream state of post-adolescence, she thought it would only take a couple of years of giving perms and highlights and eyebrow arches to earn enough money to attend college. All in a row, that was, not class by excruciating class, so that she'd be thirty-seven come Flag Day and still discouragingly far from having a degree.

Then there was the size thing. She hadn't meant to gain weight. She'd known, realistically, that she wouldn't maintain the size six she'd been in high school—size four if the clothes were expensive, which they usually weren't—but she hadn't wanted to be an eighteen-twenty, either. Hadn't wanted to hear "You have such a pretty face" said in a pitying voice, with a silent "if you weren't such a lardass" tacked on the end of it.

Another bead in the string of disappointments she'd dealt to her parents. Borrowing metaphors from the old movies she grew up on and still loved, Carol thought her mother had deserved Shirley Temple and got Jane Withers instead. But then, Dixie Whitney should have had Cary Grant, too, and Daddy had been more like Burgess Meredith.

A glance in the rearview mirror reminded her that if she had it to do over again, she'd do a little less processing on her hair. It was, for the time being, its natural caramel color, but only the careful and religious application of several different products kept it from appearing as dry as it actually was.

The car complained noisily when she started it, and she frowned at the instrument panel as if it were at fault. "Come on, Bess. Don't let me down now." Maybe she should have made a down payment on a new-to-her car instead of renting a condo on the beach for two weeks in July, but she *needed* those two weeks. Admittedly, Bess was sixteen years old, but she still had most of her own paint and never failed to start. Well, almost never.

After an encouraging pat to her steering wheel and a mumbled prayer from her driver, Bess quieted to the chirpy murmur of an old engine. Carol breathed a relieved sigh. "Good girl."

There weren't many cars out and about. Of course, a traffic jam in Peacock meant being second in line for a left turn. Those northerners who talked about how slowly things moved in the south would be dead right if Peacock were truly a microcosm of the region. Deac Rivers, the minister of the Methodist church next door to Carol's salon, always said the only time the two traffic lights downtown had stopped working, it was three days before anyone noticed.

She went through the newly added drive-through at

the Cup and Cozy, ordering her last hit of caffeine for the day. "Make it a big one, Jack. It was a long, hard day."

"You ready for that final in Tennessee History?" Jackson Winters squirted a shot of cream into her commuter cup and fiddled with the lid. "It's going to be a bitch. This lid's not going on right. Let me get you a new cup."

"Not this time. I didn't bring any money." She grinned at him. "Other than enough to pay for the coffee and your tip, that is. Don't forget study group at my house tonight."

"I'll be there." He handed her the cup. "Thank you, ma'am. Y'all come back now."

"Always do."

She almost drove past the cemetery. No one in there would go anywhere if she missed a week. She knew Grace Campbell had been there earlier—she mentioned it when she stopped in to have her bangs trimmed—but she hadn't been carrying flowers.

With a sigh, Carol stopped in front of her shop, letting the engine run in case the old Pontiac was really feeling testy. She cut iris from the bed that surrounded the sign proclaiming the salon to be The Clip Joint, using the scissors she kept in the car, then got back into Bess and went to the cemetery. She drove straight to the back on the west side, where the tiny marker rested in the shade of a crimson maple. She replaced the scarcely wilted flowers on the grave and stood in silence for a moment, letting grief settle into its accustomed spot.

Sometimes, in truth, she had to go deep to get to the sorrow. It had been so long, and three months had been precious little time to be a mother. But she came here every Wednesday to make sure she remembered the feel of her baby in her arms, the tug of a tiny mouth at her breast, the full head of blond hair that felt like silk. Sometimes she thought she could even feel the horrendous pain of her milk drying up after Miranda didn't wake up that day.

Carol gave herself a little shake. Being willing to let go of mourning didn't mean it didn't hurt. Even after nearly nineteen years, the throb from grief was as steady as the one in her legs. Only thing was, there was nowhere to rub, no anti-inflammatory to ease the pain of losing a child.

So why do you punish yourself every week of your life?

It wasn't the first time the question had ricocheted through her mind, but the answer was just as predictable. It wasn't punishment. Not really. If she allowed herself to forget, those bittersweet mind pictures of Miranda Rose might go away forever.

And there wasn't much else. That was the hard part. Even in a small town, beauticians were plentiful, just as bartenders and convenience store clerks were. Not that there was anything wrong with any of those occupations, but size-six Carol Whitney with the soft, vibrant hair had wanted—maybe not more, but different. She'd wanted an education. To travel. To live—at least sometimes—somewhere more exciting than Peacock, Tennessee.

"See you next week, Miranda. Give your dad a hug for me." Carol couldn't remember young Rand Shipper's face exactly, or the sound of his voice or how his hands had felt, but she remembered loving him. She remembered, if she concentrated, the feeling of hopeful that had been the delightful lace edging around the tapestry of their relationship.

Bess started right up, and Carol inched toward the center road of the hilly old cemetery. Far from being frightened of the place, Peacock children tended to play in it, jumping from behind grave markers with gotcha whoops and Rebel yells.

Not so many kids as there used to be, she reflected, taking a swallow of coffee, and fitting the cup into the plastic holder on the dash. The children of her classmates and their younger siblings spent most of their time inside playing video games and eating too much of the wrong foods so they could become part of the childhood obesity trend that claimed cover space on many of the magazines in the shop.

When she was an adolescent, the craze of the week was teen suicide. Parents took to reading diaries and crashing uninvited into their children's rooms to make sure they hadn't diarized plans to kill themselves or at least to give it the old college try.

Her brother Ed, three years her senior and her parents' favorite, had been one of the statistics. Rather than come out of the proverbial closet and put an end to their dreams of a having a rich heterosexual attorney for a son, he hanged himself from a rafter in the barn when he was twenty-one. A farewell note for their parents explained that the rigors of college life and his unrequited love for a pretty Yankee coed had become too much for him. There'd been a note for Carol, too, asking her to deliver a letter and a few treasured personal effects to Quinn, the lover he'd left behind in New Haven.

She and Quinn still exchanged Christmas and

birthday cards. When he and his long-time partner adopted their children, she sent them handmade quilts with the children's names embroidered in the corners. She was godmother to their youngest.

Her father, thanks to the loving duplicity of his children, died believing their son would have been a saint if he'd lived longer. Carol thought he probably also took with him the belief that his daughter would have been a prostitute if he hadn't loaned her the money for cosmetology school after she got herself pregnant by that boy who went off and got himself killed in one of those countries "over there someplace."

Bess coughed and died as she crested the last rise on the cemetery's center road before pulling into the street. At the same time, the cup-holder broke and the cup fell. The faulty lid came off and the hot contents splashed indiscriminately all over the front seat and its occupant.

"Well, damn it." Carol flinched when the hot liquid hit her legs, swiped ineffectually at the mess, and tried to maneuver the car with an unresponsive steering wheel.

And a tall, lean man with a ponytail rode a bicycle directly into her driver's door.

Chapter Two

"Son of a freaking bitch." His hip was on fire and Dillon's bike was a bent-up mess. Steven had no doubt his brother-in-law wouldn't hesitate before killing him. Of course, if he was hurt really bad, he could—he moved experimentally. "Oh, son of a freaking, *freaking* bitch." He never used the real f-word—its pure badness was one of those things from childhood that stayed in his head—but sometimes it pushed at the edges, screaming to come out. "Oh, hell, something's broken." He wasn't a surgeon for nothing—he knew these things. He knew in his heart of hearts that he was a bit of a hypochondriac, too, but this was real, by God. It hurt like hell on steroids.

The person in the car gave up on her door and clambered out the passenger side. "Steven, is that you? Are you all right?"

He squinted. Who the hell—"Carol?" She'd been his sisters' and Promise's friend all their lives; she'd been *his* friend that long—why did she drive right out in front of him?

"Yes, it's me." She knelt beside him, her knees cracking with the effort, and held up her hand. "How many fingers?"

"All of them. Why did you hit me?"

"I didn't. You hit me. How badly are you hurt? Do you know what day it is? Who's the president?"

"It's Wednesday. Or maybe Thursday. But I never know that even if I haven't been run over by a wild woman in a Pontiac. Why do you drive a car they don't even make anymore? The president isn't who I voted for, and I don't want to talk about it. How could I have hit you? Your car's a lot bigger than Dillon's bicycle."

"Probably because you weren't watching where you were going. Plus, Bess died, so I couldn't get out of your way."

"Bess?"

"My car. The Pontiac you were casting aspersions on."

"Oh, well, if she died, she did it in the right place anyway. I smell coffee."

"It's on me."

"Smells good." Oh, Lord, how inane could a conversation get? Especially when he was damn well sure he'd broken something. Son of a *bitch.*

"It was." She felt his forehead, which he would have laughed at had he not been in severe pain. That, and her hand felt nice against his skin. "Do you have a cell phone? I do, but it's as dead as the car. I'm forever not plugging it in."

"You and Grace," he muttered. He leaned up on one elbow to search for his phone and discovered another place that hurt. "She just started carrying hers recently, when Dillon spent an entire afternoon searching for her and laid down the law that she either carried the phone or he'd get a leash."

Carol snorted. "I'd have liked to have heard how *that* conversation went down."

"If you were in town that day, you probably *did* hear it. But she did start carrying the phone—she just never remembers to charge it." He found his cell phone, which explained why his hip hurt so much. He probably didn't have any broken bones, but the phone was a total loss. "Well, damn, we're phoneless. Let me see if I can get up." With a mighty inward groan, he turned with the idea of getting to his feet.

"No." She pushed him back down so quickly and efficiently he didn't have a chance to regain his balance. "I'll walk over to Malone's and call. Should I get an ambulance or call Dillon?"

"I'll never hear the end of it either way, but I don't need an ambulance, so you'd better call Dillon. I don't suppose you could call a cab instead? I'll pay."

Carol rolled her eyes. She had really nice eyes. Green. Mossy. "This is Peacock, Dr. Elliot. We don't have taxis here." Her gaze moved past him. "However—don't go away." And she was up and sprinting toward the cemetery entrance a lot quicker than he'd have expected.

A lot quicker than *he* could move right now. He tried to straighten again, avoiding his left hip and his right elbow but groaning out loud this time— since there was no one there to hear him—and made it to a seated position. The movement brought Dillon's bicycle into view, and Steven groaned one more time. If he knew his best friend, and no one knew him better, that two-wheeler wasn't a hundred-dollar one from Walmart. It was more like a special-order-let's-ride-the-trails model from the bicycle shop at the end of Main Street in Peacock.

"Steven, I got you a ride. And some help moving." Carol was coming back.

Jonah, a resident of Elliot House and a good friend,

stepped from behind Carol. "Come on, son, let's get you up. Gracie said you were home for a while, but I didn't expect to see you this way."

Once he was finally on his feet, Steven was certain no bones were broken, although his hip was still screaming at him, and he had some dandy abrasions from wrist to shoulder on his right arm.

He limped to the cemetery entrance between Jonah and Carol. "I'm going to ride in the senior citizens' van?"

"Beats walking," Carol observed, "or telling Dillon what you did to his bike."

He looked down at her. "What *I* did to his bike? I wasn't working alone there. But how are you going to get home?"

When he was seated in the middle seat of the van, his long legs spraddled to the side, Carol leaned in. "I'll wait here for the mechanic and put Dillon's bike on my bike rack. When Bill gets Bess running again, I'll bring the bike home. If he can't get her going tonight, he'll take me home."

Steven shook his head. "Don't take it home. Dillon will go into cardiac arrest. Take it to the bike shop. They'll either fix it or give it a decent burial and order a new one."

"Do we need to call the police since there's property damage?" asked Jonah.

"Dillon doesn't even know yet. He hasn't had a chance to hurt me," said Steven. "Oh, you mean the bike? No, we don't need to call the police. It's all in the family." He smiled at Carol, still standing at the door of the van. "And friends thereof. Are you all right? Is the car dented? I didn't even ask."

She laughed. "The car and I will survive. My coffee cup's broken, though, so I may need a few days off work."

Grace was back in the garden when Steven got out of the van. She approached him, hands on her hips. "What happened to you?"

He told her, walking into the house with his hand on her shoulder for support.

"Are you sure Carol was all right?" she asked. "She wouldn't have told you if she wasn't, you know."

He snorted. "Sounds like someone else I know."

His sister scowled at him. "Bite me. Want some coffee?"

The question made him think of how good Carol Whitney smelled. Not just the coffee, but whatever scent she wore, if she wore one. Or maybe it was just her.

What was he thinking? They'd been "hey, how you doing?" friends their entire lives. She'd been one of Promise's strongest pillars of support during her illness. In all the years he'd known her, he'd never once noticed whether she smelled good or not.

"Yeah, coffee would be good. Dillon here?"

"Holed up in his office. He's working on the middle part of a book, which he says takes him ten years and he hates it, hates it, hates it. This afternoon after you left, he said he was going to quit writing and go to work for Grant at the bank." She grinned in true wifely unconcern. "Means he's stuck."

"Doctors can't get stuck." Steven knew he sounded pompous. He also knew Grace expected it of him. She would worry if he was different. He sat on a stool at the island, keeping his weight off his left side as much as he could. His hip still hurt.

"Really?" She set coffee in front of him, then took a seat on the stool around the corner from him. She sipped, peering over the rim of her cup at him. "Isn't that why you're here? Because you're stuck? Somebody died, and you don't know how to go forward from that? It's the same with every loss since Promise, only it's harder every time to come back. Isn't that *stuck*, Steven?"

Well, hell. He started to bristle, to tell her she didn't know what she was talking about. But she did. Promise had been his wife, the person he loved more than he'd have thought was possible. But she was Grace's best friend, a better family to her through difficult times than her own brother and sister, and Grace missed her nearly as much as he did. If Dillon hadn't been there to tug her out of the emotional attic where she hid herself, Grace would have been stuck, too. Just like Steven was.

"I thought maybe—" He stopped. He hadn't thought at all, but the ideas were there, swirling through his mind with pictures of the kind of house he might buy and where he'd open an office. He'd always loved Peacock, although he'd never seriously considered living here fulltime. He'd lived in a city ever since leaving for college when he was eighteen and never grown tired of it.

But Peacock seemed to be calling him home, and he could find no viable explanation for it among the pictures in his mind. Peacock was pretty and friendly— people used to say *The Andy Griffith* show could have been filmed here except that Peacock was so much nicer than Mayberry no one would have believed it really existed. It was also a one-word definition of "stuck." Wasn't it?

Dillon's voice, loud and combative, preceded him into the room. "You broke my bicycle, didn't you? I saw you come home in the Old Fartmobile. I bought that bike at the bike shop. It was so expensive I had to trade my Maserati for it."

"You got rid of the Maserati because it hurt your knees getting in and out of it," Steven yelled back amiably, "and you traded it for an SUV when you and Grace decided to jump on the baby bandwagon."

The change in the room was so sudden and so intense it was as if the sun had gone down. Steven even glanced toward the windows over the kitchen sink to see if darkness had fallen without him noticing. "Gracie?"

"No baby bandwagon," she said crisply. "It remains that you and Dillon are to be the true test of my child-raising skills."

The day that had started—and continued—so wrong grew even darker. If there was ever a person who should be a mother, it was his little sister. "Have you been to—"

"You name it and we've been there." Dillon stood behind his wife, his hands rubbing her shoulders. "So we're going to adopt, and since I'm pushing forty and Gracie's thirty-seven, age has become an issue."

"What about private adoption?"

Dillon shook his head. "Maybe later. We're going through regular channels for now."

"I've talked to a few women after the birth mother changed her mind. I'm not quite up for putting myself through that." Grace set her cup down carefully, as if she was afraid it would break. Or maybe the fear was that she would break. Her pain reflected on Dillon's face, and it extended to Steven.

Damn it all to hell and back. "Well," he said, "geezy Pete." It was Grace's favorite oath, as close as she usually came to swearing. Mama's warnings against using bad language went deeper with Grace and Faith than they did with Steven. He didn't think they ever even *thought* the f-word. At least, not often.

"It'll be fine." Grace squeezed the hand that rubbed her shoulder. "Faith and Grant are coming over for dinner. Which one of you heroes is going to clean the grill?"

****

Carol was sweating buckets by the time she opened the back door of the brick house that sat on a picturesque twenty-two acres of rocks, trees, and a hayfield on a hillside at the edge of town. Peacock was small enough that walking to the end of it wasn't a hardship, but that last climb halfway up Taylor Hill took every bit of strength left in her too-many-hours-standing legs. There was a reason people called the incline Go-to-hell Hill—if you made it to its top, you thought you'd already been there. She should have hitched a ride with Jonah, but she'd expected the mechanic to wave his magic wand over the Pontiac and get her going one more time.

That hadn't happened.

"She might have another life in her," Bill had hedged, "and she might not. I'll tow her over to the garage in the morning. The wrecker's out picking up a car at the textile plant. But I'll give you a ride home, Carol, and drop Steven's bike off at the same time."

But the mechanic had been checking his watch, and Carol knew his two youngest both played Little League. The season wouldn't start till next week, but they were playing practice games now and their dad wanted to be standing at the fence beside the backstop, yelling, "Hey, batter. That's the way," not doing after-hours deliveries.

She shook her head, hoping her smile didn't reflect how tired she was. "No, you go on home, Bill. I need to run a few errands anyway."

She'd had a respite before climbing the hill, when she stopped in at Breakaway and asked the owner to pick up Dillon's bicycle.

"Sure," he said. "It's closing time anyway. Want me to give you a lift up the hill first?"

"No, I'm fine. The exercise will be good for me."

What was she thinking? She was pretty sure every muscle she had was cramped. Probably bleeding and hanging in semi-detached strings from her bones, too.

"Hi, kids. Hang on. Supper's coming." Barney, the border collie she'd rescued from a shelter, and Fred, the long-haired black and white cat who'd stopped in at the shop one day and never left, waited patiently on the back porch.

The Victorian hybrid that was her house was old-brick cool, and as soon as she filled the animals' bowls, Carol sat at the kitchen table with a glass of sweet tea and a plate of the cookies a client had given her. This would be her supper, she told herself, picking up the final crumbs with a dampened finger. She barely had time for a shower before her classmates would start showing up for study group. They would eat pizza and snacks, but she wouldn't. At least, not very much.

In her dreams, she wouldn't eat. She'd never yet

met a pizza she didn't like.

With a despairing look at the clock, she went upstairs, starting at a run and ending the climb with a limp. She went through her bedroom, ignoring the unmade bed and the pile of discarded clothes on the floor.

The bathroom, remodeled in a contract trading skill for skill—the contractor worked for free; she planned his daughter's wedding—gave her the same jolt of pleasure it always did. She gazed regretfully at the whirlpool tub before stepping into the shower.

Fifteen minutes later, with her face free of makeup, her hair still wet and in a loose ponytail, and wearing a long sundress that didn't cling anywhere, she went downstairs. She took homemade pizza crusts from the freezer and a jar of sauce she'd canned last year out of the pantry. It wasn't fair that she liked cooking as much as she did—skinny Grace Campbell, who always had someone to cook for, hated it.

Six students came to the study group. They'd just settled in at the table with pizza and class notes when there was a knock at the back door. "Anyone else coming?" Carol asked.

"Nope, this was it," Jack mumbled, his eyes on what he was reading. It was, in fact, the entire Tennessee History class. The professor had a way of scaring students right into dropping out.

Carol went to the door. "Steven?"

"Grace was worried about you." He held up a new commuter cup from the Cup and Cozy. "And I felt like maybe I owed you this. I didn't know what you drank, so it's just house blend."

"Thank you." She took the cup, smiling at him.

"Come in if you like. You can help us study Tennessee History."

He stepped inside, and even though he was basketball-player-lanky, his height made the roomy kitchen feel crowded. "I took that in the summer one year. Professor Kingman?"

"Yes. He's a piece of work."

He nodded. "Always was. He's become part of the history he tries to teach, I think. Still wearing leisure suits?"

"No. He wears denim shorts and a shirt and tie year-round. With wingtips and dress socks. It's a textile experience just going to class." She introduced her classmates, ranging in age from Reese Confer's barely sixteen to Dallas Marburger's sixty-three. "Steven has taken the class. Maybe he can tell us how to pass it." She gestured toward the empty chair beside hers. "Want something to drink?"

"Got beer?"

"I do." At least, she thought she did. Someone was always leaving the last bottle from a six-pack. She rinsed her hair with it. "I know you're a wine snob," she said, pulling the bottle from the back of the refrigerator. "I hope that doesn't extend to beer, because I'm pretty sure this is about as far down the brewery chain as you can go. Glass?"

"Bottle's fine, and it's not nearly as bad as the stuff Dillon and I made last year. Grace swore it was going to kill her flowers when we poured it out. We told her it was better to off some flowers than send people to the hospital when they tried drinking it, but she didn't really agree. You know how Grace is."

She handed him the beer, almost jumping when

their hands touched. Oh, for heaven's sake, was she going to get all hormonal now? She'd known him her entire life, although he'd never been to her house before.

"What do you remember about this class, Doctor?" asked Jack.

"Just Steven will do." He flashed the smile around the table that Carol was sure had literally charmed the pants off many of her gender. "The nice thing is that his finals—at least as far as I remember and according to what my nephews have said—haven't changed since he first started teaching. Sometime right after the Civil War, I'm thinking."

"Hard?" Dallas's brows lowered skeptically. "I already feel goofy being the oldest kid in class. I'll really feel bad if I flunk the course when I was there for at least half the history he's teaching."

"Being the youngest isn't a picnic, either," said Reese. "I keep thinking he's going to pat me on the head, and then I'd have to go home and wash my hair."

Steven gaze was thoughtful. "Not all that hard, but he leans toward the obscure, which Tennessee's got a boatload of in its history. And he has a real thing for Nancy Ward, the 'Wild Rose of Cherokee,' I think his mother told him to pick out a woman to emphasize to keep from pissing off female students and she was the first one in the history books."

Carol's stomach clenched. She'd named her baby Miranda Rose because she read about Nancy Ward while she was pregnant. It had been years since she'd even thought about the heroine from the 1700s. The mention of her in the textbook had been of the "in passing" variety, certainly not enough for the professor to hang a large part of an exam on. Not even enough to settle onto Carol's memory like an ache.

Almost as if they were on a schedule, the students began gathering their things at eight fifteen. By eight thirty, Carol was standing at the door admonishing them to be careful going home. The ones who lived in student housing took leftover pizza and the half-eaten bags of corn chips and pretzels. They said they would see Carol in class the next morning and yes, Mother, they would be careful.

Reese dawdled over gathering her things and was the last to leave. Carol stopped her on the way out the door. "Is your dad home? Do you need to stay?"

"No, he'll be home."

They'd had this conversation before—Carol worried that Reese would stay alone rather than be what she construed as trouble to anyone. "Come back down the hill if he's not. Okay?"

Reese nodded, flashing the bright smile that was a carbon copy of her mother's. Carol imagined it hurt Jeff Confer just to look at it—he'd loved the young wife he lost the same way Steven Elliot had loved Promise.

Carol would have to walk or ride her bicycle to school the next day. The shop was one thing—it was just over a mile to the Clip Joint, but campus was a mile farther and she had to walk or bike up *and* down an even bigger rise than Taylor Hill. The muscles in her calves made jumpy little cramps just with the thinking about it.

Crap!

She turned at the sound of Steven's voice— Promise used to say it sounded just like Southern Comfort tasted when you were half-drunk and wanting to complete the process. She'd forgotten he was still here.

"Nice people. Is that Jeff Confer's little girl? Isn't she young for college courses?"

"They are nice people," she agreed. "Reese is winding up her sophomore year, but she's scary smart. She's taking advanced placement classes out at the college so she'll have stuff out of the way when she graduates. Jeff doesn't pay much attention to her, but he's good about taking care of what she needs—financially, anyway. Want something else to drink? Coffee?"

"Only if you're having some."

"Go on out on the porch. The evening is beautiful—thinks it's already April. I'll bring the cups out."

She joined him a few minutes later, setting steaming mugs on the small table between the two rocking chairs she'd gotten at the flea market the week before. "It's a nice night. What brings you here in the middle of the week?"

He grinned at her, and her heart stumbled a little in purely feminine reaction. Her heart and a few other parts, if she was completely honest about it. *Good God, Carol, get a grip.*

"I brought you a new cup," he reminded her. "And stayed."

"You helped us study. That was nice of you." She sounded prim. That was good. Beat the hell out of sounding sexually needy, which she thought she probably was. "But what I meant was, why are you in Peacock in the middle of the week? Vacation? Or did you just feel like being run over in the cemetery?"

"Vacation. A long one, I think, because I was feeling as if I'd been run over even before you and your wayward Pontiac came after me. Know any good houses for sale?"

A house? Dr. Lean and Sexy wanted a house?

"There's one farther up Taylor Hill—before Sawyers' and Confers', but it's far enough off the road you can't see it. I don't know how good it is. Because, you know, definitions differ." She gestured back over her shoulder as if he could see through the bricks and mortar of her house. "It's around the curve and right across the hayfield. As the crow flies, it's probably less than a half mile, but it's closer to a mile on the road. Remember the Taylor sisters who lived up here? Never married, didn't go out much—only to church and the grocery and to have a glass of wine at Maeve Malone's. They lived in these two houses. I used to come up here and do their hair, and when Miss Letty took sick five years ago, she offered to sell me her house. She passed away before I even moved in. Miss Abigail died a couple of years ago. Her house is just as she left it, but it's a good price. The family—it's just some cousins from over in Charlotte—want to unload it."

Steven shook his head. "I don't remember them. Is it a hellatious mess?"

She shrugged. "Probably. This one was. Miss Letty tried to keep it up, but ten rooms and a barn were more than she could deal with. I've been five years working on this and there are still two rooms and a bath upstairs I haven't touched."

"Could we go up and see it? On the outside, anyway. Do you have a good flashlight?"

"I can do better than that. The power's on in the

house and I have a key. I always had it when I did her hair and the family just asked me to hold onto it in case anything happened. They'd be tickled to have me show it to you."

The idea of walking up the hill made her calves scream in protest before she even left her chair but spending more time with Steven didn't bother her at all. Well, sort of bothered her, but she wasn't going into why and how much. Not for a New York minute.

They ambled up the barely-paved road. Barney trotted on ahead, then came back to make sure they were coming. "My coffee's hotter than yours," said Carol, "on account of I have this snazzy new cup."

"Yeah, but I didn't have to make mine, which makes all the difference in the world. In case you haven't heard, it's a requisite of doctors that they make lousy coffee."

"Kind of like their handwriting, huh?"

"Exactly. It's a mandatory course in pre-med."

She laughed, then stumbled over a rupture in the pavement. Steven caught her, his arm strong and warm around her waist. "Y'okay?"

Her breathing hitched. "Fine."

She tried to draw away, but he held her firm. "My hip hurts, so you're holding me up, plus I don't want you breaking that cup. It cost me twelve bucks. I've already got Dillon upping the value of his bicycle every time his mouth opens. He was telling Grace tonight in very woeful tones that he was sorry, but he'd taken out a second mortgage to buy the bike and unless I replace it with an even more ridiculously expensive model, they'll probably lose the house."

Carol's laughter rang through the darkness even

though she tried to quell it with a hand over her mouth. "Oh, God, did Gracie threaten to kill him?"

He didn't answer, and she looked up at him. His expression was unmoving. Not angry or even sad, just silent and still. "Steven?"

"Sorry." He squeezed her waist, and she thought she liked feeling bothered, maybe even for a Tennessee minute—it would be longer than its New York equivalent. "I never realized before that you laugh a lot like Promise did. It was nice to hear."

Oh. "I'm sure you still miss her." Everybody—Carol included—missed Promise Delaney Elliot, although probably not in the same way her husband did.

"I do." He chuckled suddenly, the sound surprised, as if he didn't quite remember how to laugh. "Can you just imagine her reaction to that?"

"She would react, wouldn't she? 'Get a life—' what was it she called you?"

"Desperado."

"That was it." She grinned at him. "She also called you pain in the ass. Maybe not to your face, but—"

"Sure she did. Often." He smiled back at her, and her heart—oh, hell, it literally skipped a beat. Next thing you knew, she'd be swooning. Wouldn't that be a story to tell in the salon?

"Here's the driveway." She gestured ahead. "If you can see John Sawyer's big white colonial or the little yellow ranch house where Confers live, you've gone too far." She steered him into the tree-lined lane that led to Miss Abigail's house. "The house is around the curve."

"Oh, holy balls." Amazement swelled through his voice and he drew them to a complete stop. He stared up at the huge brick house with its center tower, mansard roof, and porches everywhere. "I grew up in Peacock, Carol. Dillon, and I ran every inch of these back roads, both drunk and sober, but I swear I've never seen this house before."

"You can't see it from the road unless you know it's there," she explained. "The trees hide it, even in winter. It's Second Empire, built in 1872 by the Taylor ladies' grandfather, or maybe their great-grandfather. I don't remember. Mine, on the other hand, is a Folk Victorian, built in 1895 by the next generation. Word has it he anticipated his wedding vows with a young lady from town, so my house was built in a hurry and added onto here and there. That's why it has a few features in its architecture that are usually associated with Queen Anne or even Gothic Revival." She lowered her voice, speaking in a confidential and somewhat scandalized tone. "It seems they kept celebrating those wedding vows for a really long time, so they had to increase the bedroom space."

Steven stopped staring at the house to stare at her, his eyes sparkling in the flashlight-enhanced darkness. "As I live and breathe, you're a walking, talking textbook. How do you *know* all that?"

Damn, there went her heartbeat again. "I'm nearly thirty-seven," she said, sounding embarrassingly breathy to her own ears. "I've been taking classes ever since I left beauty school when I was eighteen and still don't have a degree. I'm pretty knowledgeable about little bits of a lot of things."

"You were in Promise and Gracie's high school class, weren't you? Even before you joined them in their adult attempts to terrorize the town?"

"I was, but I didn't go to school my last semester. I was too busy mortifying my parents and burying my brother."

"Ed." His arm left her waist to come around her shoulders. "I'm sorry. He was a nice guy."

"Did you know he was gay?" She never talked about Ed's lifestyle—even if it mattered, he was dead. But it was suddenly very important that Steven knew.

"Well, yeah, I guess, but he just *was*. He didn't talk about it, so nobody else did, either. Or if they did, I don't remember. He was funny. Smart. Drank like a fish the way most of us did—we thought we were so cool. And he didn't take any shit off anybody. If you're thinking in gay stereotypes, Ed didn't fit. Watch your step—there's a board missing on the porch. You bring the key?"

"Right here." She handed it to him, then wished she'd unlocked the big door herself. If she had, his arm would still be around her. "He kept it a secret because of our folks. It would have broken their hearts."

"But you knew." He unlocked the door and pushed it open but didn't step inside. "You never told them?"

"Nah. He'd always been their favorite anyway, and it wasn't as if they were bad parents to me—they weren't. They just liked him better, Dad especially. At least when I got pregnant, he was able to turn his grief over his death into anger against me for a while. It was healthier for him and no more than I expected." Although she'd grown to think that was wrong—she should have been entitled to the same acceptance her brother had. Resentment still trickled through occasionally, but she tried to catch it before it became a full-scale emotional flood.

"They never expected to have children, and Dad was already in his forties when Ed was born," she went on. "They adopted me because they didn't want him to grow up alone, and they were pretty much bewildered by both of us. Mom still is sometimes, by me, and I've never taken the notion that Ed was a heterosexual saint away from her."

She laughed, the sound jittery, nervous. "I've just talked more about myself than I have in years. Let's go in and figure out what this house would be like if someone dropped a couple hundred thousand into it."

"Okay." He gestured for her to go ahead of him. "You got that much?"

"Sure, other than the last three zeroes, and even then, I'll need to go to the bank." She stepped away, although she didn't want to. "Barney, stay outside. Let me get the lights. The wiring isn't old, but if the plumbing's like mine was, it's a real treat. These houses are grand old ladies, though, just like their owners were."

The house was dusty, and neglect showed in the furnishings and window treatments. The hardwood floors were scarred and in need of repair. The kitchen was a cook's nightmare, where what might have been antique became merely old. The bathrooms were shambles of falling tiles, rusty sinks, and massive bathtubs with clawed feet and graceful, rounded ends. Even Carol, who'd never met a sow's ear she couldn't envision as a silk purse, was daunted by the amount of sheer labor restoring the "grand old lady" would command. She couldn't imagine what Steven was thinking.

"Wow." He stood in the middle of the front parlor,

its chandelier scant inches above his head, and looked around, his thumbs hooked into the pockets of his shorts. "So, I know wallpaper would be with the period, but could I get by with using paint?"

"Sure can. I did. Wallpaper requires way too much swearing and crying. Maybe drinking, too."

"Who do I talk to about it?" He grinned at her. "The house, I mean, not your cussing, bawling, and boozing."

"I have the realtor's number at the shop. It's someone in Kingsport." Peacock didn't have a real estate office, but Steven probably knew that.

"Good. I'll run by there in the morning. I'll still be hiding from Dillon anyway."

"You really want it?" She couldn't believe it. She was fairly certain he could afford any house he wanted—why on earth would he choose a white elephant perched on a hillside at the very edge of the back of the beyond?

"Sure do." He rubbed his hands together. "It'll be cool, making it back into what it ought to be, and I'm not that bad of a neighbor. I buy really good wine. Grace says you're a good cook, so I can see bartering in our future."

Carol liked bartering, and she wasn't opposed to wine. Especially the good stuff she never bought.

"Will you write me prescriptions so I don't have to go to the gynecologist every year?" she bargained.

"No, ma'am, I will not, but if you have heart palpitations while you're cooking for me, I'm your man."

"Oh, well." She exaggerated a sigh. "If that's the best you can do."

Chapter Three

Steven didn't sleep much—he hadn't since medical school when he never seemed to have the opportunity. Even so, he was surprised to wake at six thirty the next morning, considering he and Dillon had been awake 'til two discussing the tools he needed to buy for the restoration of Miss Abigail's house. As different as the two men were, they did share a passion bordering on stupidity for power tools. Jeff Confer stopped by on his way home and made it even worse—as a logger, he already had a whole bunch of fun things with sharp blades, all theirs for the asking.

Grace handed Steven coffee when he came into her kitchen. He looked around, squinting against the lighting that managed to be soft and bright at the same time. He'd have to see about installing that in the kitchen at Miss Abigail's.

The house definitely needed a name.

"What do you think of High on Taylor Road?" he asked, after the first swallow of coffee. He sat at the island.

She took her usual seat. "I think it sounds like a hangout for teenagers who are being particularly stupid. You know, kind of like you and Dillon and Jeff. Why do you ask?"

"I'm wanting to name the house."

"Oh." She reached for a doughnut. "I made these

this morning—took all the cholesterol out. Have one."

Grace didn't cook worth a damn, but her baked goods and pastries were to die for, and he probably would, because she didn't stint on either sugar or fat. He grabbed a plate and took two.

"We named this house 'Crooked Mouth' because that's what Campbell meant in long-ago Scotland. Besides which, Dillon thought it sounded like a golf course," Grace said thoughtfully. "What does Elliot mean? Our ancestors came from Scotland, too, probably wearing tar and feathers, but that's about the extent of what I know."

"The motto on the family crest is 'Peradventure,' which means 'through adventure.'" Steven chewed thoughtfully. "Elliot's Adventure?"

"Sounds like a kids' TV show. The motto on the clan badge means 'with strength and right.' What can you do with that?"

He thought for a minute of his father, who had molested Grace and left misery in his wake. Elliot wouldn't be a happy name to give to the house on the hill. "Nothing."

"It's Miss Abigail's house," she said. "Just like our house is still the Rountree place at the end of the street, even though we have a little sign on the old gatepost that says it's 'Crooked Mouth' and we have spent more money than I've ever seen before making it over to suit us."

"Then my house will continue be 'Miss Abigail's.' Thanks, little sister." He ruffled the curly hair she hadn't combed yet anyway and snagged another doughnut. "Carol said if you and Dillon want to see the house this evening, we can stop there on the way down the hill and she'll give us dinner if we wait 'til seven."

"Nice. She's a great cook. But she'll be tired. She has class this morning and works this afternoon."

"Shit!" Steven swallowed the last quarter of the doughnut in one hasty gulp and took a rubber band out of his shorts pocket, twisting his hair into a ponytail. "Her car's broke. She'll be walking all the way out to campus. Do you know what time her class is?"

"Eight." Grace's brows, so delicate in her no-nonsense face, rose. "If she needs a ride, I can take her. She'd never ask."

"I know, but I'll pick her up. She's fun to talk to."

"You're just now finding that out?" Grace was grinning, but he wasn't going to have the conversation with her the expression called for.

It was strange, he acknowledged, swinging up into the truck for the drive to Carol's, this sudden…hell, what was it? It wasn't attraction, for a whole bunch of reasons. He'd known her forever, plus she'd been friends with Promise and Grace from kindergarten on. He remembered that she'd cut Promise's long hair down to a pixie when it started falling out, then shaved her head when it became necessary. In the later, harder days, she used to make meals appear as if by magic when none of them felt like eating, much less cooking.

She'd fixed Promise's hair one last time when she died. And put on her makeup and painted the always-perfect nails. The funeral director whose wife worked with Carol had told him later that she also cried and cried and cried.

He liked her—he always had—but she was…well, she was big was what she was. She was okay-pretty along with it and he wasn't one of those guys to whom a perfect body on a woman was important, but he wasn't particularly attracted to either curviness or its too-narrow opposite.

But he still liked her, and it was different from the grin-and-greet liking he had for other women in his life. It also in no way resembled the affection he had for his sisters. The feelings he had for her were sudden to say the least, since their interaction had always been of the out-of-sight, out-of-mind variety.

You'd have thought he'd landed on his head instead of his hip.

Carol was coming out the front door of her house when he pulled into her driveway, adjusting a quilted backpack on her shoulders. "Hey," he called, rolling down the truck window, "want a ride?"

Her hesitation was so instant he felt it before she said, "No, that's okay. The walk will do me good."

"It's two miles and some to campus, and it's barely daylight." He craned his head out the window. "And it's going to rain."

She squinted up, then back at him, her gaze narrowed. "Maybe by the first of the week."

"Come on."

"All right." She came around the front of the truck, taking off her backpack. She tossed it in ahead of her, then pulled herself into the cab. "I think that maneuver would be easier if there were fifty pounds less of me," she commented, scrounging among the empty drive-through coffee cups for the seatbelt. "Of course, most things would. Why are you here?"

"Vacation."

"No, I mean, why are you *here*?"

He pulled into the road. "Didn't we have this

conversation yesterday?"

"Yes, and we didn't sound any smarter then."

She laughed when she talked, that husky sound that reminded him so much of Promise. He grinned over at her, grateful. "You don't take favors well, do you?"

"It's not that. I just don't like depending on other people. It's not something that's worked out well for me in the past."

"Well, you're going to feed us tonight, so let's just consider it a beginning to our bartering relationship." He waved at Jean Rivers as he passed the Deacon's Bench, the town's premier restaurant. "Did you hear anything on your car?"

"No, but I didn't expect to. Bill's kids had a practice game last night. He didn't sound all that hopeful, though." She sighed, a gesture he saw rather than heard, just a little downward tilt of her cheeks along with a truly pretty mouth being tucked in at the corners. "It's hard to complain—Bess is a really old car—but I didn't want to buy another one right now."

He stopped the truck in front of the building where her class was, certain it hadn't moved in the twenty years or so since he'd taken Tennessee History. "What time do you get out of class? I'll pick you up."

"I can walk. I'm going to work from class." She reached for the door handle.

He scowled at her. What was it with women that they had to argue with every blessed word a man said? "What time?"

"Eleven." He *heard* the sigh that time.

"You rolled your eyes, didn't you? I could hear it in your voice." he said cheerfully, and made a shooing motion, "Go on. You don't want to be late for this

44

interesting class. I'll see you after. What time's your first appointment?"

"This is my afternoon at the Old Fa…Elliot House. I start about noon. They eat lunch early, so they're ready for me then."

"Well, good, I need to check in on them, too. I'll pick you up here."

"Oh…" She stopped before closing the door, rummaging in her backpack, and coming up with a key ring. "You can stop by the shop for that number. I think it's in the front of my appointment book under realtor. If Kay's already in the shop, tell her I sent you. The other key is the one to Miss Abigail's house, in case you wanted to go back this morning."

"Who's Kay?"

"The other beautician in the shop. She helps me do flowers, too, and is married to the funeral director. You know her." Carol grinned at him. "She likes to work on live ones once in a while."

"Me, too. Now close the door before I get arrested for parking in a handicapped space."

"Oh, Lord, you didn't, did you?" Without waiting for him to answer, she shut the door and stepped onto the sidewalk, heading toward the building.

Steven pulled away—from the drop-off space, not the handicapped one—and drove back into the center of town. He parked in front of Maeve Malone's and sprinted across the street to the Clip Joint.

The building was old, as most of the ones in Peacock were, with large mullioned windows in its lower front and shuttered ones upstairs. Three mirrored work stations filled one side of the shop, a cozy conversational area the other. A children's play area complete with train table was behind that. In the corner, with a pendant light over it, a round table with four chairs sat. The homework table, he'd bet. Reese Confer said she spent a lot of time here, often accompanied by friends. The appointment desk and shelves of retail items were at the front. It was bright-colored and inviting.

The shop was girly. Carol cut men's hair—she'd even trimmed his a few times—but the design of the shop gave no quarter to his gender. Even the magazines in the wall rack were geared toward women. The contents of the "take a book—leave a book" display in the seating area ranged from Jane Austen to Nora Roberts to signed copies by Dillon Campbell. Steven was surprised at how many of the novels he'd read. He'd learned to *like* books for women—they tended to end better.

The shop felt like Carol Whitney's personality. It had a lot of things in it but wasn't cramped. It was feminine but comfortable, pretty and smart.

He found the phone number he needed, writing it on the back of an appointment card, and left the shop, driving up Taylor Hill Road to Miss Abigail's.

"So, yeah, I'm interested in this place," he said when a pleasant voice answered his call to the realtor. "I'll be here until a quarter 'til eleven this morning if someone wants to come over here and talk to me. Steven Elliot. Great. I'll be here."

He was even more enamored of Miss Abigail's in the daylight. The windows were tall and ornate and there were a blue million of them. A front porch embraced the front and one jutted out on each side, plus a huge flagstone terrace lay across the back. A couple of balconies snugged into architectural recesses on the second floor. The third floor was a creepy-crawly cavern of a space that Carol wouldn't go into the night before.

"It's big enough for a really nice apartment," she'd said, standing at the bottom of the staircase that led to it. "However, there aren't any lights, although it's been wired, and I don't think anyone's been up there since Sherman's march."

"He didn't come through here, remember? It was Sherman's march through *Georgia*. What was that class you're taking?"

She'd scowled at him, offering the flashlight. "You haven't seen that third story. I think maybe he started in Tennessee. But be my guest if you want to check it out. I'm staying down here."

In the end, he hadn't gone to the third floor, either, and he was anxious to see it.

He was standing at the bottom of the stairs, debating where to go first, when he heard the scratching at the door. Surely the realtor couldn't have made it from Kingsport that fast, even taking the highway. He opened half the double-door entry. "Well, hello. Are you the Welcome Wagon or the neighborhood watch?"

Fred and Barney didn't answer, just stepped inside and waited expectantly at his feet. "Just coming to check the place out? Let's go."

They followed him from room to room, never getting in the way, but not venturing out on their own, either. The house was more than he'd ever thought he'd want. It was as big as Dillon and Grace's on Lawyers Row, larger than Faith and Grant's on the other side of town. He'd never even had a spare bedroom before, so why was all this space calling to him? Did he think he'd find Promise in the big rooms? Or maybe forgiveness of himself because Jamie Scott was dead?

The boy's nasty-ass parents were planning their only child's funeral instead of helping him pick out a college. They would never tell him to be in by midnight or turn in his car keys or that So-and-so was a perfectly nice girl, but wrong for him, the son they loved more than life itself. They would never have gotten Steven's vote for Parents of the Year, not even Parents of the Afternoon, but no one raised a child with the notion that kid would die before them. Even Robert Elliot in all his meanness and occasional perversion wouldn't have wanted that.

Steven wandered through the downstairs, the black and white animals in his wake. Two parlors, a huge-ass dining room and a little, cozy one beside the kitchen nightmare. A roomy library with walls of shelves and two sets of French doors that opened out over the overgrown but still Englishy-looking gardens. Two half-baths. His Knoxville apartment would have fit into the front foyer and the formal parlor to its left.

The place even boasted servants' quarters—or a mother-in-law suite, depending on which way you wanted to go. It was a large room complete with sitting room and full bath behind the kitchen. Steven had never known anyone who had a live-in maid, although he had friends with residential *au pairs*. He'd always thought it odd that some people needed so much help with one baby while others raised entire litters without breaking that much of a sweat. He'd said as much to Faith once, and she'd given him a good half hour of explaining about emotional sweat and calling him names.

Thinking of nannies made him remember Grace's inability to have children. Sadness worked its way into his thoughts, pushing away the anger and frustration of Jamie's death as well as the smile that had emerged with the memory of Faith's lecture.

Grace could *get* pregnant, Dillon said—she just couldn't carry a child. A hard pill to swallow for a woman who had self-esteem issues anyway.

Steven had heart patients who'd been determined to carry a child despite terrifying odds. He'd done his best to talk them out of risking their very lives with pregnancy. Often, his best had been by way of being useless—his warnings had fallen on deaf ears. Although there had been more happy endings than not, the jury was still out on how much heart damage had been incurred to the strong-minded mothers. It wasn't a statistic he kept—although someone probably did. The truth was sometimes he flat out loved being wrong.

It would be really nice if Grace's gynecologist was wrong, although she probably wasn't. If Jake Sawyer, the family physician, had any doubts about the diagnosis, he'd have sent Grace to another specialist.

Steven didn't argue with the price the realtor gave him. The pretty woman in a red suit and stilettos that would eventually lead to some podiatric job security wouldn't go to the third floor, either. Standing on the terrace, she waved a dismissive arm toward the carriage house that had been converted to a garage. "It's in good condition, I believe. Have you checked it out?"

"No, but I don't care. What do you guys think?" He looked down at the cat and dog.

They took off at a trot toward the brick building.

That was just weird.

"Well," he said, "I guess they'll examine that part. I'll hear their report later, but I'm not all that concerned. There's acreage, I believe?"

"Eighty acres, forty of it in woods. The rest of it is presently being farmed by—" She leafed through the papers in her hand and gave him a name. "He lives through the woods there and farms Ms. Whitney's land, too—I think it's just up the road? I believe they have some kind of…understanding."

Her lip curled when she said Carol's name. Steven stiffened. "If they do," he said quietly, "it's certainly not of a nature that requires judgment from anyone else."

"Oh, of course." She reddened. "I apologize. Are you prepared to make an offer then?" She shuffled through the documents again.

"Yes, for the asking price, and I'll split the closing costs." He took a business card out of his wallet and wrote Dillon's fax number and address on the back. "You can either fax or messenger papers to me here or you can reach me by cell phone if you need to talk to me—or you can when I get a new one. I'll consider any counteroffer and get back with you."

By the time the realtor drove away in the funereal company car with a magnetic sign displayed crookedly on its door, Steven was in the carriage house with Fred and Barney. "I've never had property before," he said, standing in a sunny stream of dust motes. "What will I do with it?"

Fred made a long, fluffy boa of himself between Steven's feet and Barney came to sit at his side, following Steven's gaze around the four garage bays. Three of them were empty, but the fourth had a garden tractor and lawn mower parked neatly in it.

"What's upstairs, you guys?"

They still didn't answer, but Barney went to the staircase that bisected the building and waited for Steven to join him.

They were walking through the dusty rooms overhead when Steven remembered he'd promised to pick Carol up after class. "What time is it?"

Fred took off down the stairs and Steven thought he should follow. He hadn't worn a watch since college. There were clocks all over hospitals, his hands and arms spent a lot of time in water, and there was always someone around who *did* wear a watch. Well, usually. Obviously Fred and Barney weren't to be counted on for everything.

The sun in the sky told him he was probably late. She'd wait, though, wouldn't she? People were always complaining about doctors being late to their own funerals.

****

Since she'd intended to walk anyway, Carol didn't know why she was so irritated when Steven didn't arrive to pick her up. Well, yes, she did know. This damn textbook and all her other school paraphernalia—heaven forbid she only have one pen or one notebook or one water bottle—were heavy. Carrying the backpack even as far as her shop didn't excite her the first little bit.

"I can drop you off," Dallas offered. "Reese already left—she has to get to the high school."

Carol shook her head, smiling cheerfully. Dallas was a hoarder, and although she was as sweet as the day was long, there was no room in her car for a passenger and an overloaded backpack. "I'll be fine," Carol promised, wondering how often she'd said those words in her lifetime. "I need the exercise anyway, and it's a good chance to smell the flowers."

By the time she reached Main Street, she was weary of smelling the flowers, and the textbook had gained weight. Shoulders that were tired of her doing hair for a living anyway were screaming at her. Her only saving grace was that she'd drunk the entire bottle of water on the uphill side of the walk.

When the black pickup came to a screeching halt beside her, she didn't even raise her eyes.

"I'm sorry." He got out of the truck and sprinted to catch up with her. "I'm late because I didn't have my cell phone because this wild woman in a Pontiac hit me yesterday and—let me carry your bag, okay? We'll pretend we're still in high school, and I'll buy you a malted. If they still make them. Do they?" He pointed across the street, gesturing somewhere between Maeve Malone's and the Cup and Cozy. "Or a beer. Or coffee. Except you don't have your cup with you, so maybe a beer would be better."

She stopped walking. "Just stop."

"Stop what?" He reached for her backpack, but she held onto it, thinking she might smack him with it. Not hard. Just enough to get his attention and shut him up.

"I'm a grownup," she said patiently. "I can take care of myself. I'm not your responsibility or your assignment or your patient. The accident yesterday was as much my fault as yours." She met his gaze levelly. "Do you get that? You don't have to take care of me."

"But—" He fell silent, looking perplexed and then resigned. "I'm terrible at it anyway. My sisters always said they were glad I got good grades, but as big brothers went I was a D-plus on a good day."

"Yet you became a doctor? Isn't taking care of people in your job description?"

He waved a dismissive hand. "I'm a cutter. Ask any nurse I ever worked with, and she'll tell you my worth begins and ends with a scalpel."

She shifted the bag from her right arm to her left. "I've seen you on television. You've personally raised millions of dollars for research. You talked *me* into donating, and I didn't even know why I was doing it."

His eyes, as intensely warm brown as a sable coat, wore a flat expression. "That's not who I am." He took the backpack from her and she let him—sometimes independence wasn't worth making a scene over. "I'm hungry," he said. "Let's get a sandwich at the Cup and Cozy. Or did you want that beer? Malone's food is good, too."

"Cup and Cozy would be good. Did you get hold of the realtor?"

"I did." He took her hand and jaywalked, tugging Carol in his wake. Leave it to a southerner to be a gentleman even when he was trying to get you killed—an approaching car was close enough the driver was going to have to stand on it to stop. Carol was pretty sure the sound of screeching brakes was punctuated by a plethora of matching cusswords. She didn't blame the driver a bit.

"She came to the house," Steven continued, "I made my offer, and she went back to Kingsport as fast as her foot-high heels would carry her. I don't think she likes the country much. Who farms your land?"

"What?" Did this man ever talk in a straight line?

"Who farms your land?" He opened the door to the Cup and Cozy and stood aside for her to enter.

"John Sawyer. Remember Jake's younger brother? He was in my grade. He lives farther up Taylor Hill on his folks' place. He farms Miss Abigail's and Jeff Confer's, too."

"Are you and he—" He hesitated— "seeing each other?"

She turned, and he bumped right into her. She stood as close to him as his big feet and her not-small ones would allow and pinned him with a righteous glare. At least, it felt like she did, and she liked the sensation.

She *didn't* like him right then. "Did you really just ask me that question, Steven Elliot? I mean, *really*?"

"Well, yeah." His feet shuffled, bumping hers. "Is there something wrong with that question?"

"Only that John has a nice wife who's a good customer at the Clip Joint. They have three kids at the high school who don't need rumors about their dad passed around. And you'd *know* he's married, if you just pulled your head out of your ass for a split second. You were probably at his wedding. What were you thinking even asking such an asinine, none of your damn business kind of question?"

He looked delighted. "You're absolutely right. I apologize. Let's eat."

"I'm not—" Well, no, she *was* hungry. This morning's banana and cold pizza had worn off an hour or so ago, and anyone who could see could tell she liked to eat. For some people, extra weight meant slow metabolisms or medication that made them retain fluid or some other viable reason—for Carol, it meant she truly loved food. Damn it all.

They ate turkey club sandwiches, drank two tall cups each of house blend coffee, and talked about Tennessee history. Carol didn't think she'd been so comfortable with a man since Rand…no, since forever. Because even though she'd loved Rand Shipper, he'd been a boy.

Just as she'd been a girl. A size six with killer legs and hair the color of the caramel stuff you poured over ice cream. She hadn't been popular, but she'd had a boyfriend—half the social battle when you were sixteen.

"Oh, hey, I gotta go." She interrupted her own thesis concerning Andrew Jackson. "I've got four minutes to get to Elliot House, and I have to run to the shop to pick up my scissors and a permanent for Mrs. Rountree."

"They'll wait a few minutes. It's not like they're going anywhere on a Thursday afternoon."

Carol saw how he'd earned the D-plus in Big Brotherhood—he wasn't passing Nice Guy class, either. "I know they *would* wait," she said, reaching into her purse and digging for her wallet, "but I'm expected at noon. They shouldn't *have* to wait. The fact that they're retired people doesn't make their time any less valuable than mine." She came up with a crumpled twenty. "Or yours."

"Put it away." He frowned at her and snatched the check from her hand. He looked at it, obviously figuring how much to tip, then left the amount of the bill plus fifty percent. "They're all college and high school kids here," he said when she raised her eyebrows. "Always have been."

Oh. Well, maybe he was *passing*, but not with honors or anything.

The afternoon at Elliot House was often Carol's favorite day of the week. Today was no exception. She put the curlers in Mrs. Rountree's abundant white hair first, then daubed color on Maxie's roots. When Grace wandered through the small room set aside as a beauty parlor, a full laundry basket on her hip, Carol snagged her.

"If you'll rinse the solution off Mrs. Rountree," she bargained, "I can cut Mary Bridges' hair. She's so patient, but I know it's driving her nuts. Then you can wash Mary's hair while I trim Jonah's hair and clip his fingernails." She grinned at her friend. "I'll split my tips with you." That would amount to about three dollars and a dozen cookies.

"Oh, hey, how could I refuse?" Grace put her basket in the adjoining kitchen and came back to extend a hand to Mrs. Rountree. "Let's get you rinsed, Mrs. R. If you're nice to me, I'll try not to get water down your neck."

"You're a little dickens, Grace Campbell. Your mama would be shocked at how you behave," Mrs. Rountree scolded, then gave Grace a hug. "Did you read at the library today?"

"No. I do it Monday nights 'til school's out, then I'll do Thursday mornings again." Nothing in Grace's voice betrayed that this was a question she answered every time she came to Elliot House, although she exchanged a faint smile with Carol.

"You should be reading to your own babies, not to all the children in town."

"Someday." Grace helped Mrs. Rountree to lean

back in the shampoo chair. "There. You comfortable? Is the water warm enough?"

"You're not getting any younger, you know," the old lady admonished a few minutes later, as Grace helped her back to her chair.

"Sure I am. You just haven't noticed." But there was a thread of brittleness in Grace's response, and Carol gave her a quick glance. They'd grown closer since Promise's death than they had been before—Carol understood by now that Grace might have her issues, but she never let them spill over where they could hurt someone else.

"Leave her alone, Margaret," said Mary Bridges. "These young peoples' lives are none of our business." She tilted her head to get a better view of her newly trimmed gray hair. "Oh, that's such a relief. You're a genius with a pair of scissors." She got up, steadying herself with the arm of the chair, and gave Carol a hug. "Thank you, dear."

With Grace's help, Carol got most of the residents' hair and nail needs taken care of. To her surprise, Steven finished taking everyone's blood pressure and checking medications and came into the little room in time to help clip toenails, Carol's absolute least favorite part of her job. She'd never cut any of the arthritic, diabetic feet, but she was terrified she would.

"I never did a podiatry rotation," he said, "but I dated a podiatrist for a while once when Promise and I were on an 'I never want to see you again' kick, which we did about once a year when we were young." He grinned lasciviously at Mrs. Rountree. "Gave me a real foot fetish."

The old lady gave his hair a tug. "You're an ornery

one, you are."

Dinner was served at five o'clock. The residents always asked her to stay, but Carol never did. The eight elderly people loved their routines and she was reluctant to disrupt them. Besides, Steven and the Campbells were coming for dinner tonight. She was more excited by the prospect than she would have expected. She and Grace spent a lot of girlfriend time together, but they seldom socialized outside of that.

"What can I bring?" asked Grace when they separated in Elliot House's driveway.

"Something sweet," said Carol immediately, shifting her purse and scissors case from one hand to the other. "Enough of it I can have leftovers for breakfast. Not that I'm greedy or anything."

"I'll drop you off on my way up the hill," said Steven. "Do you need to stop at the grocery?"

"Yes. I need some wine." She smiled sweetly at him. "Unless you were going to bring a bottle of the good stuff."

He rolled his eyes. "I'll do that. Red, white, or rosé?"

"Whatever goes with grilled pork chops and garlic mashed potatoes. If you bring that, I don't need to stop anywhere."

"Chardonnay." He opened the passenger door of his truck and waited while she pulled herself in, then closed the door and sprinted around the front to slide in under the wheel.

"Okay." Since she didn't know one wine from another, she was open to being agreeable. Mostly, she was trying to remember if she had a working corkscrew. And there was something else. "Steven?"

He backed into the street. "What?"

"What's wrong with Grace?"

Chapter Four

Carol's question was blunt, and her green gaze held steady on his.

Steven hesitated. Grace and Carol were friends, close ones at that, but his sister was secretive to a fault. She probably wouldn't thank him for talking about Dillon's and her business.

"You can tell me," said Carol, "or if it's too personal for you to talk about I'll ask her so she can tell me to mind my own business. Wouldn't be the first time, but sometimes she needs to talk about things, and I've learned over the years how to get her to share. Occasionally I do it by yelling at her and acting as if she's hurting my feelings—which sometimes she is. Other times it has to do with the wine—we both get a little chatty near the end of our second glass."

"She can't get pregnant," he said. "No, that's not true. She can, but she can't carry a child."

"Oh." Something came into Carol's eyes that he couldn't ignore. Hurt. Old and weary pain. "Biological clock's ticking hard, too, isn't it?" Her voice was flat.

"I imagine so. She hasn't said much, and Dillon and I haven't talked about it." He and Dillon would play golf tomorrow, with Jake Sawyer and Grant, and then they would play pool at Malone's. Maybe, over beer and the sandwiches Malone's was famous for, they would get to the subject that darkened Dillon's eyes and made Grace's features tighten. Or maybe they wouldn't. They'd been supporting each other through life's slings and arrows since their first day of kindergarten, but they'd never gotten particularly good at the talking part of it. Doing was easier.

"Every now and then"—Carol gazed out the truck window at the trees that canopied the road up Taylor Hill—"life bites you in the ass."

"It certainly does that." Steven swung the truck into her driveway. "Do you want some help with dinner?

"No, but thanks for the transportation. See you all about seven, right?"

"Right." He lingered, watching her go to her porch with Barney walking politely at her side while Fred waited at the door with a switching tail. Spring flowers bloomed everywhere, like they did in Grace's yard, but his sister's were artistic in their profusion—something she seemed to achieve with very little thought, albeit much effort. Carol's were more abundant than artistic, but they were just as pleasing to the eye. The colors reminded him of her shop. Feminine but comfortable.

That was how she was, too. She was overweight and very aware of it—her conversation was sprinkled with self-deprecation—but she didn't seem to beat herself up over it. She didn't hide behind clothes that were too loose or too dark or too conservative for who she was. In a world where self-esteem wasn't always easy to find for those who didn't fit into society's round holes, she seemed to like herself.

And she was a good cook. Last night's pizza was both homemade and delicious. Steven ate his share and then some. When Carol invited them to dinner tonight,

Dillon had been euphoric enough to warrant a scowl from Grace.

Steven was anxious for Dillon and Grace to see Miss Abigail's. Maybe if his sister got involved with the restoration of the "old lady," it would take her mind off not being able to have a baby. Dillon's attitude mirrored Steven's—throw money at something until it was what you wanted—but Crooked Mouth's house and gardens were labors of Grace's love as much as the Campbells' money.

He wasn't disappointed with their reaction to the old house. "Jesus," said Dillon conversationally, standing in the middle of the kitchen, "what a mess. It's like a frat house in our day after losing in the Final Four."

"Or winning. All depends on the liquor and drug availability." Steven arrowed a frown at him. "And we're way too young to use the term, 'in our day,' Campbell."

"Grace, where are you going?" Dillon bellowed as his wife disappeared up the creaky back stairs. "You could be lost for days up there. Do you have your phone with you?"

"Are you going to make it like it was in the 1800s, Steven?" she called, ignoring her husband.

"I hadn't thought that far," he yelled back. "What do you think?"

"Well…" Her voice trailed away, and Dillon glared at Steven.

"If she's gone into the attic, you know what she's like in places like that. We'll never get her out."

"Oh, shit…" Steven hit the stairs at a sprint. "Gracie, don't go in the attic. I haven't been there yet, and I don't know what's there. Even Carol didn't know, and she's a freaking history book on this house."

"I'm not in the attic." She came out of a bathroom when his heels hit the upstairs floorboards, Dillon right behind him. "I really like this, Steven. The woodwork's in good shape under all the dirt, and even the plaster isn't bad except in the bathrooms. In those, you need to go right down to the studs—you'll have plenty of time for that while you're getting those bathtubs restored. Someone was forward-thinking when they built this house—there are actually closets. Remember the ones—" She disappeared again, into a bedroom across the hall.

He followed her, and Dillon trailed after him. "Remember what?"

She straightened from where she was bent over the contents of a cedar chest, her hair a maze of cobwebs. "In Elliot House, we had to have closets built into every bedroom. We grew up there and were used to hanging our clothes wherever we could find an available space—usually on the floor in your case—but when it became senior housing, that didn't work anymore."

"I never minded it," Steven told Dillon, who was beaming at his wife like he didn't have a lick of sense.

Truth was, when it came to Grace, that's pretty much how it was. Thank God. There were a lot of things in life that pissed Steven off, but he'd hit the jackpot as far as brothers-in-law went, and Dillon and Grant weren't too bad as husbands, either.

"Of course you didn't mind it. I was the one who had to follow you around picking up after you. *I* minded it." Grace grinned at him as she went past.

"Where are you going now? Not the attic," he

repeated.

"Okay." Disappointment crossed her features. "Well, this is cool, Steven. I think it'll be great for you. But huge. What will you do with all the space?"

"Fill it up." Steven rubbed his stomach when it growled. "Seen enough? I told Carol we'd be there at seven."

Miss Abigail's had about three times as much space as he needed—maybe five times—but he'd known last night when he and Carol came around the curve in the driveway that this was where he was meant to be. He thought he might even be able to sleep nights in the big room at the back that had once been the maid's quarters.

Carol was at her grill when they got there. She was dressed in something long and gauzy—the effect of which was compromised by a chef's apron. Her hair was up in a messy ponytail. She gave Grace a hug and appropriated the wine Steven was carrying. "Oh, my," she said, perusing its label with wide eyes. "Good thing I found the corkscrew. I'd have felt bad breaking the neck off this to get into it."

"You got anything I can snack on?" Dillon brought up the rear with a cake carrier. "Grace wouldn't let me have *any* of this, and I haven't eaten for days, I swear."

"Uh-oh. You're on Chapter Six, aren't you?" Carol shook her head sympathetically. She put a few pieces of grilled asparagus on a plate and handed it to him. "Grace says you never eat when you're there. You just whine…er…mention that whatever you're writing is a piece of shit and you should go back to—back to what, Grace? I can never remember."

"Depends on how pathetic he's being." Grace

stood beside her. "If it's real bad, he says digging ditches, but if he just wants attention, he'll say he needs to see his therapist."

"That's either the bartender at Malone's or I come and see you for a haircut." Dillon grinned at Carol. "I'm done with Chapter Six, though, so this is a celebratory evening. I'm starved." He bit into the asparagus. "God, this is so good I could almost forget it's a vegetable."

Carol laughed, and Steven stopped moving to listen to the sound on the evening air. It was, to use one of Deac Rivers' favorite terms, a balm to the spirit.

Steven realized, with the sound of Carol's laughter still whispering through his senses, that for the first time since Promise's death, he wanted to be with someone for something besides sex—although that wasn't out of the question, either. He wanted a relationship that went beyond their friendship and he wanted it to grow slow and easy and maybe—and this was a really big maybe—long-lasting. Not permanent. Oh, hell no, never permanent again, but longer than a weekend. Deeper than a shared fondness for good wine and classic rock and roll.

He had not cared, in these past three years without Promise, whether he lived or died. While he'd never considered suicide or taken more or greater risks than he ever had, neither had he given the future much thought   or   concern.   Whatever happened…well…happened.

But now, on a brick patio that smelled invitingly of pork chops and good wine and springtime in the mountains, Steven Elliot wanted to live. To share good times with people, and, come to that, bad ones. He wanted patients to be more than their faulty hearts—he wanted to sit in a consultation room with them and talk about where they were going on vacation and did they think the Titans could go the whole way this year.

He wanted to hear laughter on the wind and have it be solace rather than irritant. And he really liked the idea of the laughter being that of a nice woman. Like Carol Whitney.

But there was more to his little epiphany than Carol, and he knew what it was. "I have to run over to Knoxville Saturday," he said, accepting the platter of pork chops she handed him. "Would you like to go with me?"

****

"She was right again." said Grace with a gusty sigh. "You really are the best cook in Tennessee just like Promise always said. So I think we should just come for supper every night. I'll bring dessert and Dillon and Steven can do the dishes. That work for you?"

Carol split the last of the wine between Grace's glass and hers. "Sure does. That cake was some wonderful, my expanding waistline is here to tell you."

"I only ate a little piece." Dillon served himself another, bigger slice as he spoke.

"And three pork chops," Grace reminded him. "Plate-size."

"Small plate." Carol and Steven spoke in unison, then laughed, their gazes meeting. Reaction settled low in her abdomen and she sat still a moment, just enjoying it.

She'd been startled when he asked her to go to Knoxville with him to attend the funeral of a patient. She was even more surprised when she agreed to go.

She hated funerals, but she supposed most everybody did. Being a surgeon, Steven might be used to them, but being a widower, he might also hate them more than most.

"We probably have time to hit a bucket of balls at the driving range." Dillon peered at his watch. "Swinging clubs will work off the cake. At least a piece of it. And we won't be so pathetic when Grant and Jake set about kicking our asses tomorrow."

"Well, that's rude." Grace scowled at him. "Eating and running and not even helping with the dishes. I thought you two had been brought up a little better than that. I'm calling your mom, Dillon."

Carol waved a dismissive hand. "I'll get the dishes. You go on."

"Oh, that's it, let them get away with it." Grace shook her head at her. "I'll stay and help. I can walk home."

"Thanks for dinner." Steven followed Carol into the kitchen, carrying his plate. "And for going with me Saturday. It won't be fun."

She shrugged. "Sometimes the hardest things are necessary, though, for one reason or another." Like cooking dinner for company tonight when she'd wanted to throw herself across her bed and have a tantrum after Bill's news.

"I'm sorry, Carol, but it will cost more to fix than the car's worth and even then, there's no telling how long it would last." The mechanic's words had been on the answering machine when she'd gotten home from Elliot House.

Steven walked back to the porch with her. "Your mother lives in Greenville, doesn't she? Do you want to

67

stop by and see her?"

Carol almost said no because that was what she did when favors were offered that she couldn't possibly return. But she didn't have a car and wasn't sure when she would get one—that changed things. While Greenville was only an hour away, it was definitely too far to either walk or ride a bicycle.

Then there was the guilt. Dixie Whitney wasn't one to make her only surviving child feel remorseful about not visiting often enough, but Carol did anyway. Nothing lessened the certainty that she didn't do enough for the mother who'd had a choice between a pretty baby and one who looked like Yoda and had chosen Yoda.

"Thanks," she said, feeling awkward. *I'll give him two haircuts for free.*

"We could take her to dinner if she'd like that." He reached, tucking a wayward lock of hair behind her ear.

It took all Carol had not to turn her face into that touch.

"She would, but Aunt Jo will want to go, too." She had to force her mind into a straight line. "That's my dad's sister. She and Mom share a house. Their husbands died within a couple of months of each other and they pooled their resources. I wouldn't know how to invite one and not the other."

"Why would you? We'll do that, then. I'll borrow Dillon's car, since my truck doesn't have a back seat."

"You don't have to do that," she protested. "We don't have to take them out."

"Actually, I wouldn't want him to hear me say this"—Steven looked over his shoulder at where Dillon was talking to Grace at the door of the truck—"but I kind of like that SUV he drives. I can't admit it because I gave him so much hell about giving up the Maserati." He smiled at her, his eyes warm. "See you Saturday morning. And thanks for dinner."

He left before she could answer, meeting his sister on the way. They spoke for a minute, he laughed out loud and kissed her forehead before joining Dillon. Grace came onto the porch. "He's a goofball."

Carol chuckled. "He's a man."

That was how she was seeing him. Absolutely. Not as her friend's brother or another friend's husband or even as a tall and exceedingly sexy doctor. Although the sexy part was coming through far too clearly to not see it.

Carol and Grace washed the dishes, laughing about the empty space below the counter where a dishwasher would go as soon as Carol could afford one. For the time being, Fred and Barney napped there on an old bedspread. At least until Carol went to bed, at which time her normally quite independent animals became needy and Barney collapsed beside her bed and Fred curled up behind her knees.

"Steven told me," said Carol into a moment of comfortable silence.

When Grace stiffened like the proverbial poker, Carol laughed and put her arms around her, holding her sudsy hands out of the way. "Don't get mad. He's worried about you. So am I. I can hear the damn clock ticking, too."

Grace hugged her back, her slim shoulders shaking a little, and Carol felt tears slip down her cheeks. There'd been enough pain and loss in the other woman's life—she shouldn't have to deal with this, too.

At the let's-get-organized meeting for their twenty-year class reunion, she and Grace had been the only non-parents in attendance. They laughed about it, then sat at the Cup and Cozy and went over the list of class members to see how many of them had never had children. There were several, more than the evening's meeting indicated. They turned the laughter on themselves then, for letting something like that matter. They'd chosen not to be single mothers, after all, although Carol was certain she'd have been a perfectly happy one if Miranda had lived. But Grace had married late and Carol not at all, so being married mothers didn't look very likely, either. And that was fine—it wasn't as if they *minded* not having children.

But sometimes, no matter how hard she pretended you didn't mind, she still did.

"We'll adopt," said Grace, "which is fine with me, and with Dillon, too. It's just the waiting." Her chuckle was wry. "When I was a kid, I thought growing up meant you didn't have to wait for everything all the time. Man, was that ever wrong."

"Sure was." Carol sniffled. "I'm still waiting for another Rand Shipper to come along, and it's been almost twenty years."

Grace dried her eyes on the dishtowel in her hand. "Even *I* only waited fifteen years for Dillon to come back to town, and I didn't even know what I was waiting for."

"What about international adoption?" Carol took the carafe from the coffeemaker and lifted a questioning eyebrow. "We can drink it while we walk into town."

Grace nodded. "We've been checking all the resources. It would be hard for us to be out of country

70

for a few weeks because of Elliot House, especially with Dillon's next book coming out next month, so we can't commit to that yet. Probably next year."

"What about a gestational carrier?"

"What?" Grace frowned in confusion.

"A gestational surrogate. Someone in the shop for highlights was looking into it and she read articles to us while she waited for the color. It's not that you can't *make* babies, you just can't carry them. A surrogate would do that for you."

Grace's withdrawal was immediate. She went back to the sink to finish drying the dishes. "How would we find one?" She put down the pan she was holding and stood still, gazing out the big window. "And what would we do if she changed her mind? What would *I* do? I know I'm a coward, but I don't think I could stand it."

Carol let the water out of the sink, watching it circle its way down the drain. She sprayed the sink clean, then wiped water spots off the faucet before folding the dishcloth into a neat square. Then refolding it. And once more. She stared out at the budding lilacs in the yard, at the bush with little red flowers she loved but had never identified, at the patch of daffodils she hadn't planted but came up to cheer her every March. Kind of like the ones she'd planted near Miranda's grave. *Oh, Miranda.*

She didn't know how long she stood there looking back over the past three years. Although Grace and Promise hadn't excluded other people from their friendship, no one had ever quite been a part of it, either, until one of them got sick and worried about the other being alone.

71

Promise had drawn both Carol and Faith closer into the circle then. "When I'm gone," she'd said one day when she and Carol were alone in the shop, "will you be there for Grace? Will you pick up the ball when she drops it? She always wants to be the strong one, but sometimes she can't. She just can't."

Carol had promised.

"Promise used to say—" Carol stopped, choking. She unfolded and wrung out the dishcloth until the motion hurt her hands. "She used to say all of us sitting around the shop talking and doing each other's nails and hair did more healing than a whole regimen of chemo, remember?"

"I do." Grace smiled with the memory. "She was right, too. It got us through some bad days. After she died, I used to come in there and just sit because I couldn't stand being alone—your books and magazines have never been so orderly! You've been such a friend. I take you for granted and expect you to do the same. I love that we're able to do that."

Carol draped the dishcloth over the little basket by the sink and took a deep breath before turning to meet Grace's spice-brown eyes. Her stomach felt as if its contents were swirling around like the dishwater had, but her voice was steady and calm. "I love that, too. So I'll do it. I'll carry your baby."

Chapter Five

A lot of people in Peacock still wore black to funerals, but Carol wasn't sure what rich people in Knoxville did. Her mother had always said, "When in doubt, a little black dress is always right." Of course, Dixie Whitney had expected her daughter to remain a size six—or an eight at the outside.

Nevertheless, Carol wore the slim black dress that made her feel smaller than she actually was, black and white high heels, and pantyhose—which she walked down to the Dollar Store at the bottom of Taylor Hill to buy because she didn't have any. After sweating her way back up the hill, she had to shower again. She considered herself a pretty clean individual, but she'd scarcely ever bathed twice by ten in the morning.

She'd just finished filling a care package for her mother and aunt and was brushing cat hair from the skirt of her dress when Steven called her name from the other side of the screen in the back door.

"I'm almost ready," she called, "if I can just get Fred to keep his fur to himself—he's such a generous cat. Come on in."

They met in the kitchen, and she stared at him. He'd undoubtedly worn a suit to Promise's funeral, but Carol had been as grief-stricken as everyone else at her friend's death—she hadn't really paid attention to how anyone was dressed. This morning, standing in her kitchen with one shoe on and one shoe off, she paid attention.

Wow.

Promise Delaney always had his heart, but nearly every girl in high school yearned after him at one time or another, whether she admitted it or not. Rand used to say, hell, Elliot was so pretty that half the *guys* wanted to go out with him, too. Age had turned teenage handsomeness into something all her classes hadn't given her words for, but the tan suit he wore was a perfect frame for it.

"You look nice," he said now.

"Thank you." She slipped her other shoe on and checked her earrings. "So do you." *In, oh, holy God…spades.*

"Maybe we could just go see your mom and take her and your aunt to lunch." He spoke in a rush, running a hand through his hair and making its long disarray even sexier if that were possible. "Going to this kid's funeral can't possibly be the right thing to do, or it wouldn't feel this bad."

"Spoken like a male in arrested adolescence."

His hands dropped to his sides. "How do you do that?"

"Do what?"

"That's the same thing Grace said this morning, only not quite so politely. Was it a class you girls had in high school, how to get a guy out of himself?"

"Yeah, we had it in the biology room right after home ec. Neither class really took, but they tried."

"Home ec took with you. You're as good a cook as Jean Rivers at the Deacon's Bench, and she's awesome."

"She is. I've gone in and helped her a few times when her *sous* chef wasn't there. Working with her was like taking lessons. I've taken a few classes—in everything, come to that—but they weren't as helpful as she is." Carol snatched a lacy black shawl off the back of a barstool. "I'm ready. Will you carry the basket? It's Mom and Aunt Jo's care package. They always tell me I 'shouldn't have,' but they have fun with the goodies in it."

He took her arm as they walked to the car, and she flashed a smile at him. "Is it that obvious I don't walk in heels very much?"

"No, but with our history, there's a really good chance you'll fall off the sidewalk and twist your ankle."

"Or you'll push me."

"There is that." He opened the car door for her, then put the basket in the back of the SUV. "Nice day."

She squinted into the cheerful late March sun. "It is."

"We could always skip this and drive to the ocean. I haven't seen it in a long time."

Carol didn't even want to *think* about the ocean. She'd canceled her July vacation right after talking to the mechanic. She waited 'til Steven was in the driver's seat and pinned him with her sternest Sunday-school-teacher gaze. "No."

"Right."

They were on the highway and the Eagles were singing "Hotel California" on the CD player when Steven broke the comfortable silence between them. "So."

She knew what he wanted to ask, but she had no

idea how much he knew of the conversations she and Grace had had since night before last. "Yes, I do," she said pleasantly. "Not as well as I cook, but not badly, either. I actually do quite a bit of it if you count the quilts I make for the children's hospital. I don't like putting zippers in things, but hardly anyone—"

"Are you really planning to carry a baby for Grace and Dillon?"

"Yes." She cut her gaze to him, but he never took his eyes from the road. Nothing in the line of his body gave her a clue about how he felt. "Providing the medical questions are answered to all of our satisfaction. I'm bigger than I should be, my blood pressure is iffy, I'm thirty-seven. I've had—" She stopped, turning her face toward the window. She'd told Grace this—she didn't need to tell Grace's brother, too.

"I know your baby died, but that wasn't a pregnancy problem, was it?"

"No. Miranda died of SIDS when she was three months old." *Sudden infant death syndrome. Crib death.* Carol had tried saying it both ways, but neither one hurt any less, so she'd taken to using the acronym. Most people knew what the letters meant. If they didn't, she ignored their inquiring eyebrows and changed the subject.

"Have you had an abortion? Or more than one?" He spoke impersonally, like someone who'd just met her and didn't like her very much. She felt wounded. He should have known her better.

"No." She snapped the word off. The sharp sound of her own voice reminded her of cleaning green beans straight from the garden. *Snap, snap, pop.* The little

76

internal analogy made her smile in spite of her irritation. Then she sighed. "I had a miscarriage about ten years ago. My gynecologist said there was no reason I couldn't have more children, but I've never gotten pregnant again by either accident or design. That's one of the things that will bear consideration. I don't want to be the vehicle for Grace having her heart broken." *Or mine. It will hurt me, too, if I can't do this most basic of woman-things.*

"It's a lot to ask even from a relative, much less a friend. Why would you do it for her?"

Carol hesitated. When she finally answered, her voice sounded flat to her own ears. "I go to the cemetery every week or so. So does Grace. You probably know that. She puts flowers on Promise's grave and on your mother's. Sometimes…often…when I get to Miranda's grave, I'll find fresh flowers already there. When Rand died, and Ed, and then when I lost Miranda and wanted to die, too, Grace and Promise were right there for me. I wasn't a part of the friendship they shared, not then, but I was a part of them anyway. And they remained a part of me. Grace and I aren't as close as she and Promise were, but she's probably the best friend I've ever had anyway." *I promised your wife I'd be there for your sister, but I don't know how to tell you that.*

She looked at him, not going on until he glanced over and met her gaze. For just a heartbeat of time, long enough to connect. She told him what she *could* explain. "Grace has helped me care for my baby all these years, she's listened to me talk about Rand and Ed when I couldn't hold it inside anymore and I didn't have anyone else to listen." She blinked a couple of times because her eyes felt sticky. "Having a baby for her doesn't seem like a lot to me."

He didn't answer, didn't take his gaze from the road to mingle it with hers again, but he reached to where her arm rested on the console between their seats and took her hand. He didn't give it an encouraging squeeze or raise it to his lips or pat it. He just folded her fingers in his and held them for a long time.

****

Jamie Scott's funeral was a nightmare proportionate with the reputation and the fortune of his family. Steven recognized the officiating pastor, whose television ministry reached millions. Some of the residents of Elliot House watched his message when they were unable to attend church. Steven had sat on the arm of the chair in Jonah and Maxie's living room once and watched the show with them.

"Slick," he'd commented, frowning. "His clothes are too nice, and he's wearing too much makeup. I think his steps are choreographed every time he comes out from behind the pulpit. I expect him to do a little soft shoe any day now."

"Judge not." Maxie rapped him smartly on the arm. "He's reading out of the same Bible as we do."

Steven guessed that was true, but the clergyman's glistening white smile and immobile and artfully streaked hair made him uncomfortable. So did the loud weeping of Jamie Scott's mother and stepmother. Where had they been when nursing staff came in off-shift to sit and tell jokes and sing songs with the scared boy until he was able to rest?

None of those caregivers were in the well-dressed selection of mourners and Steven wondered if no one else on the hospital staff had received the black-bordered invitation he had. Anger stirred when he remembered the nurse who stroked Jamie's hair and recited the 121st Psalm after he died, and the one who sang hymns and wiped away tears as she prepared the boy's wasted body for transport.

Jamie's father sat silent and morose between his wife and his ex-wife, glancing at his watch when the proceedings apparently went on longer than he liked.

Steven wondered why people like this got to be parents when Grace and the woman beside him did not.

At the end of the seemingly interminable service, he was able to nod at Jamie's parents and escort Carol out into the sunshine before he had to express sympathy he wasn't sure he felt. "One of the nurses used to sing that song from the sixties, 'We'll Sing in the Sunshine,' to Jamie," he said as they crossed the packed parking lot to the car. "He used to laugh at her, and she'd say, 'You just hide and watch, youngun.' I sure hope she was right. I hope he's singing loud and clear."

When they were on the two-lane highway that led to Greenville, fresh drive-through coffee steaming from cups between them, he said again, "Thank you for going. I'm still not sure why it felt necessary, but it did."

"It was necessary so there would be someone there to mourn for him rather than put on a show." She smiled at him before raising her coffee to her lips. "Someone to help sing him into the sunshine."

****

"Why, Carolina Jessamine, if you're not the prettiest thing." Carol's Aunt Jo, as tall as Carol, gave her a talcum-scented hug and moved on to Steven.

"And you are, too, young man. My goodness, a man in an open collar with his sleeves rolled up is enough to give a girl palpitations, don't you think, Dixie?"

"If it's a man who's still breathing, he gives you palpitations, Jo." Carol's mother's voice was sharp, but her eyes weren't. They were as soft as the white hair in her ageless pageboy. "I'm so glad to see you, darlin'." Her long embrace was a reminder that as long as Dixie Whitney lived, Carol would be loved. Not understood—no, not even close to that—and not always accepted, but the love was unconditional. It would have been nice to be their natural child, as Ed was, and to have been the favorite, again as Ed was, but one shouldn't miss what she'd never had. She really shouldn't.

"Dr. Elliot, I thank you for bringing my daughter." Dixie released her and extended her hand to Steven.

"It's Steven, Miss Dixie." Steven's smile could have charmed the birds right out of the trees—it did no less with Carol's mother and aunt. "I was glad to come. I hope you don't mind that Carol dragged me along with her."

Carol smiled at him, touched that he'd made the visit sound like her idea. "We thought we'd take you to lunch."

"That would be nice, but Jo fixed a big enough pot roast for a greedy army and I baked a pineapple upside down cake—we must have known you were coming." Dixie led the way inside, and Carol noticed that she was moving slower these days. She touched things as they went into the kitchen, something she'd always done— she was both artistic and tactile—but now she held onto objects a little longer. Carol wondered if she used them to help keep her balance. The thought made her heart ache.

"Set the table, please, Carol," Jo requested. "We're eating in the kitchen. There's a mess on the dining room table. Your mother's making a quilt for Quinn's little boy for his birthday."

Carol turned from the cupboard that held the dinner plates. "Who?"

"The youngest one that Quinn and his partner adopted." Dixie held her gaze. "You're his godmother, aren't you?"

"Yes." Carol lifted down the gold-rimmed china she'd grown up with, setting four plates on the counter carefully before reaching for dessert plates. "But I didn't know you'd kept contact with Quinn."

"I haven't always, more shame to me." Dixie stirred a pot on the old stove. "Get me those serving dishes up on the top shelf there if you would please, Steven. Jo, are you ladling up the roast and vegetables or are you just going to stand there?"

"Thought I might just stand here if it's all the same to you." Jo lifted a Dutch oven from a back burner and set it on a trivet on the counter. "You need to behave yourself, Dixie. You don't want these young people knowing what an old biddy you really are."

"Mom." Carol kept her voice patient. "Quinn?"

"I was going through things thinking that after seventy-some years I might actually throw something away. I found a letter he'd written me when your brother died. Just saying how sorry he was, and that he'd considered Ed a good friend. And I remembered him, you know, remembered walking out onto the porch that day after the funeral. You and he were standing there, and he was crying." Dixie drew a long, shuddering breath. Her hands trembled, and Steven stepped forward to take the saucepan from her and pour the corn into a bowl. "Thank you, dear. One of the joys of being old is also being weak and pathetic."

Carol, carrying the plates on one arm, offered her other one to her mother. "Mom, are you okay?"

"I'm fine. My energy's kind of…well, gone to hell in a hand basket lately, to tell the truth. Jo says I'm old, and she knows all about old."

"Mother, you just said 'hell' without it having a Biblical context. What is going on here?" Carol eased her into a seat and began to set the table.

"It's always Biblical, honey, just more sometimes than others." Dixie waved a dismissive hand at her. "The napkins are in that drawer over there. Anyway, I went out on the Internet—that's just manna from heaven, isn't it? You can play games and everything. I've been playing poker with a diverse group of people. It's very interesting."

Poker? Carol's eyebrows rose. She refused to meet Steven's gaze, afraid they'd both start laughing. But who was this woman and what had she done with Carol's mother?

"I found an address for Quinn." Dixie refolded the napkins Carol gave her, turning them into pretty silverware pockets with virtually no effort. "He's a lawyer, you know, and wasn't at all hard to find. I wrote to him and he wrote back, sending me pictures of his family."

"You know then that he's gay." Carol laid the napkins at the four places, slipping the flatware inside them, keeping the pieces straight. *You could have asked me. I'd have given you the address, the kids' birthdays. We could have talked about how much he and Ed loved each other. All you had to do is ask.* She stepped back from the table, coughing into her elbow, trying to dislodge the resentment that sat hard in her chest.

"Well, yes, dear, I know, and I know Ed was, too. I think I always did. I didn't know how to face it, or how to talk to Ed or your father about it. Or even you—it didn't seem fair to you to burden you with it. It wasn't your fault I didn't know how to face things. If I hadn't been such a coward, he might still be alive." She met Carol's eyes, and the grief on her face was as fresh and new as if she'd lost her son this morning instead of nearly twenty years before. "I haven't quite figured out how to live with that."

You should have talked to me. I was always there. But Carol knelt before her, feeling a run pop into her pantyhose. "You didn't do anything wrong. You were the best mother to Ed and me, and the best wife to Dad that anyone could have been. Things were different then." Her own hurt seemed childish in the face of her mother's grief. Coming in second with a mother as loving as Dixie Whitney was still a pretty good position.

"But you knew, didn't you? And you talked to him about it. Your brother knew you'd love him no matter what. He didn't know that about Dad and me, and that was wrong."

"Of course he knew it." Carol took Dixie's gnarled hands into a gentle grip, shaking them for emphasis. "We both did. We knew we drove you crazy— sometimes we even *tried* to drive you crazy—but we knew we were loved. I still do." She hadn't been loved as much as Ed. Never that. But the words were true—she'd never once doubted Dixie's love for her. She still didn't.

"That's a great gift for a kid, Miss Dixie." Steven moved past Carol, setting serving bowls on the table where Jo's pointing finger directed him. "My sisters and I had that from our mother, but our dad—" He shook his head.

Dixie looked up at him as if she'd just remembered he was there. "Robert Elliot was a son of a bitch."

Carol was stunned into silence, but Steven's shout of laughter rolled through the room, bringing cleansing and joy to a pain-filled day. "That he was, ma'am, and your husband was not. He was a southern gentlemen and homosexuality would have gone down hard with him, but he still would have loved his son. I knew Ed pretty well. I don't believe you or his father could have changed his ultimate path."

Hope shone in Dixie's faded eyes. "Do you really think that, Steven?"

"Yes, ma'am, I do." Steven's smile was gentle. "Carol and I were just at the funeral of a boy who didn't ever have the love Ed did, and who never had the opportunity to choose his own course in life. I understand you having mixed feelings about his death, but the truth is that he chose it."

"I was so angry with him," Dixie whispered, tears rolling down her cheeks. "I thought I'd never get over it."

"I was, too." Carol's eyes stung. "Still am sometimes. And that's all right. We don't have to *like* his choices." She grinned at her mother, although her cheeks trembled with the effort. "I don't think you

84

always liked mine so well, either."

Dixie freed one hand and stroked her cheek. Carol turned into the caress. "Sometimes, though…yes, you did present challenges."

"I know. Ed was the easy one."

"He was. But you were both interesting, to say the least." Her mother grinned back at her, and Carol recognized herself in the expression.

How could that be? She didn't look like either of her birth parents, but she *did* resemble the woman who'd raised her? There was, Carol realized, a certain comfort in that.

Steven's hand came to rest on Carol's shoulder. "Could we eat now?" he asked meekly. "That roast is going to be some delicious."

"It is." Jo nodded assertively. "Because I cooked it. Dixie Whitney would have turned it into shoe leather."

"And if Jo'd made the cake, you'd have had to spoon it out of the pan instead of slicing it," Dixie retorted smartly. "Take your seats, children. Carol, ask the blessing, please, and don't cut it short. The food will still be here if the prayer lasts more than three seconds."

"Yes, ma'am." Carol sat where Jo told her to and reached for Steven and Dixie's hands as she bowed her head.

They discussed politics over the main course—Dixie was a Republican, Jo a Democrat—religion over dessert (Jo a Baptist, Dixie a Methodist, although they both attended the Church of God around the corner), and the condition of Tennessee's highway system while Carol and Steven cleared the table. Both of the women oohed and aahed over the contents of the basket Carol brought them. They said they'd serve the bottle of wine to company, but Carol noticed they didn't offer to open it.

"Mom." Carol sat beside her mother at the round kitchen table. "I need to tell you something."

Fear leaped into Dixie's faded eyes. She looked both wary and anxious. "You're not ill, are you, Carolina?"

"No. It's about Steven's sister Grace—you remember her. She can't carry babies, so I'm going to try to carry one for her. I know it may not seem natural to everybody, but it does to us."

"Well." Tears washed away the fear, and Dixie caught the moisture with the corner of a handkerchief she withdrew from her pocket. "We'll make the baby a quilt, won't we, Jo? And we'll pretend to be its grandmothers. I'll be the better one, of course."

"Absolutely." Jo lifted her coffee cup in salute. "And we'll give all kinds of advice nobody wants. Especially your mother. You know how she is."

"You don't mind?" Carol had been afraid the announcement would toss Dixie back into mourning for Ed.

"Oh, in a way I do, because I'd love to have grandchildren of my own, and I think you'd be such a good mama yourself, but no one knows better than me what a gift you're giving." Dixie leaned to hug her, and Carol drew in the scent of lilies of the valley.

That sweet fragrance and soft lace-edged handkerchiefs and the pageboy haircut that hadn't changed since Carol cut it that way while she was in beauty school—these drew the picture of her mother. This was the woman who'd never missed a volleyball game in all the years Carol played it. She'd been a Girl Scout leader until her daughter begged to be allowed to quit, at which time they'd gone to lunch at the Cup and Cozy and celebrated their freedom from green uniforms.

Resentment was like grief—you could feel it without it taking over everything else. In the end, Carol discovered every time she spent the day with her mother, love was stronger than both. It wasn't always enough, but it came close.

"Thanks, Mom." Carol sniffed. "We need to head back now. Steven will turn into a head of cabbage if we're not home before nine. Can we fill our cups with some of that coffee before we go?"

"Really good cabbage, though. I would be solid and wouldn't have that moldy-looking black stuff in my leaves." Steven shook hands with Jo. "Thanks for a great dinner. I think I see where Carol got her cooking skills."

"Come back anytime." Jo beamed at him. "We enjoyed the visit, didn't we, Dixie?" She bustled ahead to fill their cups.

"We did." Dixie pushed herself to her feet to walk with them to the door. "When are you going to the beach, Carol?"

"I'm not." Carol kissed her aunt's cheek and then her mother's. "I changed my mind."

"Oh, but you—" Dixie stopped, firming her lips. "It's none of my business how you spend vacation, but I hope you take some time off even if you don't go anywhere."

"I will. Promise." Carol held up crossed fingers. "Ready, Steven?"

"I am." He bent to kiss Dixie's wrinkled cheek. "I hope to see you both again soon, Miss Dixie."

She touched his face. "You're such a nice boy."

Carol grinned over her shoulder. "No, he's not. He's sucking up."

Inside the car, as they left Greenville's city limits, she said, "Thanks for going. I forget sometimes how lucky I am to have them and go too long between visits."

"That funeral was a reminder, too, wasn't it?" His voice was dry, pain rasping through it.

"It was." She laid a hand on his forearm, thinking abstractly that he was certainly well-muscled for such a lean man. "It's good that you went."

He stopped at an intersection and took a drink of the coffee Jo had given him, dislodging Carol's hand. "Your aunt has a way around a coffee pot, doesn't she?"

She nodded. "She taught me a lot of what I know in the kitchen."

He met her gaze, the expression way too sexy for a pompous man in an Armani suit. Of course, the ponytail, warm brown eyes, and the earring in his left ear lent him an air of—what, danger?

Yes, Carol's stomach, flipping as if she were an adolescent with a crush, warned her. *Danger.*

Chapter Six

As soon as Grace opened the door to her knock, Carol started talking. "The fertility center called the shop ten minutes ago. All systems are go. I don't know how we all passed the psychological part, but we did." She grinned over Grace's shoulder at Dillon and Steven. "Even the father. He must have lied, huh, Steven?"

"Well, I did." Dillon came forward, his arm going around Grace's waist. "But Steven helped me. Lying was how we got through junior high, but I'm not good at it anymore. Marriage reforms you." He reached past Carol with his free arm to close the door, then gave her a quick, strong hug on the way back.

Carol had known Grace since Sunday mornings in the primary class at the Old Methodist Church. They, along with Promise, had usually sat in a row of little red chairs against the wall with their hands folded in their laps because one of them—more often than not Grace—had thrown sand in another child's face or stolen cookies from the tin on the shelf. In those thirty-some years, Carol had seen Grace cry exactly twice, one of those times being at Promise's funeral. But now her face was buried in Dillon's chest, and her shoulders shook with sobs.

"Oh, hell." Like Truvy Jones in *Steel Magnolias*, Carol couldn't stand to see someone cry alone. She dug in the pocket of her Clip Joint smock for a tissue, coming up empty except for a lock of Kate Sawyer's hair. "Gracie, I'm sorry. I should have given you some warning. I was just so excited." She drew in a sniff that became a sob, and then Steven's arms were around her.

Oh, hell. Silently this time. Carol hadn't always been celibate since Rand died. She'd had two long-lasting relationships, one of which ended with the miscarriage she'd told Steven about two weeks ago. She'd also had a few short-term "things" that for the most part she didn't like remembering. But it had been a couple of long, dry years since she'd been…well, physical with anyone besides herself.

She couldn't have said it then, in this kitchen full of tears and males-being-strong, or out loud even later, but if Steven had invited her to lie down so he could have his way with her, she'd have cleared the table in the windowed alcove across the room and assumed the position.

Any position he had in mind.

Oh, hell, indeed.

He pulled a tissue from the box on the counter, tucking it into her hand, then kissed the top of her head. She reveled in his touch and drank in the scent of him, feeling like a virgin too long denied. Also feeling somehow cherished, but not the way she felt when her mother hugged her. Not that way at all.

"I'm sorry," she said again, drawing away and blowing her nose. "Grace, are you all right?"

Grace didn't answer, just left Dillon's arms to cross the room and hug her hard and close. Carol had no choice but to cry again. So did Grace.

"I have to go back to work." Carol glanced at the

clock on the double wall oven—she'd kill for an oven like that—through still-teary eyes. "Faith will be at the shop in six minutes sharp. Do you want to go with me and tell your sister what we're going to do?"

"Yes." Grace reached for Dillon's hand. "Do you and Steven want to come, too?"

"No." He smiled down at his wife, and the tenderness in his expression almost had Carol crying again. Only the gleeful smirk Steven sent her stopped a new eruption of tears. "We'll talk about it when you come back, and then we'll all talk about it this evening. Steven will cook on the grill. You go do the sister thing. Ask her and Grant to come to dinner and by the time they go home, we'll have the baby named and Grant will have set up the college fund."

"I'm on foot," said Carol as they went toward the door. "Can you drive us to the shop?"

"Sure." Grace snagged her car keys from a hook inside a cupboard. "Why are you walking? Was your car hurt worse than Dillon's bike or Steven's hip?"

Carol waited till they were outside to answer. "The car's dead. Bill gave it a Christian burial at the salvage yard a couple of days after the accident. Until I find something I like that I can afford—sometimes those terms are exclusive of each other, by the way—I'm hoofing it and riding my bicycle. I actually found a muscle in my calf the other day and fit into a blouse I didn't buy at the tent and awning shop, so it's good for me."

Inside the red Mustang, Grace buckled her seatbelt and took a deep breath. "I wish Promise was here. She'd love the whole idea."

Carol couldn't cry again—she already had a

headache. "Nah, she'd be mad because she didn't think of it first."

"Oh, she would, wouldn't she?" Grace's gaze caught Carol's before she put the car in gear. "Even if it doesn't work out, I'll never, ever be able to thank you for being willing to do this. Not just this very thing but being the friend you've been these past years. I just—nothing will ever be enough to repay you."

"You don't have to. You only have to bake desserts for me the entire time I'm pregnant. Ones without calories in them because I know damn well my weight will become an issue later if not sooner."

Faith was already in the shop, sweeping the floor free of Kate Sawyer's hair. A year younger than Steven and two years older than Grace, she was one of the most beautiful women Carol knew. Her eyes were pure jade green, not the mossy-sometimes-brown of Carol's. She had gold-streaked brown hair, a curvy shape, and a tattoo of a rosebud on her backside. She'd married Grant Hartley the week he graduated from college and had twin boys a year later. They'd spent the past twenty years being Peacock's cutest family.

"I was worried," she said when Carol and Grace came in. "The door was unlocked, and Kate's check was lying on the counter, but no one was here."

"Sorry, Faith. I was excited." Carol took the broom from her. "Sit down. Want some coffee?"

"Sure do. I made a fresh pot. Hi, Gracie." Faith gave her sister a hug and sat in the hydraulic chair, arranging a towel and a cape just so around her neck. "What's new? What were you excited about, Carol?"

Carol poured the coffee. "Go ahead, Grace. You're busting with it."

Grace didn't need a second invitation. "We're having a baby. At least, we think we are. Carol, Dillon, and I."

Faith screamed and hugged indiscriminately, then reclaimed her seat. "You're going to have to explain. I don't think Peacock has progressed to having *ménages à trois.* Or maybe that's just me. We all know what a priss I am."

Grace explained, so excited her hands kept gripping each other, then pulling apart and gesturing wildly. She didn't do *any*thing wildly, and Carol felt tears pressing behind her eyes again. *Let it happen. For her. Please.*

"We'll do the procedure in Kingsport," Carol explained when Grace had wound down. Sort of. "If it takes, I can go to whatever gynecologist you choose as long as it's not someone who gives me the heebie-jeebies." She grinned at Grace in the mirror as she flipped a comb through Faith's hair. "I've watched that movie too often."

"*The Hand that Rocks the Cradle?* The one with the creepy guy who cops feels from his patients?" Grace shuddered. "We've all gone to Maggie Leiden ever since she came to town. I'm comfortable with her if you are."

Faith laughed. "You don't usually use the word 'comfortable' when you're talking about gynecologists."

Carol nodded. "That's sure true."

A hint of sadness, obvious even in her reflection, crossed Faith's eyes and although she appeared as almost-unnaturally perfect as she always did, something was…off. Carol's scissors stilled. "Faith? Are you all right? I'm not pulling your hair, am I? I meant to stop doing that years ago. Most of the time."

Just like that, the eyes cleared. How did she *do* that? "Oh, I am! Really, I am. I'm so happy for Gracie and Dillon I can hardly stand it."

"But?" Grace's brows raised with the question.

"But I'm jealous. I wish I could do it for you instead of someone else." Faith's cheeks were pink. "Now you know just how shallow I can be."

"I know you would if you could." Grace gave her sister a hug, dodging the scissors Carol still held. "Of course, Grant fainted when your twins were born and hyperventilated when you showed him that tattoo. He'd have a cow if you decided to carry a kid for someone else."

"Only a small one if it was you," Faith argued, laughing. "It's a moot point anyway. My reproductive organs were as inefficient as yours evidently are. It was a miracle I was able to have the twins. But, speaking of twins, aren't multiple births a hazard of in vitro fertilization?"

"They are, but there are ways to address that if the situation arises." Carol hoped it wouldn't arise. She didn't like to think of those ways, but the truth was, she didn't want to carry what one article she'd read referred to as "a litter."

"Oh, there's Deac. I have to talk to him about the church garage sale. The Old Farts want to run it." Grace was out the door so quickly they barely heard her last words.

"Won't it be hard? To give up a child you've carried?" Again the sadness was in the green eyes, and Faith's voice was soft.

Carol turned the chair to clip her bangs and met that gaze. She laid down the scissors and lifted Faith's hands from where they lay in her lap. "No. Because I'm going to be her favorite aunt. You'll be vying for position, Mrs. Hartley, because after all, you have good hair and pretty nails. I think I can win because not only can I *do* your hair and nails, I also have a good arm in softball and arm wrestling."

"Ah." Faith's bottom lip moved between her perfect white teeth. "But I can play the guitar—remember I taught my boys?—and...*and* I have a tattoo. How can you possibly be a cool aunt without a tattoo?"

"Who says I don't have one?"

Faith's eyebrows quirked. "Do you?"

"Maybe. Want your hair washed?"

"Not today. I just needed to get it out of my face. It always feels so much better right after it's trimmed."

Carol took off the towel and cape. "There you go. Want to make your next appointment?"

"I'll do that when you do my nails." Faith pulled her into a hug. "Thank you. For being a sister to my sister."

"I'm not." Carol held her gaze. "I'm her friend, but just as I could never take Promise's place—even if I wanted to—I could never take yours, either. Remember that."

****

"I still don't see why you want such a big-ass house." Dillon screwed furring strips to the wavy old plaster walls in the front parlor of Miss Abigail's. The old house's new owner wasn't a purist—they were putting up drywall in every room with not-great walls.

Which was most of them.

"I didn't." Steven pulled up another floorboard. Rotted. Damn it. "I may as well replace the whole floor." He tossed the board to the pile in the foyer. "I wanted a house the size of Carol's, but then I saw this one, and I wanted it instead."

Dillon shrugged. "Good enough reason."

Steven frowned at his friend's stiff shoulders. "Something bothering you?"

"No." Dillon attached another strip. "Yes. I don't know."

"Well, that certainly clears things up." Stephen pried up another board. It broke in the middle, knocking him flat on his ass. "Son of a freaking—give me one good reason we're doing this. Why didn't I just hire a contractor to do the whole house at one damn time instead of being all heroic and stupid and trying to do some of it myself?"

"I don't know that you *had* a good reason. I'm all for you hiring a contractor, though. You wanna use my phone?"

"I have my own with me."

"No, you don't. You broke it yesterday when we were hauling drywall into the house. You need to go ahead and get them by the case, you know—it would be cheaper than buying a new one every two weeks."

Steven crawled over to the cooler Grace packed for them every day. "You want a beer?"

"Yes. Maybe two."

Steven grinned, taking in the contents of the cooler. "We're not allowed two. It's one beer apiece and enough water for an army. Is your wife out to reform us?"

Dillon took the bottle he offered and popped off its cap, not bothering to catch it. "Your sister is…damn, Steven, I can't stand to see her hurt if this thing doesn't work out with Carol. If the IVF doesn't take or she can't carry." He sat on the floor, leaning against the wall, his knees drawn up. "Gracie wants a baby so badly."

"Don't you?"

"Sure I do. I'd like a dozen of them, or at least a basketball team, but the truth is that as long as I have her, I'm good."

Steven understood that. If he'd been able to keep Promise, he was certain he'd have never asked for another thing.

Get a life, Desperado.

He started, spilling his beer over his fingers. "Did you hear that?"

"Hear what?"

"Nothing."

Yeah, right, nothing. Either Promise was haunting Miss Abigail's or…well, maybe she was just trying to get her point across. *I am, damn it. I'm trying.*

"You're underestimating Grace, Dill. If this doesn't work out, she'll wait for adoption." But his little sister would be devastated. Steven knew that, and just the knowing caught at his heart. He also knew Grace Elliot Campbell only went *through* fires—she never went around them.

He drained his beer and got back to his feet. "She'll be all right, and this will work for all of you."

"I hope you're right." Dillon went back to his driver and the stack of furring strips.

"I am, and there's something else, too."

Dillon glanced over his shoulder. "What's that?"

"As long as she has you, Gracie's good, too. There isn't any way around getting hurt, but you and she are like a little fortress unto yourselves. You'll both be okay."

Light broke in silver shards in Dillon's dark blue eyes, and his mouth lifted into a crooked smile. "You're right, we will. Thanks, Elliot. There are times when you're less than a complete asshole."

What about Carol? Will she be all right? The thought stopped Steven in the middle of ripping up another board.

The night before, he'd grilled hamburgers for Faith and Grant, Dillon and Grace, and Carol. They'd all discussed the surrogacy. They'd agreed not to talk about it outside their families until they knew for sure that Little Baby Campbell was on his way. The men had insisted that yes, he would be a boy—if he was a girl, Carol would just have to do it again until she got it right. She'd laughed along with them, but in retrospect, Steven wondered if she'd really thought it was funny that they treated her like a piece of machinery with a reset button.

Dillon left Miss Abigail's at noon, but Steven kept working at the house until his grumbling stomach told him he should find a meal somewhere. A glance at the clock Grace had put on the mantel in the front parlor so he'd quit asking everyone what time it was told him it was five-fifteen.

Carol was probably walking home.

He left his tool belt next to Dillon's on the deacon's bench beside the front door. He needed a shower, but if he took time out to do that, she'd be at her house before he could intercept her. Besides, the bathroom the contractors had done a hurry-up completion on was still clean, right down to the yellow and green towels Faith had given him—he wanted to show it to Carol before he'd had time to really mess it up.

The empty driveway reminded him he and Dillon had driven together this morning. Not only was Carol on foot, so was Steven. "Come on, Barney," he said to the dog at his side. "Let's go get your mom."

They met her at the bottom of Taylor Hill. She wore a sundress along with the sneakers and white socks she changed into before she walked home. She'd clipped her hair into a cluster of curls on the back of her head and she carried groceries in two reusable bags. Sweat slipped down her face and neck, disappearing into the deep Vee neck of the dress.

She looked really wonderful.

He took the bags before she could protest. "When are you going to get a car?" He knew he sounded like a scolding parent, but exhaustion marked her features. Not that it made her look any less wonderful, no indeedy. And the way that sweat trickled down between what he was certain were most excellent breasts was absolutely…thought-provoking. Yes, that was it.

"I'm on vacation the first two weeks of July. I might shop around then."

She didn't sound too interested. Which was ludicrous. She'd been walking up and down Taylor Hill for more than two weeks now. Her vacation was still a good nine or ten weeks away. Unless she was in training for some weird uphill-walking marathon, getting a car should be at the top of her list of priorities.

Not that her priorities were his business, but holy shit, scaling that hill would wear the balls off a mountain goat.

And probably off him, too, he decided about halfway up the hill.

"So, will the shop be closed while you're off?" he asked, panting a little bit. He noticed she wasn't even out of breath. That was a pisser.

"No. Kay will work more, plus we're getting a new beautician next week. I have three chairs, and the truth is the shop's busy enough for another operator. It's Lynn Lewis—she got laid off from the textile plant and took herself right to cosmetology school. She's a single mom who needs the work. Not to mention, I can use the booth rent and I'll probably work less during part of Grace's pregnancy, so I need to watch my financial Ps and Qs."

"Do you like being pregnant?" They were halfway up the hill. He'd only thought he'd been sweating before. Now he was *sweating.* Carol was, too, although not as much, and God knew she wore it better.

"I did with Miranda. The next time, it felt wrong from the get-go. I'm not too perceptive, and I blamed it on my life being a shipwreck, but I'm not sure that's all it was." She shrugged. "Whether you're religious or not, I think some things are just meant to be. *C'est la vie.*"

"How long before you came to that extent of 'so goes life'? Did you take a pill for it? Or was it a 'come to Jesus' moment one Sunday morning while Deac was preaching?"

Her mouth tucked in tight at the corners and her shoulders straightened. She avoided his gaze. "It took time. Grief does. No one knows that better than you, Steven."

He felt chastised, and probably rightfully so. He was surprised he didn't hear Promise's voice this time. *Way to go, Desperado. I'll bet you kick puppies, too.*

"Want to go out to dinner?" he asked. "We'll have to walk down and get my truck first, but I'll buy. We can drive around to car lots and find you a vehicle. I'll give you all kinds of bad advice, though, so you need to talk to Bill about anything I suggest. If I'd been around in the 1950s, I'd have bought an Edsel."

"Steven."

They walked another fifty feet, the bag in his left hand gained ten pounds, and that was all she said. Just that one patient word. Well, shit. "Yes?"

She stopped walking and after a few steps, so did he. He turned back to face her.

"I'm only going to say this once, number one because it's none of your business and number two because I don't like having to admit it. I can't afford a car. I mean, my credit's good, and I could get a loan, but my income isn't consistent enough to make car payments feasible, so I don't want to make them. End of story. I don't want to talk about it anymore."

When he started to speak, she raised a hand, palm out, and shook her head. "Don't even suggest loaning me the money. Definitely do not suggest that Dillon and Grace give me the money because you think they might owe it to me. They do not. Do you hear me? *They do not.*"

"So what *do* they owe you? What do *I* owe you? How do you quantify the gift you're giving?" He set down the bags and reached for the hand she was still holding up. "I'm not being an asshole—no matter what Dillon would tell you if you asked him. I really want to know. How do you put a price on what you're doing for my family?"

"Well, that's easy." She picked up the heaviest grocery bag and started back up the hill. "You don't."

****

How could such an intelligent man be such an idiot? She set the grocery bag on the counter and reached for the one Steven carried. "There's sweet tea in the fridge. Why don't you get us some while I feed Fred and Barney?"

"They ate up at Miss Abigail's." He took glasses from the cabinet and the tea pitcher from the refrigerator, as at home in her kitchen as if he lived there, a thought that gave her pause. "Fred said the food there wasn't as good as at home, but Barney didn't complain."

She took a long drink from the tea he handed her and frowned at him. She wasn't going to address the fact that he had conversations with animals—if she was honest about it, it made for points in his favor. "It's not necessary that you feed them."

"Hey, they're working at my house—I'm gonna feed them."

She choked on a laugh. She loved Fred and Barney, but— "Working?"

"Absolutely. Barney's the greeter. He meets and kisses on everyone who visits, then shows them around the house. Fred is the resident law enforcement. If you have it in mind to walk too fast, he'll wrap himself right around your ankles and toss you eyebrows over toenails into the fireplace or down the stairs."

"Well, they are efficient."

He waited expectantly, and she knew she was going to have to explain things to him. The idiot. She sighed. "It's friendship, Steven. No more, no less. Do you remember when Grace cut her hair short? It was because Promise was going to lose hers when she had chemo. We were all in the shop that day—both your sisters and Promise and me. We all cussed and laughed and bitched, but no one cried. It was one of the hardest, best days of my life. If we can have this baby, it'll be that kind of day. Because we're *friends*. It is sad that sorrow made us closer, but it did. The closeness blesses my life every single day."

His dark gaze met hers. And tangled with it. He was dirty, with sawdust on his ragged shorts and his hair hanging lank and sweaty, half free of the band he used to tie it back. His T-shirt was torn, and part of his taut stomach showed through the hole, slick and smooth and tan. He finished his tea, his eyes never wavering, and set down the glass. For a moment, he turned the glass round and round in the wet circle made by its leaking condensation. Then he studied her again.

When he took the steps that closed the distance between them, it was as if he moved in slow motion, although she knew he didn't. He took her glass from her and put it beside his. His hands cupped her bare shoulders and he drew her body right flush against his. She could smell the sweat on him, and it could have been unpleasant but wasn't. It was just hard work and attractive man and...holy good grief, did hormones have a scent?

It might be a good idea to push him away—she was pretty sure she outweighed him, and she did have that good arm she'd been bragging about earlier that day. But the arm was busy with its partner hugging his neck, and pushing him away would just be—oh, Lord, it had been way too long since she'd been kissed.

She wasn't sure she'd *ever* been kissed like this, because she didn't remember a man's lips—no matter where they happened to be touching—ever making her tingle all the way to the…well, no, not the bottoms of her feet, because she couldn't even *feel* her feet. She could feel her knees, though, because they were threatening to give way right out from under her.

"Oh." It was more a sigh than a word when he drew away. Just slightly. "Oh, my."

"I noticed." He kissed her again, backing her up to the counter so the threat of losing her balance was minimized. She relaxed a little, so that her breasts were closer against his chest. And twice as sensitized. Oh, hell, she might as well be naked.

She loosened his hair from its band, burying her fingers in it, and opened her mouth to his insistent tongue. She wondered if…what? She wondered what? Good God, her mind was complete mush.

Of course, her mind had little to do with the way the rest of her felt. His hands moved down her back, coming to rest on her hips and drawing her in closer to him. Closer to his… Carol didn't think in those terms— she'd spent too much time in her shop telling adolescent clients to watch their language. Plus, it had been way too long since she'd been up close and personal to…whatever…herself. God, he felt so good.

Response. That was it. Closer to his response! She almost giggled at the inane euphemism, but she was afraid he'd stop kissing her if she started laughing, and she didn't want that. No, ma'am.

He leaned her farther back, taking care not to bump her head on the upper cabinet, and took a little tactile advantage of the deep sweetheart neckline of her sundress. She hadn't really liked the cut of that dress bodice when she'd made it. More fool her.

The dress dipped low in the back, too, and when he moved his hands away from the exposed skin, someone made a protesting little sound in her throat—she supposed it was her. She relaxed a little more and came in direct contact with the iced tea pitcher against her bare back.

"Yow!" She jerked away, bumping Steven's chin with the top of her head, and giving herself a little shake to get rid of the gooseflesh the touch of the cold decanter had given her.

"Oh, wow." He was peering straight down at her neckline, which was by this time very crooked and scarcely decent. "Could you do that little tremble thing again? It was really impressive."

Her nipples tightened where they were barely inside the dress. She pulled the bodice up, straightening it as well as she could. His "response" was impressive, too, but she wasn't going to tell him so. At least, not now.

"Were you hunting me?" She should have waited to get her breath back—she sounded like a vamp from one of 1940s movies that were on really late at night when you couldn't sleep. "When we met on the road, I mean."

"Huh?" He sounded nonplused, and she felt like cheering. She wasn't the only one who'd been kissed stupid—he wasn't doing so well, either. "Oh, yeah."

"Yeah?" She turned away, starting to put away the abandoned groceries. If she couldn't see him, she would neither hyperventilate nor jump his bones. Maybe.

"Want to?"

Want to what? *That?* Did she *want* to? Hell, yes, she wanted to. But they were just barely aware of each other, and he was going back to his big city life and big city friends in a matter of weeks. Although he'd probably spend some weekends at Miss Abigail's and possibly even open an office in Peacock the way he'd mentioned, he wasn't good relationship material.

Even more, in Carol's mind and she thought probably in his, he was still Promise's. The thought sobered her and stilled her hands. *Oh, Promise.*

"What did you…why did you want me?" she asked, trying to insert some sense into the conversation, some mental cold water on her still-shrieking girl parts.

"Dinner." He pulled his hair back into a band he took from his pocket—he never seemed to run out of ponytail holders. "Would you like to go to dinner? And shop for cars? I know you're not going to the beach this summer, but I'll buy you a girly drink with an umbrella in it and you can pretend." He ran a finger lightly down the strap of her dress. "You can wear one of these dresses, although probably not this one since I seem to have decorated it with sawdust and sweat. Oh, wait." He held up both hands to stave off an answer. "Grace told me it was rude to suggest someone wear something in particular, so I take that back. Wear whatever you like."

"When and why did Grace tell you that?" She refilled their tea glasses and handed him his. She took a long drink, hoping the cold brew would serve to cool down her insides.

Well, that wasn't working—she was pretty sure she felt them sizzle.

"Thursday. She was going to afternoon tea over at the Old Farts Home, something they've apparently decided to have every Thursday. You stay for it, too, don't you, after you get their hair and nails all prettied up? Anyway, she had on her overalls, complete with grass-stained knees, and I said, very politely, 'Holy shit, Grace, are you wearing those?' She didn't respond well."

"I'm amazed." She shook her head.

"I was, too," he said righteously. "I was only trying to help."

Even if she could have resisted the hormonal storm that had overtaken her kitchen, Carol had no defense against his laughing dark eyes. "Okay, thanks. I'd like to go to dinner. And you're sure it's all right if I wear whatever I please?"

His gusting sigh should have made the kitchen curtains stir. "Yes. Fine. Can I use your phone to call Dillon and ask him to bring my truck up the hill?"

"Sure, or we can walk down if you'd rather." Carol was surprised at how much she was enjoying the walking these days, especially when it was downhill.

"You wouldn't mind?"

"No." She grinned at him. "But you have to take a shower. I do have some standards on dates." She gasped as soon as the words left her mouth. "I'm sorry. I know this isn't a date. We're friends who kissed…accidentally. This is dinner, not a date. Right?"

He smiled, a slow and lazy expression that turned her stomach over. And over again. "Wrong." He came over and kissed her once more. Thoroughly. "It's a date."

****

"Why did you let me eat the whole thing?" Steven groaned. "I'm a cardiac surgeon. I tell people to *avoid* too much red meat, yet you let me order *and* eat a sixteen-ounce porterhouse steak. And it was—God help me—probably the best steak I've ever had in my whole life. Or at least since that one Dillon cooked last week."

Carol stood still, hands on her hips, and tried not to laugh. "I *let* you order and eat half a cow? I *let* you? Did I *let* you order the strawberry shortcake for dessert, too?"

"No." He groaned again, not very convincingly. "You made me. I saw you staring at it in that display thing and knew how bad you wanted half of it. What kind of guy would I have been if I hadn't ordered it? I just thought you'd eat more than three little forkfuls. Do you have any Tums? Or maybe a bottle of Pepto-Bismol in your purse?"

She scrounged around. "I have a breath mint. It doesn't have hardly any lint on it. Will that do?"

He squinted at the mints she held up before he took them. "It's a new roll still in its wrapper. How could it have lint on it?"

"It doesn't, but if you can be a drama queen I should at least have the chance to perform a little, too. Give me one."

Steven gave her a mint then tucked the rest of the roll in his pocket.

"Those are mine." She held out her hand and he took it.

"Let's go over there." He pointed to the auto

dealership across the street with his free hand.

"Steven." She yanked so hard on his hand she nearly pulled him off his feet and had to stifle a laugh at his scandalized expression and dancing eyes. "I'm not getting a car right now. Not this week or next or even the one after that. The only thing I could pay cash for is the spare tire and just possibly floor mats. I'm enjoying the walking and riding my bike, so don't worry, okay?"

"What if—" He stopped. "Come on. They won't charge you for kicking the tires and complaining about the prices, and I've been thinking about trading my truck anyway. That thing Dillon drives is growing on me."

"What if what?" He was dragging at her hand now, but she held her ground. "What did you start to say?"

He hesitated, and then plunged ahead. "If you get pregnant, you can't be walking up and down Taylor Hill every day. Summer's coming on, and it's going to get hot and humid and miserable. You know what Tennessee's like."

She softened and let him pull her along. At least as far as his truck. "No," she said, when he opened her door for her. She pulled herself up into the seat and smiled into his eyes. They were amazing. They were just eyes, for heaven's sake, but they were just so…amazing. "Walking will be good for both the baby and me. If weather becomes a problem, I'll deal with it then. Not now. You don't need to take care of me or worry about me. Just be my friend the way you have been the past few weeks. It's been such fun."

"It has," he agreed. "But tonight, Ms. Whitney, you're my date."

And he kissed her again, with her absolute

cooperation, right there in the parking lot of Saints and Sinners Restaurant and didn't stop until a passing teenager suggested they "get a room, man."

Chapter Seven

Within the next few days, Steven began staying at Miss Abigail's. The big downstairs bedroom and bathroom were finished, and he'd gotten a new refrigerator and six-burner stove. The appliances were incongruous in the middle of the down-to-the-bones reconstruction of the kitchen, but they worked. Carol doubted if Steven had ever used the commercial range, but she loved it. He'd conned her into cooking dinner for them three times the first week the stove was hooked up.

She had to have injections in preparation for the in vitro procedure. Her hips got sore, with bumps under the skin where her system didn't like the abuse it was taking. Her hormones—both the ones Steven aroused in her and the ones in the needles the reproductive endocrinologist kept coming at her with—were all over the place.

"This," he said seriously one night after she yelled at him, shaking a spatula for emphasis, "is PMS on steroids. If you were my patient, I would suggest you go to bed with a nice man and soothe yourself by giving him a blo—"

"Don't say it," she warned, her cheeks quivering with the effort it took not to laugh or cry—she didn't know which. "In the first place, there *are* no nice men, and in the second place, I'm pretty sure you could get disbarred for even thinking what you just almost said out loud."

His eyebrows lifted. "Disbarred?"

"Well, you know, lose your license. Be revoked. Whatever."

"Oh. Maybe." He hesitated, his gaze dropping to the spatula she held. "So is that a No?"

The day Grace's fertilized eggs were harvested, Carol had to go home and go to bed. She felt fine. But strange, too. A little melancholy. Grace would have stayed with her but didn't question Carol's need for solitude. "I'll send supper up with Steven," Grace promised. She set a vase of multicolored daisies on the bedside table and left her alone.

Steven came at six o'clock, waking her as he clattered up the stairs. He set the tray Grace had sent across Carol's lap and went down to the kitchen for a bottle of the beer he'd taken to keeping there. He came back up and lay beside her on the bed, commandeering the remote control and at least a third of her meal. Grace must have known he would—she'd sent enough food for a small country. He was quiet and so was Carol, although they both watched and laughed at a movie. More tired than she'd expected to be, she fell asleep against his shoulder, her hand lying on his chest, wrapped lightly in the fabric of his shirt.

He was still there in the morning. When she woke, it was to find him watching her with slumberous oh-God-sexy eyes, his hair a silky tangle on the pillow, his hand holding hers where it still rested on his chest.

"Oh," she said. *Good Lord, what do I say now? There's hardly ever a man in my bed when I wake up.*

Make that never. She hadn't always been celibate,

but no one ever spent the night. At least, not in the ten years since she'd had the miscarriage. At first, it had been to keep from getting hurt—if a man was never inside her house, he couldn't get inside her heart, either—but then it had become...easier. Yes, that was it. Easier. Especially when Reese Confer spent the night or the weekend if her father was away. Carol loved her teenage neighbor, but she didn't want to have to explain why it would be okay for Carol to have a boyfriend sleep over when she'd been preaching Just Say No to Reese ever since puberty raised its ugly head.

"Actually"—he cleared his throat—"I just got here. I didn't want to be late for breakfast."

His eyes danced, and she burst into laughter, pulling free and sitting up in bed, stifling a groan when she tried to move muscles that had been too long in one position. "What do you *want* for breakfast? I'm starved. Someone ate half my dinner last night."

In that moment, she knew the procedure the day before had "taken." She wasn't particularly intuitive, but she was never hungry until she'd been up a while and had her coffee, regardless of how much dinner she'd had the night before. She never slept straight through the night, much less without moving, but her whimpering body parts told her she had done exactly that.

She didn't drink any coffee this morning, only three cups of caffeine-free apple-cinnamon tea. When Steven gave her an odd look, she shrugged and turned back to the bacon sizzling in the skillet in front of her.

For now, for at least the fourteen days until they returned to the fertility center, she would keep what she knew to herself. In case she was wrong. In case the pregnancy didn't prove to be viable. Just in case.

Carol had been the sole resident on this part of the hillside since Miss Abigail died—the Sawyers and the Confers lived farther up and around. It was kind of nice knowing someone else was nearby. Steven came down the hill some evenings and helped her weed the garden and the flowerbeds.

When Reese was there, he sat with her and helped with her homework, although occasionally the girl said he was more hindrance than help. Wads of lined paper had sailed through the air more than once. Sometimes they made Carol laugh so hard she just stayed in one ecstatic place and let it happen. If she pretended once in a while that they were her family, that was all right. No one knew but her.

There were the times he swept her into his arms, and they danced between the rows of vegetables, keeping time with the music and the joy that swelled between them. He taught Reese how to two-step and foxtrot and even, hilariously, to waltz.

Before bed, Carol sat on the porch with her hand on her stomach and talked to the life she knew she carried. She told the baby about its parents and how much they would love it. She talked about its Uncle Steven and how special he was. Fred and Barney, certain she was talking to them, sat close to her and listened intently.

Carol's parents had been loving to her and Ed as well as to each other, but there hadn't been much music or laughter in the house. She'd spent her adulthood alone, mostly by choice, and she liked it, but there was a wide empty streak of loneliness in her life she *didn't* like.

For now, that streak had narrowed down to a skinny little line she hardly noticed. The hollow space was filled in by the specialness of what she, Grace, and Dillon were doing. And the company of the man who danced with her and a lonely teenager in the garden.

****

"Oh, man, you don't want to leave Knoxville." Carter Mitchell shot Steven a dismayed frown. "You've been there ever since you got out of med school and you're one of the best cutters in the business. You'll never be content here. I mean, it's great for weekends and your friend Jake, the family practice guy, but what are you going to do? Drive across the mountain three times a week to do surgery?"

"No." Steven leaned back in the Adirondack chair he'd dragged down to the dock from the porch of Grant's cabin. "I'll come over if there's a real need, but there usually isn't, Mitch. You know that. I *am* a good cutter, but not the best by any means, and I'd like to stretch some. I want to spend the summer studying and easing into practice with Jake. He's got enough business for two of us, especially if I can do some of the surgery he'd normally send to Kingsport. Cardiothoracic is my specialty, but it doesn't have to be the only thing I can do."

"Will you still do publicity stuff if we need it? Whether we like it or not, the public does respond financially to a pretty face."

Steven hesitated. "I don't think so. At least, not talk shows or anything that requires I wear a tuxedo." That part of him had died the day Jamie Scott had, and Steven wasn't interested in reviving it.

"You know the celebrity patients will still ask for

115

you."

"And I'll come if it's urgent, but not to do a minor procedure just so someone can drop my name. I want to be a doctor, not a name."

Mitch nodded. "If you ever want to come back full time, we'll have an office for you."

"I appreciate that." And he did. Steven didn't take his professional good fortune for granted.

"I do have a question for you, though." Mitch skimmed a pebble across the surface of the stream. "Is this because of Promise? I admit I didn't know her that well, but I can't believe she'd like you quitting."

It was a fair question, and Steven wasn't entirely sure of its answer. "I think if I try to grow myself a new life, I'll stop trying to find the old one. I'm not quitting. Not really." He straightened his shoulders against the back of the chair. "I'm starting."

It had been a nice weekend of fishing. Everyone's beer coolers were full of trout to take home. Steven hoped he'd be able to talk Carol into cooking his, even though she'd probably insist he be the one to clean them.

Tomorrow was the day she, Grace, and Dillon went back to the fertility center, the day they would find out if their grand new adventure was beginning or…not. He hoped it would go well for all of them. Prayed it would.

"Are you nervous?" he asked Dillon as they packed their stuff into the truck for the drive back to Peacock. "About tomorrow, I mean."

"Yeah." Dillon waved at Grant, who was spending a few more days at the cabin with his sons, and Mitch, who had driven his own car since the lake was closer to his home than Peacock was. Jeff Confer had left earlier.

"How about you? Are you nervous about leaving Knoxville? Giving up taxicabs and pizza delivery and 'stat' meaning fast instead of 'when I get around to it'?" He opened the passenger door of the truck, hauling himself up with the help of the grab bar.

Steven climbed behind the wheel, bumping his head as he'd been doing for the four years he'd owned the pickup. "Peacock has pizza delivery."

Dillon closed his door. "Only if the owner's van starts."

"I didn't say it was reliable. I said they *have* it." Steven backed onto the narrow gravel road. "How about you? You lived in Boston for years, not to mention some residential details overseas while you were doing the journalist thing in addition to writing books. You didn't seem to suffer much when you came back to the mountains."

"I have Grace."

It fell between them, the unspoken reference to Promise's absence and the fact that Steven had run in place for the three years since her death.

"I'm not searching for Promise," Steven said carefully, braking sharply enough at a stop sign that Dillon grabbed the dash and glared at him. "I know she's gone, but I'm not avoiding the memories anymore, either. We were together—or fighting and breaking up—for twenty-some years of our lives."

Dillon nodded. "I remember when Grace got to where she could drive the Mustang. It took months, you know, after you gave her the keys and told her Promise wanted her to have it. Then one day she just got in and drove. I think she cried some and went to the cemetery and called Promise names, but she's enjoyed every mile since."

"Right." Steven smiled, a light feeling slipping into what had been a dark place for a very long time. "I'm ready to drive the Mustang."

****

Morning sickness, no matter how you tried to dress it up by reminding yourself each day that this too would pass, just sucked. The best part of it—good only because it made Carol laugh—was that Grace was sick every morning, too.

One more positive note was that Grace made a new dessert every day and delivered it to the Clip Joint. Sometimes it was just sugar-free gelatin with bananas and frothy topping, but it was still dessert, and as soon as Carol finished throwing up and brushed her teeth, she ate it.

Reaction to the news of her surrogacy was mixed. She sensed disapproval from a few people at church, but no one commented except Deac Rivers. The huge African-American man, whose heart was proportionate with his size, boomed, "Jesus said, 'Greater love has no one than this, that someone lay down his life for his friends.' You are *carrying* life for your friends, Carolina Whitney, and I am so proud of you!" from the pulpit.

After that, few clients mentioned it, but not unless they had something encouraging to say. That changed on Friday.

"I know your heart was in the right place, my dear." Mrs. Gleason, an Elliot House resident who had come to the Clip Joint for a comb-out every Friday for fifteen years, filled in her check and passed it to Carol. "However, what you and Grace Campbell are doing is a sin against God. I feel I must take my business elsewhere."

"I'm sorry you feel that way, ma'am." Carol kept her voice even with an effort. "I will still be here should you change your mind."

She stared blindly at the check after the woman left, wanting to tear it up. Fifteen years and she'd never left so much as a nickel for a tip, never responded to the Christmas gifts or birthday cards Carol gave all her regular clientele. Even when her husband died, and Carol sent flowers from the Clip Joint and took a pot of beef and noodles to her house, the old lady had sent a printed note thanking her for her kindness and moved on. Mrs. Gleason hadn't even mailed the note, just handed it to her the Friday following the funeral. And she'd kept the casserole dish that had held the noodles.

Carol was a passive person. She believed in turning the other cheek and forgiveness. She thought kindness was the greatest gift humankind had to give.

She also thought she'd like to beat the hell out of Mrs. Gleason.

Before going home, she cut some flowers and took them to the cemetery, going directly to the little grave under the maple tree. "Hi, baby. It's been an eventful week." She talked about the pregnancy, about painful bumps under her skin where she'd had injections, about the funny card she'd received from Dixie and Jo. Then she sat silent for a while, drawing solace from the peaceful place where Miranda rested. "See you next week," she said finally, getting to her feet. "Give your dad a hug for me."

She wasn't surprised to see Steven at Promise's grave. She touched his arm as she passed.

119

He caught her hand, bringing her to his side. "Carol's cooking dinner for me," he said conversationally, "and she's carrying Grace and Dillon's baby for them, too." He listened for a moment. "I think you're right." He touched the top of her marker. "Talk to you later."

"Bye, Promise." Carol spoke over her shoulder as they walked away from the grave. "I'll bet people think we're strange, talking to the ones we've lost."

He shrugged, the gesture so like Grace's habitual one it was laughable. "Let 'em."

"What'd she say?"

"Huh?"

"Promise. What did she say?"

Steven smiled down at Carol, the expression making her heart do all sorts of funny things.

"She told me I was wasting time."

Carol stopped, pulling her hand from his. "Steven, we're friends. I'm doing a favor for your sister and your best friend. I know you like me for that, but we can't—"

He set his hands on her shoulders and met her gaze. Oh, Lord, she could get lost in those eyes of his. He didn't even have to talk, although his Southern Comfort voice rubbing up against her nerve endings made being lost even more…absolute. And lovely. Oh, yes, lovely.

He talked anyway. Damn it.

"We're both single, Carolina, whether it's what we intended or not. We're of legal age, though just barely. No matter where we go from here and make no mistake about it"—he hesitated, shaping his palm to her cheek— "we will go *somewhere* from here. It will be golly-hot-damn exciting when we do, and we'll be friends at the other end of it, if for no other reason than we always have been." He set his hand on her stomach. "Dollars will get you donuts we'll be co-godparents to this kid, and Grace is going to get all persnickety about us doing it right."

Carol stared at him, trying not to think how warm the spot was where his hand lay. "Did you really just use the word 'persnickety'?"

"I did. Don't you think Dillon would be proud? He's sure three syllables are my limit, and I just used four."

She shook her head. "You're a doctor. Every word you use professionally is polysyllabic. Don't forget, I've seen you on talk shows."

"That's only on TV. The rest of the time I say things like 'toss me that knife' or 'oh, shit, he's bleeding like a stuck hog.'" He beamed at her, his eyes crinkling. "Dillon's trying to make me sound more civilized before I move back here permanently."

Carol was pretty sure all the color rushed from her face—at least, that's what it felt like. Permanently? Had he really said that?

"What do you mean?" she asked. Surely he didn't *mean* permanently. Peacock had two stoplights, three gas stations, and a thirty-bed hospital often referred to disparagingly as a first aid station. The town didn't even have a movie theater, although the local drama group had restored the old one and performed plays on its stage three or four times a year plus a Christmas pageant. The Clip Joint always had a sponsorship ad in the play programs. But what would a well-known cardiothoracic surgeon *do* here?

"It's time I came home. In retrospect, I wish I'd

done it years ago, but I didn't and there aren't any do-overs, which explains why my wife told me to 'get a life' so many times. It wasn't so much that I haven't always had a life, more that I spent so much of it regretting what I had and hadn't done. So I'm coming back to Peacock. If it doesn't work out, Knoxville's still there, but I'm not going to 'wish I had' either way."

He slung an arm around her shoulders, urging her along with him. "What are you cooking tonight?"

Carol sighed. "I hadn't thought much about it since it only came up a few minutes ago. If this tall, skinny guy comes over, he could cook burgers on the grill while I made a salad. Turkey burgers, of course, because he hates red meat."

"Dumb son of a bitch."

****

His brain hurt.

Steven handed Lois Gleason's file back to Jake Sawyer. "I don't believe I've ever given family practitioners enough credit. I apologize."

"Not necessary." Jake tossed the file on his desk and grinned at him. "I tend to think cutters all have the personality of Gregory House from the TV show. Or none at all. And I'm not apologizing."

They'd spent the day together. Steven made people laugh by telling them he was job shadowing—which he was. He took vitals while Jake's nurse was at lunch and again when she left for the day to pick her sick child up at day care. He talked to patients about the medicines they were taking and why they were supposed to take them as directed until they were *all gone*. He thought it was to his credit that he didn't once add "Goddammit" after the "all gone." He discussed the Titans' next-season possibilities with anyone who would argue the point. Which was most everyone.

When Mrs. Gleason gave him a frosty glare, he beamed back at her. He sat in on a conversation Jake had with Becky and Davis Rountree about the grim realities of ovarian cancer and wanted to go out and hit something. Really hard.

Office hours ended at four thirty. Or somewhere around there. At a quarter 'til five, Jake locked the door behind the office manager and said, "My office." He got two bottles of Sam Adams out of the refrigerator in the clinic's break room and led the way, picking up a couple of files on the way.

The beer tasted wonderful—the files were…what they were. Mrs. Gleason needing yet another new hip wasn't upsetting—she was eighty-something and meaner than a snake. Her treatment of Carol was proof positive of that. Becky Rountree, on the other hand, had been a couple of years ahead of him in school and she didn't have an unpleasant bone in her body. It seemed as if ovarian cancer could have found someone else to throw its poison lasso around. Someone like Lois Gleason.

Of course, it always seemed that way. Had since medical school days, when he saw children die and depraved old bastards live to be centenarians. Yet he'd had to treat the perverts with the same care as the innocents. At least as a cutter, Steven hadn't felt compelled to be overly polite to patients he didn't like. After one day of observing Jake, he understood that family practice was going to be different from that. Way different.

Yeah, his brain really hurt.

"You can change your mind, you know, and I won't be pissed off. I only came back here from Nashville about eight years ago. It was quite a transition. My older kids were threatening to go back to the city every time a rural challenge presented itself." He laughed. "They couldn't believe Carol's was the only place in town—at that time anyway—to get their hair cut. After the first time, though, their old friends waited 'til they came to visit so they could get a trim at the Clip Joint. She helped them with their homework while she worked and listened to all the stories of teenage anguish, and it wasn't unusual for her to have five or six high-school kids in there at once."

"She still does that—I think Jeff Confer's daughter lives there. And Carol ropes other people into the homework thing if she's busy or if it's beyond her." Steven had been annoyed the first time she asked him to talk a kid through a calculus assignment. But he'd been kind of enjoying it when she told him to get in the chair if he wanted his hair trimmed. He'd been irritated again at being interrupted.

He thought Carol enjoyed irritating him.

He liked that in a woman.

Jake's voice, amusement in it, brought him back to the present. "It's a lot different here socio-economically."

Steven grinned at him. "Still getting paid in fresh brown eggs like Doc Bridges used to?"

"It's been known to happen. And we still deliver babies sometimes—at least I do—which means the insurance costs are through the ceiling. Maggie Leiden's right here in the building and we work together quite a bit. She has young kids of her own and is expecting another and she's the only ob-gyn in town, so it's good we work so closely."

Steven had loved his OB rotation, but it had been a long time since he'd "caught one," as an Amish midwife he knew referred to delivery. Cesarean sections had changed some since then, too. Gotten better, although in his mind way too frequent.

It would be exciting, being there to meet life when it came into the world instead of fighting to keep it from going out.

But it was still Jake's practice—he had the corner office and kept his kind of beer in the fridge. Not that Steven had a problem with Sam Adams or an office in the middle of the hall somewhere between the lab and the staff restroom. "You'll let me know if it's not working for you."

"I will."

They'd known each other for a long time. Those two words were sufficient for Steven. He extended his hand. "Then I'd say we have a deal. At least 'til the end of the year. Then we can see how we feel."

Carol had just started up Taylor Hill when he drew up beside her. "Ride, Ms. Whitney?"

She got in, moving wearily. "Thanks."

Concern rippled through him. He wasn't sure he'd ever seen Carol so quiet. Even when she was sad or upset, she was verbal. In the garden, she talked to the plants. She carried on conversations with Fred and Barney. She sang when she wasn't talking, and her throaty laughter was music all by itself.

Steven was the same way. Dillon refused to go to movies with him because he never shut up. Faith still smacked him with the hymnal in church. Grace laughed because he even walked loud.

The primary difference between him and Carol, he had to admit, was that she was a hell of a listener while he was no listener at all. Not that he didn't care what other people had to say, but he'd rather osmose the elements of the conversation than catch them all at once. It had gotten him into trouble more than once while he was training, but the truth was he was better than most at hearing what patients *didn't* say. This came in really handy in medicine.

But not always in relationships.

"What's wrong?" He pulled into her driveway and killed the engine.

"Nothing." She reached for the door handle, but he stopped her with a hand on her arm.

"Carol."

She met his gaze, and he recognized the expression in her eyes, the tightness around her mouth. Grief looked the same on everyone, no matter how they tried to hide it, and Carol wasn't even trying now.

"What happened?" he asked. He'd seen the paper—no one in Peacock had died—but Carol was a beautician. Like a bartender, she'd know if something occurred before the media did.

"It's Flag Day."

Oh. Now that she mentioned it, there were extra flags flying in town—a whole row of them in front of the newspaper office, a great big one at the VFW. "Well," he said, "that's too bad."

"I'm thirty-seven today."

"Happy birthday." Even to his own ears, it sounded lame. "Happy" wasn't even in the vicinity.

She opened the truck door and got out, pulling free

of his hand. Fred and Barney waited politely on the back porch, and she walked right past them and into the house.

Steven followed her, taking time to pet the dog and cat and assure them "Mom's okay." He went into the house without knocking, something he didn't normally do even after the eight weeks or so they'd been seeing each other nearly every day. "Carol?"

She kept her limited supply of liquor in an antique dry sink under a window at the end of the kitchen. She was already there, pouring a healthy shot of rum into a glass of ice. As he watched, she popped open a can of cola and filled the glass to the top. And set it down.

"I can't." She turned to face him. "For the first time, I forgot about renting a room to Baby Campbell. I can't drink 'til he moves out." She thrust the glass at him. "Here. Drink this for me. Real fast so it will make you dizzy. If I can't have passed out on the couch, I at least want dizzy."

Steven didn't drink anything but wine and beer, and even that in limited quantities—most anything made him dizzy. He frowned at the drink he took from her and set it on the table. "I'd be willing to pass out on your couch after a rousing glass of sweet tea."

Her smile was halfhearted at best. She turned to gaze out the window, sipping from the can of cola. "Miranda died on Flag Day nineteen years ago. She was three months old." She drew a shuddering breath. Sipped again. Stared through the spotless glass at the hayfield beyond. "Rand died five months before she was born, Ed just four weeks before Rand. I go right past the days of their deaths—sometimes I don't even remember them—but then Flag Day comes, and I wonder why in the hell I'm still walking around, because I surely to God died when she did."

He put his arms around her from behind, resting his cheek against her temple. "I know," he said quietly. And he did. Promise had died in June, too. The twenty-third. He could still smell the roses that filled the high school gym the day of her funeral.

Carol swayed a little as he held her, as if to music that played in her heart, and he smiled. The mommy dance. That little rocking motion, his mother had said, came from holding babies. He didn't know how true that was, but Faith swayed sometimes. Grace never did.

"This is probably why, don't you think, for now anyway?" He laid his hand on Carol's stomach, feeling the warmth of her skin through the cotton blouse she wore with capris. "I don't know why things happen, especially bad things, only that they do. You and Grace have both had more than your share, but you're carrying her baby for her, so that she'll hear that music you hear. She'll rock back and forth like you do, and it will be because of what you gave her."

"Maybe so."

He thought of his conversation with Dillon, of Becky and Davis Rountree and what they were facing, of moving from a two-bed-two-bath apartment to a house with more than six thousand square feet not counting the carriage house turned into a garage.

"And it's time, Carol."

She angled her head so she could see his face. "Time for what?"

"Time to drive the Mustang."

Chapter Eight

Carol got lots of birthday cards, many of them including gift cards that ascertained she wouldn't have to pay for her daily Cup and Cozy fix for months to come and as soon as she got a car, she might be able to afford gas for a while. Clientele who had moved away still remembered her and included notes with cards. "Can't you come to Iowa and show my new beautician how to cut my hair so the cowlick almost lies down?" made her laugh.

With the laughter, some of the pain drained away. Or maybe the lessening was due to being held by Steven Elliot.

Who had confined her to her room.

"I know," he said when she complained about being shooed away like a recalcitrant child, "sounds kinky, doesn't it, being sent to your room when you're—how old did you say? Geezy Pete, thirty-seven? I'll be along later with the whips and handcuffs." He grinned at her, then gave her a kiss that numbed her from the neck up but made every other part of her tingle. "For now, take a bath, a nap, read a book. Whatever. I'll get dinner for us and maybe even run out to the convenience store for a donut to put a candle in. It'll be late, but that's okay, isn't it?"

Yes, it was. She took a long bath in which she fell asleep, wakened only by the landline phone ringing. It stopped almost immediately, so Steven must have answered it. She opened and read her mail, enjoying the little stack of cards, and lay on the bed with one of the books she'd received from clients today. She felt human again, as if she had, admittedly with the help of the desperado downstairs, averted a crisis.

Because she knew Grace, she knew what he'd meant when he referred to driving the Mustang. And maybe he was right. Maybe it was time.

"Carol?"

She must have dozed off, because for a moment, she had to think where she was and whose voice was calling her.

"Mom?" Carol got up and went to the door. "Mom, are you all right?" She glanced at her watch. "It's nearly nine."

"Of course, I am." Dixie drew her into a hug. "I've just come to celebrate my daughter's birthday, even if I am late. That's Jo's fault. You will let us spend the night, won't you? I can't face driving back to Greenville with her after dark."

"Of course." Carol tried in vain to remember if there were sheets on the beds in the guest rooms. Oh, well, Dixie was her mother, not a guest. "Stay the summer if you'd like. You can help me with flowers."

Her mother laughed. "Probably not the summer, but I'd enjoy a few days with you. Come on, honey, we need to go down. The Elliot boy says supper's nearly ready. Goodness, he's a dandy. I think you should consider keeping him. I believe he also said you should—let me get this right—'haul ass' because he's not waiting all night on you."

"Oh, yeah, he's a dandy, all right. And, Mom, you

just said 'ass' and it wasn't about a donkey *or* Biblical. You're getting downright lax in your language. Do we need to get the soap?" She tucked her mother's hand through her arm before they started downstairs.

"I'm just getting wild in my old age. It's from putting up with your aunt for so long."

"I heard that," Jo yelled from below. "Give her a little push, Carolina. You'll both get down here quicker."

"Aunt Jo, that's awful," Carol scolded, "and you know you don't mean—what is going on?"

The foyer was full. Of Campbells, Hartleys, and Sawyers. Maggie and Dan Leiden. Deac and Jean Rivers and most of the residents of the Old Farts Home. Lynn and Kay. Reese was there with her father. Plus one long-haired grinning Elliot.

"It's your birthday," Steven explained into her stunned silence, "and we thought you should have a party."

"But I—" She never celebrated this day. Everyone knew that—even Dixie had given up trying to spend it with her years ago.

The Mustang. It was time to drive the Mustang. Carol pasted on a smile. "I'm so glad to see everyone. Grace, did you make that cake? Do I get some even if I already had today's dessert?"

"You can have some because all the energy it's going to take to blow out this many candles is going to negate the calories." Grace was sticking candles into the sheet cake on the dining room table as she spoke. "How did we all get to be so old?"

"You blinked your eyes," said Maxie, and everyone laughed. Including Carol. It felt good to laugh on this day. It did.

I won't forget you, Miranda. I'll never forget you. Just stay with your daddy—he'll take care of you.

The thought brought tears to her eyes, but she was able to blink them back.

"I have to know," she said, when they were all seated at tables on the back porch, "how you managed this so fast. Three hours ago I was whining about what day it was, and now I have twenty-some people at my house eating a really delicious dinner that I didn't cook."

"Actually, Steven's call to the Deacon's Bench was a godsend," said Jean Rivers. "The private party in the banquet room had misjudged the number of attendees by twenty or more, so we're having leftovers. Except for the cake. I don't know how Grace managed that."

"That was easy," said Grace. "I was bringing it to the Clip Joint tomorrow morning for a Day After Carol's Birthday celebration, so it was all ready to go. Faith, of course, made the decorations from duct tape and a roll of toilet paper."

Faith flapped a hand. "Christmas lights. Plus, you know how they party at Elliot House—they had *tons* of decorations. Nothing to it."

"It's so pretty." Carol gazed around at the twinkling white lights and the flickering candles. "Mom, you and Aunt Jo haven't driven over here in forever, much less at night. That 'Elliot boy' must have been some convincing."

"Nope." Steven held up his hands. "However, in order to take as much credit as possible for this party, I will say I tried to call your mom and Jo. They didn't answer, which means they'd either already left

Greenville or if they were still home, they don't have caller ID. Because I know they'd have answered if they knew it was me." He batted his eyes at Jo. "Right?"

Dillon leaned around Grace to rap him sharply on the back of his head. "You're pathetic. Don't encourage him, Miss Jo."

Carol turned to her mother, feeling pressure behind her eyes again. She held them open wide. Her throat tickled so her voice seesawed when she spoke. "You were coming over anyway?"

"We were. It took us longer because we had to make a stop." Dixie took another bite of her dinner. "I know we should have called first, but we wanted to surprise you."

"You certainly did that." Carol smiled at the cluster of tables. "You all did. It's the nicest birthday I've ever had."

It was also the tidiest party she'd ever had. "Usually," she argued uncertainly as Jake and Deac folded tables to load them into the back of Deac's van, "guests don't clean up afterward."

"Usually," said Grace dryly, "guests don't invite themselves." She put Christmas lights neatly into a red and green plastic tote. "We'll have these out again for the Fourth of July—I don't know why we bother putting them away."

"People invite themselves to the Old Farts Home all the time." Jonah opened the door of Elliot House's van and helped his wife into the front passenger seat. "Then we don't let 'em leave."

"Not true." Lynn Lewis laughed. "I bring my kids there at least once a week so they can help in the garden, and you can't *wait* for them to leave. Could it be they haven't caught on to the helping part yet?"

"No, it's because they beat Jonah and Noah at poker." Steven offered his arms to two of the older ladies as they stepped from the porch.

Carol leaned against the post beside the steps, watching the cars make their way down Taylor Hill. Jo and Dixie sat in the wicker chairs, still sipping from their wineglasses. Steven shared the porch swing with Fred and Barney.

"There's an extra car out there on the other side of your truck, Steven." Carol squinted toward the driveway. "Did someone come alone and go home with someone else?"

"I don't think so, but I believe that's what I'll do," said Dixie.

"What do you mean, Mom? Aunt Jo's ornery, but she'll still drive you home." Carol grinned over at her mother and aunt. "Or else you can stay with me."

"I drove over here," said Dixie. "I know I don't drive often, but I still can."

Jo snorted. "That's a matter of opinion."

"Bite me," Dixie invited, giving her sister-in-law's knee a pat.

Carol choked on a laugh. "Mother, that bar of soap's coming closer and closer. So why did you drive over?" Jo had done the driving for the two women ever since they'd moved in together. "Did you rent a car for something?"

"Rent one? Oh, no. But you hadn't bought a new car yet and it occurred to me—belatedly, I'll admit—that I had one taking up space in a storage unit. It's twelve years old—you remember I bought it the year your father died—but doesn't have very many miles on it. I'd really like for you to have it for your birthday. You can use it for a down payment on a car you like better if you want to." Dixie came over to where Carol stood, carrying a small gift bag. "Here are the keys and the title."

"But I can't take this." Carol backed away, her hands waving back and forth in a vehement gesture of refusal. "Daddy would be spinning in his grave—he didn't think girls needed cars, or that women did, either. He drove you everywhere."

Dixie caught her hands, pushing the bag handle into one of them. "I loved your father, honey, and I know you did, too, but the truth is that sometimes he was just a…curmudgeon." She spoke the last word as if it was the most dreadful epithet she could come up with for her late husband, and Carol's mouth curved into a smile. Now, *that* was her mother.

"You got that right," said Jo wisely. "Steven, dear boy, is there any more of that wine? My brother didn't think women should drink, either, but I've always been rather proud of my abilities in that direction."

Steven refilled her aunt's glass, but Carol knew he was still watching her. She could feel the warmth.

"Please." Dixie's gaze held Carol's. "I'm like every other parent in the world—I made so many mistakes. Letting you think I preferred your brother over you was one of them. I can't undo that one, although I hope you'll come to know I didn't. But letting your father get by with buying a car for Ed but not for you is one I can fix even if it's over twenty years past time."

"You don't owe me anything, Mom." Carol shook her head at the same time as she shook the hands still holding hers. "You're the best mother ever."

"It's not because I owe you. It's because I love you more than anything in life. And because I want you to have it."

Carol took a deep breath. "Okay." She laughed on the exhale. "Thank you. Let's go see it. I don't even remember what it is."

She should have, though. It had been both sweet and hilarious when Dixie bought it. She'd driven it from the dealership to the handicapped parking space in front of Clip Joint and honked the horn. When Carol came outside, followed by her client still in a cape and permanent rods, she and the customer burst into laughing applause.

Twelve years later, Carol laughed and applauded again. "Steven," she called. "Come see."

He came around the back of his truck, Jo's free hand through his arm while the other hand held firmly to her glass. "Well," he said, "I told you so."

Dixie Whitney's first car was a dark blue Mustang convertible.

****

Halfway up the hill to his house, Steven spoke thoughtfully, doing a one-eighty to eye the car still sitting in Carol's driveway even though they were around the curve and he couldn't see it anyway. "It's kind of woo-woo."

Carol stopped mid-step. "Steven, you just said persnickety the other day. Now you're saying woo-woo? Dillon will never let you live it down."

"Dillon doesn't know I said it." He stopped with her, pulling her into the loose circle of his arms.

"He doesn't *now*," she agreed, "but he will as soon

as I tell him. And he'll spread it all over town. You know how he is."

"He won't spread it if you don't tell him."

She grinned at him, and he loved the laughter that danced in her eyes. Suddenly the exertion of planning and putting on a birthday party for twenty in the space of two hours was worth the effort.

"Yeah," she said, "but you know how *I* am."

He hugged her. "What is woo-woo is the whole thing with your mom and your aunt coming over here and bringing you the Mustang."

"Oh, come on, you and they cooked it up, didn't you?" She drew back. "I'm a big girl, I love surprises and the party was a great one, but you can be honest with me on this. You got hold of Mom and Aunt Jo."

"No, ma'am, I did not, although I admit I tried."

"But they haven't been here in—I don't know, *years.* What made them come today?"

"That's part of the whole woo-woo thing, but not really. Dixie's your mom. I have no doubt she knew you needed to see her today. I've been a doctor and a guy long enough to know that's one corner of woo-woo that mothers have a fairly exclusive contract on. The Mustang part, though, that's just weird. How could you have forgotten it? I mean, honest to God, Carol, it's *gorgeous*, and you forgot your mom had it?"

"I didn't think she still did. She stopped driving when she had her hip replaced and moved in with Aunt Jo—what, ten years or so ago? Who'd have thought she'd keep a car she'd only put five thousand miles on in two years? Five thousand! Can you imagine? I hadn't even thought about it since then."

"So what are you going to name it?" He started

walking again. This was a habit they'd gotten into. Carol would intend to accompany him to the end of her driveway, letting Fred and Barney have their last walks of the day at the same time. Before they knew it, she'd end up walking all the way up to Miss Abigail's with him. Then, rather than have her negotiate Taylor Hill by herself in the dark, he'd escort her back home.

"The Mustang?"

"Yeah. The Pontiac was Bess, but you don't want to call a Mustang Bess."

"I've never had a neat car before, and I've certainly never had a convertible." She was quiet for a few minutes, breathing a little hard as they walked. Steven slowed his pace.

"I know," she said, coming to a stop again. "Wilma.'"

"Wilma what?"

"The Mustang. I'll call her Wilma."

Wilma? Surely she wouldn't. "You can't do that to that car."

"I most certainly can." She planted her hands on her hips, and he was almost certain she was tapping her foot, too. "No one will know it but her and me. It's not like I'm going to get one of those sparkly license plates or anything."

He shook his head before she'd even finished speaking. "No, Carol. *I'll* know it, and I absolutely cannot see that beautiful car and know you've named her Wilma. She probably won't start once she knows about it."

"Then I won't tell her."

He grinned at her. "Maybe not, but I'll tell Dillon and he'll tell her. You know—"

"—how he is," she finished in unison with him. She started walking, and he caught up, capturing her hand in his. "What do *you* think I should name her?"

"Something spectacular."

"Julia Roberts is taken."

"How about Isabella? That's got a real ring to it."

"How about Sally? Like the song."

...ride, Sally, ride... "Not bad. Want me to sing it to you? I know at least half the words."

"Go for it, big boy." She stopped again, folding her arms in front of her.

Oh, shit, him and his big mouth. "What?"

"You heard me. You offered to sing. Let's hear it."

For an ill-advised few months in high school, somewhere between baseball and football seasons, he and Dillon joined a rock band called Feather. (They were from Peacock—what else would they call themselves?) Dillon played bass guitar. Badly. Steven was the lead singer—at least until the drummer made up with her boyfriend. The one who was the real lead singer.

That had only been twenty-some years ago, and Feather had performed in worse places than the middle of the road that climbed Taylor Hill.

So Steven sang. He made up lyrics to fill the spots he didn't know and danced like—what was that poem Promise had loved, or was it an Irish blessing? Whichever it was, he danced as if no one was watching.

But someone was. Carol was a one-woman audience, clapping her hands with his suspect rhythm, her throaty laughter a rich accompaniment to both the song and the jingle of the charm bracelet he'd given her for her birthday.

And her eyes. Lord, she had the most beautiful eyes, and they sang and danced and called out to him with every sweep of her long lashes. They were just eyes, for God's sake—they couldn't *really* make music in his heart—but they did. Oh, hell yes, they did.

He stopped singing and came to a stop standing toe-to-toe with her, his gaze locking with hers in the starlit night. "Carol?" He wasn't sure what he was asking, but when she raised her face to meet his lips with her own, it wasn't important anymore. All that mattered was her.

"Open," he whispered, drawing his mouth away for just a second.

She chuckled. "Bossy, aren't you?"

But she obeyed, and he deepened the kiss, breathing in the scent of her. His hands slid down her sides, feeling the warmth of her skin through the slick fabric of her dress. He skimmed the sides of her breasts, enjoying the hitch in her throat when she inhaled. He ended the kiss. "You feel so good."

"Not any older than I did yesterday?" Her hands tunneled through his hair and she drew his face back down to hers.

"Oh, no, ma'am." He kissed her again, pulling her so close their bodies curved into one another from breast to knees. The heat between them smoldered and coiled in its intensity. She moaned, deep in her throat, her hands slipping inside his shirt. He reacted strongly enough he had to stop kissing long enough to breathe. "Not even a day older."

He leaned back enough to stroke lightly over her breasts, then lay his hands on the warm skin above the low neckline of her dress. "Come home with me." She closed her eyes, and he brushed her lips over the lids. "Stay for breakfast."

She smiled, opening her eyes. "I'd like to." She spoke over his protest. "I would. But Mom and Aunt Jo are here. I'm not positive, but dollars will get you donuts Mom still thinks I'm a virgin."

He sighed, resting his forehead against hers. "I don't know about that, but you definitely give me non-virtuous thoughts. I gotta tell you, Carolina, I'm enjoying the hell out of them."

"Come on. Walk me back to the house so you can go home."

"Okay." He put his arm around her waist, drawing her close to his side to head back to her driveway. When they reached the mailbox, he burst into laughter.

"What?" She raised her eyes.

He pointed to where his truck sat between Jo's Buick and the blue Mustang. "I could probably drive home."

Her deep chuckle joined his. "Probably."

He walked her to the back door and spent a long time kissing her goodnight even with Fred winding impatiently around their legs. Barney had given up and fallen asleep on the porch swing.

A few minutes later, Steven was back at Miss Abigail's. He, Dillon, and the sub-contractors he'd hired had made a lot of progress in a short time. The house was well on its way to becoming a warm and welcoming place.

He walked through the night-light enhanced rooms to the kitchen, which was taking shape due to Carol's input. "If I'm going to cook for you, which you seem convinced I should do a lot of," she'd told him, waving a spatula in his direction, "you need to make it cooking-friendly. Put an island here with barstools around that side the way it is in Grace's kitchen and don't get countertop for pretty—get it for indestructible."

He'd listened. He didn't see himself ever falling in love again, but that certainty didn't apply to food—he *loved* Carol's cooking.

He poured a glass of milk and studied the cozy area. The open shelves stacked with brightly colored dishes, the cookie jar shaped like a surgeon complete with scrubs and a scalpel, the coffee mugs that fit into a row of cubbyholes above the coffeemaker—everything was comfortable and warm. Carol had chosen almost everything in the room, and it looked like her. Felt like her.

He couldn't feel Promise's presence in Miss Abby's house, because she'd never been there, he supposed. It had been hard to get used to that—she'd been a part of him most of his life. The emptiness he'd felt without her was finally going away. He still missed her and thought he always would, but "getting a life" was starting to seem like a possibility.

There were no curtains over the big mullioned window in the dining area beside the kitchen. He went over to it, gazing out at the stars. "You'd like it here, Prom." But he wasn't sure that was true. Promise had been a small-town girl, but there was a world of difference between small-town and rural, and she'd never been interested in stepping to the country side of the equation.

He located the Big Dipper and searched for the other one, the Little one—he could never find it. "No, you wouldn't like it, would you, darlin'? But you'd like it that *I* do."

She'd be glad he liked Carol, too. That thought, although he was positive of its accuracy, was unsettling.

He sat at the island and opened the newspaper that had come that day, smiling because Peacock's tabloid-size weekly was one of the things in life that never changed. It still had the column "I Can See from Here..." wherein a nameless reporter wrote about who and what he or she had seen through the office window. This week, Grace Campbell had been to the Clip Joint more than once, Deac Rivers had jumped double Dutch on the sidewalk in front of the church for donations to the church camp fund, and the Cup and Cozy had set little bistro tables and chairs outside—which meant reporters could snoop and enjoy a sandwich and a cup of the blend *du jour* at the same time.

Steven laughed softly to himself there in his empty kitchen. He'd come a difficult and winding way from reading the financial and sports pages in the *Knoxville News-Sentinel* on the run to reading every word—including the classifieds—in the *Peacock Chronicle* as he sat in unhurried and unlonely solitude in Miss Abigail's house.

An advertisement for the Clip Joint caught his eye. "Cut up with Carol, color and croon with Kay, lowlight and laugh with Lynn. Or just stop by to talk. We *love* to talk!" There were silhouettes in the ad that suggested the profiles of the stylists—a ponytail for Carol, dangling earrings for Lynn, a subdued chignon for Kay. The design of the ad had to be Carol's work. It smiled at you.

And it made you smile back. Just like she did.

Chapter Nine

Carol stayed on the porch for a few minutes after Steven's truck pulled out of the driveway. It had been the longest, best Flag Day she'd had in twenty years. Or maybe ever. To end it with mind-bending kisses from the sexiest man she'd ever known was as sweet as the icing on that splendid birthday cake. Her knees were still wobbly and the girly muscles in her abdomen and between her thighs even more so. Her breasts throbbed almost painfully in the confines of her bra.

She didn't consider herself a prude, although Jackson Winters and Seth and Drew Hartley had assured her that's exactly what she was during an off-subject and mildly obscene discussion in a study session in the shop. She was just particular, she'd told them, and she wanted to be emotionally engaged before she got sexually involved. Right, they had agreed. A prude.

It had been a long time.

Maybe emotionally engaged was asking too much. She didn't have to be in love—she wasn't even sure she'd recognize it if it came along. She had loved Rand, but she'd been seventeen and then he'd died. Her memories of him were treasured but dim, and the truth was that she hadn't loved anyone since him.

She didn't have to love Steven, nor did she need for him to love her, but she wanted to be more than friends, more than human replacements for vibrators. What she wanted was assurance that he was "emotionally engaged."

Because she was. She hadn't meant to be, but it was too late now.

There was something else, too. Carol didn't dwell on being a big girl, what was referred to by skinny advertisers as "queen-size" or "plus-size." At least she didn't think she did. But her mind did latch onto wondering what a devastatingly handsome—and lean— man would think about her naked body. She wasn't one who undressed in front of anyone or wanted the lights on during sex, but she didn't hide under the covers, either.

She and Steven were friends, and she wouldn't lie to herself—she'd like for them to be lovers, too. But what if, when things started getting hot and heavy, he wasn't attracted to her after all? What if—oh, dear God forbid—he felt sorry for her? She wanted to make love with him, but not at that cost to herself and not at the risk of a friendship she cherished.

With a sigh that reverberated all the way through her, she opened the door, holding it wide for Fred and Barney.

"Mercy sakes, what are you doing here?" Jo, with her partial plate in a glass somewhere and wearing what Carol was pretty sure was Uncle Jim's old robe, peered over her trifocals at her niece.

Carol blinked, closing the door behind her. "I live here."

"It's your birthday. Why didn't you go home with that nice Elliot boy and celebrate in style?"

"Because Mom would ground me." She looked

past her aunt at where Dixie sat at the table with a cup of…something. Carol wasn't sure she wanted to know what it was. "Wouldn't you?"

Her mother appeared mildly surprised at the question. "Oh, Lord, no, but I would probably ask if you were carrying condoms. You just can't be too careful these days."

"I have fallen through the rabbit hole," Carol muttered to no one in particular, refilling the animals' water dishes. "There's no longer any doubt about it."

"I want you to be happy, and I hate it that you're alone. I don't think that's strange at all." Dixie sipped from her cup. "Do you want some hot chocolate?"

"No thanks. I am happy, Mom, really, and I don't mind alone." *Most of the time.* "Steven's around right now, and he's fun, but I don't think he's ready for a relationship and I'm not ready for something less than that." She grinned cheerfully. "Or if I am, I'm not about to admit it to my mother."

"Well, that's right." Jo sat down and nodded wisely at her sister-in-law. "We forget, Dixie, that you were born yesterday. By the way, Carolina, did you drive that car yet? Your mother buried the needle on the speedometer coming over here tonight. You should make sure it still runs."

"The bag's there on the table with the keys in it." Dixie pointed. "And I didn't bury the needle—just pushed it. A little."

Carol stared. "You want me to drive it now?"

"No time like the present." Jo waved at her. "I'm off to bed. See you in the morning, sweetheart. Thanks for having us to stay. Are you cooking breakfast, too?"

"As soon as I get done throwing up, I will," Carol

promised.

Dixie set her cup in the sink. "I'm going to bed, too. I stopped waiting up for you twenty years ago." She came to hug Carol, drawing back to meet her eyes. "Do what you want, honey. Life's too short." She turned back at the doorway. "I think I'll sleep late in the morning. You, too, Jo?"

Jo's voice floated back from the stairs. "Oh, hell, yes."

Carol went into the little bathroom and brushed her teeth, then surveyed herself in the mirror. She took the clip from her hair, combed it, then put the clip back.

And took it out. She seldom wore her hair down. Except tonight she thought maybe she would.

It took a few minutes to figure out the interior of the Mustang, to find the buttons for the electric windows and the knob that turned on the lights. She thought about putting the top down, but she didn't know how and didn't want to take the time to learn.

She grinned in delight when she started the car. There was a lot more power under her foot than there had been in the Pontiac, although Bess had done her best. She thought about turning the other way when she got to the end of her driveway—cruising through town and maybe going out to the highway to push it, like Dixie had, "a little."

But she didn't. She turned right and went to the next driveway on Taylor Hill, the long one with the curve in it. Lights were on at Miss Abigail's. That was good—she didn't want to have to wake him up to seduce him. Not that she was at all certain she could go through with it.

Tom and Huck, the two rescue kittens Grace had

foisted off on her brother, raised their heads when she stepped onto the porch. "Hi, kids," she murmured, bending to stroke their fuzzy little black heads. "Is your dad awake?"

"He is." Steven's voice came from behind the screen door. "Evenin', Ms. Carol. To what do we owe the pleasure?"

The sound of his voice slipped warm and inviting into her consciousness, rippling up her spine and creating all kinds of sensations in her stomach. And below. What was she doing? Oh, Lord, *what in the hell was she doing?*

"I don't know," she said. "Do you want to go for a ride?"

He stepped outside, still dressed in the shorts he wore all the time. But no shirt. Holy geezy Pete, no shirt. Other women could say what they liked about hairless, shaved bodies, salivating over shiny, silky male skin, but Carol had never joined the movement. The gold-tipped hair on Steven's chest, arrowing down his belly toward the low waistband of his shorts made her…well, salivate.

Moonlight washed the porch, glinting off his hair and the light in his dark eyes. He'd taken the band off his ponytail so the dark blond mane fell messy and straight nearly to his shoulders.

That hair. He should cut it. A forty-year-old man with hippie hair…oh, holy, *holy* geezy Pete again, he looked wonderful. He should never cut it. Just keep the ends trimmed the way he always had.

She started to lean against the wall of the house— her balance was off, her knees weak. Her heartbeat was crazed, too, bouncing all over the damn place. But

Steven caught her before she could shift her questionable stance, his arm circling her waist.

"A ride?" he said, the soft southern drawl barely above a whisper. "Y'think?"

And then this mouth was on hers, his hands everywhere at once in a way that should have seemed rushed and rowdy but was simply exciting instead. "I meant," she said, drawing away just enough to speak, "in the Mustang."

His hands slipped up her arms to tunnel into her hair—she was glad she'd left it down—and his lips took hers again. What was that word that kept cropping up in the books she read in the summertime, the ones she really enjoyed that were never on college reading lists? Plundering. That was it. She'd never really liked the word, but now, with Steven Elliot's lips and tongue doing leisurely, erotic things to her, she liked it. Oh, yes, she liked it a lot.

"Oh, is that what you meant?" He smiled down into her face. "Maybe we could do that later."

"Maybe." She smiled back at him. "I've never done this whole make-the-first-move-and-seduce-him thing. Are you going to be gentle with me?"

"Hmm." He kissed her again, gathering her in close so that she swore every inch of her could feel him. And it felt good. Deliciously, decadently good. "Nope. Don't think so. That okay for you?"

"I don't know." She had her hands in other people's hair nearly every day of her life, but no one's ever felt like his. It was past midnight, but it was as if the thick strands still held the warmth of sunlight.

"Wanna go in?" He took some time with her ear, with the side of her neck, with his fingers inside the straps of her dress and bra. Coaxing time. Teasing time. "I do. I want to go inside with you."

She lifted her head, meeting his moonlit eyes, searching for…she wasn't sure what. "Yeah," she said. "I want to go in."

****

He'd actually made his bed, probably the first time since he'd moved out to Miss Abigail's, because the ladies from Elliot House had given him a quilt for it as a housewarming gift. He'd washed the sheets, then made the bed neatly and took pictures of it with his phone so the "girls" would be able to see it.

He hadn't thought the first girl to see the quilt on the king-size bed would be Carol. Or maybe he had, because it felt so right, walking through the house with his arm around her. They stopped at the dining room window, where he showed her the Big Dipper, glad he'd located it earlier so could appear knowledgeable when he pointed over her shoulder at the arrangement of stars. Then she found Orion's Belt and the Little Dipper, both of them, without even trying.

"I can never do that," he admitted, squinting, "but there it is, plain as day. Or night."

"Ed was big into astronomy. He taught me a lot. I still have his telescope."

He lifted the skirt of her dress to rub the cloth between his fingers. "Did I tell you I liked this?" He released the fabric, stroking his hand lightly up her thigh, up her side, coming to curve around a breast. "And these?" He bent his head to string kisses along the wide scoop of her neckline. "Did I tell you you're beautiful? You are, you know."

It was funny the things being a grownup did for

you. The thought caught up to him from somewhere out in left field. "Beautiful" used to be a word that came easily, not always meant, a softening-up line that always worked. It came easily now, too, but only because he did mean it. Only because it was true.

"Hey, Carol."

Her eyes, darkened nearly to gray, were cloudy and soft. "Hey, what?"

"How'd you like to see my new quilt?"

Her kiss-swollen mouth lifted in a smile, and her eyes cleared. "Sure. Where do you keep it?"

"Come on." He took her hand, pulling her along with him into the short hall that ended in his bedroom. "I'll show you."

"Oh." She drew away from him when they entered the room. "It's beautiful. Turn on the light, Steven, so I can see it better."

He didn't want to turn on the overhead light fixture—the bed might be made, but he hadn't dusted recently. Well, maybe he hadn't dusted ever, so he walked past her to switch on the bedside lamp.

"I helped with this," said Carol, going to the bed. "See those stitches in the corner, the ones that are crooked? Those are mine. The crooked ones on the other side are Grace's. Mrs. Rountree and Mrs. Willard weren't overly impressed with us. Faith's, of course, over there on that block, are perfect." She stroked the fabric.

"Of course." He grinned at her. "Don't talk about my sisters. They're not what I want in my mind right now."

"Okay." She came back to stand in the loose circle of his arms. "Tell me what you want in your mind." Her hands rested lightly on his chest, her nails short and shiny with clear polish.

"Actually." He cleared his throat. "My mind doesn't have a hell of a lot to do with anything. It's pretty well…dropped to another part of my anatomy." Her dress had buttons in the front, and he freed them one by one, his lips following the path of the opening until he encountered the silky fabric of her peach-colored bra. "You wear really pretty underwear." He slipped the straps of her dress from her shoulders and pushed it over her hips so that it puddled on the floor. "And you have really pretty skin. Soft."

She was curvy. Delectably so. Where it wasn't golden from the sun, her skin was pale, but tinged with the same peachy shade as her bra and the panties that were cut way high, exposing the smooth hip-to-thigh transition that was—bar none—his favorite part of a woman's body. A tattoo of a cluster of yellow flowers twined around a pink rose trailed over her hip, and he knelt to kiss there, captivated.

He stroked lower, his fingers under the elastic of her panties, enjoying the quick intake of her breath. Enjoying that her hands weren't exactly idle, either. She was doing all kinds of things guaranteed to drive him right out of his mind. He'd always known she was an extraordinarily capable woman. She seemed intent on proving it.

In extraordinarily capable ways.

She wasn't gentle with him, thanks be to Jesus, but she wasn't…ungentle, either. She was urgent, but not in a hurry. Earthy, but…he didn't know, but he thought sweet was a good word for it.

When they were naked, and the new quilt was

folded semi-neatly over the back of the wing chair that sat near the window, Steven said, "Are you nervous?"

God, she smelled good. Girly and warm and sexy.

"No, not much. Not now." She smiled into his eyes, her hair falling softly over her face. "Of course, the Mustang was shaking all over herself driving up here."

"I knew you'd come." He kissed her, stroking his hand down her side then up and under the weight of her breast, tracing a line up the center of her ribcage with his thumb.

"Did you now?" She raised an arm to lift her hair out of her face, then pushed his aside, too. "Really?"

"Well." He loved her arms. They were well-proportioned. Graceful. His hand left her breast to move down the outside of one and up the inside. "I hoped you would. Oh, God." Need robbed him of his voice.

"And were you nervous?"

"No." He traced the line between her ribs again. And again, going lower each time, to tease the hidden flesh between her thighs. And higher, to circle the tight, dusky pink skin of her nipples. "I was needy."

She laughed, the sound catching throaty and female on a gasp as his fingers dived inside.

"How about you?" He sounded a little air-deprived to himself. With good reason—he couldn't remember the last time he took a normal breath. "Were you needy?"

"I don't think so." Her eyes met his, and she brought her hands to his face to kiss him. "But I am now."

He moved over her, bringing them together slowly, even though there was no need—she was ready for him, moving restlessly as he took his time entering her. He knew, although she'd never said, that it had been a while since she'd been with anyone—he wanted this first time to be perfect for her. As perfect as it already was for him. Her hair smelled like vanilla. Oh, dear God. Vanilla was supposed to be plain. Quiet. Who knew it was anything but that? Who in the hell knew?

"Whoa, Sally," he said once, "we better slow the Mustang down." And they both laughed so hard they had to stop and start again.

And then there was no slowing down, much less any stopping, as need met need. Their hearts beat hard and fast and together, mirroring their movements and finally, in joyous, abandoned unison, their release.

****

"Wow." His voice was hushed, exhausted. Carol smiled with the hearing of it.

She stretched under the sheet, biting her tongue on a groan when her long-unused girly muscles complained. "Uh-huh."

His arm was around her, keeping her close. "I'm thirsty," he murmured sleepily, "but I don't want to get up."

She thought for a moment about being delicate, then gave up the notion. "I have to pee, and I have absolutely no choice about whether to get up or not."

His dark eyes, which had been nearly foggy with sleep, opened wide. "Woman, the romance in your soul truly undoes me."

She grinned at him. "Steven, you're a doctor, and I've known you my entire life. I'm pretty sure you wouldn't recognize romance if it bit you on the…if it bit you. However, bladders are something you probably understand—even given your specialty is a bit removed from them—and mine is at the present time overtaxed. Close your eyes. I'm getting up."

He blinked. "Close my eyes? After what we just did—twice, I might add, three times for one of us—you want me to close my eyes?"

"I do." Making love with the lights on was one thing—walking around naked was something else again.

He sighed mightily. "All right."

When she came out of the bathroom, he was asleep. She smiled down at him, bent to kiss him, then thought better of it. They'd avoided awkwardness so far—no use inviting it by exchanging goodbyes.

She petted Tom and Huck when she let herself out of the house, locking the door behind her.

The Mustang purred down the hill and she was in bed within minutes, stroking Fred's fur and smiling to herself. "In a few hours," she whispered to the cat, "I'll be throwing up and feeling like John Sawyer has run over me with that old saw-tooth harrow he uses sometimes when he plows everybody's gardens in the spring. But for now, I just feel pretty good. You don't know this, Fred, and you never will, but there's nothing quite like great sex."

Chapter Ten

"How long does it last?" Grace held a cold, wet towel to Carol's sweaty forehead as she took a few deep, slow breaths of her own. "If we keep puking for the next seven months, you're going to look like a basketball on legs and I'll disappear entirely. Don't tell Dillon that—he'll want me to keep throwing up 'til he finishes the next book. He says I'm a distraction."

"He likes being distracted, too. This should end in the next few weeks. It did before, but every pregnancy's different. Since we've found out there are two little Campbells in there creating gastric discontent, I don't know if that means it will last twice as long." Carol rubbed her stomach, willing its little occupants to calm down, and grinned with the memory of the day she and Grace and Dillon had found out she was carrying twins. It had been like the circus came to Peacock. "However, my vacation starts as soon as I color Faith's hair this morning, and I'm bound and determined I'm not going to spend two entire weeks being sick. We'll see if my bound and determinedness is enough to control raging nausea."

"I have faith in you." Pale as a ghost herself, Grace sat in the hydraulic chair at Kay's station. "So what are you doing while you're off? Other than not throwing up?"

"Well, I was going to just work in the garden and

can and freeze stuff, but Mom and Aunt Jo's visit has extended from a few days to a month, so they're doing most of it. Aunt Jo's even taking care of my flowers. I go home from work and sit on the porch and drink sweet tea all night." And she was loving it. Pregnancy while working full-time was more exhausting at thirty-seven than it had been twenty years before.

"No school? You *always* have school. I don't think the community college can go on if you're not there."

"Kind of like you and the library?" Carol countered. Grace had headed up story hour for kids at the library at least once a week since their high school days, when they shelved books and dusted for extra credit in English.

"Kind of." Grace shrugged, smiling. "It was always a safe place. Still is, even if I don't need it anymore. There are kids who do, the ones who'll still be in the beanbags corner reading when the librarian starts turning off the lights."

Carol nodded. That was why some high school kids came to the shop to do their homework at the table and chairs in the corner. It wasn't because she was smart enough to help them with their homework—she usually wasn't—but it was safe at the Clip Joint, and there was always food.

Reese came to the shop because no one was ever home at her house—Jeff was a logger who worked long hours and her mother was dead. Not to mention, Carol loved her. "I'm not afraid," Reese said honestly when Carol worried aloud about her being too often by herself. "I'm lonesome."

Carol replaced retail items on the shelves, pleased that sales were up. "I thought about taking one of those intensive summer courses where you go to class every day for two weeks, but they weren't offering anything I wanted. Then I thought about just going to a beach somewhere and spending a weekend in a motel, since getting a car for my birthday means I could afford to, but the idea of doing it alone no longer appeals to me like it used to."

Because of Steven. Because she saw him every day and—at least for the three weeks since her birthday—most nights. They made love. They laughed. They sat at Little League baseball games and cheered for kids they knew and kids they didn't. Sometimes they played Euchre with Grace and Dillon.

Steven helped Reese with her summer classes and took her driving because she needed practice. She had her license, but he worried about her driving alone in the hills.

They had, because Steven felt like it, gone to Maeve Malone's Saloon on a Saturday night and called everyone they knew to come for a karaoke party. He had sung "Mustang Sally" to her, with Dillon, Grant, and Jake providing tuneless but enthusiastic backup.

It was well on its way to becoming the best summer ever.

"Other than being sick with me, which I think is really nice of you, are you excited, Grace, or are you scared?" Carol saw Faith park across the street and stepped into the back room to prepare her hair color.

"Both." Grace followed her, nibbling on the biscotti she'd brought for Carol's daily dessert. "What about you?" Distress shone suddenly in her eyes. "Does this make you remember Miranda more?"

"Sometimes." Most often in the middle of the

night, when Grace's twins thought it would be a good time to give their gestational carrier a roaring case of heartburn. "But not in a bad way. What was it you said that one time when we were talking about Promise?"

"That the knives of grief had dulled?"

"Yes."

Faith came in, carrying a bag. "Good morning." She hugged Grace and looked askance at the contents of the dye bowl Carol was holding. "Purple? You're making my hair purple?"

"Yes, as opposed to the chartreuse I made it the last time. You wouldn't want me to get bored now, would you?" Carol pointed. "Dessert of the day is biscotti. Coffee's fresh."

It seemed odd, suddenly, being in the shop with Steven's sisters. She'd never thought of them that way—they'd always been her friends, and he'd always been their brother. But summer, this glorious few weeks, had changed a lot of things. She wondered how Faith and Grace felt about Carol and Steven as a couple. "Hooking up," as Jeff Confer said when she cut his hair. She'd been embarrassed and pulled his hair on purpose.

"What's the matter?" asked Grace, refilling her cup and reseating herself in Kay's chair. "You're all thunderstruck about something. Is it because you left the orange out of Faith's hair color?"

"No, I put the orange in—it was the turquoise I left out." Carol stirred absently for a minute. "Just thinking."

"About Steven." Grace nodded wisely at her sister. "She's got that 'what the hell was I thinking?' look on her face."

"Oh, she does, doesn't she?" Faith came closer to peer into Carol's face. "I think she needs a vacation, too."

"She's going to have one," said Carol, "if you'll get your rosebud-tattooed size four butt into the chair so we can get started on your roots."

Faith narrowed her eyes. "How did you know the tattoo was a rosebud?"

Grace shook her head sadly. "She's forgotten, Carol. You'll have to tell her."

Carol frowned, ignoring Faith's alarm. "Oh, but we agreed…"

"She won't remember that, either. She was pretty…you know." Grace made a seesaw motion with her hand.

"I was not," Faith burst out. "I'm never…you know." She tipped her hand back and forth in mocking motion. "At least, not since—"

"Right." Carol and Grace spoke in unison.

Faith sniffed, although she was grinning sheepishly at the same time. "That was Maxie's fault. She didn't tell me the punch at Mrs. Rountree's birthday party was spiked." She sat down, lifting her sleek brown hair so Carol could fasten the cape around her neck.

Her sister snorted. "She didn't tell you to drink twenty-three glasses of it, either."

"It was August. It was hot." Laughing herself by now, Faith met Carol's eyes in the mirror. "What else did I talk about while I was…you know."

"Yeah, we know." Carol separated Faith's hair into sections. "I think 'three sheets to the wind' is how Dillon described it. Nice you're married to a man who knows all those elegant sailing terms, Grace. That sounds so much better than 'drunk as a skunk.'"

"Or 'soaked to the gills.' I never liked that one, either." Grace grinned at her sister. "Although you were. Seth told Grant you were 'sober impaired.' I thought that was a pretty good one."

"So, what else did I tell you?" Faith sipped her coffee.

"Nothing." Carol applied cream to Faith's forehead around her hairline. "And we all agreed that we would never mention the tattoo in public, but it's just us girls here. And I have one, too. There, I've admitted it and I'm not even drunk, depending on what you put in the biscotti, Grace."

Steven loved her tattoo. He called it Jessie because the flowers were jessamine and paid toe-curling homage to it whenever he was in the vicinity of her right hip.

For just a minute, she stopped brushing color onto Faith's roots and gazed out the shop window. Steven drove past on his way to Jake's office. He tapped the horn twice, and she almost raised her arm to wave.

"He seems almost like himself again, you know it?" Faith spoke gently. "It's been such a long, lonely time for him." She smiled at Carol. "Thank you. You're good for our brother."

"He's good for me." *And he's still lonely, although maybe less than he was.* She saw it in his eyes sometimes, when he looked past her at something she couldn't see.

"So anyway, we have this house rented on Topsail Island in North Carolina for two weeks, right?" Grace spoke briskly, going to get the carafe off the warmer to refill their cups. "Because I've never spent more than a weekend on a beach in my entire life and Dillon's big on me having new experiences whether I want them or not. Then this friend of his"—she stopped to glare at Carol as if what she was about to divulge was her fault—"the tall guy who's a doctor—anybody know him?—suggested they take a motorcycle trip at the very same time because he won't be working with Jake for the next few weeks."

Faith nodded, and Carol swiped her cheek with the color brush. "Grant's going, too. He and Dillon are renting motorcycles as we speak, and we've watched both *Wild Hogs* and *Easy Rider* this week." She frowned. "I don't think that color will match my face, Carol, do you?"

"Hold still and let me get it off, or it's going to be the ugliest blusher you've ever worn," Carol threatened. "You'll have to go into seclusion 'til it wears off."

"So, do you want to go to the beach with me?" Grace asked Faith. "And, hey—" She clasped her hands in front of her as if suddenly struck with a brilliant thought. "You, too, Carol. We would have so much fun. It's too late to get our deposit back on the house, so we might as well enjoy it. Your mom and aunt would be glad to stay at your house and watch things, I'll bet."

Carol crossed her arms under her breasts, noticing uncomfortably that they were starting to grow, and stared at her.

"What?" Grace's innocent expression wouldn't have fooled anyone. "I think it's a good idea, don't you, Faith?"

Faith laughed. "I do, but you need to stop trying so hard. You can't lie to save your soul. Believe it or not, Carol," she said dryly, "this didn't just this minute enter her head. It's been coming on ever since you canceled your vacation. Then when the guys started talking about the whole riding, bonding, sleeping in a tent, don't-shave-or-shower trip, that pretty much sealed it. We're going even if you don't, but we'd rather you did."

"And since I don't have to lie anymore, we already talked to your mom and your aunt." Grace picked up the phone when it rang. "Good morning, Clip Joint. Lynn? Sure, she has some time. Ten o'clock Tuesday work for you? Cut and color? Great. Thank you." She hung up, then grimaced. "Oops, I should have gotten her name, shouldn't I?"

Carol laughed. "Just put 'mystery client, cut and color' in the book. It's not the first time. What did Mom and Aunt Jo say when you talked to them?"

Grace scribbled busily. Erased and scribbled again. "They think it's a cool idea. I wouldn't be surprised if they planned on doing a little partying while you're gone, though."

Carol went to the back room to mix Faith's highlight color. "Did Steven ask you to ask me?" she said, sticking her head around the corner.

Faith waved a dismissive hand. "That would require thought. He's really smart and all, but he didn't get the thinking gene out of the pool. He was too busy grabbing onto charm and funny."

He definitely got those. Carol had spent the last three months being captivated by them. It was a good thing she knew better than to take the charming part too seriously.

"Okay," she said, grabbing the box of foil, and going back to Faith. "I'll go, but I'm paying a third."

"No, you're not." Grace had found the ostrich

feather duster Carol kept under the counter and was flipping it over the retail shelves.

"I am, too."

"No, you're not." Faith grinned at her in the mirror. "You're the only one of us with a convertible. You're driving."

****

"You'll have fun," said Steven. He sat on Carol's bed with his back against the headboard, Fred sprawled across his lap, and watched her pack. "Not as much fun as if I was there, but still fun."

"You'll have a good time on your *Easy Rider* trip, too. I'll bet you'll have *more* fun because I'm not there."

"Damn right. You'd want to do girly things like shower and change clothes and sleep in a real bed every day. I like that one," he objected when she tossed a white eyelet blouse aside.

"Then you can wear it on your trip," she offered. "It makes me itch."

He leered at her. "Me, too." His eyes flicked to the clock beside the bed. "How long are Dixie and Jo going to be gone?"

She zipped the suitcase closed and lifted it off the bed before he could help her. "They're gone for the day. A bus trip to some den of iniquity or other with the Elliot House residents."

"Good." He shooed Fred away and pulled her to the bed, his fingers moving immediately to the buttons on her blouse. "I'll miss you."

"I'll miss you, too."

"Something we've never talked about, you know, is—" He paused, searching for a word that wouldn't

164

sound pompous. Not that he minded that sometimes, but not with her. Never with her.

"What's that?" She sat cross-legged beside him, her blouse half-undone, her hair a mess. "I thought we talked about everything and decided you were wrong about most of them."

She was beautiful. He told her that sometimes, but he didn't think she believed him, so he tried harder to show her that she was.

Nah, pompous was okay. She wouldn't mind it this once. He cleared his throat. "Exclusivity."

Her eyes widened. "Steven, this is Peacock. Nothing is exclusive here. Even at the Deacon's Bench, where people come from all around to have dinner and give parties and receptions, it's first come, first served. You know that."

He unfastened a few more of her buttons. "Would you happen to be stringing me along, Ms. Whitney?"

"Like a yo-yo, Dr. Elliot."

"Uh-huh." He eyed her, his eyes half-closed as he considered. Her feet or her ribs? Both were bare. Enticingly so. "And are you ticklish, Ms. Whitney?"

"Why, not at all, Dr. El...aieeee!" She went sideways with a shriek, ending up, as he'd thought she might, underneath him, laughing uncontrollably and trying—not very hard in his estimation—to get away.

"Laughing at me, were you?" he said, holding her wrists above her head and smiling down into her face.

She shook her head, her silky hair rustling on her pillow. "Oh, no, I wouldn't do that."

"Ah." He relaxed his hold. "I didn't think you would."

"Really?" She pulled her hands free. "You didn't?"

She wasn't the only ticklish one. He went down howling, ending with her on top, his hands moving her curvy hips to where they would be the most effective. And, oh, holy balls, yeah, were they ever effective.

Soon—though not very—when they were dressed again, and he'd carried her suitcase downstairs, he addressed the issue again.

"I don't mean to be all possessive or anything," he began. "You're a grownup, and you're certainly entitled to have sex with whomever you like. I absolutely believe you would always make sure it was safe. But, I guess…the girls always said I wasn't good at sharing, and maybe they're right." He was pretty sure he was making a mess of whatever in the hell it was he was trying to say.

He was even more convinced of that when she started laughing again. God, he could listen to her laugh all day long. Grant used to say it was a damn shame you couldn't dance to the sound of women laughing, because it was the sweetest music ever made, and he was right.

Carol filled their cups with decaf—God help him, he was learning to like it—and sat at the table with him. "You should know, Steven, that if Rand Shipper hadn't swept me off these size ten feet in my junior year, I'd likely still be a virgin. I didn't have any intention of sleeping with *anyone* I wasn't married to, *ever*. Obviously, it hasn't worked out that way, but I still only sleep with one person at a time. Wouldn't it be awful if I got confused while we were having sex and called you Albert?"

He met her sparkling gaze. "Albert?"

"Yes."

"That would probably be all right. I couldn't deal with Bertie, but Albert sounds sort of sexy." Her hair was down, and he pushed it back from her face. God, she was so…female.

She smiled slightly, turning her head enough to kiss his knuckles. "However."

Her eyes weren't laughing anymore. He gave her hair a tug. "Uh oh. 'However' is never good. It's like when your parents say 'we'll see.' "

"Exclusivity needs to be a two-way street."

He didn't know why he hadn't seen that coming, but he hadn't. The only man-woman association he'd ever had that would register on a relationship scale was the one he'd had with Promise. It had started when she and Grace were still crawling around getting into things while their mothers visited and had never stopped.

There had been other "hook-ups," both during break-up times and since Promise's death, but he had never given serious thought to waking up with anyone he slept with—at least, not on a consistent basis. No one ever asked or expected him to be faithful. No one called him her boyfriend. No one admitted they had to pee like a racehorse—it was as if the women he'd been with didn't have bodily functions other than orgasm.

Not that exclusivity was a problem. It wasn't at all.

"I don't need you to fall in love with me or promise me lifelong loyalty or any of that. I don't even expect you to consider our relationship a…well, a relationship, but I'm not much into that kind of adventure, either." She grinned sheepishly. "I know I sound like a prude, but so be it."

He knew she was no prude. She was exciting and sexy and so much fun he sometimes went days on end thinking he might actually be able to live without Promise. Not just exist, but live, with a large part of his heart intact.

"I want to be your boyfriend," he said. "No class ring—I hocked it to buy beer when I was a freshman in college. But we'll sit together at all the Little League games and the Cup and Cozy and I'll even buy—if I have any money. When you're taking care of Reese and pretending you're not, I'll pretend right along with you. What do you think?"

"I think you have your eyes on my Mustang."

"Nah, it's too little—hurts my knees—though I probably look good in it. Not as good as I do on a motorcycle, but not bad. I'll be an excellent boyfriend." He lifted her hand, turning the chain he'd given her round and round. "Boyfriends give charm bracelets."

"Well, since you did give me the bracelet and I love it, it's okay with me if you're my boyfriend. For the summer anyway." She leaned in to kiss him, her hand on his shoulder, and he caught her wrist just to touch her. He loved her skin.

"You don't think I'll stay in Peacock, do you?" He held her gaze.

"No." But she didn't seem unhappy—not even a little bit sad. "You're too—I don't know—intense, maybe. You move too fast. No one does that here. You know that. Besides, you've been gone too long. Other than a few weeks some summers and the awful time while Promise was sick, you haven't actually lived here since you left for Vanderbilt. And I don't think you've wanted to, have you?"

She was right—until this summer, he hadn't wanted to come back here. But that was before finding

Miss Abigail's. Before Jamie Scott died.

Before Carol.

"Dillon was away for years," he said. "He didn't even come and visit after his folks retired to Arizona and look at him now. You couldn't pry him off Lawyers Row with a crowbar."

Carol shook her head. "Dillon came home and found Grace. Had she not been here, he wouldn't be either."

But you're here. Steven didn't say the words out loud. He was startled to have even thought them.

She checked the clock on the oven. "It's time for me to go. I told Grace I'd pick them up at ten. When are you guys leaving?"

"As soon as everyone kisses his wife goodbye. I'll follow you into town and kiss you at the same time so you won't feel out of place or anything."

She went to the sink, rinsing the coffee carafe and their cups and draping the dishcloth neatly over the sink divider. "That's really big of you. You're not going to throw your cell phone away or anything like they did in that movie, are you?"

He picked up her suitcase to follow her out the door. "Nope. Why? Are you going to worry about me?"

"Heavens, no." She opened the Mustang's trunk for him. "I'm not your mother." She gave a little toss of her ponytail. "I'm your girlfriend."

Chapter Eleven

The GPS Dillon plugged into the cigarette lighter in the Mustang found the rental house on Topsail Island with no trouble. The women chose bedrooms by pulling numbers from Faith's straw hat, then re-chose because Faith liked the mirrors in Carol's room, Grace liked the bed in Faith's room, and Carol liked the sliding glass doors that opened on the balcony in Grace's room.

"Somehow," Grace muttered, rolling her suitcase down the hall, "I'll bet the guys aren't doing this. I am starving, by the way."

"Me, too," Carol agreed. "I haven't had any dessert today and lunch was hours ago."

"Well, then." Faith came out of her room. "Let's find a restaurant."

Carol, whose idea of deep-sea swimming was having the water more than six inches deep in the bathtub, hadn't brought a bathing suit. "I need to go to one of those beach shops first," she said. "I'd thought I'd just wear shorts, but I don't think they'll be properly beachy in all those pictures we're going to take and never print out. The ones your kids will be showing to people when we're all residents at the Old Farts Home."

"Oh, good idea." Faith was wearing her crusader look, and Carol and Grace exchanged grimaces. It didn't usually bode well for them.

"I did have a suit," Carol vowed a half hour later,

eyeing the huge and confusing selection in the beach shop, "but I think I gave it to the museum as a God-awful example of late twentieth-century fashion."

A sales associate stared at her with wide eyes. "The twentieth century? Really?" She held up a completely style-less black maillot. "How about this?"

"Or how about this?" Faith presented a green-patterned tank top and black bottoms. "It'll grow with you this summer, but it has a low neck that will keep Steven"—she hesitated—"at attention."

"Faith, I haven't worn a sixteen in five years. Is there a larger size?" Carol reached past her.

"No. Try this one." Faith pushed it into her hands.

"And this." Grace, whose taste usually leaned toward whatever her sister forced on her, gave her a teal and brown polka-dot suit. "I like this."

"But it's too small."

"Just try it. They run big here."

"Oh, no, ma'am," the associate intervened. "They actually run a little small. I have to wear a two instead of a zero."

"See?" Carol reached into the rack of eighteens, none of which were as pretty as the ones Faith and Grace had draped over her arm.

"Try those. We'll find something else while you're in there." Faith, never pushy, gave her what was very nearly a shove. No, there was no "very nearly" to it—she *thrust* Carol toward the curtained dressing rooms along the wall.

"Fine. Find me a cover-up while you're at it. Maybe a pup tent." While Carol didn't particularly mind being the size she was, she did realize a swimsuit cover-up the size of a beverage napkin wasn't going to do a lot for her.

But both suits fit. They even had a little room in the front for the space Grace and Dillon's twins were going to take up before summer ended. The tops did indeed showcase her cleavage to a nearly embarrassing point, but they did the same thing for her legs, which were long and shapely and well-muscled from all the walks up and down Taylor Hill. But they were…yes, they were sixteens!

She bought them both—plus a lacy white oversized T-shirt with a deep Vee neck to wear over them, pushing her credit card into the slot and hardly even flinching when she calculated how many haircuts it would take to pay for the purchase.

Then they went to a seafood restaurant and stuffed themselves.

****

"I don't think I've ever gotten up and not known what I was going to do that day," Carol admitted the next morning, walking along the beach with Grace. "My father lived according to a schedule and expected the rest of the family to do the same thing. We had a big desk calendar on the wall in the hallway and Ed and I had to post our daily plans as soon as we could print. Not that Dad was above *changing* those plans if he didn't approve of them—cleaning the basement always took precedence over going to the movies—but he loved predictability. Ed was smart enough to fake it so that as far as Dad knew, he was going along with the program, but I was always in-your-face rebellious." She shook her head, a float-through of sadness dimming the brightness of the sunrise. "Ed died because he couldn't face the life he had in front of him, and I've scheduled damn near every minute of the last twenty years. Life is strange, isn't it?"

"It is." Grace shaded her eyes with her hand, gazing up at a parasail being towed high above the waves. She pointed in the direction of the colorful sail. "Dillon and I did that. It was so much fun. I was scared, although I wouldn't admit it. I'd love to do it again."

Carol watched the parasail grow smaller until it all but disappeared. "I would, too. We could this week, if you'd like."

"Maybe."

But there was hesitation in Grace's voice, and the expression on her face was fear, almost dread. At the same moment, familiar nausea made itself known. *Oh.* Carol carried Grace's babies—she needed to heed Grace's fears as well. "And maybe not," she said briskly. "It's safe, I think, but these little critters of yours might kick up a fuss. I'd hate hurling right out in front of everyone."

Grace laughed, relief skittering through the sound. "I'll bet you wouldn't be the first one."

"But you and Faith should go."

"Nah, Faith probably won't. She's weird about heights. Even flying requires either a tranquilizer or several glasses of wine. There was one time they didn't have any wine, but they did have a bottle of rum left over from a party. She drank some of that before going to the airport. Drank it neat, the way Grant tells the story." Grace nodded wisely. "That's another situation she doesn't talk about."

"Sounds like a good thing to have on hand if you ever need to blackmail her."

"Oh, it is. Or if I just want to get her going. That's

fun, too."

Carol laughed, then came to a stop, watching Faith walk across the sand toward them. "How can she look like that first thing in the morning? I swear, this wind's blowing hard enough to bend my eyelashes, but she doesn't have a hair out of place."

"Just one of life's unexplained phenomena." Grace raised her voice. "If you didn't bring us fresh coffee, Faith Deborah, you could at least try to look as bad as we do in the morning."

"The coffee's brewing, and I got us a tee time." Faith beamed at them, not the least out of breath after the sandy scramble down to the water's edge.

"Tee time?" Carol exchanged a blank look with Grace. "Faith, I've never played golf in my life."

"I have," said Grace, "and it was ugly. Some woman called me 'girlie' and suggested I take up ping pong. I was going to mention something she could do, too, but Dillon wouldn't let me."

"No time like the present to learn," Faith maintained stoutly. "We can rent clubs. It will be fun and safe and good for us. Afterward, we can stop and have a drink—since we have our own designated driver—and lie about our scores. That's what the guys do."

Carol understood then the real reason for the tee time. It had nothing to do with golf or drinks or even fun—it had to do with how much Faith Hartley loved her sister. If it would keep Grace from worrying about her babies when Carol parasailed or rode a zipline, Faith would schedule shuffleboard tournaments for them every day for the entire vacation.

"It's okay, Faith." Carol draped a companionable

arm over her shoulders and did her best to mess up the flawless gold-streaked brown hair. "I'm not going parasailing or bungee jumping or even scuba diving." She patted her still-roiling stomach. "Lucy and Ethel are safe with me."

Grace grinned. "Dillon's counting on Ricky and Fred."

Faith sighed, although there was gratitude in the smile she tilted at Carol. "Does everything in our lives come with famous names? You have Fred and Barney. Steven has Tom and Huck. Gracie, you have cats named after authors."

Grace's eyebrows rose. "Is she comparing my babies to family pets?"

"Sounds like it to me. I don't think you should have to put up with it." Carol nodded decisively. "Now, when is this tee time?"

"Two o'clock. I can't believe Steven hasn't gotten you to play before this," said Faith.

They turned as one to head back toward the beach house. "It's been mentioned. I said no and offered to drive the cart for him, and he reminded me that I'd run over him in the cemetery. It was all downhill from there." And fun. They'd laughed, he'd shown her the non-existent scar on his hip, and they'd made love. He'd sung "Afternoon Delight" in the drowsy aftermath, and golf had been forgotten.

She really missed him.

****

Somewhere in Indiana, Steven propped his feet on the mattress closest to his chair, eating breakfast burritos and wondering if he could get the cherry cheesecake dessert from the deli sack before the others realized it was there.

"Are we going to admit we stayed in motels or are we going to persist in the roughing-it story?"

Dillon was propped up in the bed Steven was using for a footrest watching an episode of "M*A*S*H." He rummaged in the to-go box beside him for a breakfast sandwich. "I'm okay with lying, but I should stop shaving soon if we're going to follow through. And where are we going from here? On up into Canada? We all brought passports, right?"

"Actually." Grant seemed moody, which was nothing new. Although he was a person who was relentlessly easy to get along with—something Steven would never admit—his scholarly face wore a mad expression much of the time. "I miss Faith."

Dillon's features softened perceptibly. "Yeah. I miss her sister, too."

It was hard to mind when his sisters' husbands missed their wives. Although he wouldn't want to share living quarters with either of them, Steven was glad the men they'd married did. Then there was the other thing.

He missed Carol. Not just the physical part, although that was some of it. A lot of it. He'd gotten used to seeing her every day, to going down the hill to share coffee with her in the morning. He never knew what he'd find when he got to her house. She was in the garden some days. Other times she'd be hanging the previous day's supply of beauty shop towels on the clothesline in the side yard. Occasionally she'd be helping Reese with the homework from the girl's summer college class and, he'd get pulled into it. His favorite times were when Jo was cooking breakfast, because then Carol would sit at the table and talk and relax for a half hour before walking down to the shop.

Not that she relaxed much. Carol was never still. He hadn't yet figured out how a person who never stopped moving could be so relaxing at the same time. But she was.

He'd turned on her living room television one morning to watch the news, only to learn it hadn't worked for six months. "Why didn't you replace it?" he'd asked, carrying the old set out to his truck to take it to the recycling center.

"I thought quilting would be more fun than watching it, and it is."

When he brought a flat-screen set from Miss Abigail's so her mother and Jo could watch daytime television, Carol was grateful, but she still didn't pay attention to it. Even the set in the Clip Joint was off most of the time, unless a client wanted to see a particular show.

They played board games with Dixie and Jo, even more often when Reese was with them. The games were loud and cutthroat and more fun than he'd ever thought they could be. Sometimes at Miss Abigail's, they watched movies. But mostly they talked while she did stuff with her hands—crocheting or making jewelry she sold at the shop—and he studied. There was a whole lot involved in family practice he hadn't realized.

"So," he said, when Radar O'Reilly had saved the day by lining up Jeeps with their headlights on to create a viable surgical theatre, "what do you say we head for North Carolina and crash the girls' vacation? We could tell them we shaved because our faces itched." Which would be pretty close to the truth.

He thought it was funny when the other two didn't

even pretend to hesitate. They were on the road within fifteen minutes.

****

Carol wasn't jealous. She wasn't. She would parasail the next time she was at the beach. And rent a jet ski for an hour or so and possibly even get another tattoo. She pushed her wildly curling hair out of her face and brandished her arm at Faith and Grace as they sailed over the water. They didn't wave back, but Faith's bare feet did a little dance in the air.

Carol sighed. Yeah, she was jealous.

She pushed to her feet. At least she could walk on the sand, dipping her toes in the sea that managed to be cold no matter what the air temperature was. They'd all walked this morning—it was how they'd greeted each of the seven gorgeous mornings they'd been here— Topsail Island was like a live-in postcard. *Having a great time. Wish you were here.*

She did, truth be told, wish Steven were here. She wasn't willing to give that too much thought, but if what they were having was a summer romance—and Carol was certain it was—she would have liked being romanced on the beach.

The morning walk (and many deep breaths to convince herself and the babies she wasn't going to throw up) was followed by a breakfast a lumberjack would have sighed over. This, Faith said, was what happened when you got three women in a kitchen, two of whom liked to cook and the other who could create pastry out of a half cup of skim milk and a package of Splenda.

Carol wondered where Steven was today. He'd called her from Louisville, Chicago, Milwaukee, and somewhere in Michigan, but she hadn't talked to him yesterday or the day before. That was another thing— summer romance meant talking even on the days they didn't see each other, didn't it? Knowing Steven, he'd probably broken another cell phone.

The time on the beach made her wish she'd traveled more. She'd taken trips to Knoxville for cosmetology classes and seminars and occasional long weekends with friends, but she'd rarely left eastern Tennessee. One memorable ski trip with classmates had ended with her and Dallas Marburger nursing matching broken ankles and brandy-laced mugs of hot chocolate in the ski lodge.

There was time—being in her thirties, even her late ones, didn't push her over the proverbial hill. But she thought of Promise Elliot, who had lived every single minute of her too-brief life and enjoyed most of them. No, there wasn't always time.

Next summer, she would parasail.

She scarcely jumped when arms came around her waist from behind and a warm mouth blew a raspberry against the side of her neck. Steven's height and the scent that was his alone identified the hugger immediately. So did the leap of her heart. *Stay calm, babies. It's just your Uncle Steven.* But she didn't feel calm, either.

"I missed you," he said.

She turned into his arms. "I missed you, too."

It was amazing how life just slipped into place sometimes. She raised her face to his, getting lost for a warm, sunny few minutes in the pleasure of his kiss. It was like the Fourth of July all over again.

Amazing.

"Not to be pushy or anything"—Dillon's shoulder bumped Steven's rather firmly when he leaned in to kiss Carol's cheek—"but what have you done with Grace and Faith? No one answered the doorbell in the condo. I know they can be annoying, but Grant and I have gotten used to them."

"Oh." Carol beamed and pointed toward the returning parasailers. "That's them. I know you can't see it from here, but the purple toenails belong to Grace and the green ones are Faith's. I imagine they kind of matched her face when she first got on the boat."

Grant laughed. "How did you get her to go? Usually it takes really good booze to even get her on a plane."

"Emotional blackmail," Carol said smugly. "It's a girl thing. And it was way too early in the day for booze when they finally decided to go, although Grace suggested it."

Grant waved, and Faith's feet danced again.

"Let's go over and take them out again," Dillon suggested. "Carol, you want to go?"

"Nah." She touched her stomach. "Next year. But you guys go on ahead. I'll walk the beach again—I've only done it once today—then go start lunch." She drew away from Steven, pushing him toward the other two.

"I'll stay with you." He pulled her back to his side and waved his brothers-in-law away.

She frowned up at him when the other two had left. "You could have gone. I don't mind."

"But I do." He kept her hand in his and started down the sand. "I haven't been out here for years. It's a nice beach."

This is one of those adolescent dreams we never

outgrow—some of us, anyway—the idea of walking a beach with a guy holding your hand. Not just any guy, but one who makes other women wonder why he's with you. The only thing that would make it better is moonlight. And if I had makeup on and my hair didn't look like Medusa's. The thought made her laugh, and Steven cut questioning eyes at her.

"Just thinking."

"Let's go out for lunch," he suggested. "We never do that at home. We can be wild and crazy. We never do that, either."

"I've noticed that about you, that you're…you know, boring."

"Have you now?" Laughter rippled music-like through his voice. His breath was a warm whisper against her temple.

And she thought, *Oh, no.* Because it rippled all through her, too. Laughter. Music. Joy that danced and sang in her heart and everywhere else he touched her. *Mustang Sally's gone and blown it, babies. I'm in love with your Uncle Steven.*

This can't be good.

Chapter Twelve

"What are you doing?" Steven stood at the driver's side of the golf cart, perplexed. She was in his seat.

"I'm driving." She nodded toward the golf club he still held. "You do just fine driving with one of those, but put you behind the wheel of this thing, and you feel compelled to drag race with Dillon on the cart paths. Parasailing would be a lot safer than riding with you in this."

"Oh." He guessed that was reasonable. He walked around to get in the other side and pointed in the direction they were heading. "You can pass Dillon on the right there. It would be out of bounds so it wouldn't hurt the fairway or anything."

"We'll just follow. That's why these paths are only wide enough for one cart, you know."

"Whoa." He reared back in exaggerated surprise. "You've gotten awfully knowledgeable about golf for someone who's only played twice, haven't you?"

"Three times. Four if you count today." She stopped the cart for him to get out and squinted at the numbers on the scorecard. "Maybe I won't. Count today, I mean. It's ugly."

"I could take you parasailing, and we wouldn't have to tell Grace. I know she worries and I don't want to add to it, but I want you to enjoy your vacation, too." He got out of the cart and pulled a six-iron out of the bag on the back. "Where's your ball? I never saw it land."

"I have enjoyed it. I *am* enjoying it. I don't have to do everything on my bucket list in this two-week period, you know." She looked around. "I don't see it, either. Does that mean I can start over with zero on this hole? What do you call that? A mulligan?"

"That's what you call it, and no, you can't. You did that on the first hole. You only get one." He shook his head at her, but the laughter in her eyes stopped him cold. He stood unmoving, his six-iron forgotten in his hand.

"If you're looking for Carol's ball," Dillon called from across the fairway, "it's hiding under this bush over here. It's trembling all over. Never saw anything like it in my life."

Grace leaned out of the cart she was sitting in. "You want me to hurt him, Carol? I don't mind."

Steven laughed and glanced toward the green, impatient with the foursome who had been lollygagging ahead of them ever since they started. And saw something.

He vaulted into the cart. "Go!"

Carol didn't question, just pushed hard on the pedal.

"Go right up to the green," he ordered tersely, and leaped from his seat before the cart had come to a full stop. "Have you called 911?" He pushed between the three men kneeling beside the prone form of the fourth.

"No." The one closest to him wrung his hands. "We left the phones in the car."

"Carol, call—" But she already was.

"The seventh hole." Her voice reached him as she

came up behind him. "On the green. Yes, I'm still here. Is he conscious, Steven?"

"No. Answer her questions," Steven instructed the group of men. No pulse. *Goddamn it.* CPR. Jesus, he hadn't done it in forever, not like this anyway. All he'd wanted was a game of golf with his girlfriend, for God's sake. Breaths first. Compressions. *Breathe, damn it, don't freaking ruin everybody's day.*

"If he has any kind of condition, we don't know it. His wife is…" The voices of the prone man's friends hummed in the background, broken by Dillon's shout that they would try to find a portable defibrillator and Carol's steady tones as she asked questions and relayed information to the dispatcher.

God, he'd forgotten how exhausting it was. Dillon and Grace were speeding toward the clubhouse. Everyone else lapsed into silence. *Breathe! One, two, three…*

"I know CPR." Carol knelt beside him, ready to take over.

Why was he not surprised?

****

"I thought it was cool that the cardiothoracic surgeon couldn't get him breathing again, but the woman who cuts my hair could." Dillon beamed at the other occupants of the table. "Of course, I taught her everything she knows."

"That's right in a way," Carol agreed, reaching for her wineglass of cranberry juice and club soda. "I cut his hair while he read the Red Cross book to me. Which means half my clients can take credit, because they all read to me. If I ever get a degree, it will be in how to avoid eyestrain."

"Do they offer master's studies in that?" Grant asked. "I'm almost certain our kids are studying the same thing. They have textbooks with uncut pages in them."

"It's amazing, is all." Grace forked another piece of pizza onto her plate. "I know you take all kinds of classes, but to put what you've learned to practical use and save someone's life is just…well, amazing. The last time I read for you, when you were making me scream waxing my eyebrows, it was from an advanced psychology book." She smirked at Dillon. "Maybe I should have paid more attention to what I was reading."

"Wouldn't have done any good." Steven punched Dillon's arm. "Some patients are beyond redemption, no matter how well you read the textbook." His hand lay warm on Carol's back. "It's a great thing, what you did today. I was losing him for sure."

Carol was human—she liked attention. She was also embarrassed by it. "You wouldn't have. And you knew what to do when he started breathing—that was what saved his life, not me."

"You're a good combination." Faith passed the breadsticks.

"We are." Steven's gaze caught Carol's, and she was unable to look away. "What do you say we pretend Topsail Beach is Taylor Hill and we'll go work off this pizza?"

Actually, she'd have liked another slice, but chances were good the babies wouldn't be all that receptive to pepperoni—they were showing themselves to be picky about what she ate, starting their objections as soon as her feet hit the floor every morning. "Good idea." She got to her feet. "You all coming?"

"No, they're not," Steven said decisively, tugging her toward the sliding glass doors that led to the beach. "They're old married people and they're going to stay here and discuss their retirement plans."

"Far be it from us to remind you that you're the oldest among us," Grant said dryly.

Steven waved at him. "That's good, Grant. I knew you'd never bring it up." He dragged the door closed on a wave of laughter.

When they reached the edge of the water, Carol waded in. "I'll miss this."

"You can always put a nice wading pool out back of your house and set up a fan to create waves."

She feigned shock. "What, and have Aunt Jo inviting men in at all hours of the day and night? You know she would."

He raised an eyebrow. "She might start a skinny-dipping trend in Peacock. You must admit that wouldn't be a bad thing."

"Have you ever done that?" She knew even as she asked that it was a silly question, but she wanted to hear how he answered it.

"Yeah. Grant and Dillon and I did up at the lake all the time. Grant's dad knew. He'd sit on the porch of their cabin smoking until we snuck back inside. He never said anything about it and we didn't, either." His gaze was on the horizon, his mind somewhere she couldn't go. "Have you?"

"No." She walked on, the water dragging at her skirt. "And I've never wanted to. If I drown, I want to be well dressed while I'm doing it."

He laughed. "I was leaving the hospital through the ER one night when an arrest came in—cardiac, I mean, not DWI or something. The staff grabbed me as I was going out the door. It was a lady dressed to the nines—I don't know where she was going, but the evening got interrupted by a heart attack. Anyway, they cut her dress off and we did surgery right away. She would have died if we hadn't. A few days later, when she was cognizant and healing amazingly fast, she was very grateful. She was also some kind of pissed about that dress. She said if she'd known where she was going, she'd have worn something less expensive."

Sadness worked its way into the edges of Carol's consciousness, but she wasn't sure why. When the man on the golf course started breathing again, she felt like pumping her fist and yelling, "Yes!" The euphoria lasted through the afternoon, when she played the best golf ever, and the evening, when they'd ordered in pizza at the beach house. A phone call to the hospital reassured her the patient was holding his own. But something wasn't right.

"I wonder who he is," she mused. "Does he have a family? Is anyone sitting in the chair beside his bed?"

"He's in a coronary care unit, so someone's probably sitting beside him sometimes for ten minutes or so or standing there anyway. The guys he was with mentioned a wife." Steven pulled her close to his side. "You have to let it go, though. It's not like he's someone who'll be back in six weeks for a haircut."

Carol thought maybe there was an insult in there somewhere, but she couldn't quite pick it out. "I have to go see him."

"What?" Steven stopped walking and released her fingers to put his hands on his lean hips and give her the "you've-lost-your-freaking-mind" look she'd seen a few times before. It pissed her off every time. "Why?"

So he can leap out of bed and thank me and offer me a huge reward because I remembered what I learned in a CPR class, asshole. Why do you think? "To see for myself that he's all right." She hated the way his expression made her feel. "To make sure someone's sitting beside his bed."

"Carol." He stopped, reaching to take her hands in his. "Honey, you can't—"

"Can't what? Can't be worried about someone I don't even know? Of course I can. I worry about everyone on the news. I worry about every kid who puts on a military uniform and thinks he or she can save the world. I worry about Little League kids because they throw the ball so hard, and they don't wear chest protectors except for the catcher. I worry about people who walk past the shop because what if they left home without telling someone goodbye and they loved them? What if…" She ran out of breath and her voice trailed away. "That's what people do, Steven. They worry about other people."

"I know they do. That's one reason for me moving back to Peacock, edging my way into family practice, at least for the time being. Because I'd kind of forgotten that worrying part."

His eyes were dark with so much pain she wanted to smooth his forehead like he was a little boy. She worried about him, too, but didn't think he'd appreciate her saying so.

"But you can't take ownership of worrying about people. You just can't. It'll drive you crazy." His voice was so soft by the time he finished that she had to bend her head closer to hear him over the sound of the waves.

"I'm not taking ownership of anything. I just want to go to the hospital to see how he is. I don't want him to be alone." *Alone's not fun if you don't choose it. Alone and sick is worse. It sucks.*

"His wife is probably there by now."

"I hope she is." Carol tried to capture his gaze and couldn't. It was as if he'd left her in the time of their conversation although he still held her hands. "You don't have to go with me, Steven. My car's here, and I can find the hospital. I'm pretty sure we drove past it when we went to Wilmington the other day."

"I'll go. We could even go on my motorcycle, but Grace would be in a panic until we got back, wouldn't she? You and she are having a very careful pregnancy."

"Aren't we, though?" She laughed, relieved he seemed to have come back from the place he'd gone. Melancholy still fluttered at the edges of her mind, making her want to wave it away like an annoying mosquito. Especially since she knew the sadness was hers, not someone else's she was feeling the weight of.

The drive to the hospital was quiet. Inside the coronary care unit, Steven talked to the staff while Carol waited. A woman sat alone across the room. She didn't speak to Carol, although she glanced in her direction and nodded slightly. She seemed familiar, but people in waiting rooms always did.

Grief and fear hung in the air and pressed down on the features of the room's occupants, giving them a heavy sameness. When Carol's father had died, she'd seen it on her mother's face even before Dr. Bridges came out of the ER and took her hands in his and told her he was so sorry but there was nothing they could

189

do.

When Steven returned, he was smiling, albeit he had a wary look around his eyes. "He's holding his own and his wife and other family are here."

"Is there anything we can do?"

"Nope, although your concern was appreciated."

"Oh, phooey." She gave him a push. "Okay, we can go. Thank you for coming to check." She sketched a wave to the other occupant of the room. "Goodnight. I hope things go well."

"Thank you." The woman's gaze slipped past her to rest on Steven, darkening in what might have been recognition, but she didn't say anything else.

"Did you know her?" Carol asked as they walked to the parking garage. "She looked like she recognized you."

He shrugged. "They're from Knoxville, so maybe she did. I've been with the hospital long enough and on local television often enough that sometimes people do. I had a patient once who thought I was the spokesman for a fast food restaurant. She wondered if I'd paid for my education by making commercials."

The public portion of Steven's life was something Carol seldom considered. She'd seen him on TV a few times in the past and rolled her eyes and laughed long and hard with Promise and Grace because there was no denying that both the camera and his occasionally bigger-than-life personality were his friends when it came to the small screen.

"Thanks for coming to the hospital." She stretched to kiss his cheek, loving the sandpapery feel of one-day-beard under her lips. "I feel better."

He drew her into his long arm. "You certainly do."

****

"I think we should go somewhere." It was lunchtime the next day and Steven knew if he ate one more fried shrimp, he was going to turn into one. But no time like the present to tempt fate—he was on vacation, after all. He ate two more in quick succession. Nothing happened, so he turned to Carol's dessert. Surely she would share.

"We *are* somewhere." She yanked the pecan pie away from his encroaching fork and protected the dessert plate with an arm curved around it. "We're at the beach, which is a long way over the mountain from Peacock."

"I know, but both my sisters and the guys I've been with for a solid week are also at the beach. I think we should go somewhere that…they're not."

"We only have one car here, the Mustang, and Grace will worry if I'm on a motorcycle." An anticipatory sparkle lit her face even as she demurred. "Where do you want to go?"

"Grace is going to worry if you're in a rocking chair as a guest at a nunnery. You're carrying her dreams around in your belly and nothing's going to make that an easy scenario for either of you, but you can't stop moving until you deliver Davy and Daniel. It wouldn't be—"

She snorted, dropping her fork. "Who? Deliver who?"

God, he loved it when she laughed. "You know, as in Crockett and Boone. They're good guys, manly men. If the babies can't both be named Steven, we're talking good alternatives here."

"I was thinking Gloria and Susan."

"Who?"

"You know," she mocked, "as in Steinem and B. Anthony? Womanly women?"

"Oh, them." He chuckled, trying to imagine Gloria Steinem and Susan B. Anthony in the same picture. "It's probably a good thing we're not naming the little Campbells, isn't it?"

"Probably." Carol laughed. "Faith suggested Hope and Charity and if they're boys Hopeless and Charity Case—she doesn't get to name them, either."

"Are you still okay with it?" Something in her eyes troubled him, but he couldn't identify what it was. She'd answered this question before—more than once, but he wondered if her answer changed as the pregnancy progressed. "The idea of having them and sending them home with someone else, I mean. I know you've been through the testing and all that, but do you feel as you're giving up your own babies?"

She smiled, the expression so tender his hand reached of its own volition to cup her cheek. Her skin was soft all over, a thought he didn't want to visit right now, but especially her face. He stroked gently, tracing the shape of her upper lip with his index finger.

"Not at all," she said, sounding surprised that he would ask. "It's such a privilege, other than the throwing up part, and such a happy thing, other than the fat part. I imagine I'll have little regret twinges after I have them, but it's not a big deal if I do. Anyone who's lived their life *without* regret twinges hasn't really been living."

"Well, then, I think you'd regret it if we don't get on my bike and ride off for a few days by ourselves." He dropped his hand from her face but held her gaze.

"Please. I'm fine with being a brother and a brother-in-law and a best friend. Matter of fact, I'm as-God-is-my-witness grateful for those relationships and the people I have them with."

Her eyes were so…welcoming. He thought he might get lost in them. And in her. Preferably soon. "But I want to be a boyfriend for a while. Please," he said again, for good measure. He wasn't all that when it came to expertise with women, regardless of his reputation, but he had learned they liked the word "please." It was right up there with "thank you" and "God, you look good" on the Saying the Right Thing scale.

"Okay, but you need to talk Grace into not worrying. I don't want her to be upset."

"Nope." He leaned across the empty shrimp plate to kiss her. "Dillon needs to talk her into it. When they got married, things like that became his job. Where do you want to go?"

****

"Surprise me."

I've never been a tourist before. It's fun!

Carol wrote the words in the flower-bedecked travel journal she'd bought in a gift shop at a Civil War battlefield. It was her fourth entry although it was less than twenty-four hours since their visit there. First had been the date and location and the weather. Then, while Steven gazed at surgical instruments in a museum at yet another battlefield, she'd noted all the places they'd stopped. The third had been a slightly profane limerick about riding shotgun on a motorcycle. In between, she'd written postcards to Dixie and Jo, Reese, and the shop.

"I haven't either." Steven's voice came, muffled, from within the towel he was using to dry his hair.

"Haven't what?" she asked.

"Been a tourist."

"Oh." She hadn't even realized she'd said the words aloud when she wrote them.

He tossed the towel in the direction of the bathroom and sat on the bed beside her, bumping her hip until she made room for him. "I've been places, but I've never really *seen* them."

"Really?" She put the journal and her pen into the side pocket of her purse and drew the blanket up over her knees—Steven didn't consider a motel room comfortable unless it was cold enough to hang meat. "Didn't Promise housesit in the summer in all these great places?" She used to cut Promise's hair the week before she left for her housesitting destination. They drank coffee—or wine if Promise was the last customer of the day—and pored over travel brochures about wherever that particular summer's house was.

"She did, and I'd go wherever she was and spend some time, but I only wanted to see her and catch up on the sleep I'd been missing since the last time I took time off. She usually didn't care—she was happy doing the tourist thing on her own—but she spent the last summer before she got sick in Ireland. The only things I saw when I was there were the pub and Cong, the town where they made that John Wayne move, *The Quiet Man*."

"I love that movie," Carol said, twining her arm with his. His muscles felt tense. "In my next life, I'm going to look like Maureen O'Hara."

He chuckled, but there wasn't much humor in the

sound. "I only saw Cong because Prom insisted, and we were on a tour bus so I couldn't back out in the middle of it. We went past this little field—of course, there are a gazillion little fields in Ireland—but this one had wrought iron around it instead of rock walls. It was a cemetery from the potato famine, where they'd buried people in big mass graves. Prom was pretty quiet for a while, then she asked me to make sure her grave had her name on it. She didn't want to be cremated, she said, because she was afraid of fire. I laughed at her. It's one of those regret twinges you were talking about."

"It is." She turned his face, forcing him to look at her. "She knew you'd take care of anything like that, whether you laughed at her or not. But if you hadn't gone to Ireland, hadn't gone on that tour—bitching all the way, I have no doubt—then you'd have more than a twinge, wouldn't you?"

"Probably." He squinted at her. "You don't mind it, do you?"

"Mind what?"

"When I talk about her."

"No." Because it reminded Carol that he was only a boyfriend for the summer and the neighbor who lived up the hill. Even if she loved him—and she did, she surely did—when summer's romance ended, she'd have to let go of that love as well. She'd done it after Rand died—she could do it again. And it would be easier this time. She didn't have to bury Steven.

"Promise and I were friends, too," she reminded him. "I like thinking about her. Remembering what good times we all had—God, she was *so* much fun. It would be a little unrealistic if I didn't expect you to like it, too." She kissed him and turned onto her side. "I'm sleepy."

"We're in a motel room by ourselves with no family members in the vicinity and you're sleepy?" He leered at her and drew her close, his hand drawing a long line of heat from her shoulder to the yellow flowers on her hip. "Think I can wake you up?"

No, not while Promise is in the room. "Probably not," she murmured. She opened her eyes, meeting his. "When we talk about her, she's still here, and you still belong to her. That's okay, but I can't be your girlfriend then."

He frowned. "I don't hang onto her in that way. I'm not still her husband." But his gaze slid away from hers as he spoke.

"Maybe not." She stroked a hand through his damp hair and held her eyes wide to keep the tears back. Some part of her wondered if she was going to cry every single day of this pregnancy—wouldn't Promise get a hoot out of that? "But I'm still her friend. When we talk about her, that's what I am."

He didn't move, but she felt his withdrawal as certainly as if he'd left the room. She wasn't sleepy anymore, but she closed her eyes again anyway. For the first time since the day her car and his bicycle collided in the cemetery, she was lonely.

****

"You'd have made an excellent saloon girl," Steven observed, looking at the picture of the two of them. In the sepia-toned eight-by-ten, he wore a duster, a crumpled western hat, and a six-gun. He sat in a straight chair with Carol's truly elegant black-mesh-covered leg across his lap. The satiny dress the photographer's assistant had fastened around her did amazing things to her cleavage.

"I used to be one."

The answer, coming from the bathroom in the cabin where they'd spent the previous night, surprised him. "You did? When?"

She came out carrying the zippered plastic bag she kept her toiletries in. "I worked weekend nights at Maeve Malone's for several years when I was in my early twenties. I wanted to get my shop paid for, and it was the only way I could do that and take classes at the same time." She grinned. "My dad wasn't happy about it—he'd rather have just given me the money I needed—but even he admitted I mixed an excellent bloody Mary."

"I never saw you there." He slipped the photographs into the stiff mailer and set it aside with her day's allotment of postcards so they could stop at a post office and mail them home.

She shrugged. "It was another time. You were the gorgeous young doctor with the even more beautiful girlfriend. I never lost my pregnancy weight and had bleached hair and makeup thick enough I needed a trowel to put it on and take it off. My girlfriends were always the same ones—still are—but it was different with guys. The ones I knew were—at that point in my time anyway—big on the wrapper but not real interested in what was inside the package. My wrapper was…suspect, to say the least."

"I like your wrapper." She was smaller, trimmer than she used to be, but it didn't matter to him. He'd liked her body as much twenty pounds heavier as he did now. He couldn't say he'd liked *her* as much, because the truth was that he liked her more every day. Every single damn one.

Well. Where did that come from? And what could he do about it? He liked having a girlfriend—he even liked *being* a boyfriend—but not beyond the summer. Not beyond liking. He'd been that route already in his life, and he wouldn't give up a minute of either the absolute happiness or the excruciating pain of it for anything less.

But not again. Never again.

"You wouldn't have liked it—or me—then." She zipped her duffel bag closed and picked it up, then put it back down, meeting his eyes across the width of the bed. "That's wrong. I didn't mean that. You were always nice to me."

"It's okay." And it was. He'd been a shallow son of a bitch. Still was, sometimes, about some things. But not her. At least, not anymore.

"Ready to go back to the beach?" he asked when they had checked out of the state park resort.

Regret—at least, he thought that's what it was— flashed over her eyes, but she nodded. "It was fun," she said, so softly he had to bend his head to hear her. "These past few days with you, being a tourist. It's as much fun as I've ever had." She smiled at him and stretched to kiss him. "Thank you."

He caught her close, making the kiss last. Not deepening it. Not asking for or expecting anything. But he reveled in the taste of her, the feel of her in his arms. There was a wholeness to being with her he'd never thought he'd feel again. A word Promise had used the summer she'd first become ill came to mind— *connection.* It had been a season of joy and unimaginable pain for the Elliots and the Campbells and the Hartleys, but they had found and maintained a connection unbreakable even by death.

With Carol in his arms, Steven thought he'd found a new link in life's creaky chain. Now if he just knew where to go from there.

Chapter Thirteen

The thing about vacations was that they ended.
You knew they were going to and you'd prepared
yourself to go back to work, but there was something
sad about actually doing it.

Carol made her bed, thinking she'd gotten a little
too accustomed to Steven being there when she got up.
"It's good to see you guys," she told Barney and Fred,
"but sometimes you're short on conversation." She bent
to pick up Fred and give Barney a rub before going
downstairs. "He goes to the bathroom by himself, too.
That's always a plus. Let's see what Grandma's serving
up for breakfast."

When Carol returned from letting the animals out
her mother handed her a plate of pancakes. "We went
into the shop on Friday and Lynn and Kay said
everything went fine while you were gone. Your first
appointment is at nine this morning and, apparently,
you're pretty well booked up for the week. Lynn said
the client wanted you at eight o'clock, but she told her
you were unavailable. She wasn't happy about it, so
you'll probably start out with a cranky one. She's
getting a perm, so she'll be there half the day."

Carol sighed. Vacation was definitely over. "Who
is it? Do you remember?"

"Yes." Dixie looked apologetic. "It's Lois
Gleason."

"Oh, hell." Not only was vacation over, it was over with a bang. "Apparently the elsewhere that she took her business didn't work out."

"The way Lynn tells it, every beautician within driving distance is too expensive, totally insensitive, too young, too old, not clean enough, or shockingly rude," Jo listed from where she sat at the desk in the corner of the kitchen. Her grin was hopeful. "If you just pop some bubblegum while you're doing her hair, or tell a dirty joke, she might fire you again."

"Kay offered to do her hair, but Lois said Kay and Lynn were both too inexperienced. Drink your milk, dear. It's good for your bones." Her mother sat at the table. "Aren't they as old as you are?"

"Kay's seven weeks older—which I take care to remind her of every year on her birthday—and she's been doing hair as long as I have. Lynn's close to my age, too, but she doesn't have that much experience yet." The pancakes, delicious as they were, were setting up a protest. "The bad part is, there's a part of me that's kind of pleased no one else could make her happy, either."

"Human nature." Jo nodded wisely. "Your mother's been preening about it ever since the girls at the salon told us. I think she's going to write a book. You know—*Hairdressers Who Can't Be Fired* or something like that."

"They can still quit, though." But she wouldn't. Carol knew she was good at what she did, but most of her competitors were, too. She had the advantage of being a home town girl in a convenient location—it wasn't something she forgot or even took lightly. She once went to a client's house after work to refresh a comb-out because even though the customer was satisfied, Carol wasn't. She sold good products and kept her markup reasonable and donated as much professional time as she could afford to causes dear to her heart.

She pushed her plate away. "I'm sorry. I just can't." She got up, getting her tote bag from the back of her chair. "I'm going to walk to work. The Mustang deserves a break. She performed admirably on vacation. Steven even offered to buy a surfboard to put in the back seat to make us all look younger and as if we deserved to be riding around in such a cool car." She hesitated, her gaze lingering worriedly on her mother. "Mom? Are you all right?"

"Of course I'm all right. I'm old, is all, and getting older by the minute. And you know what it's like living with your aunt. It nearly sends a body over the edge." Dixie walked her toward the door, an arm around her waist. "Be careful walking and have a good day."

"Your mother's not a nice woman," Jo commented. "I don't know how I put up with her." She smiled. "Have a good day, Carolina, and don't take any crap off that Gleason woman. Reserve crap-taking for sisters-in-law and men who are worth it."

"I'll remember." Carol kissed her mother's cheek and bent to pet Fred and Barney as they hurried inside. "Take care of Mom and Aunt Jo while I'm at work, okay?"

She was sweating by the time she reached the Clip Joint. "I think maybe walking when the heat index is all set to go past a hundred degrees was a mistake," she admitted to Lynn, taking a bottle of sweet tea from the refrigerator and pushing the cart filled with curlers to her work station.

"I'll take you home." Lynn flipped the hair dryer down over Dallas Marburger's foiled hair and narrowed her eyes toward the front door. "You ready to contend with Mrs. Gleason?"

Don't take any crap. Jo's voice echoed in Carol's mind. "You know, I think I am. You might want to go out for more coffee. It could get ugly in here."

"I wouldn't miss it for the world." Lynn grinned at her. "I've got your back, boss."

Reese poked her head out of the back room, where she was putting away supplies. She grinned. "I'll sit on her and squash her. I must outweigh her by about fifty pounds."

Dallas ducked out from under the dryer. "I'll help Reese with the squashing. I'll probably need your help next semester."

"I knew I could count on you girls." Carol pulled open the door. "Good morning, Mrs. Gleason. How are you?"

"I'm getting a hip replacement next week, and I'm about sure my cataracts are coming back. I hope you still have those permanents I like." Scowling indiscriminately at both Carol and Lynn, the old lady limped to Carol's chair and sat down with a stifled groan.

"I still have them." Carol approached her, carrying a fresh cape and a clean towel. "But the price has gone up." She quoted an increase that made Lynn roll her eyes.

"Gee, boss," the other beautician mumbled, "you keep that up and you'll almost make minimum wage."

Mrs. Gleason's already-thin lips nearly

disappeared. "That's scandalous."

Carol hesitated with the cape. "No, ma'am, it's not. It's the first time I've charged you more for a permanent since you started coming here fifteen years ago."

"Will you give me any samples?"

"One shampoo and one conditioner, just like always. We have a new kind Kay got from the supplier this month."

Rage reddened the woman's faded eyes. She sniffed. "I need waxing, too. I suppose the price has gone up for that as well."

"Yes, it has." Carol beamed at her in the mirror. "Shall we go ahead, or would you care to—"

"No, no, I'm here now. I'll pay it. But it's outrageous."

"You want a trim, too?"

The sigh was so deep, it seemed to shake the chair. "Well, of course I want a trim. What do you think I'm paying you for, girl?"

Don't take any crap.

"Well, I'll tell you what." Carol turned the chair and looked into Mrs. Gleason's wrinkled face. Without the mirror as a filter, she had to steel herself against the pity that rose inside for the lonely old woman. "You're paying me for cosmetology skills, which I'm more than happy to provide, as well as free drinks and snacks while you're here. And you're paying me to be both professional and polite, but there's another half to that story. You can either be polite to Lynn and Kay and me, as well as anyone else who is in the salon when you are, or we will no longer provide our services. That's your choice."

It was what was known as a Mexican standoff, with the third opponent in the triad being Mrs. Gleason's pride. If it fell first, Carol would win.

"All right." The words came, little more than a whisper.

"Fine." Carol smiled at her. "Coffee? Reese just brewed a fresh pot."

"Well, of course I—" Mrs. Gleason stopped abruptly. "Yes, please."

"I'll get that for you." Lynn turned off Dallas's dryer. "You, too, Dallas?"

"Sure do, because unless I'm mistaken, Grace and Dillon are coming with Carol's daily dessert." Carrying the newest issue of *People*, Dallas went to open the door for Grace. "Whatever that is, I want seconds."

"Me, too." Steven followed his sister and brother-in-law into the shop, carrying a second container. "Morning, ladies." He set the pan down and bent Carol over his arm and kissed her senseless.

He took his time about it, and she lifted her arms around him both to keep her balance and to feel the play of his back muscles under her hands.

"Wow," said Dillon mildly. "Grace said you were raising your prices for the first time in a hundred years or so, Carol. Is there an extra charge for the show or is that free?"

"Oh." She straightened, pushing her hair out of her face and meeting Steven's laughing gaze. "Well."

"Who wants key lime cheesecake?" Grace saved her. "We had this in North Carolina and it was so sinfully good we thought we'd have to go to confession even though we're not Catholic, but I found a recipe that's lower in fat and calories but still tastes really wicked."

"I had mine already." Steven stroked the backs of his fingers down Carol's cheek. "See you at your house tonight. Aunt Jo's cooking."

"Okay." Her stomach was still jumping around from the kiss. Cheesecake would help. Surely it would.

****

"Normally I wouldn't stick you by yourself your first day after vacation." Jake Sawyer handed Steven a pile of notes. "But I promised Becky Rountree and her doctor that I'd be there for her surgery."

Steven nodded. He'd rather have Jake's assistance in the OR than anyone else's he knew, so he didn't blame Becky's surgeon for feeling the same way. "Not a problem." He grinned past the other doctor at the office manager. "I'm pretty sure Ms. McGrew will keep me in line."

The woman nodded sadly. "It's a heavy load, but someone's got to do it."

As the day went on—busy in the way Mondays always managed to be—Steven became more certain family practice was a good career choice. He missed the exhilaration of a big hospital and the staff he'd worked with in Knoxville, but not as much as he'd thought he would. He couldn't deny the leap of adrenaline and the urge to hurry back when Mitch called him concerning a case, but the attachment to Peacock and Miss Abigail's—and the neighbor who lived just down Taylor Hill—grew more powerful every day.

It was interesting connecting patients to people he'd known growing up here. "Your mom," he told the last patient of the day, a young football player in for his pre-season physical, "was so hot. Your dad didn't deserve her. I'll bet he still doesn't. Tell him I said so and to meet me at Malone's or the Cup and Cozy one of these days to talk about it. I haven't seen him—other than driving the baler in the hayfield—since he had all his hair and mine didn't have any gray in it."

Ben Sawyer, who was Jake's nephew, was aghast. "God, Doc, she's not hot. She's my *mom*. She's *old*."

Steven drew back and grinned at him. "Before she was your mom, she was hot, and she's not old. She's younger than me, and I'm nowhere close to old. Don't forget I can make you turn your head and cough over and over again if I'm just not sure."

"Ah, geez…"

"Didn't say I would, just that I could. So Reese gave you a ride? You two seeing each other?" He hoped so. It was hard being a heavy girl—high school hadn't changed that much since he went. Having a hunky boyfriend would help.

"Nah. She lives out by us—you know that. My car wouldn't start today and hers would, so she drove me."

"She's a pretty girl."

"We're just friends. She's kinda…thick."

Steven's eyebrows rose. "Thick?" He knew what the kid meant, but he wanted him to say it. The little asshole. Hunky didn't mean shit.

"You know. Heavy. And she knits. My *grandma* knits."

"Oh." He thumped Ben's head a little harder than necessary. "I knew it—you really do have rocks in there. You and your buds don't like 'thick,' huh? Or girls who knit?"

"Oh, hell, no." The boy rubbed his head. "I mean, she's a nice enough girl, just not who you want to be going out with."

"So skinny's better than nice." Why was he doing this? Steven didn't care who John Sawyer's kid went out with. Only now he was glad it wasn't Reese. She deserved better than this judgmental little prick.

"No, man, not better. Just…when you were in high school, your girlfriend was the prettiest one around. I remember her. I mean, Miss Delaney taught me in school and she was always so cool and pretty and all. I'm really sorry, you know, that she died. But she was hot, wasn't she, Doc? She wasn't heavy or anything."

"Nope. She was great looking, and I have a sister who was that way, too—we used to rag on Faith about being born with a homecoming queen crown on her head. But I've got another sister who wasn't, and a girlfriend who's not skinny. Part of being grown up, I guess, is seeing beyond the packaging." He patted the boy's muscled shoulder, doing his condescending best to be as pompous as Dillon always said he was. "You'll get there." And if he didn't, John Sawyer would have no problem jerking a knot in his son's supercilious tail. The thought made Steven grin.

He accompanied the boy into the waiting room and tossed his file onto the counter. "This kid wore me out. I'm going home, and I think you should, too," he told the office staff, and felt himself lighten when he saw who was sitting with Ben's young chauffeur. "Hey there, Miss Carol, are you here to see me?"

She smiled at him, and he thought her green eyes were probably the nicest thing he'd seen all day. "Actually," she said, "I thought maybe you could take me home. Lynn was going to give me a ride, but I had to see Maggie after work today. She told me I ate too much on vacation. I said it shouldn't count because I threw up every morning just like clockwork and besides, I'm eating for three. She didn't care. Acted like she'd heard it all before. Then I gave her a piece of that cheesecake Grace made, and she said I shouldn't eat that at all—I should bring such things to her rather than succumb to temptation."

"Oh, well, you know how doctors are. Hi." Steven grinned at Reese, who had a lapful of lavender yarn with sparkly things in it. The yarn matched her eyes. He wondered if the football player had noticed that or if the dumbass thought her worth rested in the size of her hips. "You can take him home now, or you can make him walk. It would help him with the two-a-days coming up here in another couple of weeks."

Ben shook his head. "Don't listen to him, Reese. Come on. I'll buy you a coke over at the Cup and Cozy. You want me to carry that stuff?"

"No, it's okay. The lavender would look goofy with your shirt." The girl got to her feet. "Thanks for the help, Carol. I think you're right about the highlights."

"Check with your dad first," Carol warned.

Reese waved a dismissive hand. "He wouldn't notice."

Carol's gaze followed the teenagers as they left the office. "He wouldn't, either," she murmured. "Jeff tries, I think, but he hasn't the least idea what to do with a girly girl."

"That's too bad." Steven thought of Jamie Scott. His parents hadn't known what to do with him, either, and the kid had died with the only certainty of love in his life coming from hospital staff. "Dammit." Why couldn't he have done more? Why hadn't the kid gotten a heart in time? "Let me help get the office closed up, and we can go home. You just wanted to ride the motorcycle again, didn't you?"

"I'm wearing a dress. What do you think?"

He swooped in to kiss her. "I think it's a good thing I drove the truck."

Chapter Fourteen

"But I *like* having you here, and Fred and Barney will probably go into a decline without you and Aunt Jo to spoil them. I'll even have to admit to Steven that I'm not really that good of a cook." Carol held her eyes wide and took deep breaths. Feeling the need to burst into a torrent of tears was nothing new to her—she'd been doing a flood of hormonal crying since the day she learned she was pregnant with Grace and Dillon's twins—but she didn't want her mother and aunt to leave with the image of her sobbing fresh in their minds.

"Honey." Dixie took her hands and held her gaze. "It's the end of October. We've been here over four months. If we don't go home soon, we won't be able to come for Thanksgiving because we'll still be here."

"But you could move here. Peacock's your home, Mom, and Aunt Jo loves it, too." Carol straightened her shoulders. "Good Lord, did that whine come out of me?" She shook her head, smiling at her mother and her aunt, although her cheeks trembled with the effort. "Have a safe trip. Call when you get there. I love you both." Was that quavery sound really her voice?

She waved until Jo's car was out of sight, then went into the house, frowning at the silence. How was it that a woman who'd lived nearly her entire adult life alone—and for the most part liked it—was suddenly lonely? Not just a little bit lonely, but crushingly so.

When the time had come to sign up for the fall semester, she hadn't done it. Having houseguests, a beach vacation, and a boyfriend kept her busy and entertained. But Steven became more and more immersed in his work as summer slipped into fall and now Dixie and Jo were returning to Greenville.

They'd left the house spotless, the garden cleared of all but the latest produce. Even the flower beds were freshly weeded and full of autumn blooms.

The two rooms and bath Carol hadn't touched since she moved in had been completely refurbished, right down to a handicap-accessible shower in the bathroom. "It's money I'd have left you anyway, Carolina," Jo said over Carol's objections, "and unless I figure out a painless way to off myself when I become a liability to you, you're going to be stuck taking care of me when I'm *really* old instead of just sort of." She grinned wickedly. "Of course, you'll have your mother, too—that'll make me seem like a piece of cake."

Dixie snorted from the doorway across the hall. "A piece of crab cake that's sat out in the sun too long, maybe."

Carol chuckled with the memory and bent to pick up Fred, giving Barney a head-rub while she was down there. "Come on, guys. I need to wash the towels for the shop."

Today was Thursday. She wasn't working this morning but would spend the afternoon at Elliot House. She'd decreased her working hours on the advice of the gynecologist and hoped she wouldn't grow too used to three-day work weeks—they'd have to end once the babies were born.

Twenty-six weeks into the pregnancy, she was relieved at how well it was going. She was big—oh, Lord, was she big—but still within the prescribed weight gain.

She was hanging the towels outside when Steven came around the corner of the house, attended by Fred and Barney. "What are you doing here in the middle of a Thursday morning?" Carol asked.

"I have to go over to Knoxville. There's a patient whose family insists I'm the only one he can see. It's Jamie Scott's uncle—his mother's brother. Remember him?"

Something clicked into place. The reason the woman in the visitors' lounge in the hospital in Wilmington that night had looked so familiar. It was because she'd been at the funeral. "The man on the golf course? He was Jamie's uncle?"

"Yes. His mother's brother."

"You didn't recognize him at the time, did you?"

"No. I barely recognize patients, much less their families or shirttail relatives I've only seen at funerals."

"Do you want me to go with you?" She could rearrange the Elliot House afternoon if she needed to, although she'd miss the time with the residents. Even Lois Gleason had taken to having her hair done on Thursday afternoon instead of making her way to the shop.

"Nah. I'll probably spend the night and come back tomorrow morning. I just wanted you to know where I'll be."

Carol pinned the last towel to the clothesline and lifted the basket to her hip. "What's wrong?" she asked. Because something was. His features were anxious, his already-dark eyes nearly black. Even his whiskey voice sounded strained.

"Mitch called me because Jamie's folks are going to sue the hospital and me for more money than I knew existed." Steven took the basket from her and laid his arm around her shoulders as they walked toward the back door. He was so tense his body felt like it hummed against her. "He's not the first patient I ever lost, and I've been sued before. It's what people do when they're grieving, and they don't know what else to do when a lawyer calls them and says, 'Hey, we can get you a million or so bucks because that bad doctor didn't do his job.' They think a lawsuit will somehow fix things. But this is different."

Inside, she went to the coffee pot. "Different how? You want a cup?"

"Sure." He took the basket into the laundry room, his voice floating back to her. "Different because this family's already as rich as Croesus. Different because they knew from the get-go that Jamie was close to the end. He was *born* close to the end—it was a dedicated staff of caregivers who kept him alive past puberty. His family is suing because they felt—as hospital investors and rich sons of bitches into the bargain—they should have had preferential treatment."

"But that's—*really*?" She made the coffee, pouring the dry grounds back into the coffee canister when she lost count of scoops. She turned to face him when he came back into the kitchen. "Can they *do* that?"

"The lawsuit probably won't go anywhere—I don't even know why the Scotts are going through those particular motions, other than they like publicity a lot. But what they *can* do, and very effectively, is withdraw their support from the hospital, which would be devastating. The pediatric unit, a very good one, was built largely by their generosity. Jamie spent months of his life there."

"I don't get it. How can they talk about suing with one breath and demand your professional services with the next one?" She took down their cups, plus a commuter cup for Steven. It was a cheap one, bought from the clearance cart at the Dollar Store. She put it back and took out the one he had given to her. She'd miss it in the morning on the way to work, but his coffee would stay hot all the way to Knoxville.

"Because it's a way they can lock me in. I won't do anything that will cause damage to the hospital and they know that."

"Why didn't they just ask you to see him?"

"They did, shortly after we got home from Topsail Island. Jake was at the emergency room with Becky Rountree trying to keep cancer's damnable treatment from killing her, and I had an office full of fall-sports physicals and an ugly siege of daycare diarrhea. When Mitch called, I told him that and said if they wanted to see me, they needed to make an appointment just like anyone else and come across the mountain to Peacock. It didn't go over well."

"So what happens now?"

He shrugged. "I see him. If he needs surgery, I do the operation. I'll even do the follow up, although I hope they'll come across the mountain for that—the practice here has become a professional priority. That, with any luck at all, will be the end of my association with the Scotts." He didn't look hopeful.

"That's hard, isn't it? Do you feel like you're

backing down?" Disappointment flickered, then ignited and burned. *Don't take any crap.* Why didn't he stand up to the Scotts? This wasn't the Steven she knew.

"I *am* backing down," he admitted. "It's all well and good to stand up for principles, but you have to weigh the costs. I can't penalize the hospital because some rich bastard pisses me off." He held her gaze. "There comes a time for choosing your battles."

If you were really coming home to stay, you'd disassociate from the hospital. She didn't know where it came from, but once it was in her mind, in bold, repetitive words, she couldn't unthink it.

"You're going back, aren't you?" She handed him his coffee, her hand shaking. "This has all been a game. A summer in the old hometown because you were bored with the big city and the big hospital. You've never given up your apartment or your gym membership."

"What are you talking about?" He sipped, his gaze never leaving hers, although the expression in his changed. Impatience created an extra line in his forehead. "What does my hardly-ever-used gym membership have to do with anything?"

Why hadn't she seen this coming? She should have figured it out when she'd seen the bill from the fitness center in Knoxville lying on the counter in his kitchen, but she hadn't. She'd believed him when he said he was home to stay. He'd bought a house, for heaven's sake, and spent more money remodeling it than she made in five years of cutting hair and waxing unwanted mustaches.

What had made her forget that she was only a girlfriend for the summer? Was it the fact that summer had passed, and he'd seemed settled into practice with Jake? Or that he still spent nights of love and back-rubbing with her?

"Does Jake know you're going back?" She didn't want to do this—it wasn't as if they'd committed to each other beyond their agreed-upon sexual exclusivity. But she did it anyway, driven by a sense of betrayal. And aloneness.

"He knows I'm still affiliated with the hospital. You knew that, too. So what makes you think I'm going back to Knoxville to stay?" Anger darkened his eyes and drew his mouth into a thin line. "Where's that coming from?"

"You backed down. You never back down." She was repeating herself, but this was important. If he gave in to the demands of a rich bully, what *wouldn't* he give in to? Steven looked almost exactly like the father even Dixie had referred to as a son of a bitch. For the first time, Carol wondered if he shared some of Robert Elliot's moral deficiency, too.

Steven sipped his coffee and walked away from her, going to stand at the window. The morning sun came in, throwing his lean body into silhouette against its brightness. "I back down all the time. Everybody does. Knowing when we have to is how we get from one day to the next."

The sadness in his voice was nearly her undoing. "But where—" She had to clear her throat. She took a drink of coffee, then set down her cup and poured the rest of the pot into the commuter cup. "Where do you draw the line? When do you stand up?"

He turned back to face her. "When I was a kid driving Noah Bridges around the summer he had a broken ankle, he talked to me about a lot of stuff, about the Hippocratic Oath and what it did and didn't say and what it did and didn't mean. He told me then if I remembered 'first do no harm' even knowing it wasn't actually *in* the Oath, I'd do all right. I had no idea how hard that was going to be. To answer your question, I stand up when it means not hurting anyone else. Means I don't get to wear a cape or sing 'here I am to save the day.' I don't get to look at things in nice, easy-peasy black and white, but that's the way it is."

She handed him the commuter cup. "Do you want me to feed Tom and Huck?"

"No. I left plenty of food and water. I'll be home tomorrow afternoon."

"Drive carefully."

He nodded. "See you when I get back. Thanks for the coffee."

She raised her face to his. "This is a blip, right?" Her voice was unsteady.

His kiss was warm. Affectionate. Short. "You bet." He laid a hand on the roundness of her belly. "Take care of all of you."

The loneliness she'd felt when Jo and her mother left materialized again when Steven's truck pulled away. It rose up in dark and somber silence and became a life unto itself in the sunny, empty day. Carol got the keys to the Mustang and her bag of beauty supplies and drove down into town.

"I'm sorry, sweetheart. I forgot flowers. I'll come back tomorrow." She wept at Miranda's grave as if she'd lost her baby the day before instead of half a lifetime ago. "Rand." She sat beside his grave, still crying. "I didn't love you long enough, and now I don't know how to do it right with someone else. But he didn't stand up like you would have. How can I love a man who doesn't stand up?"

****

Steven loved hospitals. All hospitals. He wasn't sure he would if he had to clean one or be a nursing assistant in one or—God forbid—be an administrator or, even worse, a patient. He didn't even want to be a department head. Neither did anyone else in the Department of Cardiothoracic Surgery, but Carter Mitchell drew the short straw.

"I wanted the money," he complained when Steven walked into his office, "not the extra responsibility." He stood, extending his hand across the width of his desk.

Steven shook the hand, thinking working with Mitch was one of the things he liked about this particular hospital. "You should have thought of that before you had four kids who were all going to be in college at the same time."

"Thanks for coming. I know you didn't want to do this."

"I still don't. I take it pressure's coming from higher up?"

"Oh, yeah." Mitch rubbed a hand through his hair. "And in all honesty, I can't say as I blame administration this time. The Scott money is huge."

"Greg's still here, right?" Gregory Muehlhausen was five years younger than Steven and an excellent surgeon.

"Yes, but the family insisted on you."

"Okay. They here for the consultation?"

"Just the patient and his wife."

"You need to understand that I'm done after this."

Mitch frowned. "Done? You can't give up surgery altogether, Steven. I know you better than that."

Could he? Steven didn't know that for sure. "I've enjoyed working here, and you're great to work with—so is the staff. I've learned a lot and have had a better career than I ever anticipated, but any moral or ethical debt I owe this hospital will be paid in full after this surgery." The thought of never coming back here left a hollow feeling, but that was nothing new—he'd been walking around with emotional empty spaces ever since Promise died. "I don't want to do the politics anymore."

"There are politics everywhere." Mitch looked sad, and older than the fifty years Steven knew him to be. "Just do me a favor—another one. Don't burn any bridges yet. I'm not arguing any indebtedness points with you because you're right. You don't owe this hospital or this department anything. But wait until this case is over and done with to decide for sure."

"All right. That I can do." *Jesus, I have no balls at all. Maybe Carol's right. Maybe I can't stand up.* "Let's go see them." Although he didn't *want* to see them. He wanted to get back in the truck and drive home to Peacock, taking the long way over the mountains because he needed the peace of mind that came from the Appalachians. He was ready to feed Tom and Huck, spend some quality motorcycle time, watch an old John Wayne movie, and make careful love to his astonishingly pregnant girlfriend.

Not specifically in that order.

He hoped she was still his girlfriend. They'd never had a "blip" before, unless one counted her shouting "shut the door!" when she was being sick, and he only wanted to help. He didn't like it one damn bit.

The consultation was uncomfortable, which Steven knew was his fault because he was formal to the point of unfriendliness, but he didn't care. These people were wasting his time for no other reason than because they could. He agreed to perform the surgery, attending to the scheduling himself while Brady and Kendra Holt waited in the chairs across from his desk and Mitch made polite conversation. Holt kept looking at his watch the way his brother-in-law had at Jamie's funeral, and it pissed Steven off enough that he took his time about making the arrangements.

If he'd been only slightly angrier and a lot more arrogant, he would have told the Holts the surgery could be done by a high school kid who knew his way around a filet knife. But Mitch didn't deserve the blizzard of flak that would almost certainly bring about.

Steven entered all the pertinent information into the computer and hit print. "When you leave, everything you need for admittance will be at the desk. You'll need to read everything and follow the instructions implicitly. Do you have any other questions?"

The man shifted in his chair, took a pack of cigarettes from his pocket, and put them back. "The woman who was at the golf course with you—I'd like to express my gratitude for her help, although it was probably unnecessary. The hospital in Wilmington refused to give me her contact information. Is that something you could take care of?"

Steven only heard one word. "Excuse me, but did you say *unnecessary*?"

"From what we understand," Mrs. Holt said, "she's a beautician from a small town in the hills. If Brady's situation had been all that serious, surely she wouldn't have been able to revive him. I read on the Internet that eighty percent of cardiac arrests die before they reach the hospital. I doubt a hillbilly hairdresser would have been able to make that kind of difference with Brady."

Steven stood, although he wasn't sure how because he couldn't feel his feet. He couldn't feel anything except a humming rage that threatened to become a roar. "Mitch, would you finish up here? I need to head back to Peacock. And those bridges we talked about in your office? They're getting hot."

It was dark by the time he drove up Taylor Hill. He'd meant to go on home to Miss Abigail's, but the truck turned itself in at Carol's, parking in the grass beside the drive because the graveled area was already full. He frowned, hoping the collection of vehicles didn't mean she had a problem other than a boyfriend she was losing faith in.

Dallas Marburger came to the door when he stepped onto the porch. "Come on in," she invited, beaming at him through the screen. "The American History class has a test coming up in the class on Andrew Jackson and Carol had already passed it, so we brought pizza and ice cream and begged her to help us."

The kitchen table was crowded with food and all the members of the study group from Carol's spring class plus a few newcomers. Jack Winters sat in the corner on a barstool cadged from the counter. He was wearing a dunce cap fashioned from an empty Cheerios box.

Steven hooted, stopping behind Carol's chair, and laying a hand on her shoulder. "What did you do to deserve that hat?"

"All I said," Jack proclaimed haughtily, "was, 'hi,

222

Carol. My, but you've grown' and she took offense. Can you beat it?"

"I don't think this has been a good man day for her," Steven said ruefully. "I started it off wrong, for which I apologize to everyone who has exacerbated the situation by being male."

"And stupid," Dallas mumbled from her seat beside Carol. "Male didn't do it on its own."

Jack ignored her and the laughter that followed her remark. "No problem. If you can figure out a way for me to pass this test on Old Hickory—who I'm not all that fond of, by the way—all will be forgiven." He smiled brightly. "Or if you could manage to take the test while I performed surgery on a patient you aren't too concerned about keeping, that would work, too. I like to do my share."

"I've always heard that about you." Steven grinned at him and sat in the chair on Carol's other side. "What's the test about?"

"His relationship with his wife. I feel like I'm taking a class on a historical soap opera, and not a very good one," Jack complained. "He killed someone for insulting his wife—I just can't make that real in my mind. Carol, may I come to the table now?"

"Probably not," she said cheerfully. "I think you're about to talk yourself into another hole." She didn't pull away from Steven's hand, but she didn't meet his gaze, either.

Steven leaned back in his chair to read the notes of the student sitting next to him. "Considering the time and place, Jack, did he do the wrong thing? Not killing the guy necessarily but fighting a duel for her honor." He tightened his hand on Carol's shoulder, feeling the softness of her hair floating over his fingers. "You know, standing up."

Chapter Fifteen

"Of course you're out of breath. You're twenty-nine weeks pregnant with twins and you're as big as a house."

Carol narrowed her gaze at Maggie Leiden. "Have I mentioned that you're a real bitch?"

The gynecologist waved a dismissive hand. "Several times. My husband says the same thing. But look, girls, we need to talk about something."

"We already talked about your husband, Dillon, Steven, your kids, and the fact that you manage to look like a girl instead of that house you mentioned even when you're nearly as pregnant as I am. What's left?" Carol moved from the examination table to sit beside Grace in the consultation area of the room. "Sweet potato recipes? I'll share mine. We are southern women after all—sweet potatoes are important."

Maggie's eyebrows rose. "Who's being a bitch now? You know my cooking is…suspect."

"Your cooking should be outlawed." Carol had tasted it. She knew.

"I think it has been. Isn't that why we're going to Steven's house for Thanksgiving? Where I assume you're cooking?"

"I am. He's got a great kitchen, plus I'm not too adept right now at tossing twenty-some-pound turkeys around. You can bring the wine and something boring you and I can drink. Grace is bringing desserts for the masses. What did you want to talk to us about?"

"Delivery." Maggie's hand moved over her own swollen belly and rested there. "I'm smaller than you, but I may not be around to deliver Hope and Crosby. I plan to be, but Jake seems to think my own little darling might have other ideas. I'll have a locum here from Kingsport, but if you'd be more comfortable with Jake, no one's going to be offended. He's as good at delivery as most GYNs I've ever worked with."

"I would. He's my doctor for anything non-girly, so I expect he could deliver—what did you call them?"

"Hope and Crosby, as in Bob and Bing." Frowning, Maggie put the blood pressure cuff around Carol's arm again.

Carol laughed. "These babies are going to be the most-named children ever born. Does that mean they're boys? You can tell me—I won't let Grace know." She grinned at Grace, then turned her attention back to Maggie. "Just raise your right eyebrow for boys and your left one for girls. If there's one of each, do the Groucho Marx thing with both of them."

"It doesn't mean anything except that I like old movies and think Bob Hope was the funniest man ever born. At least until I married Daniel Leiden. And I can't tell you if for no other reason than my eyebrows don't work independently and they're way too plucked to do a Groucho anyway. I don't even know what *I'm* having this time, although Dan says if it's a fourth girl he's going to have me tested to find out if I'm really the baby's mother."

Carol snorted. "Don't make me laugh. I'll have to pee."

"You doing that a lot?"

"Laughing? I'm pregnant, remember? Of course I'm doing that a lot, when I'm not crying. Aren't you?"

"Yes, but my blood pressure's not elevated and my feet aren't swollen beyond recognition. And I was talking about peeing, not laughing."

"I'm pretty sure these babies are playing jump-rope on my bladder—probably double Dutch, the way it feels—so, yes, I pee a lot. Or I did, anyway. It seems to be slowing down now. My hands and feet only swell occasionally, unlike your chest. You have graduated to a D-plus cup, right?"

Maggie scowled at her. "You are not a nice person. That's all there is to it. Keep your feet up more, rest more, take your blood pressure. If you don't have a cuff, stop in here or at the drugstore and do it." She rolled her eyes. "What am I saying? That long drink of water you hang out with travels with a sphygmomanometer—have him check it." She sobered. "About the breast milk thing. You remember that drying up is a tough time."

Carol did remember that. She'd sat up in bed over and over after Miranda's death, her breasts tight and painful, murmuring, "I'm coming, baby girl," before she came fully awake. The memory was still unbearable. Her voice was breathy when she said, "Should I pump for Grace's babies?"

"You can. It's a generous thing to do and not uncommon for a surrogate." Maggie's gaze moved from Grace to Carol. "You're going to see these babies all the time, so separation will be a little more complicated than if you and Grace weren't friends. Are you up for the continued importance factor of providing their milk?"

Carol felt like she could breathe again. At least for now. "I'm up for whatever they need. Except sweets. That's up to their mother. I need a way to ensure that I will indeed be their favorite aunt. Faith has blood relationship and great hair going on for her, plus she can play the guitar. I'm not above courting favor with breast milk."

Steven and Dillon were in the waiting room when the appointment was finished. "Why did you let them in here?" Maggie asked the office manager.

The woman shrugged. "Since Steven works here, it was hard to keep him out. And Dillon gave me a copy of his new book. One of those advance ones that makes you look like you know somebody famous even if you only know him because he was a pain in the ass in high school. He even signed it."

Steven glared at Dillon. "You haven't even given me one."

"I gave yours to her." Dillon gestured at Ms. McGrew. "I owe her money for her kid's fundraiser, and I won't owe you any until we play poker on Thursday night." He drew Grace into the circle of his arm and smiled at Carol. "Are you all healthy?"

"We are. One of us is disgustingly fat, but other than that, we're in good shape." Carol laid a soothing hand on the twins who had graduated to doing cartwheels as she spoke. "Forget I said the word 'shape.' It's something I try not to even think about."

"No sweat," Grace said. "I have this dandy double stroller picked out. You and I will walk the babies until you're thin again, and I figure out another way to make them quit crying at the same time. Faith and I did that with Seth and Drew, even in the middle of the night. Grant was so paranoid about us being outside in the dark that he used to follow us in the car."

"Nah, he wasn't paranoid. He's just a stalker by nature." Carol laughed. "I haven't been thin since high school, which you know, but walking the babies sounds like a good idea."

****

Steven was amazed at how beautiful Miss Abigail's was. The closest he'd come to hiring a professional designer was the day right after he bought the house when Carol, Faith, and Kay walked through the rooms carrying tumblers full of wine and chose paint colors for the walls. He had followed them for a while, and in the dining room had suggested off-white for the entire first floor.

The idea hadn't gone over well. They'd suggested he either busy himself elsewhere or hire someone he'd have to pay very well to tell him off-white would be lovely. Since they were only paid in wine, they'd tell him straight up it was boring.

So the room colors were both vivid and fairly representative of the time period when Miss Abigail's was built. When the time came to furnish the house, he'd assigned different rooms to different people, thinking rightly that all he'd have to do was write checks. He hadn't really bargained for the *size* of some of those checks, but the library Carol and Grace finished with 173 dollars and furniture from the attic nearly made up for the hand-built-in-the-mid-1800s Windsor chair Faith bought to place beside the fireplace in the front parlor. The rocker was older than the house and too uncomfortable for anyone to sit in, but he'd been unable to resist the look in her eyes when she saw it.

Steven hardly ever went upstairs after the rooms were finished. He'd kept his room in the maid's quarters behind the kitchen, finding he could make it out of bed and to Peacock's small hospital in a matter of minutes if the phone rang in the middle of the night. He didn't always look very good when he got there, but that didn't really concern him.

"What on earth are you doing up there?" he hollered on the Wednesday afternoon before Thanksgiving. "For all I know, it's haunted."

"It's the attic that's haunted, goofball, not the second floor. I'm just making sure there are towels and toilet paper in the bathrooms and flowers in the bedrooms. You're going to have a full house tomorrow night." Carol came down the stairs as she spoke, carrying a duster and flipping it over the banister rails. "There'll be twenty-six for dinner and half of them are spending the night."

He reached for her hand. "Let's go check your blood pressure."

Her eyelashes fluttered at him. "You're the one who's shouting. *My* blood pressure isn't the issue."

"Then you can take mine after I take yours." He pulled her toward the kitchen.

"That sounds like foreplay."

"We can arrange that." Although they couldn't. They'd stopped the actual act when it became uncomfortable for her, although they satisfied each other in different ways. He loved how she thrived on being pregnant. She was completely unembarrassed by her body, and he liked that, too. Being a physician had given him an unending fascination with how the human body worked—having a pregnant girlfriend only served to increase that interest. Although it was a whole lot more personal now.

He fastened the cuff around her arm. "Be still. And don't do the eyelashes thing. It messes with *my* blood pressure."

"I need to go home."

"Hush." He frowned first at her then at the reading. "I want you to lie down for a while."

She shook her head in protest. "Mom and Aunt Jo will be here any time. I need to check on dinner and make sure their rooms are ready."

"I'll come with you and do that."

"You have guests coming," she reminded him.

He swung his arm in an all-encompassing gesture. "Tomorrow morning, not tonight. Well, except for Mitch and his wife, who are going into empty nest withdrawal because none of their kids are making it home. But they won't be here before nine o'clock at the earliest—he hasn't made it out of his office on time in all the years I've known him. By then you'll be on the couch with your feet up, and I'll be back here acting like I've done all the work to get ready for company."

"Okay."

Her quick agreement made him frown. Although he wouldn't classify Carol as the controlling type, she didn't take kindly to *being* controlled, either. Even when he tried to act the stern and knowledgeable physician when he talked to her, she usually laughed at him and did things her way.

The drive down the hill took only a couple of minutes, and she was on the couch with a quilt and a pillow in a few more. "Just check their rooms," she requested. "I know they're clean, but Fred and Barney want to act like guests once in a while and take naps on top of the beds and they never smooth out the wrinkles when they get up."

"Lazy asses."

She sniffed. "Yes, unlike Tom and Huck, who need to go on diets because someone overfeeds them, and then they spend all their time holding down the porch swing."

He sat beside her, fastening the blood pressure cuff around her upper arm once more. "Don't forget the energy they expend watching birds. They're probably exhausted. Is your face puffy?"

She glared at him. "You may not have noticed this, but I'm puffy all over. I haven't worn rings in weeks, and I'm pretty sure my earlobes are swelling up around my earrings."

"Keep lying on your left side and stay down," he instructed, trying to tell if the skin around her eyes was swollen or if he was borrowing trouble. "Have you had any nausea lately?"

She latched onto the first part of what he'd said. "Stay down how long?"

"'Til Maggie or I tell you it's okay to get up."

Mutiny settled across her features. If he hadn't been so worried, he'd have laughed, because the expression just didn't fit. "Tomorrow's Thanksgiving. I'm cooking."

"Nope. You're not. Headaches?"

"Steven, I need to—" She stopped, disquiet replacing the rebellion on her face. "Headaches?"

"Yeah. Have you had any lately? More than usual,

I mean." Although he didn't think she got headaches. The date on the bottle of Naproxen in her medicine cabinet was expired. He *did* get headaches, and he'd looked.

"Yes," she admitted. "Not bad ones, never bad enough to take anything even if I had stuff to take. But frequent."

"Does Maggie know?"

"No. I didn't think of it when I saw her—we were too busy discussing my weight and her cup size." She started to sit up, then leaned back against the pillows propped at the end of the sofa, taking care to stay on her side. "What's happening, Steven? Are the babies all right? They're still moving all the time. Kicking up a storm."

"Did you have any problems carrying Miranda?"

"No." Her expression was confused. And frightened. "We've been through all that. It was what you medical types call a textbook pregnancy."

"And the miscarriage? Do you know what caused that?"

"No. It was fairly textbook, too, I think. The pregnancy felt wrong from the beginning. I didn't even make it through the first trimester. Doc Bridges said sometimes your body just says no." She smiled, but her eyes were sad. "I felt really betrayed by that. I'd heard *no* often enough already. It wasn't that I really wanted to be pregnant by the sperm donor in question, but since I was, I certainly did want that baby."

Jo and Dixie arrived then, and Steven went out to carry their things in. "She needs some coddling," he said on the way into the house.

Dixie flashed a smile at him that gave him a

glimmer of the pretty debutante she'd been in the picture that hung in Carol's living room. "What do we need to do for my daughter?"

"Make sure she stays down. Keep her occupied. Monitor her blood pressure." He spoke over his shoulder. "Jo, you travel with a cuff, don't you, from when you were a volunteer in—what was it, the Crimean War?"

"Young man, you are a smartass." She swatted him with a tote bag that seemed to contain at least one lead pipe. He'd bet it left a bruise. "I was a nursing assistant in a veteran's hospital while I was in college and law school. But I do travel with a blood pressure monitor because Dixie's old and I'm—"

"—even older," Dixie interrupted. "We can do that. What else?"

"Don't let her boss you around—she'll know you're worried if you do." They reached the porch, and he stopped to meet their eyes in turn. "I'm afraid she's got preeclampsia. It's not a terrible thing, but it's not good, either. I don't want to say anything to her 'til Maggie's seen her and gotten some blood."

"She'll figure it out, you know," Jo advised. "My niece is no dummy." She sniffed. "Other than about men, that is."

Steven grinned at her. "Present company excepted, by any chance?"

She opened the door. "We'll see."

Acting as if he'd cooked the whole thing—and to give himself due credit, he *had* warmed the dinner rolls—Steven set up the long table that usually sat behind the couch as a buffet. "Just lie there," he ordered Carol. "We'll fix your plate."

"Don't let Jo do it." Dixie brought dinner plates from the kitchen. "She hogs the okra then blames other people."

****

"I am so sorry." Grace's eyes, large and brown and half-framed by dark semi-circles, looked miserable. "This is more than you bargained for."

"Stop." Carol shook her head at her. "When you sign up for pregnancy, you take it as it comes. I'm not saying it's fun or I don't wish *you* were the size of Dumbo the elephant and puking like Fred with hairballs instead of me, but it is what it is."

Grace's smile was small, but it was there. "I'm going to tell Dillon you said that. He thinks it's the worst new old adage he's ever heard." She set a cup of decaf on the table at the end of the couch. "We all missed you at dinner at Miss Abigail's, especially Steven. He's champing at the bit for everyone to go home so he can come down and see you."

"Your little darlings are being a little rough on my holidays." Carol sat up to drink her coffee, amazed she could be exhausted by simply lying down for what felt like days even though it had only been about twenty-four hours. "I was throwing up on Memorial Day weekend and the Fourth, couldn't go to Faith's Halloween party because the flu had started its trek through town, and had to miss the first Thanksgiving at the Retreat. Goodness knows what they've got in mind for Christmas. Then they'll probably want to be the New Year's babies and will grow up with one feeling inferior because he wasn't born first."

"Oh, cool!" Grace beamed at her. "Something new for me to worry about. That's good Mom practice, isn't it?"

"It certainly is."

"What is your due date, Carolina?" asked Jo, handing plates holding pieces of pumpkin pie to Carol and Grace. "I know it's sometime in January."

"Another holiday being taken over," Carol mourned. "If they go full term, they could be born on Groundhog Day. I won't be able to watch that movie with Bill Murray five or six times if I'm in labor."

"Not that you'll make it that long," said Dixie briskly, joining them in the living room. "but they have a TV right there when you're in labor. You know, in case the doctor or the nursing staff get bored." She looked around. "Oh, shoot, I forgot Steven wasn't here to take offense. I just wasted a zinger."

"It's all right, Miss Dixie. We'll tell him you said it." Grace went to the kitchen and came back with the coffee carafe, refilling cups. "How long are you ladies staying? I know Carol would like it if you just moved in, and it would be nice for the babies to have grandmas close by for when I panic in the middle of the night."

Jo snorted. "The Old Farts Home is right down the street from you. They'll all be on call, unless they're parked right in your living room, that is."

Carol listened to the quiet murmur of women's conversation, punctuated with laughter, and ate her pie slowly. Savoring. Thinking, in spite of herself, of Steven. Of spending her days and nights with him in a home they shared. Of sharing middle-of-the-night baby duty with him.

Babies.

She didn't remember all of the days of Miranda's short life. Time had—perhaps mercifully—given her a faded view of much of that time. But there were moments that still rose up as if there had been no empty years in between. Moments and hours and sometimes full days.

Like when Faith had come to visit, pushing the double stroller with Seth and Drew snoozing inside to Carol's little apartment above the building that became the Clip Joint. She'd brought the baby a soft pink romper, complete with matching bonnet and booties. The name "Miranda," with a rosebud beside it had been embroidered on the front in a rainbow of pastel colors. The outfit had been too big, but Carol had put it on her anyway. She'd set Miranda in her bouncy seat and taken at least twenty pictures of fleeting smiles and inadvertent bubbles blown and Rand's blue eyes.

It had been the last day, and the joy and the anguish of it were even now unbearable to recall.

But it would be even more so to forget.

It was nice, to lie here on her left side and remember. Just for a little while. To rest her hands on the huge bump that was Grace and Dillon's babies and tell them in low murmurs how much they would be loved. To think, as memories of Miranda slipped back into the safe place she kept them, that in only a matter of weeks she would see her feet again.

Sometime during that long night, the blood pressure cuff surrounded her upper arm and her legs grew warm where someone sat beside them. "Steven," she mumbled, bringing her hands back to her swollen belly, "we were sleeping. All three of us."

"Sh." His hand shaped her cheek. A moment later, the cuff released its almost painful pressure. He sighed so quietly she wasn't sure she'd heard it. He kissed her forehead and her cheek and, briefly, her lips, and his weight lifted from the side of the couch.

"Don't go." She was surprised to hear herself say the words, but too sleepy to be embarrassed by them.

Sounds, thumps that were soft even on the hardwood floor, reached her ears. She opened her eyes long enough to see the recliner beside the couch where she lay. "You'll be so uncomfortable."

"Sh," he said again, taking her hand. "I'll be here. I've slept in worse places." He raised the hand he held to kiss her fingers. His lips were so warm, she wanted to curl herself around the sensation. "Rest warm, girlfriend."

Chapter Sixteen

"It's preeclampsia, but don't panic, okay?" Late Monday afternoon, Maggie Leiden smiled at Carol, then scowled at Steven. "We'll leave that to the tall guy over there. You just need to stay in bed, on your left side as much as possible. We'll try working together with nature—like you do with hair color—and see what happens. The babies are viable, so if they decide it's time, we'll go along with what they say. I'd like them to wait at least 'til New Year's, but I don't think that's going to happen. I imagine Laverne and Shirley will be in a bit of a hurry to celebrate."

More than a bit, Steven thought but didn't say. He'd been pretty sure of the diagnosis, but he didn't like hearing it.

"Will you tell Grace, Maggie? And make it so she won't worry." Carol tried for a smile, although the effort fell short. "She won't believe you, Steven, no matter what you tell her, but she thinks Maggie's more trustworthy. At least, she does now. Her calling the babies Laverne and Shirley might push their mother over the edge."

"It's that girl thing, isn't it?" Steven sighed dramatically. "But you're right. I'll talk to Dillon, though. He has faith in me."

"That would be good—the guy thing," Maggie said wryly, then returned her attention to Carol. "Are your mother and aunt still at your house? I know you're a big girl, but you do live in the boonies—I'll be more comfortable if you're not alone."

"They're there, but I don't want them to have to take care of me."

Maggie ignored that. "Do you have a downstairs bedroom?" She slipped the blood pressure cuff onto Carol's arm again.

Carol's sigh came all the way from her swollen feet. "Yes. I used to call it the living room, but somehow the couch became a daybed and my favorite place to sit and read became a recliner with a remote control damn near attached to it. Fred keeps walking around and around because he's not sure it's still his house."

The doctor waved a dismissive hand. "Living rooms are overrated. Ours is a campground, complete with Barbie tents, sleeping bags, and marshmallows. The girls never sleep in their rooms anymore. Dan and I just huddle at the kitchen table, wondering when life got out of control."

Steven snorted. "Dan should have thought of that before he let you have three girls."

"Let me?" Maggie nodded and released the cuff. "Good. It's staying pretty stable, but we still need to watch it. Did you really say 'let me', Steven?"

Oh, hell, he had, hadn't he? "Yeah, but I didn't mean it. He hasn't *let* you do anything in forever, right?"

"Good answer." She nodded at him. "Take care of my patient, okay? Carol, I'll see you next week and the week after but then I'm going on my own pregnancy leave. I'm going to have campouts with my girls and finish the quilt I started in college and read the fifty-five books that are stacked up beside the bed. Heaven knows there'll be no chance for anything like that *after* he's born."

"He?" Carol raised a brow at Maggie. "Did you give in and open the envelope?"

The gynecologist shrugged, grinning. "Or she. You can go home now, Ms. Whitney. Lie down and turn on a shopping network on TV. You can get all your Christmas shopping done while there's someone there to wrap it for you. No working at all 'til after you've delivered—I don't care *what* Lois Gleason's hair looks like."

Carol was quiet on the drive up Taylor Hill, her attention focused somewhere outside the passenger window of Steven's truck. The withdrawal wasn't unusual—she'd grown increasingly moody as the pregnancy progressed. Sometimes the air around her fairly crackled with touchiness. Today, however, she seemed more melancholy than irritable.

He hated it when she was sad.

"You'll be okay," he said. "Frank and Jesse will, too."

"I know." But she didn't look like she knew. Her eyes were more gray than green, her skin pale, her smile dim. Even her hair color—which she had explained to him at great length was different than what she used when she wasn't pregnant—seemed washed out. When he'd suggested she stop coloring it altogether, he was glad they weren't in high school, because he was certain she'd have flung his class ring at him. Promise did that a few times—those things could do some serious damage.

Terror moved through him before he could stop it, before he could remind himself this wasn't Promise with breast cancer, but Carol with an exhausting pregnancy. For a moment when he pulled into the driveway, he sat still, afraid to shift and disturb his own fragile balance.

Her questioning look made him move, although his legs felt weak. He walked her inside, waving at Dixie and Jo where they sat at the kitchen table cutting out Christmas cookies. He arranged a pillow behind Carol's back, then rearranged everything so he could sit at the end of the daybed and put her head in his lap. "Tell me what's wrong," he insisted. "I'm your boyfriend. I have rights."

She turned her head so her gaze met his. "Excuse me? You have what?"

Make her laugh. If you can just do that, it'll be okay. "I'm your boyfriend, and I have squat for rights, but I worry about you. Better?"

"Absolutely."

"So." He stroked her hair. She said it was coarse, but it felt soft under his fingers. The skin of her cheek did, too. Soft and wet. "Carol?"

"I'm just—" She stopped, sniffled, and shook her head, the movement slight and warm against his legs. "I'm waiting for the other shoe to drop."

He understood that—it was how he'd spent the last six months of Promise's life. Telling Carol yet again that "it's going to be okay" was the wrong thing to do, but he didn't know what the right one was. "What do you think is going to happen?" He tucked her hair behind her ear, feeling dampness on his pants where her silent tears seeped through.

"That's what scares me. I don't know."

The idea of her being afraid worried him. "Just rest," he urged. "I'm going to make Dixie and Jo give me some cookies, then I'll get out of your way."

"I think I sleep twelve hours a day," she protested, but her eyes closed even as she spoke.

He got up carefully, placing a pillow under her head and drawing a quilt up over her shoulder. He kissed her cheek. "See you tomorrow."

"Ummm…" Her eyes opened. "Steven? Go see Grace. Make sure she knows the babies are all right."

"I'll go there now." He kissed her again.

His cell phone rang as he got into his truck. "Grace says come by for supper if you're not eating with Carol," said Dillon without preamble.

"I'll be there in a minute." Steven appreciated the invitation, although he'd been going there anyway. After a weekend of company, Miss Abigail's was shockingly empty. He needed to explain preeclampsia to Grace in a non-panic-inducing way anyway.

Which he didn't do very well—that became obvious the minute the plate she was holding hit the floor.

"Good job, Elliot," Dillon muttered, picking up his barefoot wife and setting her on the kitchen counter. "Stay there."

"I've seen movies." Grace's eyes were huge in her thin face. "I know what preeclampsia is. We're going to lose them, aren't we?"

Steven got the broom and dustpan from behind the basement door. He handed the dustpan to Dillon and swept the hardwood carefully because Grace never wore shoes—he used to say he'd done his first surgery rotation stitching up cuts in her feet. "No, we're not going to lose them. We're not going to let that happen." He kept his voice calm. "Carol's up the hill going crazy because she has to lie down all the time until she delivers. Do you know what bed rest is like for someone who thinks sleep is a total waste of time? Somebody who buried a baby twenty years ago?"

"Steven." Dillon shook his head from where he knelt holding the dustpan. He reached to clasp his wife's slender calf in one hand. "Grace doesn't need that."

"No, he's right." Grace sat still. "I wasn't even thinking about Carol, and I *know* how awful bed rest is for her. We just talked about it Friday, before she even knew it was an ongoing thing." She frowned. "We haven't talked about Miranda in a long time, though. Years. Maybe we should."

Steven met his sister's eyes. Grief held her features in rigid captivity, and he knew if he could see into a mirror, his reflection would look the same way. The time since Promise's death disappeared in a moment of shared pain.

"Maybe I should." He couldn't believe he was saying it. Meaning it. He didn't talk about death unless he was able to separate himself from it by leaving his office or going away for the weekend. Or moving back to Peacock. He took a deep breath and put the broom away. "Maybe I should stop pretending it's a closed wound and see if I can help her make it feel better."

****

"Bed rest is expensive." Carol finalized the purchase of yet another Christmas gift from an infomercial retailer. "Aunt Jo, did you really *want* six-for-the-price-of-one bras that are guaranteed to make you look bikini-ready without exercise or diet?"

"Or plastic surgery," Dixie added.

Jo ignored her sister-in-law. "Of course, I did, Carolina. You did include the black and the peek-a-boo lace in the order, right?"

Dixie snorted. "Like you'd remember what to do with it."

A knock at the back door was followed by Steven's shout. "Anybody here? Barney said I could come in." He came into the living-room-bedroom sock-footed, tossing his coat over the back of the couch. "Maxie said to tell you ladies there was bingo at the Old Farts Home tonight and that they were almost positive the punch had some medicinal additive in it. And if it doesn't, she'll see that Jonah puts it in. If you go, you need to stay down there, though, because additive means no more driving for you."

"Carol's doctor doesn't want her left alone," said Dixie.

"I'll stay with her. She can clip my fingernails so that she feels useful," Steven added magnanimously, sitting at the end of the daybed with Carol's feet in his lap. "I just washed my hands the day before Thanksgiving, so they're pretty clean and all."

She raised an eyebrow at him, trying not to laugh. "You know, I have really big feet and they could do a lot of damage where they are."

He grinned at her, wrapping her feet in the quilt at the end of the couch and stroking her calf under its cover. For a moment she forgot they weren't the only ones in the room.

"We'll go." Jo got to her feet. "Come on, Dix. I

haven't played bingo since I got old enough to think it's fun."

Steven escorted them outside and walked Barney before coming back into the house. "You want hot chocolate?" he called from the kitchen.

"Only if you're going to start a fire in the fireplace."

"I can do that."

Waiting for him, Carol looked around at the cozy room. She loved her house, loved its eclectic furnishings and warm colors, the hardwood floors she'd sanded and refinished regardless of their imperfections, the carpeted areas where the wood had been beyond redemption. It wasn't enough, she didn't think, to fill her days and nights when the summer romance with Steven ended. But it would help. Surely it would.

Steven came in. He set the two cups of hot chocolate on the table between the daybed and the recliner and went to light the fire he'd laid in the fireplace last week when he'd shared a pickup-load of firewood with her.

She arranged herself in a sitting position to drink her chocolate. Sometimes she concentrated so hard on lying on her left side the way Maggie had encouraged that she ended up numb on that side, her arm tingling, and her ear sore from the pressure.

When Steven sat down, he held the framed photograph of Miranda that always sat on the mantel. Carol had taken it that last day. The baby's curls shone gold and her smile was gummy and bubbly, caught at the perfect second. Her eyes were open wide and sparkling, and if Carol ever found herself forgetting what Rand Shipper looked like, she had only to look at that picture.

Steven set the frame between them. "Tell me about her."

"What?" He knew about Miranda already. He knew Carol usually went to the cemetery every week, that the baby had lived just three months, that sometimes when Carol stared into space, she was remembering. And wishing. What else did he want to know?

"I don't *know* her," he said. "I knew Rand and Ed. Knew your dad. I'm crazy about your mom and Jo. You know my family, were close friends with my wife, are carrying my nieces or nephews or both." He held the frame up, smiling at the image of the baby. "She was undoubtedly the most important person in your whole life, and all I know is that she was born and she died."

Carol flinched and sat in silence while she tried to think of what to say. "She lived," she said finally. "She lived and breathed and had just started to laugh. Her voice was going to be deep, like mine—I could tell. She had chubby legs and little starfish hands and a strawberry birthmark on her right shoulder that Noah said would probably go away in time only it never got a chance."

Once she started, she couldn't stop. Everything she had stored unspoken in the empty place in her heart seemed to need to come out at once. Her voice sounded scraped and raw and she had to sip at the too-hot chocolate to make it work, but she kept talking.

"She weighed just seven pounds when she was born and the water weight I'd counted on losing amounted to about a cup. I stayed awake all night the night I brought her home because I was afraid I wouldn't hear her cry. She had a full head of curly blonde hair and she didn't lose hardly any of it. My dad—oh, he was so mad at me for getting pregnant, so mad at me for moving out on my own and going to beauty school—but he would sit and hold her for hours at a time. When Mom would offer to take her, he'd say, 'oh, in a little while, Dixie,' and go on holding her."

Carol had to stop and breathe, to mop her face with the tissue Steven handed her. "Whatever my schedule was, and believe me, it was a nightmare in those days, Miranda went along with it. When I worked nights at the Cup and Cozy, she slept in the booth at the back or sat in her bouncy seat and charmed everybody while I was working. One time, Lois Gleason called the police and told them I wasn't fit to be a mother because I was raising my child in a coffee shop. The sheriff then was Jake Sawyer's dad—remember him?—and he came down and held Miranda while I mopped the floor. He told me about Vietnam and how he was afraid to come home because people called them baby-killers but no one in Peacock did. Or if they did, he never heard about it. And he told me it wasn't where you raised a child but how much you loved her while you were doing it. He told me Lois Gleason was one mean bitch. He said she was the one with the problem, not me."

Steven's laugh, deep and gentle, interrupted, and she looked over at him, nonplussed.

She'd forgotten he was there.

"Go on," he said. "Did you pierce her ears?"

"Oh." She smiled, remembering. "No. I was going to, but I couldn't do it. Her little ears were so perfect the way they were. Mom insisted she inherited them from her even knowing that couldn't be. But I bought earrings, tiny little gold beads, for when it was time. I had them on layaway at the jewelry store that used to be where the Dollar Store is now when she died. Mr. Engel said I could have my money back or apply it to another piece of jewelry, but I got them anyway. They're in the keepsake chest my father made for me when I was in high school, still in the velvet box and wrapped in the fancy paper the store always used. Mr. Engel gave me a little baby ring to put on her finger in her casket. I put Rand's and my class rings in there, too, and a picture of us together so that when she got to heaven, they'd know who her family was and could take her right to her daddy. I was worried...I was so afraid she'd be scared, you know?" She stopped on a gasp, covering her face with her hands.

She was aware, dimly, of Steven's arms around her. She thought how long it had been since anyone had held her while she cried over Miranda. Dixie had sought to spare her—Carol knew that—but sometimes she needed to revisit the pain in its fullness in order to feel the pleasure that time had been.

"It was the shortest three months of my life," she whispered. "I thought I could never be joyful again, after Ed and Rand had both died, and instead I was happier than I'd ever been. Or than I've been since."

"I'm sorry." He smoothed her hair, bent his head to kiss her. "I'm so sorry to have made you hurt again."

"No." She turned her head, meeting his reddened eyes. "It's good to talk about her. I just thought about the last day on Thanksgiving, remembering the little outfit Faith had given her. It's in the keepsake chest, too, along with booties Rand's mother knit for her and a little quilt my mother made. She was buried snuggled in a soft blanket Dad bought for her."

"Was it a good day, that last day?"

She nodded. "Do you remember that scene in *City Slickers* when the guys were talking about their best days ever? The one guy told about his best day and when his buddies asked what his worst one was, he said 'same day.' That was the way Miranda's last day was. It was perfect. But at three o'clock the next morning, when I got up wondering why she hadn't woken up to nurse, it became the worst." The tears that had stopped momentarily started again, trailing down her cheeks. She reached across Steven for another tissue. "I have faith. I believe Miranda's with Rand and I'll see them again someday, but that doesn't mean I understand."

Steven chuckled. She felt the vibration of it, then his kiss on the top of her head. "Yeah. I've had a few conversations with God that I'm sure had my mama rolling her eyes and telling the Lord I don't really mean what I'm saying."

"She'll run interference for you. That's what mothers do." Her throat was dry, and Carol reached for her chocolate. "You want to heat this up again?"

"Will do." But he didn't get up right away, just stayed still and held her. "Is that what's been wrong the last few days? Has the forced inactivity made you miss Miranda more?"

She sat silently for a little while, then shook her head. "Do you remember when I had the in vitro, and I told you later it was like I knew by the next morning that it had taken? It was so weird, because I never feel things like that. I'm more of the 'hit me in the head with a brick' type than intuitive."

He grinned—she felt the lift of his cheek against

the side of her head and thought what a silly thing that was to find comforting. But comforting it was. "I think I've hefted a few of the bricks," he said.

She smacked him, and he caught her hand, holding it against his chest. His heart beat firm and steady, and his skin through the flannel of his shirt was warm against her fingers. Oh, yes, comfort.

She cleared her throat. "Promise not to say anything to Grace about this, because she tends to feel guilty about everything—I think you Elliots have a Jewish mother somewhere in your ancestry."

"I promise."

"Once I got into my thirties and hadn't met Mr. Right, or even Mr. Okay-I-Can-Live-With-That, I never truly planned on having children. But I didn't really plan on *not* having them, either. Carrying Jake and Elwood has been such a gift, and I started to think about having a baby on my own after them. There are a whole lot worse things than being a single mother."

Although the knowledge had been floating through her head for days now, since long before the bed rest, she hadn't said it out loud. The words came out slow and painful. "But when I started thinking about that, when I sat down and figured up how I could be a family instead of a single woman on my income, that was when I knew there wouldn't be any more pregnancies or any babies after these. Sometimes your body talks to you—you know that as well as anyone—and mine's been telling me that for a while now. I just didn't want to listen."

She smiled at him. Her face felt swollen, but there was a new lightness in her, too. "Thank you for listening to the things I needed to say. And for letting me hear myself. All my life, it's hurt me knowing I took second place with my parents. It took remembering how they mourned for Miranda to know I never did. Grief is just so heavy that sometimes it outweighs other things."

Chapter Seventeen

"I appreciate you doing this, Reese." Carol watched from the daybed as the teenager sat cross-legged on the floor and wrapped Christmas presents. "I know gift bags are easy, but there's nothing like opening a present."

"I like doing it," Reese assured her, curling ribbon with a scissors' blade and a sweep of her arm. "Oops, sorry, Fred." She petted the cat she'd just knocked off the chair. "Did Lynn or Kay bring you pictures of the Clip Joint? We decorated it the Saturday after Thanksgiving, and it looks beautiful! Kay told her husband—he substitute teaches at the high school sometimes if he doesn't have any funerals going on— and he told my art teacher. I got extra credit for it. Isn't that cool?" She got up from the floor, her movements awkward, and brought her cell phone over to Carol. "See?"

Carol looked at the pictures on the miniature screen. "It's a great job, honey. I'm glad you got extra credit." She handed the phone back. "What are you and your dad doing for Christmas?"

"He's going hunting with his buddies up in Canada."

"What will you do? Spend the holidays with your grandparents?" Jeff's parents were both dead, but Hilary's lived in Knoxville.

The girl's shrug was elaborately casual. "Not this year. They're going on a cruise over the holidays. I'll be okay," she said, maturity and sadness fighting a fine war in the timbre of her voice. "I'm sixteen."

"But, Reese, the holidays…" Carol stopped, not sure how to word what she wanted to say. "Why don't you come here? You can spend Christmas Eve night and Christmas day with us. Steven and his family will be here some of the time and other people will stop in, too. Actually"—she warmed to her subject—"you can just spend your whole vacation from school. We're not exciting, but the food's good, and you could do the up-and-downstairs running since I'm stuck in bed, and it's hard for the others to go up and down that much. You could also run errands for Mom and Aunt Jo. They think they don't need any help with anything, but sometimes they do."

Reese hesitated, but longing etched itself on her face. It reminded Carol of the girl's expression sometimes when she looked at Ben Sawyer. "I don't want to be a problem, Miss Carol. It seems I've been a problem for someone my whole life, starting with my mother, and…you know, it gets old."

"You've never been a problem." Carol reached, pushing the girl's highlighted hair behind her ear where it never wanted to stay. "Circumstances suck sometimes. That's all there is to it, and there isn't much you can do about it. But if you decide to live your life as a victim…well, that's up to you. I'd like you to come and spend the holidays, but you'll be more than a guest—you'll have to be a temporary family member. No one's going to make your bed or pick up after you, and you'll eat what's on the table or do without."

"I'd like to come."

"Good. But you need to check with your dad."

"He won't care."

It was unfortunate, but the girl's flat-spoken comment was probably accurate. Jeff Confer loved Reese—Carol was sure of that—but he was a "wallet daddy." He liked showing off pictures of his little girl, but that was about as far as it went. His wife had died when Reese was still a baby, and sometimes it seemed as if all the emotion in him had died at the same time. In recent years, Reese had spent more time at Carol's house and the shop than she had at home.

"Are you sure I wouldn't be in the way? What if you go into labor or something? I won't know what to do." Reese grinned ruefully. "I've seen lots of babies being delivered on TV, but I think there's probably more to it than that."

"Honey, you can be the kid. Mom and Aunt Jo are staying here, plus Steven is here more often than not. We're having an open house on Christmas afternoon, and you can have friends stop in, too. You can roll your eyes and talk about how lame grownups are."

As if on cue, Reese rolled her eyes. "You're falling behind on name tags. Who is this for?"

Carol frowned, thinking about the delicate china cup and saucer in the package. She'd found it at a garage sale in the fall. "Lois Gleason."

"You give her a Christmas present? She's mean."

"I give all clients Christmas presents, including you. But yes, she is mean, so she needs presents more than most."

"Oh." Reese didn't sound convinced, but she attached the name tag Carol handed her. "What did you get Dr. Elliot?"

"A tire pump, a patching kit, a helmet, and a new water bottle."

Reese snorted laughter. "Why?"

"He wanted a bicycle like the one Dillon rides that he had to replace because I ran over him in the cemetery, but I couldn't afford that—it would have been like buying a new car, I swear—but his family went together and bought him one. I just bought the spare parts."

"What do you hope he got you?"

"Oh." Carol hadn't thought about that. Christmas was like her birthday—she always got a lot of cards and presents from clients, plus gifts and nice checks from her mother and aunt. It had been a long time since she'd had a boyfriend over the holidays. "I don't know."

Maybe another long summer of going steady, of having someone to laugh with and make love with and tell things to that I can't tell anyone else. Someone to go parasailing with and let me drive the golf cart. Someone who wants to know Miranda.

She brought her attention back to the girl with the wistful eyes who was wrapping presents on the living room floor. "What about you, Reese? What do you want for Christmas?"

Reese shrugged. "Nothing, really." She curled a long green ribbon. "Can I ask you something?"

"Sure." Carol grinned at her. "I'm quite an expert on where babies come from, if you want to discuss that, but it might not match up with what you already knew."

Reese blushed and dipped her head. "Do you hate being big?"

Carol had to lean forward to hear the question.

"Sometimes," she admitted. "I have a guilty fear that this preeclampsia thing is partly weight-related. But my size is okay with me because *I'm* okay with me. I'm not who I thought I'd be when I was your age, but I'm happy with who I am." *Most of the time.*

"What about when you're not dating anybody? Aren't you lonely?" Reese's fingers, slender and pretty, folded a lacy knit shrug neatly into a box.

"I get lonely sometimes, sure, but not because of my size. And sometimes I get lonely even when I *am* dating somebody. Being part of a couple isn't a paid ticket to being happy all the time."

"Is that why you never got married?"

It had been years since anyone had asked her that question straight out—anybody sober anyway. Carol knew some people thought her single state was because she was overweight. Or too picky. Or a lesbian. Rand's mother thought it was because she'd never gotten over Rand.

"I think I never got married because I was never with anyone I wanted to wake up next to for the rest of my life. I cared for a couple of men after Rand—I won't deny that—but not enough. Never enough."

Until now. Until she loved a man she wasn't sure would stand up when he needed to—at least when she thought he needed to. But then, "perfect" hadn't even been in the top ten on her list of man requirements the last time she looked. Neither had a ponytail, a pierced ear, or a motorcycle.

But sometime in this long summer of being Steven Elliot's girlfriend, the list had changed.

Carol shook her head before she found herself crying yet again and looked at her watch. "Now that you know my deep, dark secret and now that you have most of my presents wrapped, young lady, I want you to go home and talk to your dad about coming here as soon as he leaves. Or before, if you want to. Tell him to call me if he has any concerns."

"Okay." Reese put the gifts under the big Christmas tree in the corner, separating clients' gifts from family-and-friend ones. "You're sure you want me to come?"

"Positive."

****

There was a note of something different in Mitch's voice when they talked two weeks before Christmas, but Steven wasn't sure what it was. "They want you to come to Knoxville for a follow-up."

"What did you tell them?"

"That you were no longer affiliated with the hospital."

"And that went over how?" Steven leaned back in his chair, propping his feet on the file drawer of his desk.

"I didn't wait to find out."

Glee, that's what it was. Mitch sounded gleeful.

"You might be looking for a job," Steven said, laughing. "Sounds like you enjoyed that way too much."

Mitch chuckled. "No such luck. I did tell them where you were practicing now, since it's a matter of public record. I wanted to warn you about that and thank you again for doing his surgery in the first place. You were absolutely good for this hospital, but I'm kind of glad you left it—I've come around to thinking it was the right thing for you."

"I think it was, too." And he did—that was the nice thing. He wasn't just saying what he thought Mitch wanted to hear. It was really, truly good to be home. The regret twinges—well, he could live with them.

"How's Carol?"

It was Steven's turn to chuckle. "It depends on when you ask her. And whatever mood she's in, my sister is in the same one. Dillon and I spend a lot of time playing pool at my house because it's safer than being around them."

"Well, just be agreeable, Elliot. I know it's hard for you, but you can do it for a few more weeks. Have a good Christmas."

"You, too. Take care."

There was a curious finality in their goodbyes. "That's weird," he told Jake, when they were having their beer-and-files meeting at the end of the day. "We're friends. We worked together for years."

"It's different, though." Jake tossed him a folder. "I worked in Nashville for fifteen years, and I can count on one hand the people I still see. There are a few I refer cases to, but even then, we only talk about the patients. My friends now are the same ones I had in high school, who either came back here or never left. I can't explain it, but that's the way it worked out. Sometimes life's a strange kind of circle."

Steven stopped in at the Clip Joint to pick up the Christmas flower arrangements Kay had assembled for the cemetery. The shop was warm and busy, the air practically crackling with Christmas cheer. "Carol misses this," he said, looking around.

"We miss her." Lynn waved a brush. "So do her clients. If you want to take that basket, that's the

Christmas gifts that have been dropped off for her so far. Tell her Kay and I just kept the best edible ones. She wouldn't want us to do without."

"Are you sure you don't want me to take these over to the cemetery?" asked Kay, shrugging into her coat to help carry the floral arrangements out. "I'll be delivering more every day."

"Nah. I need to make Carol's and my weekly visits anyway." Steven smiled at her and held the shop door open for her to precede him outside. "Peacock needs a florist. You're running yourself ragged."

"I know, but I hate to tell anyone no. It was a lot easier when Carol did the flowers and I just helped her. No one knew just how much she did until she had to stop doing it for a while." She laughed breathlessly when Steven took the last grave blanket from her, and brushed pine needles off her gloved hands. "Even Lynn and I didn't know, but we do now, believe me." She shivered in the sub-freezing air. "I'm going in. Thanks, Steven. Tell Carol to let us know if we can do anything to make the time go faster. We'll be glad to bring her all kinds of work she can do while lying in bed on her left side."

He laughed and gave Kay a hug. "Yeah, I'll tell her that, all right, and I'll let you know just how it went over."

At the cemetery, he decorated his mother's grave. "Sorry I'm not being real neat here, Mama. You know Gracie and Faith will come along and do it right." He touched the top of the granite marker and moved on to where Miranda was buried, taking extra time arranging the little grave blanket. "Your mom couldn't come," he said, "but you know she thinks about you all the time.

Misses you." He made sure the little Christmas ornaments in the pine branches were secure. "She talks about you, so I know you now, too. She'd have been such a great mom, Miranda." He touched the small monument as he had his mother's. "She loves you. Me, too."

At Promise's grave, he listened for a moment to the bamboo wind chime hanging from the shepherd's hook. "Liking the music, darlin'?" He put the arrangement of cedar and roses on top of the marker. "God, woman, I miss you, but you know that, don't you? Loving you, being with you…it was the best anything could ever be. We had…oh, holy balls, we had so much fun. It was just the luckiest damn thing. I love you, Prom. I do." The back of his throat ached and burned. "I always will. And I love Carol. But you know that, too, don't you? You're dancing your ass off and saying, 'Told ya, Desperado,' aren't you?" He took a deep breath. "We've said our goodbyes, done all that good stuff. It's okay that you're always going to be a part of me, that you were, oh, Jesus, the love of my life. And it's okay that someone else is, too."

The chimes pealed again, the sound resonating through him. He felt lighter. He felt happy.

"Merry Christmas, Prom."

Chapter Eighteen

While it was by no means original to the house, there was no denying that Carol's furnace was very old. Its warranty, she explained to Steven when he complained about it only being sixty-three degrees in the house, had been written on stone tablets. When the time came—as it had the previous fall—to replace it, the well went dry at the same time. Faced with the choice of not-very-efficient heat or hauling water in buckets from the creek, she had chosen to spend the winter months sitting around the fireplace in sweats and invested a great deal of her retirement account in a new—and very deep—well.

Therefore, it stood to reason that during an ice storm on December twenty-first, when she was confined to a daybed in the living room and her elderly relatives and a teenager whose father had been amazingly willing to give her up for several weeks were all staying with her, the furnace stopped working altogether.

"You'll need a new one, Carol. You know that." The voice of Parker Wendell, the contractor she'd worked with ever since she'd bought the house, sounded crackly and far away. "But no one can get up Taylor Hill with this ice. Do you have any space heaters?"

"No. Just the fireplace and the oven."

"Plenty of wood?" He sounded worried now, and she was sorry she'd called him—she'd known there was nothing he could do.

"Yes, and Steven's here."

Parker laughed. "He won't burn well—he's too green. Let me talk to him a minute."

She handed Steven the receiver, then listened to one side of a cryptic conversation she was certain she'd have resented if she hadn't been so glad he was there.

"We can," Steven said to the unheard voice. "Dillon and Grace are here, too. He was proving Grace that his new truck really would drive on ice, so we'll see how it does going to my house."

"Your house?" said Grace when he hung up. "Why don't we go down to ours? If we're going to be iced in, wouldn't it be better to be in town?"

Steven shook his head. "We can't get down the hill. Trees have fallen across the road since you came. If there's an emergency and Jake needs me at the hospital or if Carol decides going into labor would be the thing to do right now, the sheriff's office can probably get us out on the old logging road through the woods, but Taylor Hill Road is way down on the list of priorities in an ice storm."

Carol glowered. "You really think labor's timing is a *choice?* Didn't you tell me you were a doctor?"

"I did, when I was trying to have my way with you, but I made it up. I really spent all that medical school time mowing lawns to help my tan and learning the words to 'Mustang Sally.' I'm a guy. I do have my priorities."

Her side was numb, and she had a crampy thing going on, too. She wondered what particular organ the twins were intent on abusing now. She tried not to wince, something she'd gotten better at in the past few weeks, because when she flinched, so did everyone else. It was kind of like a delayed and awkward form of the wave. After a while, she'd started to feel guilty. "Have I mentioned that you're a goofball?"

"Many times," he said sadly. "Many, many times, but I was sure you didn't mean it." He kissed her. "I'm going to let you get up, after all, even if you don't have to go to the bathroom. I think that should make me your hero."

"You're always my hero," she assured him.

The drive up to Steven's house was slow in the two trucks. Ben Sawyer appeared with his father's tractor to see if they needed help with anything, and Reese rode up to Miss Abigail's with him, blushing when he helped her into the cab of the big John Deere.

"I never realized Taylor Hill Road was all that narrow," Carol observed, looking down from her position in the passenger seat of Steven's truck. "Or that it would be that far down if we happened to slip off the side of the mountain."

"This is a good time to embrace the positive." Steven cut his eyes to her briefly. "You doing all right?"

"I'm fine." And she was. Sort of. Discomfort had become so commonplace she wasn't sure when it had crossed the threshold into pain.

Not yet, she sincerely hoped. Although Steven's house was beautifully restored, and she knew from reading its history that several babies had been born there, she had no interest in adding to that particular statistic.

However, whether she wanted to give birth in it or not, Miss Abigail's was as snug and cozy as a 140-year-old house with ten-foot ceilings and towering windows could be. Carol relaxed on the couch with the cup of spiced tea Reese brought her, realizing this was the warmest she had been in days. "Maybe years," she muttered, and winced at the pain that slipped sharply across the lower part of her back.

Not yet. Please.

Dixie and Jo cooked vegetable soup and baked chocolate cake while everyone else played Trivial Pursuit, which Carol won. After eating, they played Monopoly. Grace bankrupted her husband and brother handily. Steven and Dillon, pouting, went to play pool.

They drifted back into the living room when Dixie and Jo started telling stories. Steven sat at the end of the sofa with Carol leaning against his shoulder. Dillon shared a recliner with Grace while Reese sat in the other one with Barney and the cats. Dixie and Jo took possession of the rocking chairs on either side of the fireplace—Steven told Jo the one she was sitting in was older than she was, but not much. Lights from the Christmas tree added even more warmth to the room.

"I wore saddle shoes and bobby socks, and I wanted a poodle skirt, but my mother wouldn't let me have one because she thought they were too flirtatious," said Dixie, her knitting needles moving with a rhythmic click through soft mint green yarn. "She didn't want me to be a cheerleader because of all that leaping around they did, but I convinced her I could jump in a ladylike manner."

"And could you?" Steven sipped from the cup of mulled wine Jo handed him.

"I don't know." Dixie met Carol's eyes, her own brimming with laughter. "I never tried."

"Were you a cheerleader, Carol?" asked Reese, her expression wistful.

"No, ma'am." Carol shook her head. "But I did everybody's hair and makeup in drama club. And one year, when there was a talent show, Promise, Grace, and I sang 'A Reason to Believe'. We didn't win, but we always thought we should have. We may have been a little less talented than Wilson Phillips—or maybe a lot—but we *were* three girls and our hair looked really good."

"The basketball team did a cancan dance and got everyone laughing so hard we didn't have a fair chance," Grace complained. "Even when Promise and Carol offered to do a striptease as an encore—"

"Grace Campbell!" Carol threw a skein of Dixie's yarn at her. "We did not."

"I wish we'd known," said Steven. He kissed the top of Carol's head. "Dill and I would have come home from college. He could have played the bass, and I could have sung 'Mustang Sally' while you and Promise did your thing. What were you going to do while they threw their clothes around, Gracie?"

"I was going to pick up all the money people threw on the stage so I could bail them out," said Grace primly. "I was always a very good friend," she added to Reese, "even when others didn't appreciate it."

Eventually, the fire died down and everyone drifted off to bed. Carol was reluctant to sleep in Steven's bed with her mother and Reese there, an observation that caused everyone to roll their eyes.

"I think you're gorgeous," Steven said with a

perfectly straight face, helping her to her feet and supporting most of her considerable weight, "but your virtue is safe with me."

"I've been giving him husband lessons," said Dillon, drawing Grace to him. "Any second now, he's going to say, 'No, you don't look fat' and then he's going to put the seat down in the bathroom without you even getting your nightgown wet."

"Come on, Mr. Perfect. Let's see you practice what you preach." Grace waved a goodnight at everyone and tugged Dillon toward the staircase. "It's really easy putting that seat down," she assured him as they walked away. "I've been doing it for years."

Snuggled beside Steven under the Elliot House quilt on his bed, Carol looked down at her shape. "I can't wait, you know it? I have great looking, classy feet, and I can't wait to see them again. I'm going to polish my toenails a different color every day for a month, and I'm going to just sit and look at them and think how beautiful my toes are."

Steven chewed thoughtfully at his bottom lip, staring in the direction she was almost certain her feet were. "Okay." He turned her face up to his and kissed her just as long and leisurely and oh, holy Mary, sexily as if she weren't seven years pregnant. "Want me to suck on them?" he offered. "I've read about that before, and I think it would probably be all right if we marinated them in something first. Maybe beer."

"Has anyone ever told you you're just sick?"

"It's been mentioned." He kissed her again and grinned at her. "Get some rest, or I'm going to be in big trouble with Jake when he sees you. He has to report to Maggie, you know, and she's as cantankerous these days as you are."

She rolled to her left side, gasping when a cramp stopped her in the middle. "Soon," she murmured, stroking her stomach.

Steven rubbed her back. "Pain?"

"Discomfort."

"Wake me if you need anything."

She nodded sleepily, curving her arm around her belly. "We'll be fine."

****

Even as a joke, Dillon's remark about the wet nightgown hadn't been all that funny. An hour before sunrise, when the wind was still making icy tree limbs crackle and pop, it was even less so. The pain that had slivered across Carol's back the evening before became a tight band that woke her with its intensity. She lay still for a moment, thinking maybe it was a dream. But Steven's hand rested warm on her hip and her left shoulder was numb. She looked for a clock, wondering what time it was, then shook her head against the pillow. Just as Steven never wore a watch, he didn't have clocks in usual places, either. But that wasn't the worst of it. Even the pain wasn't the worst of it, although it played havoc with her breathing.

No, the worst of it was that the wet nightgown was a reality.

Oh, hell.

It was too soon. She was just over thirty-four weeks. She was huge, but that didn't mean the babies were big enough. And even if they were, they might have trouble breathing. They'd need the neonatal unit in Kingsport, but Peacock's minuscule obstetrics unit would be preferable to Miss Abigail's in an ice storm.

The pain subsided slowly, but the nightgown was still wet, which Steven was going to tease her about forever and ever—or at least 'til their long summer of love was over, at which time he'd probably get grossed out and buy a new mattress.

"Steven."

He woke instantly, not even startled by her voice. "Labor?"

"Water broke."

He kissed her cheek and reached behind him for his cell phone, thumbing in a number as he laid the fingers of his other hand against the side of her throat. "Jake, will you get first responders up the hill as soon as you can? Carol and Stan and Ollie have decided it's show time." He listened, his hand rubbing Carol's arm after he'd evidently determined she had a pulse. "Okay. See you then."

When he'd disconnected, he got out of bed. "Be still. I'm going to assemble the troops." He went toward the bathroom, his phone once again at his ear. He didn't close the door, and light sifted into the room.

He was back in a few minutes, wearing scrubs, his hair tied back. He handed her a plastic cup of water and her toothbrush. "You were going to ask me for it, weren't you?"

"I was," she agreed, "but mostly I want to be dry. Will you help me up so I can change the sheet and me?"

He helped her, laughing as he pulled an ancient Vanderbilt University football jersey over her head. "I love it when you dress sexy."

She'd just returned to the dry bed when the pain came again, more quickly than she'd expected. And more gripping. Yes, gripping was the word and it was…oh, hell, *intense*. She thought maybe the twins were having a wrestling match in there. "Hmm," she murmured. At least it sounded like a murmur to her. It may have been more of a grunt because Steven looked faintly alarmed.

The door bursting open preceded Grace's panicky voice. "Carol?"

"I'm really glad I got dressed," said Steven. He grinned past his sister at Dillon. "Everything will be okay, but it looks like you're getting your Christmas presents a few days early."

"Isn't it too soon?" Grace voiced Carol's fears in a wobbly voice. "Steven? Can you deliver a baby? Can you deliver two?"

"Yes, I can. I was there when Lucy Maud had her kittens, wasn't I? How hard can it be? And it's not too soon. Another couple of weeks would have been nice, but Paul and Ringo have decided they don't want to wait." Steven gave Grace a hug. His movements were relaxed, his expression natural, but Carol saw the tension in the veins in his neck, and the way his hands opened and closed.

Jo's voice came from the hallway. "What do you want Reese to do, Steven? Dixie's making such a racket coming down the stairs she's going to wake her. Good morning, Carolina. I see you felt like being an early bird."

"Morning, Aunt Jo." said Carol. "I hadn't actually planned it." She tried to push herself up. She'd always heard that back labor wasn't for sissies, and she had a sneaking suspicion those rumors were true. Even when the pain eased, it left shrieking little echoes in its wake. "Steven, can I sit up for a little bit?"

"Sure." He helped her, stuffing pillows behind her, then sat beside her to take her hands in his. "The boyfriend's got to be the doctor for a while. I need to get real close and personal here in a minute." He grinned at her. "I'll try not to get all excited."

"Are you taking my pulse?" It was okay with her if he was. Him holding her hands was comforting.

"Just in passing." He leaned across her, reaching for the blood pressure cuff. "And now I'm going to do this. There's just no end to my deviant ways."

"I didn't want to say that." She started to smile, but one of the babies must have thrown the other to the mat and was holding him there. "Yowch."

"Pretty soon," said Grace, sitting cross-legged and pale on the bed beside her, "you can start yelling 'I hate you!' and 'You'll never touch me again, you rat bastard' at Dillon just so we can keep this realistic."

"You can do that." Steven wrapped the cuff around Carol's arm. "Grace does it all the time without even being in labor."

"She does," Dillon agreed. "It's a real turn-on."

"What can I do?" Grace twisted her hands, and Carol thought on some level this labor was harder on the babies' mother than on their Aunt Carol.

"Time her pains." Steven watched the blood pressure monitor, his face expressionless. "Both how long they are and how far apart. Seems to me they're kinda close for no longer than she's been at it. I'm going to examine her now, though." He looked around. "Dill, you want to make sure the outside lights are on and the ambulance can get close to the house?"

Steven's leather medical bag seemed to appear from nowhere. He pulled a packet of surgical gloves from it and tore it open with his teeth.

"I didn't know doctors still carried bags." Dixie came closer to the bed and gave Carol's fingers a squeeze. Her hand was soft and warm, and Carol closed her eyes, absorbing the love in her mother's touch.

"He does," said Grace.

"Yeah." Steven looked sheepish. "I got out of the habit, other than carrying a scrip pad and my laptop, but that day on the golf course, the only thing I had with me was a determined girlfriend. I hauled the bag out of the back of the closet and filled it up again. It comes in handy if anyone goes into labor or even if I'm just trying to impress somebody. Let me see, babe." He examined Carol, his expression unchanging.

"How are we doing?" She drew in a sharp breath. "Damn, Gracie, there's another one. They're prizefighters, I'll tell you. Maybe you better call them Rocky and Diamond Jim."

Steven hesitated, then frowned at her. "You seem to be in a hurry."

"From what I've heard," said Grace, glowering at her brother, "most pregnant women aren't. They just want to stay pregnant for years on end. Is that what you had in mind, Carol?"

Carol laughed, although hitches in her breathing made it sound funny. "Why, yes, that's what I thought. Especially since bed rest and lying on my left side are such fun. Can I have some ice?"

"I'll get you some." Dixie, looking haunted, fled.

"This is rough for her." Carol smiled at Grace. "You, too."

"Whereas it's a piece of cake for you." Steven reached to stroke her hair back from her face.

People came and went in the room as daylight broke on what appeared to be a brighter day. The wind finally stopped blowing, and the ice began to melt under the stern direction of the sun.

Steven's cell phone rang, and he left the room to answer it, coming back a startlingly strong pain later. "There are still trees across the road. They moved some last night, but more have come down. The logging road is a mess, too, so it'll be a while yet. Jake told me to have a beer and go back to bed. What do you think of that, Carol?"

She twisted, searching for a less-uncomfortable position. "Go ahead. Have one for me. I'll just lie here and suck ice chips and call you a rat bastard."

He looked pained. "No, that's Dillon. I didn't have anything to do with it. I am the angel of mercy."

"I never knew the angel of mercy wore a ponytail and an earring. In my day, she was a girl and looked like those paintings of Florence Nightingale where she walked around the battlefield with a lamp in her hand." Jo stood in the doorway.

"That was the war you were a nursing assistant in, wasn't it, Jo?" Steven smiled over at her. "Did you know her personally?"

"I was going to tell you the coffee was ready," she said, "thinking I would try to be nice to you since my niece seems to think you're redeemable. However, it's obvious she's wrong."

Reese appeared behind Jo. "What can I do now? I fed the animals and explained to them that you would be all right even if your doctor was a little on the strange side."

Steven snorted laughter. "A flat flannel sheet,

young lady, without further editorializing," he said, then looked back at Carol. "Unless you have receiving blankets handy?"

"I do. I made them myself so they're prewashed and everything." Carol lifted herself so Steven could put something dry under her. "They're on the top shelf in the linen closet in a gift bag that says 'baby' on the outside because you never know when you might need a shower present. However, since they're at my house, it's probably not a good idea."

"Just get the flannel sheet and have it available so it can be warmed if we need it," Steven instructed when Reese looked like she just might take off down the hill. He swung his gaze back to Carol, his features softening. "And don't tell me—you probably have diapers somewhere, too."

"Actually, we have some in the truck," Grace intercepted. "They were on sale, so we bought a bunch."

"So we're set if we need to be."

Carol thought she should have been more alarmed than she was, and maybe if she hadn't gone into the next stage of labor with its attendant nausea and pains that seemed intent on tearing her in two, she would have been. As it was, she thought in the blurry minute between contractions, virtually everyone she loved was here and she was as comfortable as possible.

"Steven," she said. "Do you remember everything from when Lucy Maud had her kittens? Because I think Grace and Dillon's litter is about to make an appearance.

Chapter Nineteen

They were perfect.

Steven had known a few doctors who waxed rhapsodic over the process of delivering babies. He'd tried to talk several obstetrical nurses into coming to work in cardiology because they had a way with tenderness not everybody could lay claim to. He'd seen tears among staff when babies were born because sometimes it was all just…awe-inspiring. It was.

But he'd never been overwhelmed by childbirth, never felt his eyes grow stinging and wet the times he'd been in attendance during at-risk deliveries. Not even when he'd been in med school and exhausted and overwhelmed all the damn time.

Except that when Dillon and Grace held their little four-pounders for the first time before the babies were whisked into the ambulance for the trip down Taylor Hill, he had to kiss Carol's forehead, and then go into the bathroom and blow his nose. Repeatedly.

Dillon and Grace stood, so close together they were touching, holding the perfect squalling babies, and passing them back and forth so they could each bond with both of them before Jake and the EMT took them from them.

"We need to go," said Jake. "You and Dill could come with us, Gracie, but I want Carol in the hospital, too. I don't trust her blood pressure at all."

"I'll be fine," Carol murmured with a drowsiness Steven didn't believe for an instant. "Let their parents go. I'll lie here and be good. I'm starving, remember, and pathetic, and I've worked hard. I didn't eat any chili last night and I want some."

Jake eyed her. "Tell you what. If you'll let us get you into Steven's truck, you can come down the hill with him and Grace and Dillon can ride with Oscar and Felix. How's that?"

The girl half of the Campbell twins cried louder.

"He didn't mean it, sweetheart." Dillon touched the baby's cheek with a finger that still trembled. "But he's a doctor like your Uncle Steven and doesn't know any better."

"No respect." Steven shook his head and smiled down at Carol. "You up for riding down with me? Eclampsia's still something to watch for. We can pretend it's a date and go through the drive-through at the Cup and Cozy and get you something sweet and frothy. I won't even get mad if you spill it in the truck."

"Okay."

Her quick agreement bothered him, as did her pallor. He realized she was exhausted, but there seemed to be more. He exchanged a look with Jake and saw his concern echoed in the other doctor's dark eyes.

"You can come home later today," Jake promised, "or tomorrow. Just let us be sure about things."

She was shockingly weak and offered no objection to being moved on the stretcher from the ambulance. "There's still ice out there," said Steven. "We don't want you sliding down the mountain."

"You're a goofball," she murmured, her eyes closing. And flying open again. "The babies? They're really all right? Gracie?"

"They're beautiful." Grace was beside her instantly, her face awash with more happiness than Steven thought he'd ever seen there. "They're perfect."

****

Late that day, Steven sat beside Carol on the hospital bed. "Did Jake talk to you already?" He reached to stroke the petals of the flowers from Dillon and Grace. Why hadn't he sent her flowers? That was a boyfriend's job, and he was screwing it up.

"He did." She folded her hands over her stomach, not meeting his gaze. "No more pregnancies. It wasn't a surprise."

It hadn't been to Steven, either, but he still hurt for her, wished he knew how to fill the emptiness in her mossy eyes. "Jake's going to cut you loose in the morning. You ready to go home?"

She smiled, or at least made a brave effort at it. "Yes. Poor Reese. I invited her for the holidays, and then subjected her to pure drama and the ongoing love-and-war between Mom and Aunt Jo. I'll have to make it up to her."

"Reese is fine. I imagine it's the first time in her life she's been more wanted than tolerated, and Dixie and Jo are eating it up. It's all grandma time for them."

"Something they've never had." Her eyes widened. "Oh, I forgot. The furnace. We're still at your house, aren't we? Should we go to a motel or something? You'll want to spend Christmas with your family."

Did she think his family didn't include her? "The furnace will go in your house tomorrow. You'll be home for Christmas if that's what you want. That's not what I want," he added. "I want you to stay at Miss

277

Abigail's."

"Oh, you shouldn't have…" Embarrassment lent color to her pale cheeks.

"I knew you'd say that, so I didn't. Parker called over at Kingsport and ordered what you needed. You know very well he can get eleven dimes out of a dollar." This much was true, but this time Steven had just told him to get the highest-efficiency system he could. He'd rather not lie about his part in the purchase, but he could if Carol's stiff neck demanded it.

"The babies—they're still all right?" She looked at him, urgency a mask on her pale features. "How long will they have to stay in the hospital?"

"They're doing fine. They'll need to stay until they've mastered jaundice, eating, and breathing, but Grace is prepared to pitch a tent in the second-floor lounge until that time."

"Good. I was so afraid, you know, when they came early…" Her voice drifted off, and her gaze shied away from his again.

"Do you want to be by yourself?" *Say no. Let me stay with you until you stop feeling empty. Or longer. I'll stay longer.*

"I do. Just for a little while." She raised a hand to stroke his cheek. "I was a self-contained threesome for over seven months, Steven. I have no regrets, but I still have to readjust, go back to being just me."

He clasped her hand, holding her gaze. "You're not just you—you have a boyfriend. You know, he's a doctor, and he's tall and even if he's a pain in your ass a lot of the time, you really like him."

She smiled again, but her eyes remained expressionless. "Go home, tall doctor, or take Dillon out for a beer so Grace can hog both babies at once. I'm fine. I am. But I need to sleep." Her voice dropped to a whisper. "I need to sleep."

****

"Give it up, girlfriend. I know you're awake."

Carol didn't open her eyes. "Have you been called a bitch today?"

"Probably," said Grace's voice cheerfully. "Dillon's with Steven and Grant so it might even be three times by now."

"Open your eyes and sit up." Faith's voice, always soft and sweet, was nonetheless commanding. "We brought booze."

Grace snorted. "It's white zinfandel in a commuter cup, but you need to drink it quick before it gets yucky."

"You've forgotten I'm pumping milk for George and Martha." Carol gave up, opening her eyes and smiling at the two women who had become more than just friends in the preceding months. "Have you named them yet, by the way?"

"You can have this—I asked Maggie." Grace pushed the button on the side of the bed until Carol was in a sitting position. "She said you can have two glasses, one for you and one for her, but you should drink them right after you pump so that there's no alcohol in your milk. She's pretty pissy, by the way, about you already delivering and she still hasn't and she is—oh, way big. Dan said the words 'freight elevator' and she threatened to divorce him and give him the children, including the one that isn't born yet."

Carol sipped from the Cup and Cozy commuter cup. "That does taste good. Thank you. Now, Grace, either tell me their names, or I'll tell them about when their mother and their Aunt Promise got suspended from school for smoking cigarettes."

"Which belonged to Steven. It was all his fault." Grace grinned, the expression so blissfully happy Carol had to blink back tears. "Regardless of that, our boy's name is Fergus Steven Campbell, after Dillon's father and his best friend. Our little girl is Abaigeal, spelled the Gaelic way because it was what Faith, Promise, and I always said we'd name the first daughter any of us had. She'll have to spell it for people her entire life, and she'll probably hate us for it, but them's the breaks."

Faith gave her a hug. "She'll love it. What's her middle name?"

Grace looked at Carol. "She's Abaigeal Rose, because we wanted her to have a name that was dear to your heart, since we know she'll always have a place there."

The tears overflowed, and Carol reached for a tissue and passed the box around—they were all a bunch of crybabies. "She will, and so will Fergus. You do know people will call him Fergie, don't you?"

"That's okay." Faith blew her nose. "I have no doubt Abby will beat the hell out of them. It's what we had to do when people called our brother Stevie, didn't we, Gracie?"

"You bet." Grace nodded, wiping her eyes, then took a long swallow of her wine. "Over and over again. It got worse when he grew the ponytail and borrowed Faith's lipstick."

"You're making that up," Carol accused without heat.

"Some of it," Faith admitted, taking an airplane-size bottle of wine from her purse and splitting it three ways. She dug deeper in the quilted tote and came up with napkins and cookies. "Of course, he didn't like my lipstick, so we had to do a little training with blue eye shadow. While he was asleep."

"He wasn't asleep," Grace corrected. "He was drunk. But we took pictures, which we'll be glad to share if you ever need them for reasons of keeping the good doctor in his place."

"I'm going home in the morning." Carol couldn't think about Steven right now. She just couldn't—that would be the true meaning of sensory overload. "But I'll pump and freeze so you'll still have the milk."

"We appreciate that, all of us." Grace turned her head suddenly as though listening, and Carol knew that was exactly what she was doing. "I need to get back. Come on, girls. They need aunt visits, too. I can tell by the way they're yelling."

"You go on," Carol urged. "I'm fine here."

"No. If you're going home in the morning, you need to be up and moving." Grace's eyes were pleading. "And I need for you to see them. Please. I've already asked more from you than I had any right to, but I need to know"—She hesitated—"I have to know you're really all right, and I'm not going to be sure 'til you've seen them."

"Okay." Carol reached to hug her. "I'll go, but I'm telling you, if Faith starts telling them the favorite aunt story, I'll make a scene right there."

"They already know," said Faith smugly. "Today while you were sleeping? I told them all about it, how I can play the guitar and have that tattoo. I know you have one, too, Carol, but it's not a rosebud."

"No, it's jessamine *and* a rose, which is so much cooler than your dinky little rosebud. And don't forget that I drive a Mustang, which has it all over your SUV."

It hurt to walk, but not much. The twins' delivery had been less eventful than anyone could have anticipated, even with their uncle in charge. Returning to pre-pregnancy life would be easier than if she'd had surgical recovery time.

The babies were tiny. And beautiful. Abaigeal, wearing a fuzzy pink hat and with her thumb in her mouth, was sleeping peacefully.

Fergus was squalling.

"Oh," said Carol, charmed. "Oh. Just like his Uncle Steven, isn't he?"

A nurse stuck her head around the door, her smile broad. "You want to gown up, Mrs. Campbell? I think he wants you."

Carol and Faith stood together outside the window, watching until Grace reappeared in a gown to scoop her baby into her arms. She sat in the rocking chair and held him, reaching inside Abaigeal's Isolette to stroke her lightly. Fergus fell silent, and Carol let out the breath she didn't know she'd been holding.

For the first time, she knew, in that deepest of all places in her heart, why she had not died when Miranda did.

Chapter Twenty

"What are you doing here?" Carol stood in the doorway, Fred and Barney at her feet. They all stared at Steven. "Why aren't you with your family?"

"I was. We had dinner together and exchanged gifts. I'll see them again in church at midnight. Aren't you coming with me?"

She always went to the Christmas Eve service, but she'd begged off this year. Reese was driving her mother and Jo, and Carol planned to go to bed. Having a baby—or two—wasn't a restful thing, and she was tired.

It seemed as if she'd always been tired.

"I wasn't going to go." She knew as soon as the words left her lips they were a mistake. She should have sounded more definite, should have worked at edging the door closed despite Fred's obsequious winding around Steven's ankles.

"But now you are." He beamed at her and came into the house, pulling the edge of the door gently from her hands so he could close it. "Hi, kids." He bent to pet the animals, then straightened. "You're still gorgeous."

"Steven, I'm wearing sweatpants, socks with holes in the toes, and a shirt with hair dye on it. I haven't had makeup on in three days. The only saving grace is that my hair is clean, and I took a shower. How can you look at me and say—"

She was interrupted by a long and oh-hell-yes-enthralling kiss that had her toes curling against the hardwood floor and her arms curving up around his neck.

"There." His breathing, she was delighted to note, was erratic. "I think it would be nice if you put on something without that godawful shade of orange on it, but if you want to wear that, it's okay with me."

"Steven, I really—"

It worked. He kissed her again, leaning back against the closed door and pulling her flush against him. He felt cold and warm at the same time and smelled wonderful. Although she was still achy and sore from delivery and her abdominal muscles were in what she feared was a permanent state of squish, desire moved through her in delicious leaping-around spasms.

"I'll change," she said, "though I have no idea what will fit."

She found the black slacks she always wore to work when she felt bloated and a silky red sweater that was snugger than she liked but still looked festive. With her hair twisted into a messy updo and makeup on her face, she felt human again. Even more, she felt like a girl.

"Did you eat dinner at the hospital?" she asked, coming down the stairs. "I know Dillon and Grace are there most of the time."

"We did, and you'll be happy to know that Fergus and Abby both gained weight today. Grace said that was the only present she wanted, and Dillon offered to take back the year's worth of massages he gave her for Christmas." Steven shook his head. "The girl has no sense of humor, I swear." He stopped to look down into her eyes, his lips lifting into a smile she could only have described as tender. "And I was right. You're gorgeous."

"And you're on the south side of crazy." She loved it that he was. Loved him. The ache in her soul told her their long summer was winding down, but she would carry its memories with her forever.

As usual on Christmas Eve, the sanctuary of the church was standing room only. Faith and Grant's twin sons, sitting with their parents, relinquished their seats to Carol and Steven.

The service was simple, the music traditional. Deac's message came from the Gospel of Luke, relating one more time the miracle of the Christ child's birth. Carol rested a hand on her empty abdomen and wondered what the next chapter in her life would be. The babies had been part of her for long enough that there was a definite emptiness—beyond the physical—where they'd been.

Two pews forward, Reese sat between Dixie and Jo, tilting her bright head whenever one of the women spoke. Once, the girl's shoulders shook with suppressed laughter, and Carol wondered what outrageous thing Jo had said.

Steven's grin told her he'd seen it, too, and he whispered, "Reese may never be any trouble when she stays with you, but I'm pretty sure Jo makes up for that."

Carol nodded. His fingers slipped through her hair in a casual caress, and she leaned into the touch in spite of herself.

No matter how late it was, or how tired everyone was, eating after church on Christmas Eve was a tradition. Carol found herself, along with Reese, Dixie, and Jo, in Grace's huge kitchen at Crooked Mouth.

"We shouldn't be here," Carol demurred, dipping thick vegetable soup into bowls. "It's your family."

Grace cut crusty bread in generous slices, laying them beside the soup bowls. "Which is exactly why you should be here." She stopped, seeking out Carol's gaze. "We'll always be friends, no matter what happens with you and Steven. We have some shared joys and pains that stitch friendship together with unbreakable thread, but there's more now. Fergus and Abby are Dillon's and my babies—we know that—but they're yours, too. They always will be."

Carol glanced into the family room, where Reese was playing a loud video game with Seth and Drew. She remembered, for the first time in a long time, sitting between Ed and Rand on her parents' living room floor while the boys annihilated her at Pac Man and Tetris.

What huge empty spaces they had left inside her. Ed, the quintessential big brother, and Rand, whose love had been unconditional from her first day of kindergarten when he'd helped her cross the street. A big boy in the second grade, he'd already known how. The sharp sensation of missing them was overwhelming, but the memory was still sweet.

"Families are convoluted," she said, smiling when Seth and Reese high-fived each other as Drew buried his head in his hands and groaned.

Grace, as small and compact as Carol was not, stood beside her, following her gaze. "They are that," she agreed. "And connected. Always connected."

****

"I wrapped it myself."

Carol looked down at the envelope in Steven's hand. "I'm proud of you," she said. "You didn't waste hardly any paper."

"Are you going to ask me to breakfast?"

He looked past her as he spoke, and she knew one of the other women in the house would invite him if she didn't. "Come in. Have you even been to bed?" He'd been called to the hospital in the middle of Christmas Eve's late supper.

"For a couple of hours on a couch in the nurses' lounge. I was on my way home, but Miss Abigail's seems too big and empty on Christmas morning. I thought maybe since you invited me for dinner anyway, you wouldn't mind if I was"—He lifted her arm to look at her watch—"a little early. Maybe six hours or so."

That was the hell of it. She didn't mind. The day that had already promised to be full and fun suddenly promised to be fuller and even more fun.

"How's the furnace working?" he asked, following her to the kitchen.

"Wonderfully. Of course, Parker said it should since it was the top of the line. How was it he put it? 'All they had available on short notice.' That was it." She turned so suddenly he plowed right into her, which her healing girl parts certainly enjoyed. "Seems funny that was all they had, and at a bargain price, too."

"Lucky's what it is, not funny." He stopped her under one of the sprigs of mistletoe Reese had hung all over the house and kissed her. "Don't you think?"

She wasn't fooled—she knew he'd done something, but she didn't know what. Right now, it didn't matter. After Christmas and New Year's, once she'd gone back to work and begun the scramble for normalcy, she would stand on her own feet again. But right now, it felt good to be supported by friends and family. It felt lucky.

"What did you get me for Christmas?" he asked.

"Nothing." She beamed at him. "I was lying on my side on bed rest. I didn't have a chance. I did try to knit you a scarf, but I couldn't figure out how to stop, so we insulated the house with it instead—it was a really big scarf."

"You're a crazy person."

"Steven, dear, you're here in time to open presents." Dixie came into the hall with a coffee tray. "You did get me one, didn't you?"

"Yes, ma'am, which you know since it's been under the tree for two weeks, and you've shaken it three hundred times." Steven took the tray and kissed her cheek. "What did you get me?"

"Oh." She widened her eyes and turned to Carol. "Were we supposed to buy him something?"

Carol nodded. "You and Aunt Jo were. I didn't have to because I'm his girlfriend and because of the bed rest thing."

"Oh." Dixie looked nonplused, albeit phonily so. "Well, maybe Jo did."

"Did what?" Jo came into the hallway—which was getting crowded. "I'd like to have some coffee sometime today if it's all right with you. Oh." She waved at Steven. "Good morning, dear. Did you get me a present?"

Steven locked eyes with Carol, the laughter rolling silent and lovely between them. "Your whole family's a study in mercenary."

"They've just watched *Arsenic and Old Lace* too often, plus they played the aunts in the local theatre production." Carol nodded solemnly. "I think they took it real seriously, too. When I bought this house, they spent hours in the basement measuring out spaces for—how did you put that, Aunt Jo?—oh, yeah, cold storage. That was it."

Reese's head appeared around the doorway into the living room. "Do we get to open presents this morning or do we have to wait for—oh, hi, Steven. Did you get me anything? Is it something I can drive to school?"

"What a good girl." Carol gave her a hug. "You're so well-taught."

Having a teenager in the house gave Christmas morning a whole new dimension. Reese was quietly pleased with the generous gift cards from her father and grandparents, but she squealed with delight when she opened the cross-body bag Dixie had given her. She immediately donned the sweater from Jo and tugged on one of the new pairs of jeans from Carol and paraded around the living room with her nightshirt hanging out below the hem of the sweater.

"Oh, oh." She ripped open the box from Steven. "Oh, look." She jumped up again, pulling on the tall leather boots over her bare feet. "They fit perfectly. Or they will when I have socks on. Oh, how did you know? My dad had a cow when I asked for these. He says fat girls can't wear boots, but they can, can't they? Don't you think?"

Carol, whose hormones were still swinging like an out-of-control pendulum, had to go into the kitchen to refill the coffee carafe. Once there, she stepped onto the back porch and stared at the snow on Taylor Hill until she was almost certain she wouldn't cry. When she came back to the living room, she set the pot down and went to hug her mother. "It didn't matter how big I got after high school," she said close to Dixie's ear, "or how mad Daddy was at me, neither of you ever called me a 'fat girl' like that was all I was. Thank you."

"Well, come here." Steven tugged Reese into his arms. "Wait a minute." Still holding her, he pulled his cell phone out of his pocket and thumbed the screen a few times until music began to play. "Let's see if you can dance in them. Come on into the hall on the hardwood."

The others watched through the restored French doors as Steven and Reese danced the length and width of the house's center hall, Barney cavorting around their feet. Fred sat on the bottom step with a frown of what looked like concentration on his face, appearing to be judging the quality of the dance. The music sounded tinny through the mullioned glass, but the laughter did not.

Carol snatched her camera from the top of the piano and went into the hall to record the impromptu dance, capturing the joy that ricocheted through the room on pieces of mirth and music. *How could I have thought for even one minute that this was a man who wouldn't stand up?*

"Okay, she can dance in them." Steven gave Reese a final twirl and snatched Carol with an arm around her waist. "Sorry, honey, I think I found a new prom date."

"Just because she's got cooler boots than me?" Carol sniffed disdainfully. "I have experience on her. Not to mention stretch marks and roots whose colors revolve right before your very eyes. Hers can't do that."

"We want to open our presents, too," Jo called from the couch. "We're so old—or at least Dixie is—that we could easily die while we wait for you three to quit lollygagging."

Even as a joke, the thought of losing her mother and aunt was upsetting. Carol scowled at Jo. "You're not going anywhere. At least, not 'til after the New Year's party at Steven's."

"Where?" Steven raised his brows.

"Oh, didn't we tell you?" Carol sat cross-legged on the floor by the Christmas tree and grinned up at him. "Faith has it all planned out. Grace and I just went along because we're scared of her."

They opened presents most of the morning, taking their time and liking everything from the complimentary calendar Parker had left when his crew installed the new furnace to the watercolor Reese painted of Dixie and Jo sitting on the back porch cleaning green beans. Steven had had it framed in Knoxville. Carol looked at it for a long time before she could speak.

He gave her a new bicycle—not as fancy as his but much nicer than the one she'd bought seven years ago at a farm auction on the other side of town. He gave her a helmet, too—a smaller version of the one she gave him, and, Reese snapped pictures of them straddling the new bicycle in front of the fireplace with their helmets in place.

When Reese adjourned to the kitchen with Dixie and Jo to prepare a late breakfast, Steven tossed the envelope he'd brought with him into Carol's lap.

"Oh." She looked at the unfamiliar writing. "It's not from you."

"No." He sat beside her. "It's from Brady Holt."

"The golf course guy? How's he doing?"

"Fine. He quit smoking and is getting a divorce—his life expectancy is increasing by the minute."

She smacked him with the card. "Did you see him the last time you went to Knoxville?"

"No. He came down for his follow-up. We even ate lunch together at the Cup and Cozy and talked about hospital fundraising, golf, and his nephew. It was a good day."

"You never mentioned it."

He grinned at her. "You've been busy."

Well, that was certainly true. She tore open the envelope and bent to pick up the slip of paper that fell out, laying it aside to read the note written inside the card.

It's hard—no, impossible—to repay the gift of life, but I wanted to try by giving you something you couldn't get on your own. Lunch with my surgeon and a conversation with a certain Jackson Winters convinced me there wasn't anything like that. Here then is at least enough to finance something you want, and I'll leave the getting of it to you. You can go to Hawaii, finish your degree, or—if you'll let me know so I can be an investor—you can leap onto the entrepreneurship train and make Carol's Clip Joint into a chain. The choice is yours.

Best wishes and Merry Christmas. Thank you with all my rescued and repaired heart.

Brady Holt

Only very occasionally, as in the case of the two new pairs of bling-decorated jeans and the cashmere sweater she'd given Reese for Christmas, did Carol's gift-giving costs venture into the three-digit range. She gave many presents and put a great deal of thought and often much labor into them, but they were never expensive.

The check from Brady Holt was for fifty thousand dollars.

"Oh," she said. "For heaven's sake."

Steven cocked an eyebrow at her. "What will you do with it?"

"Send it back."

"He wasn't trying to be insulting."

"I know. Money's not an insult. But it's not something I can accept, either. If I needed it, maybe, but I don't."

Dillon had wanted to give her money, too. Not after the twins were born, but earlier, when she offered to carry them. She'd accepted recompense for her loss of earnings and, laughing uproariously with Grace in the consignment shop, clothes to get her through the last two trimesters. She hadn't wanted to be paid for being a friend, and she didn't want to be paid for being in the right place at the right time, either.

"I was so lucky to have been adopted by my parents," she explained. "Not that I always made them happy or that they fulfilled my every want or even need, but we were all just lucky to have had each other. Even if I were rich, though, I wouldn't try to pay Mom for that luck." She grinned. "She'd smack me one just for offering."

"But if she met your birth mother, I'll bet she'd want to pay her."

"We did meet her." Carol hadn't thought of that day in ages. "I got curious in high school, so Ed found her for me. He said he did it so he could send me back. I told Mom I wanted to meet her, so she took me to Charlotte, where I was born, and we had lunch with her. She was nice. She answered my questions and asked her own. But she was married to a man who didn't know about me and she had no other children. She was glad to know I was all right, but she didn't want a relationship. She gave me her phone number in case I ever needed to contact her for health reasons, but I've never used it."

Steven frowned. "That had to hurt."

"Mom said she would have given her everything she and Dad owned if she'd just stay out of my life, but when she wanted to do just that, it made her mad. Who did this stranger think she was turning her back on the most wonderful daughter in the world?"

Carol laughed softly with the memory. "I *was* hurt, because I thought there'd be this great reunion straight from an afternoon talk show on TV—one of those you used to go on, remember?—but it wasn't like that at all. Then Ed said, what, he couldn't send me back because she wouldn't take me? Dad said—and you must remember this was a man who never, ever used even fake cusswords—he said the woman was a danged idiot."

She sat quiet, thinking, the check in her hand. "I guess," she said quietly, "money can't give me back Miranda or Ed or Rand. It can't improve on my straight-laced father calling my birth mother a name because he loved me that much. It can buy famous artwork, but not that picture of Mom and Aunt Jo Reece painted. I just don't want it. Is that goofy?"

His gaze met and mingled with hers, warm and

exciting at the same time. "Probably," he said. "But your dad was right. She was a danged idiot."

Chapter Twenty-One

With the new year came normalcy. Sort of. Carol stopped saving milk for the babies when they were a few weeks old and becoming downright greedy with their formula. While it was a relief, she cried when she retired the breast pump. Grace responded by plunking Abby and a bottle into her arms and telling her she was nowhere near done with the baby-feeding business.

Jo and Dixie returned to Greenville the day after New Year's. Reese went home when her father returned from Canada a week later. "I love my dad," she said. "I do. And he loves me as much as he can. But sometimes our house is so lonely, like it died when my mama did. Can I still come see you at the shop?" She looked around the porch and down at the animals, sitting worriedly at her feet. "And here? Can I come here, too?"

"Whenever you want. For as long as you want." Carol hugged her close. *Don't cry until she leaves. She doesn't belong to you.*

Sometimes, it seemed like nothing really belonged to her.

While she didn't mind her own company, the house was too quiet—even Fred and Barney seemed bored. When Steven stopped in for coffee on his way to work, Carol and both animals stood on the porch and waved as he drove off. On the fourth day of silence, she dressed in black yoga pants and a white camisole with a black and white tunic over it and drove to the shop.

"It's too soon," said Kay, swirling a cape around Kate Sawyer's shoulders. "You delivered three weeks ago, for heaven's sake."

"It's too soon." Lynn came out of the back room with the elaborate dye concoction that helped make Jean Rivers one of the most elegant-looking women in town. "I've had two kids and gone back to work after six weeks and thought I was gonna die."

Carol sat at the front counter and opened her calendar. "The house is too empty," she said. "I have to get used to it again." She looked around the shop, already bare of Christmas decorations, and was surprised at how good it felt to be back. "I'll start back tomorrow. That way it won't be a full week." She hesitated. "Actually, I'm going to try a four-day work week for a while. Monday through Thursday noon, still spending the afternoon at Elliot House. I think I got a little spoiled by having long weekends."

"Do you want to close the shop for three days a week?" Lynn sounded shocked. And worried. She worked at least five days a week and an occasional sixth because she needed the money.

"No, I want to close my chair." Carol got up, pulling on her coat. "Let's have a meeting at my house. Dinner included. We can make us a real for sure business plan. The kids can come along—Fred and Barney need someone to talk to. Sunday night?"

She drove to the college campus, parking far away from the registrar's office because she needed exercise. She didn't want it, but she needed it.

"It's the very last day." The advisor laughed, but

frustration shredded the sound, as if it had been a long week already and it was only Tuesday. "If you'd come in earlier, you could have taken classes you need for your degree. As it is, they're all full—with people waiting to get in."

Carol waved a dismissive hand. "I'm thirty-seven. The degree is—for the moment anyway—a non-issue. I'm thinking 'Quilt making in Tennessee' and 'Appalachian Cooking.' I like regional classes and I haven't taken these."

"There's a new one. Did you see it?" The advisor pointed. "'Tennessee Women in the Twentieth Century.'"

"Is it still open?" Carol had never met a history course she didn't like, even the one with Professor Kingman.

"It is."

"Kingman isn't teaching it, is he?"

With the ghost of a grin, the advisor shook her head.

"I'll take it. Skip the cooking. Any chance these are Friday classes?"

"That one is. The quilt one is Thursday night. Convenient for you since it has a group of instructors, half of whom live at Elliot House. Some of the sessions will be there."

On the way home, Carol had lunch at the Cup and Cozy with Faith and Grace and got to smile into Fergus's dark blue eyes. She stopped at the grocery store and the library, went into Breakaway to sign up for the first women's ride of the season, and went home to cook supper.

Somewhere, she thought as she moved between

fridge and stove and sink and danced to the oldies on the iPod Jo had gotten her for Christmas, she'd lost herself. The independent woman she'd worked to become seemed to have been parceled out. Some of her had gone home to Greenville with her mother and aunt, another portion was with Reese in her father's lonesome house up the hill, a tender and still hurting part was with Fergus and Abby. Much of who she was—

She stopped in mid-moonwalk, her gaze moving unerringly to the snapshot magnet-bound to the refrigerator door, the one Dillon took with the fancy camera he bought to photograph babies. It was of her and Steven walking up Taylor Hill Road toward Miss Abigail's Retreat. Their hands and heads were together. Dillon said when he looked at the picture he swore he could hear them laughing.

Carol could hear it, too. Could feel it. And she knew just how much of her was Steven Elliot's girlfriend.

It was a lot.

****

"So what do you think about family practice? You've delivered your first babies, lost a patient or two, and won the football pool at the hospital." Jake passed Steven a beer.

Steven nodded his thanks. "It's more work and more exciting than I anticipated, which I like a lot. I get enough cardiac work to keep my hand in and enough 'what the hell is this?' work to keep me learning. The head nurse in a thirty-bed hospital is as knowledgeable and humbling as the ones at Knoxville, and the office manager here is just as scary as the one in the cardio unit there, too. How about you? How do you like having someone else in the practice?"

Jake grinned at him. "The beer's gotten better. I mean, I like my Sam Adams, but the microbrewery stuff you bring in is…special. Kate likes that I sometimes actually take time off now, and I can say all our kids' names without a reminder. I'm still working on getting the right name with the right face, but it's coming."

He paused for a moment, turning his bottle in a circle of condensation on his messy desktop. "The last time Davis came in with Becky, he brought me some partnership papers. They're nothing special—pretty much nameless, dateless copies of the ones Noah Bridges had written up when he took me into the practice, but any time you'd like for us to add those names and dates, I'd be pleased to offer you a partnership."

For a painful thread of time, Steven hesitated. How much would it have meant to Promise if he'd come back to Peacock while she was alive and well? If he'd shared more than bits and pieces of himself and his life with her?

The truth was he couldn't do anything about that, and he'd lived long enough to know regret was an ugly taskmaster.

But what would it mean to Carol? Would she be glad if he made that in-writing-commitment to the medical practice or would she expect him to take off when the going got tough? Which it would. It always did.

He was forty. More and more silver streaks replaced the gold ones in his dark blond hair. The leg he broke in two places while skiing in college let him know loud and clear when rain was anywhere in the tri-state area. He still had broad shoulders and a presentable six-pack of abs, but his skin was looser and softer than it had been five years ago. He still loved sex, and had missed it greatly these past weeks, but once was usually enough. After a thrilling one time, he was happy to sleep with Carol's cheek pillowed on his shoulder, his arm keeping her close.

Somewhere along the bumpy, crooked line the last eight months had drawn, he'd been able to stop reminding himself not to call Carol by his dead wife's name. He didn't wake up with his surgery schedule going through his head, either, nor chug Mylanta in secret or sit in the dark and drink beer alone. He'd even stopped blaming himself because Jamie Scott died. Most of the time.

The thoughts startled him.

He extended his hand to Jake just as he had over six months ago. "If you'll have me," he said, "I'm in." Before releasing Jake's hand, he added, "You're not going to retire in a couple of years like Noah did, are you?"

"I'm forty-five, so probably not. If I was home all day, Kate would make me do stuff I don't want to. What are you going to do if they want you to host a medical spot on a news show on TV?" Jake challenged.

"If it's local or a one-off, I'll do it. If it requires frequent travel to cities with more than two stoplights, I won't."

"Works."

"Good."

Both their cell phones rang at the same time and

they shared a resigned shrug as they answered. "On my way," they said in unison, leaving the office so quickly they nearly jammed in the doorway.

They reached the hospital within minutes, running the red light at the corner of Main and Broadway with their horns blaring. They parked their trucks haphazardly within the parking spaces reserved for doctors and ran in the emergency room entrance, pulling off jackets and tossing them onto the nursing station desk as they passed. Steven followed Jake into the second of the two cubicles without meeting the gaze of anyone who waited in the little waiting room at the end of the hall.

Emergency care was a favorite when he was in training. He loved the nonstop activity and adrenaline rush of it. His hallucinogen experiments didn't go beyond marijuana, and he supposed his emergency room rotation was responsible; the high of working the night shift in a large city trauma center beat the hell out of the good nap he took after smoking weed. Had he never watched a heart transplant and worked and begged his tired and skinny ass into a cardiothoracic residency, he probably would have made trauma care his specialty.

But that was long ago and far away. He was a lot more tired now. A lot less hopeful. He'd seen too much. He hadn't lost that many patients, but even one was too many. Jamie Scott was more than he could bear. The kid was, good Christ, seventeen. Steven hadn't realized at the time that losing Jamie had been his last call—he'd operated on other people, even Jamie's uncle, but his heart wasn't in it. He denied it in conversations with Dillon because he liked to get Dillon's goat, but his surgeon's hand needed a heart connection in order to work right.

That connection had been lost. Or moved, to be more accurate, because family medicine held his doctor's soul now. Not as tightly as cardio, maybe, but firmly. Happily.

But this wasn't happy. This was Jesus freaking awful, and he wished he could be anywhere but where he was. Wished he was Dillon stuck on Chapter Six or Grace staring in foggy-eyed amazement at her babies or even Grant at the bank where he'd worked his entire adult life, his job in jeopardy because he refused to foreclose on anyone until he'd found every single borrower-protecting loophole there was.

"Don't you even think of dying, you stupid son of a bitch," he muttered even as he kept trying. Trying. Trying. Although there was nothing he could do to halt the inevitable, an inevitable that had been sixteen years in coming.

This patient wasn't that young, and unlike Jamie, he had some control over what happened to him. He knew what he was doing when he drove his pickup— one old enough to have neither seat belts nor air bags— into a tree on a muddy, seldom-traveled logging road.

He was forty. They were in the same class, their desks three apart from kindergarten through senior year. They protected each other in football and were starting and second five in the same position on the basketball team. They went to the same parties, accepted the knowledge of Ed Whitney's sexuality without comment, and stood—along with several others— against a faction that wanted to make something of it. They both married their high school girlfriends.

And they both lost them.

"Goddammit, don't die on me!" The words broke loose, not muttered this time. He saw tears in one of the nurses' eyes, heard a sob from another.

"Elliot." Jeff Confer's voice was faint but clear.

"What? I'm right here. Don't give up, you sorry piece of shit. Don't you do it."

"Shut up." His eyes, the same light brown as Reese's, glinted with a macabre kind of humor. "This is what I've wanted for sixteen years. You know how that is. We both know. You found your way back, but I didn't. But Reese. You and Carol—you'll take care of her, right? Davis…Davis Rountree has everything written down and Grant's got all the money where it needs to be. Just call them."

"Damn it—"

"Please."

"Okay. Okay."

"Tell her her daddy loved her. Just never could do it worth a damn."

"I will." And as Jeff's life slipped inexorably away, he said it again. And again.

With a nod to the attending nurse, he pronounced him and stepped away, going to the phone on the wall, dialing a number. "Will you come to the hospital right away?"

"Sure." The sound of Carol's voice changed within the word, and he knew she was getting up, moving toward the door. "What's wrong?"

"Reese needs you. Her dad just died."

Chapter Twenty-Two

Kay was with Reese when Carol came into the emergency room lounge. "We'll take care of things and see you tomorrow when you're ready." The sometimes-beautician, sometimes-florist funeral director's wife kissed the girl's forehead. "Hang tough, darlin'. You're not alone."

Carol hugged Reese's shoulders when Kay walked away. "Y'okay, kiddo?"

"I will be."

Steven came into the room, still dressed in the jeans and sweater he wore in the office. He wrapped his arms around them both. "He loved you, Reesey, the best he could. He wanted you to know that."

"I know he did," she said. "I always knew. Even my grandparents, Mama's parents, understood that. But he never really wanted to live without her."

Damn you, Jeff. Grief and anger made Carol's fingers tremble. *She's always going to know she was never enough.*

"I can't keep staying here," Reese said when Carol took her home from the hospital. She shook her head as she hung her coat in the closet and went to stand in front of the fireplace. There was no fire, but she rubbed her hands together anyway, as if trying to warm them against the pervasive coldness of grief.

You can for now. Carol almost made the polite

rejoinder, but then remembered what Steven told her about Jeff's final request. So she said, "Yes, you can. It's your home for as long as you want it to be. We're your family for as long as you want us to be." She put her arms around her and held her, swaying side-to-side in what Steven called the mommy dance. Thoughts of Miranda and Reese rolled together in a way so painfully soft and strong she thought it must be what angina felt like.

Reese drew back. "Can we have some hot chocolate? And a fire? I'm so cold."

"Absolutely."

When Carol came back with the chocolate and a plate of cookies, Reese was on the couch wrapped in one of the quilts that was always there. She was sobbing like the wounded child she was. Carol put down the tray and sat beside her. She took her in her arms again and cried with her. When Steven came in a little later, he took Reese's other side, meeting Carol's eyes over the girl's bright hair. *Here we are.*

Yes.

That was the first night.

Dixie and Jo arrived by noon the next day. "What do you say," Carol said, hugging them both, "you sell the house in Greenville and just move in here? There's lots of room and we have a girl who needs a family. Besides that, I'm anxious every single time you're on the road driving here and back home. And I'm too old to worry."

The two women looked at each other. "*She's* too old?" said Jo mildly.

"We're not," said Dixie, "but I'm getting a lot older riding that far with you, so I think we should stay."

Jo scowled at her. "Do we have to admit I already listed the house, and we changed our address with the post office?"

"No, she doesn't have to know everything." Dixie gave Carol's hand a squeeze. "Now, where's Reese? We're here to be grandmothers."

And they were. While Carol and Steven walked with Reese through necessary decisions, appointments, and phone calls, Dixie and Jo cooked and baked. They sorted out the food people brought to the house. Dixie told stories of when Jeff and Hilary Jason Confer were in high school. She remembered their wedding, how happy Hilary was when she was pregnant, what a pretty baby Reese was.

Jo talked about it being all right for Reese to be mad at her dad. Yes, he was dead, but he'd been stupid, and it was completely understandable to have a full ration of pissed off in there with the grief. Why, her husband, Carol's Uncle Jim, died of a heart attack and she still got angry at him from time to time. Just because. They'd agreed to die at the same time, after all, and Jim went and blew it.

Davis Rountree made a conference call to Carol and Steven, and they stood outside and talked to him on their cell phones until Carol's fingers nearly froze and Steven's nose took on a Rudolphesque hue. When they came inside, they sat in Carol's half-finished library with Reese and talked to her even longer.

Grace and Dillon came with the babies and Grace handed Fergus into Reese's arms. "You wanna feed him? Wear a towel—he spits up almost every time. Takes after his dad."

Dillon followed, carrying Abby. "I think you should take this one instead. She's probably wet. She usually is. But she's really sweet." He mussed Reese's hair gently. "She takes after me, too."

Ben Sawyer came with his mother when she brought a casserole. "Hey," he said, going to where Reese stood at the window. "Want to go for a walk?"

"Sure." She got her coat from the back of a chair—they'd come and gone so much the past few days no one bothered with the closet or even the antique coat tree that stood in the entryway.

He held the pea coat for her. "It sucks about your dad."

"Sure does," she agreed.

"Wear your gloves."

Reese stared at him. "My gloves? You're worried about me wearing gloves?"

"Well, sure." He stroked a finger down the soft cheek of the baby in Dixie's arms. "You can't be touching babies with cold hands, and I know you, Reese Confer. You love messing with babies."

Carol watched as they walked away from the house. When they approached the end of the driveway, Ben's hand captured Reese's. "That'll help," she said to Ben's mother. "Thanks for the food, but even more for bringing Ben."

"He wanted to come."

"I'm impressed."

His mother grinned sheepishly. "I am, too."

That was the next day.

Carol couldn't fit into her black dress yet, although she probably came within five pounds. She was set to drive over to Kingsport and buy a new one, but Reese wouldn't hear of it. "This is my dad's funeral, remember?" she said. "You should wear jeans and a Tennessee Titans sweatshirt. That's what I'm going to do."

So Carol got on the phone and online and created what she'd heard called a "rapid dissemination" message. There would be no viewing, she told and typed, but the funeral would be at the church with beer and brats to follow at Carol's. Wear jeans. Spread the word.

"You can have it at Miss Abigail's," Steven offered, eating potato chips from Reese's plate. "There's more room."

"Dad's friends would end up swinging from the chandeliers," she demurred. "At Carol's, they know if they do that, they'll have to fix what they break. They're not as scared of you as they are of her."

Steven glowered at her, but his dark eyes danced. "Missy, are you making fun of me?"

"Why, yes," she said, blinking owlishly at him, "I do believe I am. You're so easy I can't help myself."

He shrugged. "I'm okay with that." His gaze turned lascivious when he looked at Carol. "Did you hear that? She says I'm easy."

She grinned at him, leaning in to kiss him on her way to the laundry room with a basket of towels. "Where do you think she heard it?"

Later, when an exhausted Reese was in bed, Carol's cell phone rang. "All right," she said to the caller. "I'll meet you there in ten minutes."

Steven, putting on his coat to go home, gave her a questioning look. "Everything all right?"

"I hope so. That was Reese's grandparents."

"I'll go with you."

She didn't argue. He was the one who'd heard Jeff's last requests. "They've lost so much in their lives," she said on the way down the hill. "They didn't always like Jeff, but there was attachment there because he loved their daughter and was Reese's father. She's all they have."

But Carol didn't want Reese to live with them, although they were fine people who loved her. They lived in a nice house in a good neighborhood in Knoxville, but they didn't like noise and loud music and the way kids danced. Reese couldn't wear makeup at their house because her grandmother thought she was too young. They didn't allow her to drive or use a cell phone or spend useless afternoons at the mall. It wasn't enough that she attended church—they were insistent she go to the early, traditional service they favored.

"Thank you for coming," said Mrs. Jason when Carol preceded Steven into the Cup and Cozy. "I know it's late for coffee, but other than Malone's Pub, there was nowhere else open in town to meet."

"It's all right."

"Go ahead and sit down," Steven urged, his hand on Carol's back. "I'll get your coffee. Anyone else?"

"We're good." Mr. Jason was grim. "We need to get this conversation over with. Tomorrow's going to be a long day. We're hoping to get back to Knoxville before dark."

With a two-o'clock funeral, Carol didn't think that was likely, but she didn't say so.

When Steven returned with cups for Carol and himself and sat beside her, Mr. Jason got right to his point. "We're certain that Jeff died intestate, so we hope you'll take care of selling his house and seeing to it that the proceeds go to pay for the funeral and maybe even establish an account for Reese. That way, we can take our granddaughter home with us tomorrow and she'll be able to start a new life with us."

"Jeff had a will—Davis Rountree has it," Steven said quietly. "His funeral is already paid for and most of his money, which started with your daughter's life insurance, is in trust for Reese."

"Jeff was a logger. Where would he get that kind of money?"

Reese's grandfather's disdain for his son-in-law's livelihood considerably altered Carol's opinion of the older man. "He saved," she said. "He always did. Jeff had his faults, which most of us who knew him tended to spell out to him at every opportunity, but he took care of his money. He took care of Reese."

Mr. Jason cleared his throat. "Well, that's good. Surprising, but good. Our financial manager will be able to invest the money wisely. I believe that's all that needs to be said. If you'll see to it that she's ready to go with us tomorrow—" He moved to rise.

"No." Carol sipped deliberately from her coffee, made exactly how she liked it and put in an extra-tall go cup. Jackson must be working tonight.

"Excuse me?" His brows, still dark although his hair was white, came together. He sat back down.

"Jeff asked us to care for Reese," said Steven simply. "Both right before he died and, Davis says, in his will."

"You've done that, and we so appreciate it," said Mrs. Jason, "but we're her grandparents. Surely you realize she needs to be with us."

311

"She needs to *see* you," Carol corrected gently, "and spend time with you, but she needs to be here. With her friends and with us. That's what her father wanted. That's what she wants."

"What about what you want?" asked Mr. Jason. "It's not easy taking on someone else's child. We have to rearrange our lives every time she comes just to visit. It's a hardship."

"But we don't mind." Mrs. Jason spoke hastily, her eyes teary. "We love Reese."

"Of course you do. But it's *not* a hardship for me. For us." Carol met Steven's eyes in the dim light of the coffee shop and knew beyond all doubt she was safe in using the plural. The long summer wasn't over yet. "We love Reese, too, and we want her, and I believe she wants us."

"There are no opportunities here," Reese's grandfather objected. "She'll end up serving coffee or booze or doing hair. Or taking classes at that satellite college on the edge of town to learn how to do taxes for people every spring. She deserves better. And more. She's not a pretty little thing that a suitable man's going to want to—"

"Charles!" Mrs. Jason's voice, cold and furious, interrupted him. "That's our granddaughter you're talking about and you've said more than enough. Steven and Carol are right. Reese *will* be better off with them. Jeff loved Hilary, and he loved Reese. We have no need and no right to question his judgment now." She gave her husband an impatient and downright unfriendly push. "Let's go. We'll help her bury her father tomorrow, then step out of the way of her making a life for herself."

"We need to be a part of that life," her husband argued.

"And we will. Won't we?" The woman's eyes were dark with grief, but her smile was brave as she met Carol's gaze across the table. "But we'll be crotchety grandparents who offer inappropriate gifts and unwanted advice instead of reluctant guardians. That's what Jeff wanted for her, isn't it? It's what her mother would have wanted, too."

"I think so." Carol held the older woman's gaze. "We love her, too."

Mrs. Jason got to her feet and reached for Carol's hand. "I know."

It was after midnight when Carol climbed into bed, her girl parts clamoring from the kiss goodnight she'd just shared with Steven. She sat with her back against the headboard and looked at the photograph on the night stand. "I think you have a sister," she whispered to Miranda.

Even as she grieved for Reese, and even as she knew things were probably going to get crazy from time to time, her heart sang.

****

Steven leaned against Carol's porch post and watched the last of the cars move slowly down Taylor Hill Road. The line of taillights was long and rhythmic in its descent, a final farewell to Reese's father. It was amazing how quickly life could change. He'd had a beer with Jeff Confer less than a week ago. They'd talked about their wives, their losses, about Carol and about Reese and what sons of bitches teenage boys were. They'd parted with handshakes, with casual promises to "catch you on the flip side."

Looking back, which he couldn't seem to stop himself from doing, he was certain there'd been no indication Jeff planned to kill himself. The insurance company didn't think he had. "There was a ton of ice out there," said their representative, "and skid marks right along with it. If he was driving too fast, well, he just was." Steven wanted to believe that badly enough to accept the adjustor's verdict in grateful silence—Reese didn't need to deal with the possibility of her father's suicide.

The ice was all gone, melted by an unseasonably bright sun and the resultant warmth. People perspired today in their Tennessee Titans sweatshirts and joked that if Jeff were here, he'd be the first one to suggest swimming in the frigid river water.

Reese laughed with them, accepted hugs and condolences, and promised she would be fine, just fine, because Dad wouldn't settle for less, would he?

But she wasn't fine yet—Steven knew that. Reese was about the same age he'd been when his mother died, and he hadn't been fine for a hell of a long time. He looked around, wondering where she'd gone. Jo and Dixie were in the house, plastic-wrapping and aluminum-foiling the leftovers. Carol was—he looked around.

There she was, walking slowly up the driveway with her arm around Reese, their heads together. He could hear the quiet murmur of their conversation over the noises of the night that surrounded them. The sound made him remember Dillon's and Grant's faces when they heard his sisters' voices—that expression that fell somewhere between ecstasy and idiocy. He thought he was probably wearing the same look.

The long and aching silence of love lost was over, and he wasn't even sure when it had happened. He and Carol talked sometimes about their long summer of being boyfriend and girlfriend. They laughed and sang old Beach Boys songs and sometimes—not always—they withdrew from each other. Afraid, maybe, to feel too much. Afraid to give up that silence that—even when it got lonely—was preferable to the unutterable pain of their losses.

He stepped off the porch, going to meet them.

Chapter Twenty-Three

"If you could have just one dream come true, what would it be? No limitations."

It was the Question of the Day at Carol's Clip Joint, posted on a chalkboard on the wall in the "study corner." Clients answered the question, standing thoughtfully in nylon capes with chalk in one hand and a cup of the coffee of the day—brought from the Cup and Cozy in thermal pump pots—in the other.

People also came in just to answer the question. A few of the answers had gained the shop some free advertisement by appearing in the *Peacock Chronicle.* A couple of them had been hastily erased due to the PG rating of the shop.

The planning meeting Carol, Kay, and Lynn held the Sunday after Jeff Confer's funeral was productive. Their new schedules gave them all better time off and the hiring of a fourth stylist to work the day's empty chair provided better service. At the conference, they'd all mentioned a need to make the Clip Joint more "of the day," a phrase they used so often it became the theme for the changes. They had Coffee of the Day, Service of the Day, Joke of the Day, and numerous other of-the-days.

The shop even had a Suggestion of the Day. People dropped submissions into a box on the counter. One of those got Lynn a date with Parker Wendell, where she held the flashlight for him while he did an emergency repair on the Methodist Church's furnace. When he promised the second date would be better, she said she'd liked the first one just fine—she could go to the movies any time, but watching a nice man doing the right thing didn't happen to her every day.

The Question of the Day started at Elliot House one Thursday when Jonah put a new white board up in the room Carol worked in and wrote, "Question of the day: What do you wish you'd done when you were young?"

The answers ran the gamut from funny (Maxie wished she'd slept with Cary Grant) to poignant (Lois Gleason wished she'd loved her husband.) The next day a chalkboard was delivered to the shop. No one admitted having sent it, but Carol thought Steven and Dillon both looked guilty.

The question about the dream come true, asked in the middle of March in belated regard to Martin Luther King Day, drew an unprecedented number of responses. When the board got full, Carol set out sticky notes, and soon there were pastel paper dreams stuck all over the wall.

"Carol carried ours," said the piece of paper Dillon stuck to Carol's forehead when she cut his hair.

"Four kids instead of two."

"The NFL."

"Two kids instead of four, only I don't know which two I'd send back, so maybe my dream did come true, and I just wasn't looking."

"Hair color that highlights itself so you'd quit putting foil on my head and laughing at how I look. What's in this coffee anyway?"

"An A in spelling so I woodn't half to do homework wile my mom gets her hare cut instead of playing games on her fone. And a new gitar like Seth and Dru play at chruch."

"Size two. Or zero."

"Straight hair."

"Curly hair."

"No more zits."

"Always having enough to eat." That one prompted the entry of a "bounty box" to the Clip Joint—the carton from the new microwave covered in gift wrap. Its contents would be donated to the food pantry maintained by the churches in Peacock.

"Having a real *Leave It to Beaver* family."

Carol took a picture of the chalkboard before she erased it and put the notes in a neat little stack—Dixie had started scrapbooking and the answers were great fodder for her. But the last note, the turquoise one with round purple printing, Carol slipped into the side pocket of her purse before stepping out of the shop and locking its door behind her.

The wind was brisk, but warm. It would be a good day to walk home—if she didn't take her time, she could get there before dark.

Steven joined her before she'd gone the first block. "I thought you walked today," he said, taking her hand. "You do remember it's March, right?"

"But it's seventy degrees!" She smiled at him. "Did you put your dream on the board today? I didn't see it."

"No, I didn't, but I stole one." He held up a piece of paper. "Someone dreamed of parasailing. I thought that was one I could make come true as soon as we both have a long weekend at the same time and we don't have to be at the high school for something Reese is doing."

Carol laughed. "Or volunteers us for."

She loved it, though, working in the concession stand at basketball games and doing cosmetology demonstrations for the home economics class. She was a "team mom" for the swing choir and had discovered an inability to sleep until Reese's bedroom door closed for the night.

"She'll be spending the first weekend of spring break with her grandparents. Maybe we could go then," he suggested. "We can pick her up on the way back."

It would be fun, and Reese was very careful not to interfere in Steven and Carol's relationship. She ended nearly every request with an anxious "if that's okay?" She never asked questions when Carol spent the night at Steven's house or showed resentment the few times either of them had refused her anything. When Carol grounded her after a particularly blatant abuse of curfew, she said, "You're right. I'm sorry," and went off to bed.

Carol thought she'd have preferred a tantrum.

Having a real Leave It to Beaver family.

It was time.

"You know—" She stopped, uncertain how to go on.

"Probably not." His glance was questioning. "Something wrong?"

"Not wrong." She took the note from her purse and handed it to him.

He looked at it, his expression questioning. "Reese?"

She nodded, then put her hands on his face, holding

his gaze. "I think summer's over, Desperado."

"Why? Reese is happy. We're happy." He frowned, impatience drawing a line between his brows.

"Reese is accepting, and she loves us. We love her, too. That's not the problem. The problem is that she wants what I had. My dad was unreasonable sometimes and my mom didn't always stand up when she should have, but it was the very best of *Leave It to Beaver*. I can be June Cleaver, Steven. I *am* June Cleaver, but there's no way you want to be Ward." She laughed, although it trailed off. "You don't even own a cardigan or a four-door car."

"Hey, I've looked him up. I *do* play golf, and I *do* go to church sometimes." His smile was crooked, his eyes sad. "But you're right. I'm not much of a stayer, am I? And I'm probably too set in my ways to be a fulltime dad. I'm better at being the goofy but cool uncle with the ponytail and the motorcycle."

He was so much more than that, but she didn't know how to tell him so.

"Maybe you'll meet Ward," he said. "You deserve that."

But it's not Ward I want. It's you. I want summer to go on forever. Say the right thing, Steven. You're so good at that. Do it one more time.

But everything had changed. Being Aunt Carol to Reese wasn't enough—she wanted to be her mom. Maybe she was late starting, but that was okay because Reese would be patient while she learned. And she wanted to be married. Marriage might not be the only kind of commitment, but it was one that mattered to her.

"Just being together was fine," Quinn said when

she and Steven and Dixie and Jo attended his wedding to his longtime mate. "Being married won't make us better parents or even better partners, but it's the life that's right for us and for the kids. It may only be that 'piece of paper' that people talk about, but it's a stone tablet to us."

Carol wanted to share a stone tablet with someone.

"When Grace broke things off with Dillon, that year before they got married, she didn't think she was good enough for him. I wanted to shake her senseless, because that was so not true. It's not true for us, either. We're good enough for each other, so that's not even an issue." Carol cleared her throat and widened her eyes, not wanting to cry. Not now. "But good enough doesn't necessarily mean right, does it?"

He put his arms around her and pressed her head to his shoulder. "Maybe not," he said, his usually smoky voice sounding splintered.

"We have to still be friends." It was muffled, but her own voice was so steady she was amazed at herself. "We're Fergus and Abby's godparents and you're still Reese's goofy but cool uncle."

"Friends is good. I can live with that." He kissed the top of her head and drew away. "And any time you want to do a friends overnight, it's okay with me."

****

"Being friends sucks. We're not exactly in high school. It's stupid." Steven glowered at Grace. "Your gender is totally fu—messed up."

"Right, you're *not* exactly in high school, so grow up." His sister glared back at him. "You're both responsible for Reese, and you both love her, but Jeff was proof positive that sometimes love and responsibility aren't enough. Carol wants commitment. Is that really so much to ask?"

"It's the twenty-freakin'-first century, for God's sake. Marriage, no matter what kind of romantic cast anyone puts on it, is a piece of paper. I thought we were pretty committed to each other without it. At least I was," he added sulkily. He picked up Fergus, shifting him expertly into the curve of his elbow, and reached for the bottle Grace was holding. "Promise and I got married. Look at how peachy that turned out."

"Oh, no you don't, Desperado." Fury and grief darkened Grace's nutmeg-colored eyes. "You know Prom didn't die because you were married. She *loved* being married to you. Do you seriously think losing her would have hurt less if you *hadn't* been married?"

"No." Nothing could have made it hurt less. Nothing. Even now, when he'd built a dandy new life for himself, when Carol had filled more empty spaces than he even knew he had, he could be caught up short by a wave of sorrow.

The back door opened, and Dillon came into the kitchen carrying Abby. "She's hungry," he said, handing her to Grace, "and she could hear you yelling all the way out in the office. So could I." He turned his dark blue gaze toward Steven. "Do I have to kick your ass for yelling at my wife?"

They had the same conversation every time Steven and Grace had words. It cooled the heat of anger every time. "I think it's time you started standing up for your best friend." Steven delivered the expected line on cue.

"Your best friend's an idiot." That wasn't what Grace was supposed to say, so maybe she was still mad, although her face softened when she looked at Abby.

"I guess I don't understand what your problem is." Dillon measured scoops of coffee into a filter. "You've committed to living here. You have a house, a partnership with Jake, even a regular seat at the poker table on Thursday nights. You love Carol. You love Reese. Why not—" He was a writer—there was nothing he liked better than a good metaphor, unless it was a bad one. "Why not eat the whole cake instead of trying to only get the parts out of the middle? The edges," he added with a smile at his wife that made Steven feel like a voyeur, "are where the flavor's at. The crunch. The extra bit of sweet."

"You were here." Steven lifted Fergus to his shoulder. He was an expert burper. He concentrated on patting the baby's back, closing his eyes as Promise's laughing image infiltrated his heart. "You were here the year she died. You saw her suffer, saw Gracie suffer, pulled me out of whatever damn pit despair is. I can't face even the thought of going through that again, and you know I can't. It would be even worse now, because Reese is part of the equation, too."

Dillon took cups from the glass-fronted cupboard. "You're right, honey," he said mildly, nodding at Grace. "He is an idiot."

A soft snore from his shoulder made Steven smile even if he didn't want to. He kissed Fergus's dark head and laid him in the portable crib that resided in the kitchen. "I'm not an idiot. I'm a coward. There's a difference."

"So you're going to live life from a distance—isn't that one of those songs with words that rip your heart out?—and I guess living that way will keep your heart from actually *being* ripped out. Do I have that right?"

Grace swayed as she fed Abby, doing the mommy dance, and the sweet contentment in her face made Steven want to weep.

He'd cried so much in the year following Promise's death that when he finally stopped, he'd thought tears were a permanent part of his past. Even when his throat ached with emotion or anguish built a freaking boulder in his chest, his eyes stayed dry. But Grace and Dillon and their babies had evidently softened that particular hard place, because this wasn't the first time in the four months since their birth he'd come perilously close to sobbing like a girl.

He turned away, going to stand at the French doors that led into the backyard.

It was raining, not at all unusual in April's waning days. Grace's cats lay on the wide wood porch, waiting for the sun to come out.

Sometimes, a persistent voice in the back of Steven's mind insisted, if you waited too long, you missed it altogether.

"You know, I came back here because a boy died, and there was nothing I could do to change that. I'd known him for years. I cared what happened to him. But I didn't love him the way I do Reese. I gave up a specialty I loved and was good at because Jamie Scott died, and I just couldn't do it anymore. What would I do if something happened to Reese? To Carol. Jesus." He shook his head. "I lived through it once. That was enough."

"No, you didn't."

Grace's words brought him up short. He turned to face her, frowning. "What?"

She laid the snoozing Abby beside her brother and

took the coffee Dillon handed her. "You didn't live through it."

"How do you figure?"

She stared back at him, setting down the cup and putting her hands on her hips. "You're a cardiothoracic surgeon, one of the best in the country. Maybe the world for all I know. But you gave it up because a patient you hadn't even operated on yet died and because another patient and his wife were insufferable." She squinted. "I mean, really? In all those years, you hadn't faced that over and over again? I understand you being tired. I'm thrilled to death you came back here to live and to practice, but to give up your specialty entirely? Oh, no, Steven, you didn't live through it."

"You don't know what you're talking about."

Dillon handed him his cup. "Sure, she does. And losing Promise? You didn't live through that, either. Oh, you finally let her go, but the best part of you went with her. It's probably good that Carol cut you loose because there sure isn't enough left over to be good for her or anyone else. Gracie's right. You didn't live through it. You're just"—he gestured at the TV on the counter—"like those 'flat Ernie' or whoever advertisements. A poster-board facsimile of who you used to be without any of the substance."

"You are a sanctimonious bastard, you know it?" Steven sipped from his cup, scalding his tongue. "Son of a bitch."

"Watch your language," Grace ordered.

"Sorry." He went back to the French doors. "Is she happy, Gracie? I know Brady Holt came back here to try and give her money again, and she went out with him. She seems fine when I see her. Of course, she's so damn busy, that's not very often." He turned back, meeting his sister's unexpectedly sympathetic gaze. "But is she happy?"

"No."

Chapter Twenty-Four

Life was fine. No, really, it was.

Carol slid into a booth at the Cup and Cozy. Her feet were killing her, her calves throbbing so hard she thought she could hear them. Plus she had a headache.

"Long day?" Grace sat across from her. "You looked tired when you came into the quilting class."

"It *was* a long day. Our new scheduling works out great, except for when it doesn't. I don't usually start working on Thursdays 'til nine thirty, but this morning the mother of a bride, a friend of Kay's, was convinced her gray roots were at least two inches long and she needed a touch-up and more highlights. Kay was at the funeral home today, which she couldn't avoid, so I went in at seven thirty to do the color." Carol bit back a groan, more exhausted than she'd been since the week Grace's twins were born. "I didn't eat lunch because I was busy. Then I had to run Reese out to the high school for play practice—her car was already there from when she rode home with Ben yesterday—so I didn't have time for dinner before quilting class. Now I'm tired and I'm starved, and I even have a headache." She grinned over at Grace. "And I'm whiny. Don't let's forget whiny."

"So whining aside, how's it going?"

The sympathy in Grace's eyes was nearly Carol's undoing, but not quite. "Fine. You know, it's not ideal, but life usually isn't. I love having Reese, love that Mom and Jo live there. Steven's great for Reese, too, much more available than Jeff ever was. But—" She shrugged. "I miss him for myself, there's no denying that. I do what I always do, fill my days up so I won't notice the empty parts, but it's not working all that well sometimes."

"He's an idiot," said Grace flatly. She smiled thanks at Jack when he set a cup in front of her. "This is decaf, isn't it, Jack? Did Dillon call you?"

"He did," said Jack, walking away, "but you didn't hear that from me."

"Steven's not an idiot." Carol shook her head. "He was the best boyfriend in the world. It's not his fault I decided at the ripe old age of too damn close to thirty-eight I wanted to be a bride instead of the perpetual hairdresser to the wedding party."

"Have you seen Brady Holt again?" Grace turned pink. "I know it's not my business, but I'm sure there's a pinky swear somewhere in our history that says it's okay to be nosy."

"No. I only went to dinner with him that night because he wanted someone to talk to. If you don't have a bartender around, someone who cuts hair is the next best thing."

They talked a while longer, then Carol looked at her watch with a sigh. "I need to get home. There isn't any class tomorrow for some reason, and I'm thinking I might spend the morning in bed."

"I need to get back to the twins, too. They love Faith and Grant, but I still go into withdrawal after a few hours." Grace grinned. "Actually, I'm afraid they'll like you or Faith better than me."

"Not gonna happen," Carol scoffed, leaving money on the table for Jack and pushing herself out of the booth. "I'll see you Sunday."

Then, without warning, nausea clutched at her stomach, the snug interior of the Cup and Cozy did a swirly thing, and Jack's voice rang oddly in her ears.

Carol said, "Steven?"

And that was all.

****

Steven hadn't yelled in the emergency room since he left Knoxville. The staff there knew him personally or by reputation and jumped to do his bidding, but the staff in Peacock's emergency room had likely known him since kindergarten, and his reputation meant nothing to them.

"Steven." Carol's voice came to him from the bed, although he couldn't see her past the personnel who were in his way pretending to do their damn jobs. "Please tell him I'm all right." She sounded airy and weak—it scared the hell out of him.

"He doesn't deserve to be told you're all right, even if you are. Just be calm, honey. Let us take care of you right now." The nurse who spoke was Deac Rivers' sister. Deac made two and a half of Pat, but he was still scared of her. So was Steven. Usually.

"Steven." It was Jake's voice this time, and Steven didn't really appreciate the thread of laughter that ran through it. "Go out in the hall with Grace and whoever else has shown up by now. Carol had low blood sugar because she didn't eat all day and was exhausted, something you've seen at least once or twice during your career. She'll be done here in just a little bit and you can take her home."

"If you're lying to me, I'll have your ass, Sawyer."

"And if you don't get out of here, I'll kick yours," said Jake equably. "Close the doors behind him when he goes out, Pat, and if you want to give him a little extra push, no one will mind."

Steven went into the waiting room, stumbling a little when the door thumped his back. He called Carol's house. "She's fine, honey," he said when Reese answered. "I'll bring her home as soon as I feed her and yell at her. Or maybe in the morning. Either way, she's with me, okay?" He listened for a minute, smiling. "I'll tell her. Give Jo and Dix squeezy-hugs from us. Love you, pretty girl."

How natural that was to say, he thought, disconnecting the cell phone and going to stand over Grace. Why was committing himself to loving and raising a kid so easy? "Hey," he said, pulling his sister to her feet. "She's okay. Why don't you go on home? You can see her tomorrow, and you need to get back to the babies before Faith kidnaps them—you know how she is."

"I will." Grace wrapped her arms around him. "Love you, big dumb brother."

"Same goes." He kissed the top of her head.

When he went back into the exam room, Carol was sitting up on the side of the bed, combing her hair and making the staff laugh. "You laugh now," she said, pointing her comb at Pat Rivers-Davies, "but just a few more years of history courses and I'll be nearly qualified to hand out maps at the Tennessee Welcome Center out on the highway."

Steven stopped and watched, as charmed by her as he always was. This was her gift, he realized, that she made people feel better just by being there. As a beautician and a friend, all she had to do was enter the room and it was as if even flat wall paint suddenly got sparkles in it. The best part of it was she was completely genuine.

"I passed the chemistry exam!" Reese had squealed at semester's end, flinging herself into his arms. "Partly because you and Ben helped me study, but mostly because Carol said I could, and she wasn't entertaining any other outcome." Tears had flushed her eyes then. "She always did what my dad couldn't. In a way, she's always been my mom."

Yeah, she was an expert at doing the mommy dance, and she loved every swaying step of it.

"You ready?" he asked, shouldering away from the door frame. "The Mustang's still down at the Cup and Cozy, but it will be safe there tonight."

The ride home was quiet. When he reached for her hand, she didn't pull away, and he kept her fingers clasped in his all the way up Taylor Hill. He hit the horn twice at her house but kept on going. "Will you stay with me tonight?"

"Yes."

At Miss Abigail's, he set her at the sturdy and scarred kitchen table that had "Peacock Furniture Factory 1875" carved on its underside and poured her a tumbler full of wine.

She frowned. "I really don't like red all that much."

"It's good for your heart." Although her heart was strong and flawless.

He cooked bacon and eggs, the only thing he had any real skill with, stuffing slices of Grace's home-baked wheat bread into the toaster so they popped up the minute he set the plates on the table. He buttered the toast lavishly—praying for forgiveness from God's council on cholesterol the whole time. "Are you feeling okay?" he asked when he sat across from her.

"Yes, I am. I promise. I hadn't done anything dramatic for a while so I thought fainting in the middle of the Cup and Cozy was just the thing." She sighed theatrically. "How much will I have to pay Jack to keep him from broadcasting it all over the college campus?"

He laughed, although he didn't feel like it. He was, even now that he could see her and touch her and know she was all right, scared out of his mind. What in the hell would he have done if she *hadn't* been all right? If Jake's expression had been sad when he met Steven's eyes over his mask instead of half amused and half exasperated? He couldn't face it again. Dear God, not again.

She looked so right, sitting there. She still wore the claret-colored dress she'd worked in. Her walking shoes—bright pink with rhinestone-embellished laces—looked…well, right, that's how they looked. This was Carol, after all, and how damn lucky could one guy get that twice in his life he could love someone so much that facing the loss of her was so much worse than dying?

"It took me something like seven minutes to get to the hospital when Grace called me," he said. He laid down his fork and met her gaze. "I bargained with God all the way down the hill. Promise used to laugh at Grace and me for doing that, because she knew as well as anyone it didn't work, especially since I never keep my part of the bargain."

"I know." She smiled at him. "I offered myself up

when Ed died, because I thought losing me would be much easier for Mom and Dad than losing him. Rand told me I was way too much trouble so I might as well forget it. I remember yelling, after he died such a short time later, 'you think *I* was trouble? Rand Shipper— now *there's* trouble for you!' I was so mad."

She didn't mention Miranda, but Steven knew thoughts of the baby were always there when she talked about Rand. How had she survived those losses? Not only survived but thrived.

Maybe because loving someone who loved you back like Promise had loved him or Rand had loved Carol gave you no other option. You were decimated beyond belief when you lost them, but you were still bigger and better because of what had been. Carol had carried Miranda under her heart for nine months, in her arms for three, and it had given her the ability to give Reese that kind of place. To do the mommy dance even with a child of sixteen or with twin babies she'd carried and then handed over.

If he lost her, he knew he'd want to die, too. He'd been there and done that. It had taken years to "get a life," and even then he'd been afraid to share that life. No, he wasn't an idiot, like he'd told Dillon and Grace, but he was a coward. But *was*—well, that was the operative word.

"I love you," he said. He picked up his fork. "Will you marry me?"

She'd been sipping the wine. She set the glass down carefully, then picked it up again and gulped a good inch from its contents. "You don't have to feel that sorry for me. I only fainted."

"I'll only feel sorry for you if you say yes, but not

sorry enough to let you out of it." He pushed their plates aside and leaned his elbows on the table between them, holding her mossy green gaze. "Don't you love me, Mustang Sally?"

"I do." Even when she whispered, her voice was throaty. Sexy. God, he wanted her. Forever. Please, yes, forever. "Oh, yes, I do."

He beamed at her. "See how easy that was?"

"You realize I'm a package deal, right?" she warned, light coming into her eyes. "Not only Reese but Mom and Jo and the Clip Joint, too. And I'm never going to be a size two or six or even a ten. I gain weight just by walking down the ice cream aisle at the supermarket, and that's not likely to change anytime soon."

"You can sell the shop if you want to. Finish school and get that psychology degree you've been working on all these years. And I really don't care what size you are as long as I'm walking down the ice cream aisle with you."

She shook her head. "The truth is, I love doing hair and I love the shop. I like taking classes, too, but only to learn things—I don't care about the degree. Are you okay with that?"

"I am. You'll cut my hair for free, right?"

"Will you go back to working in Knoxville one day a week the way Mitch has been asking you to and Jake has said go ahead and do? How am I going to be able to brag about being married to a cardiothoracic surgeon if you're not one?"

He hesitated, but only for a moment, then laughed. "Yes," he said, and was surprised at the relief he felt. He loved family practice, but that didn't mean he didn't still love being a cutter.

He'd never thought he could love another woman as much as he had Promise, but he did. He did. "What do you say?" he asked.

She laid her hands in his, and it was as if his heart slipped into place. "Yes," she said. "I say yes."

A word about the author...

Retired from the post office, Liz Flaherty spends non-writing time sewing, quilting, and doing whatever else she wants to.

She and her husband Duane live in the old farmhouse in North Central Indiana they moved to in 1977. They've talked about moving, but really…forty-some years' worth of stuff? It's not happening. It would require removing old baseball trophies from the attic and dusting the pictures of the Magnificent Seven, their grandchildren.

https://windowoverthesink.blogspot.com/